The Burglar of Sliceharbor

THE FIRST FOUR EDGEWHEN® NOVELS:

The Dragonslayer of Edgewhen
The Artificer of Dupho
The Klindrel Invasion
The Burglar of Sliceharbor

AND COMING OUT AT THE END OF 2015:

The Bladesman of Darcliff

Edgewhen®: Fantasy adventure stories of heroism and friendship.
Learn more at **edgewhen.com**.

The Burglar of Sliceharbor

JASON A. HOLT

Edgewhen® is a registered trademark of Jason A. Holt.

Published by the author.
JasonAHolt.com

print ISBN: 978-0-9860717-7-5
epub ISBN: 978-0-9860717-6-8

For all the women in blue.

2 Yellowmonth
Summer 1670

IN THE PORT OF SLICEHARBOR, all the buildings are thatched with palm fronds. Local thatching techniques can be divided into two schools: the orange and the blue. And because this is Sliceharbor, where oranges and blues have been living together for hundreds of years, many of the orange-skinned thatchers subscribe to the blue school, and many of the blue-skinned thatchers subscribe to the orange. The people under the roofs don't much notice, as long as the thatch keeps the rain out.

But Bendoko the Crane noticed. He spent a lot of time on rooftops. Not only could he tell the difference between the orange school and the blue, he could also spot the dozen-or-so variations within each school. On this sticky summer night, he was lying on a roof thatched in the style he called "whole-stalk batten-weave". He did not know what professional thatchers called it, because he was not a thatcher. Bendoko the Crane was a burglar.

It was a good night for burglary. The silver moon shining through the misty clouds gave Bendoko enough light to see the stalks he was unweaving. Of course, anyone looking at the roof could see Bendoko, but no one ever looked at roofs, especially not on hot summer nights when every sane person in Sliceharbor was either at home sweating through a stupefying sleep or relaxing in one of the city's many bathing pools. The rain had passed, the mosquitoes were out, and no one would be taking an evening stroll in the Palace District.

Bendoko carefully undid the thatcher's work and set aside the cluster of palm fronds. They smelled of fresh rain and roof mold. A tiny gecko near Bendoko's hand began gobbling up the ants that scurried out of the disturbed thatch.

Everybody's got to eat, Bendoko thought.

He lashed his climbing line to the exposed ridge pole and peered inside the hole he had made.

Inside was a second roof, made of wood, sloping leeward—a hurricane roof. Good. He was pretty sure the rest of the palace had only a single roof. The hurricane roof indicated he was indeed above the palace's library wing. The library needed the extra protection. Irreplaceable documents could be destroyed if the roof leaked.

The space between the two roofs was big enough to crawl into, but too small to stand up in. And it was dark.

Well, I've got to eat, too, Bendoko decided. He slipped off his straw sandals, brushed the mosquitoes off his arms and legs, and crawled inside.

The boards of the hurricane roof were tarred and caulked, like the deck of a ship. Bendoko had a tiny saw on his tool belt, but he hoped to find a hatch. There should be one, somewhere. The librarians would need a way to access the cramped space if the attic fauna became too stinky or belligerent. A few spiders and lizards were to be expected—even encouraged—but you wouldn't want pack rats to set up shop above the largest scroll collection in Sliceharbor.

Bendoko felt his way along the sloping boards, brushing his bald head against the poles that supported the framework for the thatching above. The small patch of silver moonlight did little to illuminate the space under the thatch. He hoped he wouldn't find any snakes.

He didn't. But he didn't find any hatch either.

Mendu, I hope you haven't set me up, he thought.

Bendoko knew he was an easy target. He worked alone—no partners-in-crime, no bosses to pay taxes to. In other words, no protection. If he were imprisoned, he would not be missed.

And Mendu was a criminal. He helped merchants smuggle goods into Sliceharbor without paying the port tariffs. That made him a bad person, like Bendoko. One of the drawbacks of Bendoko's profession was that he did not get to deal with good people. Good people, by definition, never needed anything stolen.

As Bendoko groped in the darkness, searching for the elusive hatch, he told himself, *That's what you get for taking a job you didn't scout yourself.*

But Mendu had seemed to have all the answers. Mendu had a map. He knew the library was unguarded. He had offered one hundred imperials, fifty up front.

Bendoko wondered if he should have asked for more. The up-front money had been enough to buy off his sister's landlord for another year, but was fifty imperials enough to guarantee that Mendu wasn't setting him up? It was probably spare change to a guy like Mendu. Then again, what would Mendu get out of the deal? Who would pay fifty imperials to get rid of Bendoko the Crane? There were cheaper options.

Bendoko's toe bumped against the corner of something. The hatch! Right where he had thought it would be—almost.

So Mendu wasn't setting him up. Of course not. No, Mendu just had a job that needed to be done.

The hatch had been tar-sealed to keep the hurricane roof water-tight. The seal was no problem. Bendoko took his putty knife from his tool belt and slipped it into the tar. The night had not yet cooled off—nights never really did cool off in Yellow-month—and the tar was sticky soft.

When Bendoko had the hatch loose, he took a moment to recall Mendu's map. He guessed he was breaking in about *here.* The scroll should be over *there.* Right?

Yeah. That was probably right. Bendoko opened the hatch.

The air inside smelled crisp and clean, nothing like the stinky tar or the musty thatch. Bendoko poked his head through and took a deep breath.

It was as dark inside the library as it was in the attic. But that was good, right? It meant no one else was in the library. So no one would ask him why he was crawling in through the ceiling.

Bendoko tugged his climbing line to be certain it was still secured. Then he lowered himself into the room. His feet touched the filmy cotton gauze that Sliceharbor residents hang from their ceilings to catch stray insects. Bendoko parted the gauze with expert toes.

His torso was only partway through the gauze when his feet landed on a flat surface—probably the top of a scroll hutch. Mendu had told him to expect the hutches everywhere.

Bendoko let go of his line and crouched down so that his bald head was below the gauze. It was time for light.

A sprinkle of quicklight powder atop a candle. A quick flick of the flint striker. The spark hit the powder and the flame sparkled to life. Bendoko shut his eyes against the brightness—too late: the image was burned into his vision—and when he opened his eyes, the room was lit by the clean glow of a beeswax candle.

Well, actually, the candle didn't light the *entire* room. The room was huge. Bendoko was indeed atop a scroll hutch. A short distance away was another scroll hutch. And lurking in the shadows were still more hutches, as far as the light would reach. The room had looked much neater on Mendu's map.

Bendoko climbed down to the stone floor. This was easy because the scroll hutch consisted of many rows of cubby holes. Each cubby hole held a wooden cylinder. Inside each cylinder, wax-sealed against the damp and the mold, was a scroll. All Bendoko had to do was find the right one ... among hundreds and hundreds of scrolls.

Ancient religious texts, accounting records from the Imperial days, historical documents of famous legal judgments—every scroll Bendoko passed was worth a few imperials to somebody. But he wasn't tempted to scoop up any extras. How would he find a buyer? And how could he sell anything without having the theft point back at him? No, Mendu was the man to handle problems like that. Mendu had contacts; that was his job. And it must pay pretty good if he was offering a hundred imperials, fifty up front.

Bendoko arrived at a hutch in a corner. This was it. Or at least, this *could* be it, if he remembered the map right—if Mendu had drawn the map right. How good was the inside man, anyway?

Bendoko held the candle flame up to the cubby holes, looking for the scroll case marked by a golden sun.

"It is not here."

Bendoko jumped. The candle flew from his fingers and extinguished itself before it even hit the floor.

From no more than ten feet away, the voice said, "The item you seek has been moved."

Bendoko's heart was pounding in his chest. He wanted to run, but without any light, he would just run into a scroll hutch.

Damn you, Mendu!

Bendoko edged away from the voice, trying to be quiet, but his breaths came in noisy, panicked gasps.

"If you would care to relight your candle, I could direct you to the current location," the voice offered.

He was male—and probably blue, because he sounded like he was the same height as Bendoko. If he'd been orange, his voice would have come from two or three feet higher.

His accent was strange—not just the fancy words he used, but also the way he said them. He wasn't from Sliceharbor. Maybe he was attached to one of the senators who were staying in the palace.

And he wasn't threatening. Bendoko realized he had just made contact with Mendu's inside man.

"Wait a moment," Bendoko muttered, shuffling his feet along the floor, searching for the candle. He found it, warm and soft, against the base of the scroll hutch.

Bendoko picked up the candle with his toes and passed it to his hand. He took the flint striker from his tool belt and began flicking sparks. The bright flashes in the darkness were too brief to illuminate the inside man, although they were more than adequate to reveal Bendoko's position.

The candle wasn't lighting. Bendoko took the time to straighten the wick, and then he remembered to use the quicklight powder. This time, the candle sparkled to life. Bendoko held it out toward the stranger, but he was gone.

"This way," called the voice.

Bendoko followed. It wasn't a setup. It couldn't be. Too complicated. Simpler just to call in the palace guards. Mendu said the Republican Navy guarded this place. An intriguing thought. Bendoko the Crane had stolen many things from the good citizens of Sliceharbor, but this was his first crime against the entire Lunaslip Republic.

"In here," said the voice, and his hand thumped twice against wood—a cabinet, Bendoko saw, as he came around the corner. By the time he reached the cabinet, the inside man had retreated to the shadows.

Bendoko studied the cabinet doors: polished mahogany, with a stylized magnolia carved into each knob; no other ornamentation except for a brass plate with a keyhole in the middle.

Bendoko tried the doors. "The cabinet's locked," he said.

"Is that a problem?" the inside man asked.

"No," said Bendoko. "No, it will just take a little more time."

Bendoko didn't like being watched while he worked, but he didn't think the inside man was offering him a choice. He looked around for a good place to set his candle and discovered that he was standing next to a desk with a lampstand that was just the right height. He set the candle on the lampstand and then felt around his tool belt for his lockpicks. This looked like a job for picks 5 and 7.

The lock was well-made, but not particularly tricky. Bendoko raised the catch, slid back the locking bar, and pulled the doors open. Behind the doors was a small hutch of cubby holes—most of them empty. Of the few scroll cases inside, only the one marked with a golden sun caught the light.

Bendoko removed the wooden cylinder. It was light—hollow, but not empty.

He flashed the golden sun in the direction of the man in the shadows. "This it?" he asked.

"That is it," the inside man affirmed.

Bendoko wondered who wanted it. But it was none of his business.

"Should I give it to you?" he asked.

"No, no," the voice said gently. "Continue with the original plan."

Bendoko shrugged. Meeting the inside man hadn't been part of the plan—or maybe it had. Mendu couldn't be expected to tell him everything. Bendoko dropped the scroll case into the shopping bag on his back and pulled the drawstring.

Before putting away his picks, he locked up the cabinet. It was always best to hide the theft if possible. People didn't come looking for things they didn't know were missing.

"I'm going out the way I came in," he said to the darkness. "Do you need help getting out?"

"I shall be fine," the inside man assured him.

"All right then." Bendoko could have added, "Nice meeting you," but it hadn't been—and anyway, he didn't think the inside man wanted to be met.

Bendoko made his way back through the labyrinth and up through the ceiling.

* * *

No one saw Bendoko weave the thatch back into place. No one saw him creep away through the palace gardens. On that hot Yellowmonth night, the soldiers of the Urban Cohort had orders to patrol Sliceharbor's more troubled neighborhoods.

Tisha was patrolling the Canal Road. When she had joined the Urban Cohort, the Canal Road had been an assignment for rookies to keep them out of trouble. The neighborhood was upper middle class: single-family houses, prosperous shops boarded up for the night, private pool houses catering to moderately well-off clientele. Crime was rare, and the people on the Canal Road had not been prone to disturbing the peace.

But war and politics had changed things. Now, even a nice neighborhood could be the scene of a low-class brawl.

Tisha heard raised voices ahead. She looked up at Gusty, her orange partner.

Gusty sighed heavily, which meant he had heard the shouting, too. They quickened their pace.

Tisha and Gusty had just reached the corner of a high privacy fence when a man came flying over it. He was a blue, wearing nothing but a wet loincloth. He landed awkwardly on the sandstone-paved street and emitted a pained whimper.

Tisha ran to his side. He seemed to be conscious, but he was in no hurry to get up.

She looked to Gusty. He was peering over the fence.

The fence was a pine-pole palisade, designed to screen the

private pool on the other side from public view. It was over nine feet high, so that even oranges couldn't see over it—unless they did as Gusty was doing. He had put his club along the top of the fence and then chinned himself up. His feet dangled a foot or so above the ground.

"Stop!" he shouted. "Urban Cohort!"

The voices on the other side grew louder and angrier. Gusty turned to Tisha and gave her a pleading look.

Tisha hurried over to give Gusty a boost. He was nine feet tall, but he was lighter than he looked. Just very heavy, not incredibly heavy. It was a good thing he only needed a little bit of help.

Gusty's iron knee-covers and cane shin-guards clattered against the fence. Then he had his legs over, and he dropped to the other side with a solid thump.

Tisha took another glance at the man in the street. Only an orange could have thrown him over that fence, so Gusty wasn't alone in there. But blues always outnumbered oranges in this part of town, especially in the pools. Tisha left the man in the street and ran for the pool house door.

"Urban Cohort!" she told the doorkeeper, although her rapier, her sword-breaker club, her combat knife, her cane skirt, her cane-plated bodice, and her copper-finned helmet made it abundantly clear that she was not just here for a swim.

The doorkeeper backed out of her way. She raced down the passageway to the pool.

The pool house was fancier than the one Tisha usually swam in. The passageway—arching high above to accommodate orange patrons—was decorated with a seascape mural. The floor was ceramic tiled. Even the smoke pots—a necessity for driving away mosquitoes, especially this time of year—smelled nice here.

But the patrons were behaving like Lowtowners.

A crowd of a dozen or so blues—men and women—encircled two oranges—both men—standing by the wooden fence. Gusty stood in front of the oranges, holding the heavy short paddle that served as his club. Only a few of the patrons remained in the pool. They looked at Tisha worriedly, hoping she could do something before someone else got hurt.

Gusty had the blues at bay. They had numbers, but he was bigger and he had a club. Also, he represented the law. Blues prided themselves on their respect for the law.

Tisha knew one of the orange men had thrown the blue man over the fence, but neither looked inclined to assault anyone now. They looked worried. Tisha realized they were looking for a way out.

"All right, it's closing time," Tisha said. "Everyone not involved in the fight can go get dressed."

The crowd of blues turned to look at her as she strode toward them.

"You." She pointed to the nearest woman. "Did you hit anyone?"

"No," the woman said, surprised.

"Then you can go," Tisha said. "How about you?" she asked the next man.

"I— I didn't hit anyone."

"You can go," Tisha said. "Everyone *who does not want to have been involved in the fight* can go." She said the words slowly and clearly, letting them sink in.

The crowd of blues began to melt like a pork tallow candle. The people in the pool began climbing out.

Gusty lowered his club, resting the end casually on the ceramic tiles in front of his sandaled feet. The two oranges behind him looked at each other warily.

Only two blues remained, a woman and a man. She looked angry. He looked worried.

"Now: what happened?" Tisha asked.

"These brutes threw my husband over the fence!" the woman said.

Tisha nodded. "I see. That's very serious." She turned to the blue man. "And what is your role in this?"

The blue man looked at the woman. "I'm her other husband," he said.

Tisha nodded and tried to think of how she would feel if one of her spouses had been thrown over a fence. She'd be angry. She'd be worried that her spouse had been hurt.

Of course, she'd also have to recognize her duty to restore

the peace. But these people weren't foot soldiers in the Urban Cohort. She couldn't expect civilians to stay as calm as urbies.

She asked the husband, "What did he do to get thrown over the fence?"

"Well ..."

Yeah, Tisha thought. *He had it coming, didn't he?*

"He told my brother to go back where he came from," one of the oranges said.

Tisha looked the two giants over: bushy tufts of curly orange hair atop their heads, orange skin a bit yellower than Gusty's, bellies somewhat paunchy over their wet loincloths.

Tisha had trouble telling them apart, so she was glad to know they were brothers. She didn't want to be one of those blues who thinks all oranges look alike.

Tisha checked Gusty's reaction. His broad, orange face was blank, which meant that he had decided not to react. Tisha tried to think of how Gusty would feel if someone had told him to "go back where he came from." He'd be angry. And hurt.

"Ask him where he comes from," Tisha told the woman.

"But I—"

"Ask him where he comes from."

The woman set her jaw and looked the orange brother in the eye. "Where do you come from?"

"We live with our mother on Spinning-Glass Street," the orange brother answered.

"So why did your husband want this gentleman to go back to Spinning-Glass Street?" Tisha asked.

"Oh, they were just arguing," the woman said. "That one said the Senate should authorize naval support for the Reconciled Queendom, and that one said we had a duty to protect the culture 'that had given us so much.'" She spat the words, as though Sliceharbor's rebellion against the Empire of the Reconciled Queendom had happened only last week instead of 130 years ago. But all sorts of long-hidden animosities were rising to the surface lately, like corpses floating to the surface of Zeemo's Eddy.

"And that's when your husband chose to interject his opinions on the matter?" Tisha asked.

The other husband nodded.

"I see," Tisha said. "You two should get your clothes—and your husband's, too. He might be reluctant to come back inside."

"That's it?" the woman asked. "A man is assaulted, and all you have to say is, 'Go get dressed'?"

"If you want justice, you can find a judge in the morning," Tisha said. "Nothing can be done about it now."

"You could arrest them," the woman said.

"Only if they present an immediate danger to the public or an immediate threat to the peace," Tisha said. "I think they've cooled off. What do you think, gentlemen?"

"We've cooled off," one said. The other eyed Tisha suspiciously, but he nodded.

"Good night," Tisha said to the blue couple.

Scowling, the woman allowed her other husband to lead her away.

"So we're free to go?" asked one of the brothers—Tisha thought he must be the older one since he did most of the talking.

Tisha shrugged. "For tonight. She might seek a judgment against you in the morning."

"We're honest men," he said. "We'll accept a fair judgment."

"If there is such a thing in this town," the younger one said. "You know the judge will be blue."

Gusty frowned.

"We'll worry about that in the morning," said the older one. "Let's go get dressed."

"We'll walk you home," said Tisha.

"That won't be necessary."

"We'll walk you home anyway," she said. "We need the exercise."

* * *

Bendoko knocked on the door of a warehouse near the docks. Big sandaled feet shuffled on the other side, but no one opened for him.

"It's the Crane," Bendoko said.

The door opened. It had been designed to accommodate orange people, but the figure in the doorway made it look small. His muscular shoulders filled the width. His bushy-haired head brushed the top. Scant light leaked around his silhouette into the shadowy street.

Bendoko kept his voice steady and said, "I'm here to see Mendu."

Sunny Too-Tall shook his head—a gesture that reminded Bendoko of an irate ox.

"It's late," Sunny said. "I'm not going to wake him."

Bendoko glanced at the gauze-covered window that faced the street—the window of Mendu's office. It was illuminated.

"He's not asleep," Bendoko said. "He stays up all night counting his money. You go ask him. He wants to see me."

A voice spoke up from inside: "Close the door. You're letting out my air."

"It's the Crane," Sunny called over his shoulder. "He wants to see the boss."

Another huge pair of sandals shuffled to the door. Sunny stepped aside so his brother could get a look.

Tiny Too-Tall was a head shorter than his brother, but still plenty tall enough to look down on Bendoko.

"The boss doesn't do business this time of night," Tiny said. "You know that."

"He sent me to fetch something," Bendoko said. "He told me to bring it here as soon as I got it."

Tiny looked up at Sunny and shrugged. "I got no problem with that," he told his brother. "You got a problem?"

"I guess not," Sunny said.

Tiny looked down at Bendoko appraisingly. "Now maybe the boss will have a problem, but if he has a problem then it won't be our problem. It'll be the Crane's problem, right?"

"I guess," Sunny said. "More work for us, though."

Tiny patted his brother on the shoulder. "You can handle it. He's skinny. It's not like heavy lifting."

Before taking up with Mendu, Tiny and Sunny had been shakers—they had made their living by catching smaller people and shaking them until their money strings fell off. It was the sort of terrifying, nonlethal assault that only oranges could pull off. Now that they worked for Mendu, they had a reputation for terrifying, lethal assaults as well.

Tiny disappeared into the warehouse. Bendoko didn't like being left alone with Sunny. The man's navel was at Bendoko's eye level.

"What are you wearing?" Bendoko asked.

Everyone in Sliceharbor wore a sari. It was easy to take off when you needed to swim, and it was easy to put back on—just pleat the skirt, wrap it around your body once or twice, and drape the excess cloth over your shoulders. A sari was loose enough to let the air circulate around your skin, and the flopping fabric would brush off mosquitoes as you walked down the street.

Everyone in Sliceharbor wore a sari, except that lately a lot of oranges dressed like Sunny. Sunny's back and shoulders were bare. In front, he wore some sort of scarf that wrapped around his neck and fell down to his round, orange belly. The end of the scarf was attached to a wooden ring centered on his navel.

The ring was big enough that Bendoko could have put his fist through it. He didn't. He didn't want to be anywhere near Sunny's navel.

The bottom end of the wooden ring was secured by a strip of fabric that came up from Sunny's loincloth. Bendoko's observations stopped there. He certainly didn't want to know any details of Sunny's loincloth.

"I am wearing a mongzhi," Sunny said. "It is the traditional dress of my people."

"What people? Oranges wear saris like the rest of us."

"Maybe here, in the blue people's town. But in the Motherland, we wear mongzhis."

The blue people's town? Sliceharbor? Everybody knew that Sliceharbor had more orange people than any other port in the Republic.

From somewhere behind Sunny—and his skimpy mongzhi—Tiny called, "Let him in."

Sunny took a palm frond from its hook by the door and handed it to Bendoko. Bendoko brushed his mosquitoes off and handed the palm frond back. Sunny nodded and stepped aside.

The air inside the warehouse smelled sharp and tangy. Tiny and Sunny could create smells that drove away mosquitoes. It was a little bit of common magic that all oranges knew—like blue people's ability to sense water currents.

The door to Mendu's lamplit office was open. Bendoko stepped inside. He shut the door behind himself, glad to be leaving the presence of the Too-Tall brothers. Normally, he got along with oranges, but Sunny and Tiny had never been interested in getting along with anybody except Mendu.

Mendu looked like a skinny man who'd been given a fat man's skin. It hung loosely from his arms and his neck. His scalp—shiny blue in the lamplight—was wrinkled like wet laundry.

Fine hairs coated Mendu's jowls. Bendoko wondered how old he was. Blue men started growing hair on their faces when they reached their forties. Mendu's beard was white, which meant he was well over sixty.

Ink on Mendu's fingers betrayed the fact that he had been going over his accounts. But his desk was clear now—no ledger, and no sign of the money he had been counting.

"Job go smooth?" Mendu asked.

"Yeah, real smooth," Bendoko said. He dropped his shopping bag on Mendu's desk and took out the scroll case. "Do you have my money?"

Mendu held out his hand. Bendoko gave him the scroll case. Mendu examined it, turning the lacquered wood in his hands, running his blue fingers along the carvings.

"I have your money," Mendu said. "And I'll be keeping it a little while longer."

"Half up front, half when the job is done," Bendoko said. "I did the job. So give me the other half."

Mendu slapped the scroll case thoughtfully into his palm. "No, Crane, it *looks* like you did the job. But the job isn't done until my client says it's done."

"What does that mean?"

"It means I won't pay you until I've handed this off to my client."

"You said you have the money now."

"I do," said Mendu. "But how can we be sure this is the right scroll? Are *you* an expert on holy scrolls? I'm not. We'll have to see what my client says."

Bendoko chewed this over. "Your inside man said it was the right scroll."

Mendu looked up. "What inside man?"

"He was in the library," Bendoko said. "The scroll got moved after you made the map, and he showed me where it got moved to."

"I thought you said the job went smooth?"

"It did go smooth. He just, you know, gave me a little help … to make it smoother."

"Did you see his face?" Mendu asked sharply.

"What? No," Bendoko said. "He kind of didn't want to be seen."

"You listen to me, Crane. You saw no one, got that?"

"Right, right. I didn't see him."

"Didn't see whom?"

"Ah … no one. Because … there was no one there to see?"

Mendu relaxed a little. "That's right. That's right, Crane. You did this job alone, because you're the best, right?"

Bendoko nodded. "Right."

That part was true at least. He *was* the best.

"Good," said Mendu. "Because—Crane, you're my friend, so I want this to be clear—if anyone hears that anyone was in on this job except you and me, my client can squish us both like bugs. Like bugs, Crane. He's that big. You got it?"

"I got it."

"Good."

"So … when do I get my fifty imperials?"

Mendu shook his head. "Come back tomorrow night. All right?"

Bendoko shrugged. "All right."

He didn't like waiting, but he knew Mendu would come through. Probably.

* * *

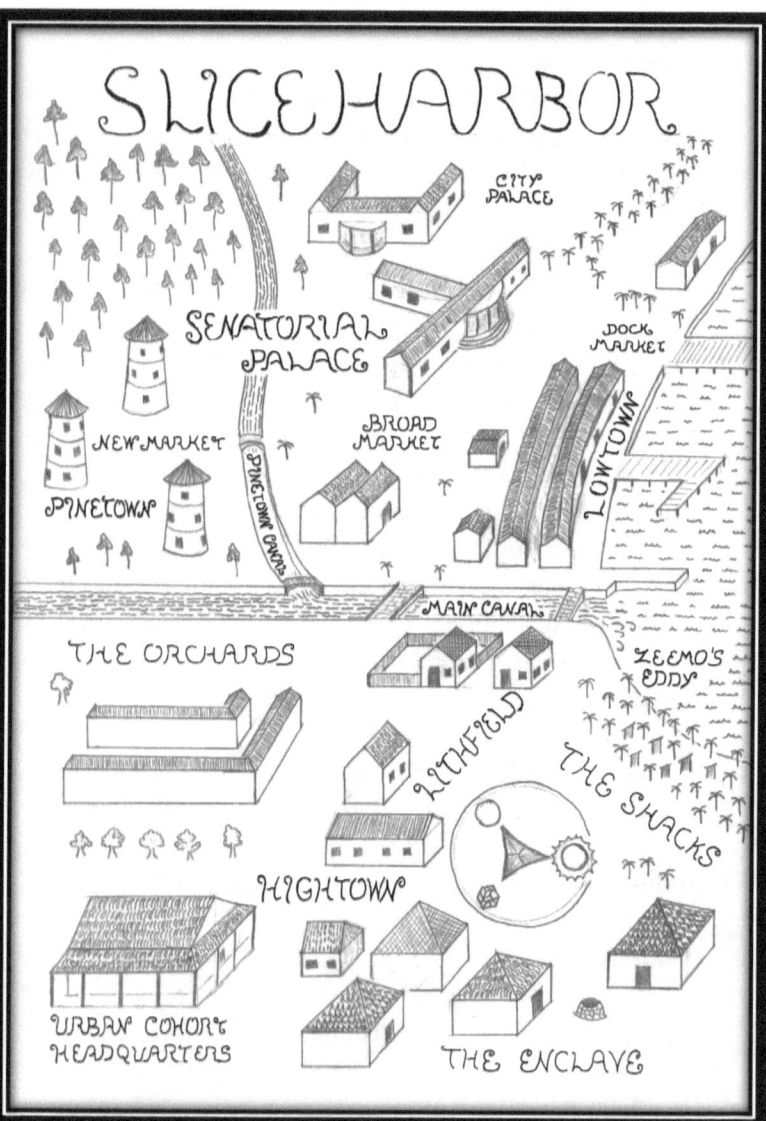

To Gusty Longbread, Spinning-Glass Street felt like a neighborhood that didn't know what it wanted to be. It was near the Palace District, but the streets weren't wide enough to be pompous. It had the hard-luck feel of Lowtown, but it lacked Lowtown's dark, twisted alleys and baffling dead ends. The lingering scents of barbecued goat and chicken reminded him of Tisha's Lithfield—except Lithfield was for blues and the houses on Spinning-Glass Street had been built for people Gusty's size.

"This is it," the older of the two brothers said, indicating a house that looked like it hadn't been remodeled since the Imperial days. The paving stones in front smelled of chicken droppings.

"I guess we don't need to knock," Tisha said.

"Yeah, you don't need to stick around, either," the older brother said.

Tisha looked up at Gusty.

Gusty shrugged.

They had escorted the boys safely home from the pool house. In the morning, urbies might come knocking to escort the boys to a judge, but that was up to the man they had thrown over the fence. Gusty and Tisha's job was done.

"Well, good night," Tisha said.

Tisha turned to leave. Gusty turned to follow her. But then the door opened.

The mother of the house stood there, eyebrows lowered in a frown.

"What happened?" she asked.

She wasn't talking to her sons. She was addressing Gusty.

"I'm afraid your sons were involved in an altercation at the Green Lagoon pool house," Tisha said.

The woman's gaze remained on Gusty, as though Tisha hadn't spoken. She stepped out onto the street.

"Get inside," she said.

Her boys disappeared through the doorway.

Now that she was in the moonlight, Gusty could see that her shoulders were bare and her navel was exposed. She was wearing a mongzhi.

Oh no, he thought. *She's one of those.*

The mongzhi was the traditional dress of the Queenies, the oranges who still lived in the Motherland under the rule of the Reconciled Queendom. Sliceharbor oranges wore mongzhis only at weddings and funerals—at least, that was the way things had been until two years ago. The war had changed everything.

"I said, 'What happened?'" She still didn't look down at Tisha.

"Someone at the pool told your sons to go back where they came from," Tisha said. "So your younger son threw him over the fence."

"And what did *you* do?" she asked, still addressing Gusty.

"I climbed over the fence to stop the fight," Gusty said.

"If you laid so much as a finger on my boys—"

"He didn't," Tisha said.

Finally, the woman looked down at Gusty's partner. "I didn't ask you, urbie. I'm talking to him."

"He's an urbie, too," Tisha said. "He helped me calm the people down, and then we brought your sons home. They're fine."

"I suppose I'll be taking my boys to a judge tomorrow," she said with a sneer.

"Possibly," Tisha said. "That's not up to us."

The woman said, "They do this on purpose, you know. They pick fights with orange boys, and then when they get beat, they can call in their judges. When was the last time you heard of a blue judge ruling in favor of an orange person?"

Gusty didn't know. He didn't think the judges were out to get orange people, but they wouldn't show any sympathy either. Not in this case. Her son had thrown a man over a fence. That was assault. A blue judge wouldn't be able to see it any other way.

"I've got a friend whose sister used to go to that pool on Nailmaker Street," the woman said. "You know the one?"

"Yeah," Gusty said. He and Tisha had often been assigned patrol duty in Lowtown.

"She can't go to that pool anymore. You know why?"

"Yeah," Gusty said.

"Why?" Tisha asked.

"Because the owner has closed the pool to oranges," the woman said.

"What?" Tisha asked. "All oranges?"

"Too many fights," Gusty said.

"Are you sure?" Tisha asked.

"Yeah," Gusty said. How could she not have heard? All the urbies had been talking about it last week—the orange ones, anyway.

"They *want* us to start fights," the boys' mother said. "They *want* us to get thrown out of their pools. And *you're* helping them."

"We're just doing our job," Tisha said.

"I'm not talking to you; I'm talking to *him*." The orange woman shook her head. "There's a war going on, and you're gonna have to choose a side. And their side doesn't want you."

She turned her bare back on them and shut herself up inside her house.

Gusty and Tisha stood in Spinning-Glass Street staring at the door. After a while, Tisha suggested, "Back on patrol?"

Gusty grunted.

They started walking.

Tisha asked, "She got to you, didn't she, Gus?"

Gusty grunted. Yeah, maybe she had gotten to him a little. But she was wearing a mongzhi. You couldn't take her kind too seriously.

The orange urbies called the mongzhi-wearers "navel oranges". It was a joke name, but the situation wasn't very funny.

Back in the Motherland, people exposed their navels to show respect for their mothers. In Sliceharbor, orange people exposed their navels to show support for the Queenies. The Reconciled Queendom was at war with Mogadwen.

Mogadwen was a land of red-skinned Children of Lith. Being servants of the god of battle, the Mogadrel tended to get into fights. Many of them were pirates. And Mogadwen tended to tolerate the pirates—even to the point of offering them safe harbor.

Two years ago, the Queen had decided that her people wouldn't take it anymore. They put together a force and invaded Mogadwen. The Queenies had size and strength on their side, but the Mogadrel had skill and numbers. They had driven out the Queenies easily. Then they had followed up with an invasion of their own.

The Lunaslip Republic had remained neutral. Mogadwen was as far from the Republic as a person could sail and still be on the Sunward Coast. And the Queenies' Sun Island was across the Sunward Sea. Gusty didn't blame the blues for wanting to stay out of a foreign war.

Some blues even sympathized with the Mogadrel, and Gusty could understand that, too. After all, the Queenies had once invaded Sliceharbor and conquered all the coastline that was now in the Republic. Everyone, blue or orange, was descended from people who had rebelled against the Queenies and driven them off so that people on the mainland could be free. At least, that was the story blues told themselves.

It was true. Mostly true. But they always left out the *good* things the Queenies had done.

Before the Empire, Sliceharbor had been just another port town. Under the Reconciled Queendom, it became the capital of the mainland province. The Empire had built new docks. They had put in the shipyards. They had engineered the Main Canal. The Revolution had given Sliceharbor its freedom, but the foundations of its grandeur had been laid in Imperial times.

At least, that was the story oranges told themselves.

It hadn't been a problem being orange before the war. But now …

Every month, Sliceharbor saw a new boatload of refugees—most of them children sent to live with relatives until the war was over. Every week, Gusty heard news of another battle lost to the Mogadrel. Every day, orange boys got into fights with blues who cheered the Queenies' defeats. And many of those orange boys went down to the docks and caught ships bound for the Sun Island. Even some of the urbies were talking about leaving to defend the Motherland.

Because they couldn't stand by while the Motherland took a beating from the Mogadrel. They just couldn't. And there was no way the blues could understand.

"Have you heard any news out of the Senate?" Tisha asked.

Well, if anyone could understand, it was Tisha. They walked

the Canal Road together every night, cleaning up the messes this foreign war had made.

Gusty shook his head. "The Senate won't do anything."

"They might," Tisha said. She was a hopeful woman.

If the Senate were to offer the Queenies even the tiniest bit of support, the people of Sliceharbor might calm down a little. But the oranges had been hoping for months, and hope had gotten them nowhere.

"No," Gusty said. "They won't do a damn thing."

Tisha brushed some mosquitoes off the back of his leg.

"Well, I guess it's not up to us," she said. "The Senate will do what it has to do, and we'll just deal with the consequences."

Gusty sighed and continued walking up the Canal Road.

3 Yellowmonth

THE LIBRARY BENDOKO BURGLARIZED is just one chamber in one wing of the great Senatorial Palace. The palace also houses the Chamber of Legislation, some administrative offices, a dining hall, and a wing of residential suites. In even-numbered years, these suites are occupied by the Senate, the nine men and women who represent the eight ports of the Lunaslip Republic.

Sliceharbor's senators (the city has two—one blue and one orange) also stay at the Senatorial Palace, sacrificing the comforts of their nearby homes so they can spend more time with their colleagues. The goal is to develop a strong camaraderie that enables the Senate to govern wisely, responsibly, and justly. "Save the rhetoric for the Chamber" is a common Sliceharbor saying, and it means, "You and I need not score debating points, because we are friends; let us talk this over and see what we can work out."

Senator Fanjei, representative of the ancient port of Thom-Hizo and admiral of the Republican Navy, gave no credence to Sliceharbor sayings. He liked nothing about Sliceharbor.

His colleagues in the Senate attributed his attitude to rivalry—or jealousy—but they were wrong. Senator Fanjei was not a petty man. His distaste for Sliceharbor was based on a fundamental issue of justice: Every other port in the Republic had one senator, but Sliceharbor had two.

The Children of the Sun Goddess claimed that Sliceharbor needed an extra senator so that their people would not be without representation—as though the criteria for wise and just government were somehow different for different peoples. Why did they think they were special? Children of the Sun in other ports were content with their port's senator. Citizens elected Children of Justice not because Fanjei's people outnumbered

Children of the Sun, but because Fanjei's people were more qualified to govern. The God of Justice had created them to be just. Whereas the Goddess of the Sun had created her people to be, merely, big.

Senator Aura, for example, was nine feet tall with legs like trees and arms like alligators. Her head was topped with curly orange hair—more like an animal's fleece than a person's smooth, bald, intelligent scalp. Her only qualification for the Senate was that she had been elected by "the oranges". She followed him to his suite after breakfast, demanding that he listen to her tired arguments one more time.

As they entered the receiving room, his secretary, Hesho, glanced up sharply from his desk in the corner. Hesho's face registered alarm. It was his duty to shield Fanjei from the unpleasant task of speaking with this woman, and Aura's presence indicated that—this morning, at least—Hesho had failed.

Fanjei chose not to acknowledge his secretary's distress. Instead, he turned his attention to Senator Aura and offered her a seat.

Her hairy eyebrows lowered into a frown. "No, thank you. I'll stand."

Well, it was not Fanjei's fault that she was too big to fit onto his stools. The furniture in the receiving room was just the right size for anyone Fanjei wanted to talk to.

Hesho squeaked something about attending to correspondence as he scuttled away through the door to Fanjei's study. Fanjei wished that he, too, could hide from this huge nuisance of a woman.

Instead he settled himself on a stout oaken captain's stool. He felt he needed the stability: Aura's arguments were always so far off base.

She took a gale-force breath and said, "If we don't take action soon, the streets of this town will become violent."

"I'm confused," Fanjei said. "Are you saying that instead of doing what is right, we should govern according to the whims of one port's most aggressive agitators?"

Her scowl deepened. "These aren't 'whims'. These are principles."

"If so, they are misguided principles," Fanjei said. "You asked the Navy to attack Mogadwen."

"I asked the Navy to send one ship—one ship!—to help the Reconciled Queendom defend their coastline."

"The action of a single ship is the action of the Navy. If you had ever served, you would know that."

"Well, I'm not asking for that anymore."

Of course not, Fanjei thought. *The others follow my lead when it comes to the Navy. Once you realized that, you had to back down.*

"What you are asking for now is equally impossible," he said.

She shook her huge, curly head. "I don't think so."

You do not know what I know … but I will play this game.

"You are asking for the Republic to hand over a sacred text to the Reconciled Queendom's diplomat. The Senate will not support such an action."

"I have three other senators aboard, and the fourth will be aboard soon."

"They will retract their support once I have spoken with them. Consider: Did not the Goddess of the Sun instruct the scroll's transcriber to keep the contents secret?"

"Only until the time of greatest need."

Fanjei shook his head. Why were Children of the Sun so obtuse? "The time of greatest need will be when the demons break out of Hell. Surely you know your theology? The Moga-drel are fierce, but they do not serve the demons."

"The Mother Goddess's words were given to her people, and it is her people who have the authority to decide when the Sun Scroll should be opened."

"I disagree."

"You don't have to agree, Senator Fanjei. The others are wavering. Our colleagues are realizing that the Reconciled Queen-dom may have a legitimate claim of ownership."

"The question of ownership is irrelevant," Fanjei said. "If the Reconciled Queendom intends to use this divine revelation—whatever it may be—against Children of the God of the Lith, then it is the duty of the Republic to keep this scroll from them. It must not be opened before the proper time."

"We've had this debate in the Chamber," she said. "You keep

losing ground. The next time I raise the issue, the vote will go my way, and you know it."

Fanjei did know it. That was why he had been forced to have the scroll stolen. He had feared this was the wrong thing to do—that the God of Justice would punish him for it after death—but now, confronted by this huge orange woman and her zeal, he felt confident that Judgment would fall in his favor. The scroll held a sacred revelation of some military power that should be used only against the demons. No pious person could let the Reconciled Queendom use that power against another deity's children.

"But there is another way," Senator Aura said.

"Another way what?" Fanjei asked. He had trouble following her incoherent thoughts.

"Another way we can calm things down," she said. "Just give me the smallest thing. It doesn't have to be a ship. Just any sign of support for those who are defending their homes on the Sun Island. We could close a port to the Mogadrel. Just one port! Thom-Hizo could stay open. Or we could provide transport for citizens who want to join the defense. Even something as simple as a war orphan's fund might be enough. Just one little thing. Is there nothing you would concede, Senator? If you propose it, I know the others will support it."

"You say you have the votes to give away the scroll. Why should I offer the Reconciled Queendom anything more?"

Aura clenched her fists and took a step toward him, nearly brushing her head against the hanging oil lamp. For an instant, Fanjei feared he had pushed her too far. She was a senator, but that did not mean she could control her violent impulses better than the rest of her kind.

"I don't have to call for the votes," she said, shaking her head and stepping away from the heat of the hanging lamp. "If you suggest some other concession—a more acceptable concession—then the scroll can stay here in the library."

Suddenly Fanjei understood the reason for this visit. Aura did not want to give the foreign diplomat the scroll. Even Aura realized that this was the wrong thing to do. She just wanted to coerce Fanjei into violating the Republic's neutrality.

He wondered if she intended to go through with it. If he said no, would she allow the scroll to be read before the proper time? Oh how he wanted to find out! This was an opportunity to learn so much about his adversary.

But Senator Fanjei never learned whether she was bluffing. The theft of the scroll had already been discovered. Senator Aura's secretary knocked on the door of Fanjei's suite and informed them that they were both needed in the library.

* * *

At the request of the Senate, Bampo the librarian had moved the Sun Scroll from its place in the library's filing system and secured it inside the lockable cabinet the night before.

Upon arriving the next morning, he had noted that the cabinet was still locked. But later, when he opened it, the scroll was no longer inside.

Aura Wisebrow's first thought was that Fanjei had stolen the Sun Scroll. Her second thought was that everyone would think *she* had stolen it. Her third thought was that Fanjei had stolen it to make everyone else suspect her.

The senators began exploring various theories: Perhaps Bampo was mistaken, and the scroll was still somewhere in the library. Perhaps someone had obtained a copy of the key. Perhaps the cabinet had been left unlocked for a time on the previous day.

None of them were making eye contact with her. Of course, they were all much shorter than she; eye contact wasn't easy. But even Senator Washirko, representing the blue half of Slice-harbor, seemed to be avoiding her gaze.

It was Senator Shigo who finally had the courage to point out the obvious: "Whether the scroll has been misplaced, or whether it has been stolen by someone with access to the library, the most likely place to find it is right here. We need to search the Senatorial Palace."

"Every room?" asked Senator Kampei in a worried voice.

"Every room," said Senator Washirko.

"Good idea," said Aura Wisebrow at the same time that Fanjei said, "An excellent suggestion."

He scowled at her. She narrowed her eyes at him. Finally: eye contact.

Washirko looked from one to the other. "I'm sure all the senators are above suspicion," he said, "but when we consider how many servants and support personnel have access to each suite, it only seems prudent to request a search that is very thorough."

Not all the senators contrived to appear pleased at this suggestion. In particular, Senator Kampei opened her mouth to object. All heads turned her way.

She swallowed what she had been about to say and instead said, "Very well."

One by one, all the senators agreed to the search. They would send for judges to oversee the investigation. The guards would be told to prevent anyone from leaving the palace without authorization.

So they were trusting the palace guards.

Aura couldn't object. The guards were sailors in the Republican Navy, the only military force that derived its authority from the Senate. Theoretically, the Navy was the force that the Senate could trust the most.

But Fanjei was their admiral. And it had not surprised Aura that the sailors Fanjei had assigned to guard the palace were all blue. Even if Fanjei had nothing to do with the disappearance of the Sun Scroll, this would be a bad situation.

"I suggest we also request help from the Urban Cohort," she said.

Washirko looked troubled. "The Urban Cohort has no jurisdiction here," he said.

"No," said Aura. "But they can act as neutral observers."

Washirko nodded. Fanjei scowled. A few of the others looked puzzled. Typical. Some blues always needed these things explained to them. Aura explained:

"The Sun Scroll is sacred to the orange citizens of Sliceharbor."

"If it's so sacred, why do they want to give it away?" Fanjei muttered in a voice quiet enough that he could pretend he had not meant to be heard.

Aura continued, "Its theft will outrage many of them. Once they learn that the blue senate has asked blue judges to oversee an investigation assisted by blue guards, some of them may suspect that the senate is interested in only the *appearance* of justice. We need some impartial orange observers."

Washirko asked, "Does anyone object to asking a few soldiers from the Urban Cohort to act as observers?"

No one objected.

He turned to Aura. "Would you send the request to Captain Kosho?"

"I will," she said.

Aura thought back to her days as the city treasurer, when a young urbie assigned to guard the City Palace had helped her uncover a pair of embezzlers. Most urbies were just soldiers, but she knew of one who would be very useful to have at the palace today.

I will ask Kosho to send me Gusty Longbread.

* * *

Gusty Longbread awoke to the smell of baked bread. It was not the yeasty smell of rising bread, nor the steamy smell of baking bread. Gusty smelled *baked* bread, with a whiff of wind-stirred ash from the ovens outside. This meant it was about noon.

Gusty rolled out of his hammock. The stone floor felt cool on his feet. He wrapped himself in a white sari, strapped on his sandals, and went outside.

Hot sun blazed down on his head. Gusty didn't mind—it was the caress of the Mother Goddess. Besides, he had thick hair. He wondered how the blues were able to stand it on their bald heads.

A blue stood under the awning of his mother's bread stall, admiring one of the long loaves from which the Longbreads took their name. He stretched out his arms to measure it. The loaf nearly exceeded his armspan. He smiled in approval and said something over his shoulder to an orange colleague, who nodded.

The blue paid for the bread and hoisted one end of the loaf onto his shoulder. The orange took the other end under an arm.

Together, they walked toward the mixed group of city pavers who were redoing the stones on the edge of the market.

You didn't see a lot of blues in this part of town. The district had been built by orange people for orange people. Originally, it had even had its own independent government. That was why it was called the Enclave, even though it was now as much a part of Sliceharbor as Pinetown and Lithfield were.

Gusty's mother smiled as Gusty approached. "Orange or blue, everybody likes good bread."

"Yours is the best, Mother."

"Here, take a handloaf," she said. "I made too many, and they won't sell as well in the afternoon."

"Thanks." Gusty took one. It was crunchy, and still warm. Of course, everything was warm in Yellowmonth.

His mother gazed around the marketplace. It was quiet. Most people were inside eating.

"Feeling better?" she asked.

"Huh?"

"You looked a little glum this morning."

"Oh."

Gusty always got home from work when his mother was taking the breakfast baking out of the ovens. They never talked then—he was too tired and she was too busy. But apparently, she wanted to talk now. Gusty finished off the last bite of the handloaf.

"It was just the same old thing, Mother. Some blues said something stupid. Some oranges couldn't keep their tempers."

"And you had to arrest the oranges and let the blues go free," she said.

"This time we didn't even have to arrest them. We just walked them home. Then their mother started in on me."

"Who's their mother?"

"It's all right," Gusty assured her.

Gusty's mother was not so easily pacified. "What did she say?"

"Just the usual," Gusty said. "There's a war going on, and we have to pick a side. That sort of thing."

"Navel orange?"

Gusty grunted an affirmative.

His mother lowered her voice. "They're trouble, Gusty. I'm not saying they're wrong, but they're trouble."

"I know."

His mother said, "Right now, they're mad at the Senate. Mad at the blues. But soon they'll get mad at the urbies, too. Don't trust them, son."

"All right," Gusty said. He didn't need to be warned. He'd been in the Urban Cohort for six years. But there wasn't any reason to contradict his mother. It was good advice.

If that woman last night had been any indication, they were already mad at the urbies. She'd told him to pick a side, but Gusty didn't want to play her game. The sides weren't orange and blue. The sides were peace and violence. Gusty's job was to keep the peace.

Really, looked at that way, the Senate was right to keep the Republic out of the war. Of course, looked at another way, they should be doing something to stop it. Would a ban on Mogadrel ships really be so bad? They were murdering oranges in the Motherland. Did the Senate expect Sliceharbor's oranges to welcome them as trading partners?

"One of your friends brought you a message," Gusty's mother said. She pulled out a small rolled-up piece of paper that had been tucked into the waist of her sari.

Gusty took the message, slipped off the string that bound it, and unrolled it onto an empty corner of his mother's display table.

He read it.

"This is from the captain," he said.

"Is it? Your urbie friends just said it was for you. I knew you'd be waking up soon, so I said I'd give it to you then."

"I guess they didn't know what it was about," Gusty said.

"I should have woken you up?"

"Yeah. Senator Aura Wisebrow wants me to report to the Senatorial Palace."

"Really?" Gusty's mother beamed. "I told you she'd remember you. What's this about?"

"I don't know," Gusty said. "But I'd better go get dressed."

"Take some handloaves to Tisha's," his mother said.

"Yeah," Gusty said. "Thanks."

That was a good idea. Captain Kosho's message hadn't said anything about bringing Tisha, but whatever was going on at the Senatorial Palace, Gusty didn't want to go alone.

* * *

Bendoko had a place in the Shacks, the cluster of squalid, slapped-together buildings on the mudflat down by Zeemo's Eddy. All sorts of detritus coagulated in Zeemo's Eddy, and all sorts of cast-off people coagulated in the Shacks: sailors who'd been dismissed from their ships, criminals like Bendoko, even honest villagers who'd come to Sliceharbor for a better life and discovered that their wages could provide food, clothing, or shelter, but not all three in the same month.

Bendoko's place was nicer than most. He had a real wicker bed that he'd stolen from a house in Lithfield. The roof didn't leak unless it rained really hard. Of course, the thatch was maintained by Bendoko, not by a landlord. People in the Shacks didn't have landlords. They just paid into one of the protection rackets. Bendoko didn't mind. It was cheaper than rent, and most of the money went to Big Zeemo, whom Bendoko considered to be a good cause.

The day after stealing the Sun Scroll, Bendoko awoke a little after noon. He set out to get some breakfast in the city. No one sold food among the Shacks, and no one kept food over night unless they wanted to attract vermin.

Bendoko entered the city near the Dock Road Bridge. He set down his shopping bag, slipped out of his sari, and jumped into the canal to wash off the grime and the mosquitoes.

He wore his tool belt under water, and also his money string, of course. Bendoko's money string was actually a silver chain. Normal money strings were too easy to cut.

His tool belt was made of cloth, and someone had cut it once, at the Dock Market. The string-cutter had been expecting a handful of coins to drop into his palm and instead he'd cut free an assortment of tools for unlawful entry. Once he'd realized he was trying to rob a thief, he'd dropped the tool belt and run away. Bendoko smiled every time he remembered the expression on that kid's face.

Bendoko didn't swim long. He just stayed in long enough to soak his skin and sop his lungs. The water in the Main Canal wasn't the cleanest water to breathe, but it wasn't as bad as rich people thought it was. You just had to find a clean current.

Before coming out, Bendoko slipped a few coins off his money chain so he wouldn't have to fumble with it on the street. Then he surfaced, expelled the water from his lungs, climbed out, and dressed on the bridge.

On his way past Big Zeemo's shrine, he dropped a flatring into the donation box. The shaman on duty murmured a blessing.

Heavy white clouds were building up over the ocean, promising another afternoon storm. Commerce was slowing down, but the street vendors were still out. Bendoko bought an orange, and then a wheat bun to take the sticky juice from his fingers. He washed the bun down with a cup of small beer purchased from a window stand. Bendoko slept in the Shacks, but that wasn't where he *lived*. He lived on the streets of Sliceharbor, with the fishmongers, the fruit vendors, the swanky merchants, the sight-seeing sailors, the canal muckers, and of course the criminals like himself.

The Dock Market was quiet because the fishing boats were still out with the tide. A local cloth buyer was discussing business with a sea captain half his size—a Child of Wealth. Two orange fishmongers were playing Sliding Stones while they waited for the day's catch to come in. A blue woman was showing cheap jewelry to three off-duty sailors who were probably more interested in the woman. Other sailors were sitting under the palm trees eating citrus they'd just purchased from a nearby vendor.

It looked like everyone was in the mood for the afternoon nap—which had been Bendoko's favorite time to visit the market back when he worked as a string-cutter. But now he was a prosperous burglar, and he could nap with the others if he wanted to.

The three sailors moved off, joking about their purchases.

One held his brass bracelet up to catch the sunlight. The jeweler began packing her wares into her handcart.

Bendoko thought of offering to help her pack up, but he decided against it. She would probably tell him to heave off. Her jewelry was cheap, but her business was honest. No honest girl would be interested in him.

The jeweler frowned and glanced at the fishmongers—the orange ones who had been playing Sliding Stones. They'd been joined by a third orange man, and now they were all grumbling at each other. A blue fishmonger stood nearby, plainly trying to overhear without getting too close. One of the oranges flexed his bicep and slapped his fist with his hand.

When the orange men noticed they were being watched, they lowered their voices. The jeweler hastily finished her packing. The blue fishmonger retreated to his stand, where he began murmuring to a citrus vendor. Bendoko decided he needed a lemon.

"What is that all about?" he asked the blues.

"It's nothing good," said the citrus vendor. "The oranges think a senator stole their holy scroll."

Holy scroll? Hadn't Mendu said something about that?

"What's so holy about it?" Bendoko asked. "Scrolls are just scrolls, aren't they?"

"Don't you follow politics?" asked the blue fishmonger.

Bendoko shook his head.

"Under the Empire, there was this temple out in the jungle," the fishmonger said. "A temple for oranges, right?"

Bendoko nodded. He'd heard of the place. Its ruins were still there. People in his line of work sometimes stayed there for a few weeks when they needed a place to hide.

"Well, one of the priestesses had a revelation—like a dream, except that she spoke with the Goddess of the Sun."

"And I'm an alligator."

"No, really. That's what they say."

"Goddesses don't talk to people," Bendoko said. "Not anymore."

"That's what makes this scroll special," the fishmonger said. "The Goddess of the Sun revealed secrets that would help the Imperial Army defeat the demons."

"What demons?"

"You know: the demons."

"The Empire was under attack by demons?"

"No, no. That's the thing, right? The priestess wrote it down for the future—when the demons come to destroy the world."

Bendoko knew that people expected the demons to invade someday, but he intended to be long dead before that happened.

"All right," said Bendoko. "So this scroll has important writings from the Goddess of the Sun. Why didn't somebody just make a copy?"

"Because the priestess said no one should open it until the demons come."

"And now it's gone," said the citrus vendor.

"Yeah," said the fishmonger. "And the oranges are mad. You see, the Queenies sent an ambassador to fetch it."

Bendoko, never afraid to start a rumor that might be to his benefit, said, "So maybe this ambassador stole it."

"Maybe," said the fishmonger. "But the oranges think the Senate was planning to give it to her."

"Why should we give it to the Queenies?" Bendoko asked. "It's our scroll, right?"

"It *was* our scroll," the fishmonger said. "Someone's stolen it."

"See, now that sounds like something an orange would do," the citrus vendor said. "Our people don't steal."

Bendoko stayed silent.

"Don't they have oranges working in the library?" asked the citrus vendor.

"I don't know," said the fishmonger.

"I think they do," the citrus vendor persisted. "You know those professional purifiers? The ones who take the mildew out of rich people's houses? Wouldn't the library need one of those?"

The fishmonger nodded slowly. "I see what you mean."

"They'd have to have one of those, wouldn't they?"

"Yeah. Yeah, they would."

The citrus vendor clapped his hands and showed them his palms. "There's your thief! Go in. Clean out the mildew. Take the scroll. Hand it over to the Queenies." He turned to Bendoko. "Plain as day, right?"

"Yeah," said Bendoko. "Right. Plain as day."

* * *

Tisha lived in the middle of Lithfield. To Gusty, the middle-class district had the feel of a big village. The blue-sized wooden houses stood separate from each other, on small lots with palm trees and vegetable gardens. Houses and fences got a new coat of paint every year.

Tisha's house was brown with two palm trees for shade and a leafy green garden for food. Her neighbors' chickens were foraging in the street. Two of these were fighting over an unfortunate snake.

The noisy giggles of Tisha's children came through the gauze-covered window. Tisha's kids were so loud they could have been heard through the wooden door. Gusty knocked.

He hadn't expected to be heard above the noise, but Tisha's husband opened the door promptly.

Sander was— Well he was small and bald, like every other blue person. They weren't that easy to tell apart. But he had a relaxed air and an easy smile that Gusty would recognize even in a crowd.

"Gusty! What brings you here?"

His eyes took in Gusty's weapons and armor, but his demeanor was curious, not unsettled. Gusty had visited Tisha's home before, but usually in civilian dress.

Gusty reached into the bundle of handloaves, pulled out one for Tisha, and handed the rest to Sander. "My mother sent you handloaves," he said.

"Thank you!" Sander said.

"I'm afraid the captain has assigned Tisha and me an extra watch today," Gusty said. "Is she in?"

Sander nodded. "Still asleep. I'll go wake her."

He disappeared into the darkness of the house—it smelled of pine smoke, diapers, and goat's milk—and Vernda replaced him at the door, observing, "Better him than me. Would you like to come in, Gusty?"

"I think I'll wait here," Gusty said.

"I don't blame you," Vernda said, rolling her eyes at the noisy giggles behind her.

In truth, the kids didn't bother Gusty. He just didn't want to squeeze his armor through the door.

Vernda came out to stand in the sun beside Gusty. She was Tisha's wife. Kind of. She was definitely Sander's wife, and the kids were definitely Vernda's. Which meant they were Sander's, too, unless they had come to some other arrangement that was none of Gusty's business.

Blues liked their marriages to be complex. Gusty had visited homes with six spouses and two dozen kids. Maybe they knew whose kids were whose, but they never seemed to care. Tisha was just as much a mother to the two kids as Vernda was. Well … maybe Sander was the second mother and Tisha was more like a father. Regardless, they were all married and the two kids belonged to all of them. It didn't have to make sense to oranges.

"So what's this about?" Vernda asked.

"I wish I knew," Gusty said.

Vernda looked worried.

"It's nothing dangerous," Gusty assured her. "We're just helping with an investigation."

"Sometimes that means chasing murderers," Vernda said.

"We won't be chasing any murderers," Gusty said. At least, he didn't *think* there'd been a murder at the Senatorial Palace. Because the request came from Aura Wisebrow, he expected she wanted his help investigating some sort of graft.

He could see Tisha now, inside the house, wearing only a loincloth and breastband, stumbling toward the doorway. She stopped well short of coming outside and squinted up at him. "Whassa thing now?"

"We're helping with an investigation," Gusty said. "I'll tell you on the way." *After you wake up*, he added to himself.

Tisha nodded and said, "Mmrrf."

She disappeared from view. After a moment, Gusty heard the rattle of a blue urbie donning cane armor.

Gusty felt deep affection for Tisha, but as a patrol partner, not as a woman. She wasn't really attractive in that way. To

Gusty, there wasn't much difference between a blue woman and a blue man.

Tisha wore a breastband, but blue women hardly had any breasts to band. True, Tisha had curvy, female hips, but … well, they were blue. She had a frog's complexion, not a woman's. And her height reminded Gusty of his little sister at age ten. Not attractive.

But Tisha was a great patrol partner and a good friend. If he'd ever find a blue woman attractive, Tisha would be it. But she wasn't it.

Tisha came out of the house fully armored. In the glare of the sun, her face scrunched up like a prune. "All right," she said. "Let's go."

"When will you be back?" Vernda asked.

"How the Hells would I know?" Tisha said.

Gusty gave Vernda an apologetic shrug. Tisha wasn't married to just Sander and Vernda. Like Gusty, she was also married to the Urban Cohort.

* * *

Some thieves lie low after committing a crime. Bendoko the Crane preferred to lie high.

Very early in his career, he had discovered that the best place to hide was on an alley-side rooftop. If the building was high enough and the alley was narrow enough, not even oranges could see onto the roof. It was his own private world up here— just him and the thatch bugs, and the lizards that ate the thatch bugs, and the birds that ate the bugs and the lizards.

The silver clouds were beginning to gather overhead. Soon they would turn gray. Sliceharbor's only relief from the summer heat was a regular afternoon thunderstorm. The rain would cool the paving stones a little. Bendoko hoped it would be enough to cool people's tempers, too.

It wasn't his fault. Not really. Sure, people were excited about "the Sun Scroll", but that was just a symptom, right? Bendoko hadn't *caused* any problems. The problem was the Queenies' stupid war and the way the oranges got so worked up over it. Any day now, they'd hear that the Queenies had surrendered or that the Mogadrel had retreated, and then things would be back to normal in this city again. One little theft shouldn't make an entire city grouchy. It just wasn't natural.

"Do you think she likes me?"

"She likes you."

"How do you know?"

The voices floated up from the alley. Two sets of footsteps were approaching, one walking double-time to keep up with the giant strides of the other.

"All right, you know how her friends kept looking at you and giggling, but she just looked at her feet? That means she likes you."

"Yeah?"

"Yeah."

The insecure one was probably orange. His voice was deeper—more or less. Both voices had the erratic harmonics of boys turning into men.

"I wish I could talk to girls like you."

"It's easy, Foggy. You just be yourself ... except, you know, more talkative."

"Huh!"

"You can do it."

"I never even know what to talk about."

"Same stuff you talk about with boys. Girls aren't any different."

"Maybe *blue* girls aren't any different."

"All girls are the same, Foggy. Blue, orange—it doesn't make any difference."

"So what did you and Tavi talk about?"

"Oh, you know. Just stuff."

"What kind of stuff?"

"Just ... stuff."

"Like what?"

"Oh, well ... you know. That scroll that got stolen."

"Oh."

"I guess you heard about that."

"Yeah, I heard. My mother's pretty mad."

"Mad? What's she mad about?"

"She thinks it was a senator that stole it."

"It was the Queenies that stole it. Everybody knows that."

"... My mother says it was a senator."

"Which senator?"

"One of the ones who doesn't want us to help the— the Queenies."

"A blue senator?"

"Well, yeah."

"Blues don't steal."

"What's that supposed to mean?"

"Nothing. Just that we don't steal. We can't. It's not in our nature."

"And I suppose all oranges are thieves, is that it?"

"I didn't say that. Damn, Foggy. Why are you so worked up over a stupid old scroll?"

"It's not stupid! That scroll can help the Queenies win the war!"

"Well who gives a damn about the Queenies?"

"I do!"

"Aw, the Queenies are a bunch of big, fur-headed— uff."

A soft body slammed into the wall of the alley.

In the sudden silence, Bendoko could hear his heart pounding.

Heavy sandaled feet shuffled away.

Had the blue boy been killed?

No. Bendoko could hear him sobbing.

Bendoko crept to the edge of the roof and peered down.

The boy sat in the shadowy alley like an abandoned heap of rags. Bendoko didn't want to get involved. It was none of his business.

The boy's shoulders shook with his sobs. What if his leg was broken and he couldn't move? Would anyone find him in this alley? And would he be found by a good person or a bad person? Bendoko put on his iron climbing claws and climbed down.

The boy was too intent on his own troubles to notice Bendoko. Not until Bendoko dropped to the ground did the boy look up.

The boy's eyes widened, round and white in the alley's gloom. His body tensed. He was no longer sobbing.

"Do you need a healer?" Bendoko asked.

The boy shook his head slowly.

"Can you stand up?"

The boy did so, pressing his back against the wall.

"It's all right," said Bendoko. "I'm not going to hurt you." He took the climbing claws off and dropped them into his shopping bag. "Do you need a healer? I can take you to a healer."

"No," the boy said. "I'm all right."

"You don't sound all right," Bendoko said.

The boy shook his head and his shoulders sagged. "I'm not hurt," he said. "I just ... feel awful."

* * *

Gusty Longbread led Tisha toward the Big Bridge, the place where the Palace Road crossed the Main Canal. But when they reached the Palace Road, Gusty forgot all about the bridge. Coming down the road, from the direction of the Enclave, was a group of two dozen orange people.

The walk and the loaf of bread must have been doing their part to wake Tisha up, for she saw the oranges almost as soon as Gusty did.

"Gus?" she asked. "Is there gonna be trouble?"

Gusty grunted. The oranges didn't have weapons, so they weren't a mob. But they walked like they expected people to get out of their way. And most of them wore mongzhis.

"All right," Tisha said. "Let's go find out what they want." She strode toward the advancing oranges.

Gusty hefted his paddle-club and followed. The paddle-club was supposed to be especially good in riot situations. But they were outnumbered twelve to one. Gusty hoped Tisha could keep this from turning into a riot situation.

As they neared the oranges, Tisha put her hands amiably behind her back and called, "Good afternoon."

The oranges slowed their advance and began muttering to each other:

"Urbies."

"Small fish. We want the big fish."

"Let 'em try to stop us."

But Tisha had already stopped them. They had halted in the middle of the street, still twenty feet away.

"Is there something we can do for you?" Tisha asked.

A spokeswoman stepped forward. Her earrings were gold, not brass, and in the latest fashion. No jewels in them, but she obviously earned a good living. Gusty recognized Lily Trueknife. Last year, she had been just another healer in the Enclave. Now she was one of the leaders of the oranges who demanded support for the Reconciled Queendom.

"We're going to speak to the Senate," Lily Trueknife said. "You can't stop us."

"Of course," Tisha agreed. "Everyone has the right to petition the Senate. Can you tell me what the issue is?"

Lily Trueknife stared at Tisha. "Child, if you don't know, there's no help for you."

A man muttered, "We want our scroll back, you ugly frog."

Tisha either didn't hear, or was very good at pretending.

"What scroll?" Gusty asked. "Is this about the Sun Scroll?"

"What else would it be about?" someone asked. "Stupid urbie."

"Has the Senate made a decision on the Sun Scroll?" Gusty asked.

"We heard the Sun Scroll has been stolen," Lily Trueknife said. "Have you heard differently?"

Stolen? Gusty was stunned.

"We haven't heard anything yet," Tisha said. "This is news to us."

Captain Kosho would have mentioned it in his message, Gusty thought. *Unless the Senate thought they could keep the theft secret.*

Secrets had a way of leaking out. Lily Trueknife's people were watching the Senate intently.

Tisha looked at Gusty. "I think I should tell them," she said.

Gusty grunted. He trusted Tisha's judgment.

"We've been called in to help with an investigation at the Senatorial Palace," Tisha said.

"It's not an investigation," said Lily Trueknife. "It's a sham. Some senators have hidden the Sun Scroll because they fear the majority will vote to return it to the Reconciled Queendom."

"Senator Aura has asked us to help make certain the investigation is not a sham," Tisha said.

That could be the reason Aura Wisebrow had sent for Gusty, but he couldn't be certain until he spoke with her. Tisha was assuming a lot.

"Who's your mother?" Lily Trueknife asked, directing a piercing gaze at Gusty.

"Pearl Longbread."

"I don't know her."

"She's a hard-working baker on Turnback Street."

Lily Trueknife gestured at Tisha. "Is she telling the truth? Will there be a real investigation?"

"There will be," Gusty said. If the Sun Scroll had been stolen, he wanted to get it back.

"Will you give us time to see what we can find out?" Tisha asked.

Lily Trueknife looked over the faces of her people. She returned her gaze to Tisha.

"Tell Aura Wisebrow that we want a complete account tomorrow morning."

"We will pass that message on," Tisha promised.

"People are angry," Lily Trueknife said. "Tell her that may be all the time she will get."

* * *

Tisha didn't follow politics as closely as Gusty did, but she knew that the Sun Scroll was important. It was a sacred document that was supposed to be preserved unopened until the time came to fight the demons. There was no way it could be entrusted to the Queenies, but some oranges wanted so desperately to stop the war that they were willing to do anything to help. She couldn't blame them for wanting the Queenies to have an advantage in the war. But Tisha knew that letting the Queenies open the scroll would be a crime against the Sun Goddess herself.

Once they were a safe distance from Lily Trueknife's people, Tisha asked, "Do you think it was really stolen?"

"I don't know," Gusty said. "But I mean to find out."

His voice held determination. He wasn't the same slump-shouldered man that had allowed an angry mother to berate him last night. Now he was striding up the road with his gaze fixed on the Senatorial Palace.

They passed through the Broad Market, and Tisha didn't like what she saw. People were clustering in small knots, murmuring to each other. It was natural for people to gossip after a big crime. That didn't bother Tisha. No, what bothered her was that the groups were either orange or blue, never mixed.

At the Senatorial Palace, the guards—sailors from the Republican Navy—were all blue. The Navy didn't mix orange and blue sailors. Their approaches to seafaring were too different: Oranges rowed galleys, while blue sailors propelled their ships by magically creating water currents.

Most blues were sensitive to water currents, but moving a big ship took special talent. And the sailors knew it. They wore pompous green bandanas and swaggered about Sliceharbor as though they ruled the place.

Well, they *did* have some authority here, at the Senatorial Palace, but Tisha didn't think they needed to display it so flagrantly. They stood guard with a wide, cocky stance. Their sword hands were loose and relaxed, ready to reach for the rapiers on their hips.

As soon as Tisha put her foot on the first step, a beefy-looking sailor announced, "The Senatorial Palace is closed to all visitors."

His green bandana was decorated with a white cord. Tisha thought maybe he was a bosun or something.

"We're with the Urban Cohort," Tisha said, as politely as she could. She didn't really think the greenscarf had overlooked their shiny iron helmets with the bright copper fins, but perhaps he wanted Tisha to be formal.

"The Senatorial Palace is closed to *all* visitors," the maybe-bosun repeated.

"We are here to assist with the investigation," Tisha said.

"Thank you," said the bosun. "But your assistance is not required. Move along."

Typical pompous greenscarf. Just because they could move ships with water magic, they thought they could order everyone about on land, too.

"Show him the order, Gus."

Gusty fished the rolled-up message out of a hollow inside his breastplate and handed it to the arrogant bully.

The greenscarf took it, unrolled it, and read it.

"I don't recognize the signature stamp," he said, handing it back.

Gusty frowned at him and rolled the message up again. The greenscarf ignored Gusty's frown. That took courage.

Tisha said, "It's signed by our commander, Captain Kosho."

"Is he a commander or a captain?"

"He's a captain," Tisha said. "In command of the Urban Cohort." This guy was making her tired. It wasn't just the early start to the day; greenscarves were insufferable.

"City government has no jurisdiction here," the greenscarf said. "Move along."

Gusty growled. "Did you even read the message? It says we're to report to Senator Aura Wisebrow."

"Anyone could have written that."

Yeah. And Captain Kosho did. So let us in, you arrogant fool!

But she didn't say that out loud.

All right, Tisha. Calm down and think. This guy wants to show he's in charge. That's all he really wants. You can give him that. I know you can. It only costs you your pride.

"Perhaps there has been a misunderstanding," Tisha said. "Our captain was led to believe that Senator Aura requested assistance from the Urban Cohort. Perhaps we are mistaken. Do you have the authority to send a message to the senator?"

"I do," said the man in the green bandana with the white cord. "But I won't waste a senator's time."

"Excellent," said Tisha. "We're agreed then. We also do not want the senator to waste any more time waiting for the Urban Cohort to honor her request. Do you think you could send someone to ask if she still requires our presence?"

She figured she had him now. He could either show off his power to grant favors or he could risk offending a senator.

"Chokimber, go ask if Senator Aura requested any assistance from the Urban Cohort."

The greenscarf named Chokimber placed three fingers to his right ear—a typically pompous naval salute—and left the ranks to enter the Senatorial Palace.

"You'll leave your weapons here," the maybe-bosun said.

"Of course," Tisha said, unbuckling her weapons belt.

Gusty shrugged and set down his paddle club.

Neither of them commented on the fact that the bossy bosun had gone from pretending they had forged their orders to assuming that the senator would ask that they be let inside.

Chokimber returned, glanced uncertainly at their weapons lying on the steps of the palace, and said to his superior, "The senator asked me to escort them to her."

"Do so," said the bosun.

Chokimber put three fingers to his ear, then turned to Tisha and Gusty. "If you would follow me?"

Tisha kept her mouth shut. Captain Kosho would owe her double pay for this watch.

* * *

Gusty Longbread and Tisha were escorted to the library. It smelled strange.

Gusty had never been in a library before. His mother had taught him to read and write, of course. All Sliceharbor children were prepared for public service, even if their parents were bakers. But writing was mostly used for messages and short-term record keeping.

Because in Sliceharbor, sooner or later, paper got damp. Then it got musty. Anything you wanted to save had to be recopied before it started growing mold.

Mold. That was the strange smell in the library—the smell of no mold. A purifier had been here recently.

Purifiers combined air and life magic to kill fungus. Their techniques were far more complex than the common air magic orange children learned to keep away mosquitoes. Purifiers were rare, and they could charge well for the service.

Because purification was expensive, the library would need to keep its good air inside as long as possible. That explained why the expansive room had no windows. It was like being in a box. The afternoon storm was beginning its sweep of the city, but the booms of thunder seemed distant, and Gusty could barely hear the rain.

As Gusty took all this in, Tisha was introducing herself to Senator Aura Wisebrow, explaining how long she and Gusty had been patrolling together and discussing their mutual acquaintances, most of whom happened to be orange urbies. Women always had lots to talk about.

"Well," said Aura Wisebrow, "I must say I am quite pleased that Captain Kosho sent me two investigators, even though I asked only for one."

"Oh, I'm not an investigator," Tisha said. "Not like Gusty."

Gusty grunted. He wasn't really an investigator, either, but he was pretty good at figuring stuff out.

"In point of fact," said Aura Wisebrow, "the official investigation is in the hands of three local judges who have been summoned by the Senate. Officially, you are here only as observers. But Gusty, dear, I was wondering if you might not look around and tell me what you observe?"

So it was like that, was it?

"Well, the first thing I observe is that the three judges aren't here."

"No," said Aura Wisebrow. "They are supervising the search of the senatorial suites." She gave a small shudder. "The search of my own quarters was quite thorough."

"Have they found anything yet?" Gusty asked.

"No." She lowered her voice. "And I don't think they are likely to. All the senators agreed to the search with very little protest."

Gusty grunted. That didn't mean the senators were innocent. Perhaps one was guilty, yet confident that she or he had hidden the scroll well.

"Has the library been searched?" Gusty asked.

"I believe the librarians are still searching," said Aura Wisebrow. "Here: let us ask."

She led them to a worried blue man who was removing scroll cases one by one from their cubbies and inspecting the ends.

"Bampo, these soldiers from the Urban Cohort are here to observe the investigation. Could you tell them what you have done so far?"

The blue man straightened up and gave them worried looks. His wrinkled face and thin, gray beard suggested he had devoted many years to the care of paper documents. Plainly, he was disturbed that one of them had gone missing.

"My assistants are recataloging the entire collection," he said. "And I am double-checking their work. If the Sun Scroll has been misplaced, we will find it ... but we aren't going to find it."

"How do you know?" Gusty asked.

"Because I know I locked the Sun Scroll in the cabinet last night, and this morning it was gone."

"May we see the cabinet?" Gusty asked.

"Of course."

The librarian led them to a desk near the doors. It held several lamps.

"Why all the lamps?" Gusty asked.

"Visitors to the library often forget to bring their own."

"All right," said Gusty.

The librarian set his own lamp on a lampstand built onto the desk and gestured at a wooden cabinet.

"This is where I put the scroll yesterday, after the Senate requested I lock it up."

Gusty looked to Aura Wisebrow.

"It was Senator Washirko's suggestion," she said. "But we all agreed it was a good idea."

"Who else knew the scroll was kept here?" Gusty asked.

"Well, the other librarians," the librarian said. "And possibly some of the senators' assistants. Really, I don't think it was a secret." He looked toward the doors as an orange woman came in. Quietly, he added, "I suspect even *she* knew." Then he glanced at Aura Wisebrow, as though fearful he had said too much.

But Aura Wisebrow's attention was focused on the new arrival. She puffed up like a hen preparing to defend her flock's scratching place. The other woman's reaction was similar.

Aura Wisebrow affected a smile. "Matyu Gloria! I'm surprised to see you here."

Incredulity registered on the other woman's broad, flat-nosed face. "Is that why you told the natives to keep me out?"

"In fact," said Aura Wisebrow, "I asked the Navy to let you in if you came, as a special favor to me. And they consented, provided you did not bring your soldiers with you."

"I left most of my soldiers guarding my rooms in the City Palace. Apparently, some of the natives wish to paw through my belongings."

"Oh," said Aura Wisebrow. She frowned. This time, her facial expression seemed genuine. "For now, we have only authorized the search of our own palace," she said. "Unless you had access to the library last night, you should not be under suspicion."

"I should not be under suspicion because I am your guest," the woman said. "And because I am a matyu. And because I am of the Sunrise line."

"Of course," Aura Wisebrow said.

But Gusty realized these were precisely the reasons the woman *was* under suspicion. She was Matyu Gloria Sunrise, the ambassador from the Reconciled Queendom. She had been tasked with taking the Sun Scroll to the Motherland, and she was the one who had the most to gain from stealing it. Of course, she also had the most to lose if it had been stolen.

Gusty had never seen a real matyu before. Ambassador Gloria Sunrise looked like a matyu should: tall, imperious, with a golden circlet nestled among the curls of her carrot-orange hair. She even had the flat nose and broad face associated with the caste that ruled the Motherland. Matyus were able to converse directly with the deities, and throughout the Sun Island's history, they had used this gift to rule.

Gusty wouldn't kneel before her. He was a Sliceharbor boy, free of the Queenies' castes. But he couldn't help admiring her. She was a matyu.

Aura Wisebrow said, "Ambassador Gloria Sunrise, I would like you to meet Gusty Longbread and Tisha, soldiers of the Urban Cohort. The Senate has invited them as observers of this investigation."

"Good afternoon," said Tisha, with a smile.

"Good afternoon," said Gloria Sunrise, with no smile. She turned back to Aura Wisebrow. "I hold you personally responsible for finding my family's scroll, Senator. Do not attempt to hide behind your subordinates."

"Gusty and Tisha are not my subordinates," said Aura Wisebrow. "They are servants of the city of Sliceharbor, as am I. And I'm a big woman. I can't hide behind anything."

Gloria Sunrise looked Aura Wisebrow up and down, her gaze lingering on Aura's golden earrings. On the Sun Island, earrings were the mark of the middle castes. Matyus wore circlets.

"You are not as big as you think," Gloria Sunrise said. "But you are the biggest fish in this pool, so I am glad to hear that you accept your responsibility."

"I do."

"And I trust you will disabuse the Senate of the notion that they can ransack my quarters?"

"I'm sorry, but under our law, an investigation must be followed wherever it leads."

"Then see to it that it does not lead to me. Do I make myself clear?"

"Is there something I can do to help?" Tisha asked.

"You?" said Gloria Sunrise. "What can you do?"

Tisha said, "Senator Aura has already said that you had no access to the library last night. If I could arrange for one of the judges to take your testimony here, in the Senatorial Palace, then perhaps they would have no need to visit your quarters."

"My testimony is of no use to them. I did not steal the scroll."

"Of course not," said Tisha. "And don't you think they will be less inclined to suspect you once you have spoken with them?"

"Why should I so waste my time?"

"Is it really a waste?" Tisha asked. "You've come to ask for the Sun Scroll. It's been stolen. You can't get it back unless the judges find out who took it. It's in your best interests if their investigation is as efficient as possible. You can help them by telling them what you know."

"Even though I know nothing?"

"Yes," said Tisha. "Once they understand that, they can focus on more fruitful lines of investigation."

"I thought you were a soldier."

"I am."

Gloria Sunrise frowned down at her. "You are too clever to be a soldier. And you are persuasive enough to be dangerous."

Tisha said, "I am only pointing out things you already know."

To Aura Wisebrow, Gloria Sunrise said, "I shall be watching the native women more closely in the future." Then, to Tisha: "Very well. Take me to these judges of yours. Let us get this over with."

As the two women left the library, Aura Wisebrow said, "The ambassador was right: Tisha is clever."

Gusty concurred.

Then he turned to the librarian and asked, "How do you think the ambassador broke in?"

"I don't know," the librarian said.

"The ambassador's rooms are in the City Palace," Gusty said. "Did any of the sailors on guard see her enter or leave this building last night?"

"Not as far as I know," the librarian said.

"Then why do you suspect her?"

"I'm sorry," said the librarian. "Maybe I shouldn't speculate."

"Maybe you shouldn't," Gusty agreed. "Let's stick to the facts. What do you *know*?"

"Well, we know the thief had a key."

"How do we know that?" Gusty asked.

"Because the cabinet is not damaged."

Gusty came around the desk and inspected the cabinet's keyhole. "Hand me a lamp," he said.

The librarian did so. A dollop of warm wax dripped onto Gusty's sandaled toes.

"Why is there wax on your lamp?" Gusty asked.

"It's from the lampstand," said the librarian. "I think someone set a candle there last night."

Gusty looked around the library. "Where did the candle come from?"

"Sometimes the senators' assistants come in with candles. Messy things."

Gusty assumed he was referring to the candles.

"I noticed the wax this morning and didn't think too much of it," the librarian said. "But after a time, I realized that the lamp-stand would be the ideal place to put a candle if one were opening the cabinet. So I opened the cabinet, just to check. And I discovered that the Sun Scroll was gone."

"Open it now, please," Gusty said.

The librarian looked to Aura Wisebrow.

She gave a confirming nod.

The librarian slipped a cord from his neck. It held a single, ordinary key. He inserted it into the keyhole and unlocked the cabinet, revealing a small scroll hutch with most of the cubbies empty.

"Where was the Sun Scroll?" Gusty asked.

"Here, I think."

"You think?"

"It has a gold seal on each end," the librarian said. "I was not worried about overlooking it."

"How many other scrolls in the library have a gold seal?"

"That was the only one."

Could the thief have stolen it just because it was the prettiest?

"Are any other scrolls missing?" Gusty asked.

"Possibly," said the librarian. "The senators want their secretaries to have access to the library over night. They are not allowed to take scrolls out of the library, but sometimes they, ah, forget."

"So you can't be certain that only the Sun Scroll was taken?"

"Not yet. We're still doing the inventory."

"All right," Gusty said.

He inspected the lock from both sides of the cabinet's doors. He turned the key. The bolt slid out smoothly. There was no sign of damage.

"How many people have copies of this key?" Gusty asked.

"I thought this was the only copy," the librarian said.

"What if you lost it?" Gusty asked.

"I wear it at all times," said the librarian.

"Even while swimming?"

"Well, no," the librarian admitted. "I hang it up on a peg by the door every night when I come home. I suppose by 'all times' I mean 'at all times when I am acting as the Librarian of the Lunaslip Republic'. But you don't wear your armor all the time, do you?"

"I'm not criticizing," said Gusty. "I just want to know when someone could have gotten a copy. Has anyone broken into your house recently?"

"No," said the librarian. "At least, not that I'm aware of."

"But someone got the key long enough to copy it," said Aura Wisebrow.

"Yes," agreed the librarian. "The thought disturbs me."

"Don't worry about it too much," Gusty said. "There are other possibilities."

"Like what?" the librarian asked.

Like lockpicks. Or a lazy locksmith who makes her locks too much alike. Or a locksmith who keeps copies of every key and doesn't admit to it.

"Just other possibilities," Gusty said.

He inspected the droplets on the lampstand. They smelled like beeswax.

Bending down, so that the lamp was near the floor, he shuffled toward the library door.

"What are you looking for?" the librarian asked.

"More wax," Gusty said.

"I found a spot of wax in the corner," said the librarian.

"Show me."

The librarian led him deeper into the library and showed him a spot on the floor. Gusty scraped it off and sniffed it. It smelled the same. It was recent, too. Or at least, there wasn't much dust on it.

"Anything important back here?"

"Actually," said the librarian, "this was where we kept the Sun Scroll until yesterday afternoon, when Senator Washirko asked me to lock it up."

He pointed to an empty cubby in the scroll hutch.

"Have these scrolls been inventoried yet?"

"Yes," said the librarian. "And the Sun Scroll is the only one missing from this hutch. I double-checked."

Gusty played it out in his mind. The thief enters the library late at night, puts a candle on the lampstand, and opens the cabinet. The thief takes out the Sun Scroll, locks the cabinet, and then comes back to where the Sun Scroll had been. Why?

Why come back here at all, if you knew the scroll was in the cabinet?

So maybe the thief didn't know. Maybe the thief looked here first. Which meant that the thief probably wasn't one of the senators: They knew it had been locked up.

That line of reasoning pointed toward the ambassador, who might not have known the scroll had been moved. Gusty didn't like that line of reasoning. He wanted the thief to be blue.

But what if the thief had been orange?

He looked up at the ceiling. Sometimes oranges disturbed the ceiling gauze. But not here. The Senatorial Palace had been designed to accommodate both peoples, and the ceilings were high, with the gauze well above the copper fins of Gusty's helmet.

The librarian was also looking at the ceiling and frowning. "Is that a leak?"

They listened. The afternoon storm sounded distant because of the wooden ceiling, but the occasional drip of water from the thatch was quite distinct when it hit the wood.

"It sounds like you have a hole in your thatch," Gusty said.

"Not a big one," said Aura Wisebrow.

"But it must be fixed right away," the librarian said. "I'll need to send for a thatcher."

"Of course," said Aura Wisebrow. "I'll see to it that the guards know."

"This leak is new?" Gusty asked.

"The roof didn't leak during yesterday's storm," the librarian said.

Gusty studied the high wooden ceiling. It looked tight. And difficult to break through.

"Is there any access to the thatch from inside the library?"

"Well, there's a ceiling hatch," the librarian said.

"Show me."

The librarian led Gusty to the scroll hutches where his assistants were doing their inventory. Gusty raised the lamp. Yes, he could see the hatch in the ceiling. And directly below it was a hole in the gauze.

He smiled. The hole in the gauze was too small to have been made by an orange person.

"Oh," said Aura Wisebrow. "Do you think the thief came in through the roof?"

"It looks that way," Gusty said.

"So perhaps my colleagues are innocent?"

And you, too, thought Gusty, although he didn't say so.

"Perhaps," he said.

But it still had to be someone with inside knowledge of the library—someone who knew where to look, and then knew where to look when the Sun Scroll wasn't where it should have been.

"I didn't know thieves could break in through the roof," said the librarian.

Gusty grunted. He had seen storm shutters that had been sawed off their hinges. He'd seen a door that had been unbarred by drilling a hole through and inserting a lever to lift the bar. He'd even heard of a case where the thief had enlarged a natural limestone tunnel and broken into a house's cellar. And he'd seen a few thefts where the burglar had come in through the roof.

"My colleagues didn't like the idea that someone we trusted had stolen from the library," said Aura Wisebrow. "But I think they will be even less pleased to learn that criminals can enter the palace through the roof."

"I know it's disturbing," Gusty said. "But a rooftop entry is not that easy. Most burglars aren't that determined."

"But someone was," said Aura Wisebrow.

"Yeah," agreed Gusty.

He wasn't sure who had done this job, but he knew the man he needed to talk to: Bendoko the Crane.

* * *

Bendoko walked along the street. He was thinking about the boy sobbing in the alley, but he didn't feel guilty. No. It wasn't his fault the boy had made his friend mad.

So the kid was afraid he'd lost his friend. Big deal. He could get along without him. Bendoko had *never* had any friends, and he got along all right. So he didn't feel guilty.

And anyway, he couldn't afford to feel guilty. He did bad things for a living.

When he stole something, he got richer and someone else got poorer. That was just the way it worked. As a burglar, he had to accept that the way he earned his living would cause strife for someone else.

Of course, a job usually didn't cause so much strife. If he cut a man's money string in the market, he only hurt one man. And the guy could still earn more money afterwards. Bendoko might break into a house and take a woman's jewelry, but women with jewelry—especially orange women—tended to have a lot of jewelry. And they didn't really need any of it.

Not that Bendoko considered himself a virtuous thief who stole only from the rich and greedy. He'd steal from the poor if he was short on coins himself. That was, after all, how he earned his living. He was a bad man.

So he didn't feel guilty about the tensions at the Dock Market nor about the grumbling oranges who gathered in knots about the city casting suspicious eyes at their blue neighbors. And he sure didn't feel guilty about what happened to some kid, even though that kid was probably the same age as his little brother.

No. Bendoko didn't feel guilty. Not really. But maybe, just maybe, he felt a little sorry.

Maybe he even felt responsible.

It was easy to say, "Hey, it was Mendu's idea. I didn't know it was some holy scroll." Easy to say, and even true. But Bendoko knew that the trouble between the two kids really *was* his fault. They wouldn't have argued over who stole the scroll if he hadn't stolen it. He hadn't just stolen from the librarians. He had stolen from the entire town—from the entire Republic!

He had the uneasy feeling that bad things were going to happen. Not little bad things, like two boys arguing, but big bad things that were going to hurt a lot of people. And when the bad things happened, he would know he was responsible. He didn't think he would like that.

The frustrating thing was that he had no way to sort this out. He was a bad man, so even if he tried to do the right thing now, it would turn out wrong anyway. He couldn't go to a philosopher for spiritual guidance. Philosophers could only help good people.

He could seek help from Big Zeemo, but Big Zeemo was not a good spirit. Oh, Big Zeemo required his people to follow a certain *code*. He was *honest* in his way. But he wouldn't be able to help Bendoko be *good*.

Not that a bad person like Bendoko *could* be good. But maybe, just this once, he should have been.

Ah, Bendoko, he told himself, *you know you won't figure this out walking the streets. Quit stalling and go see Puji.*

* * *

Bendoko and his siblings had grown up in an apartment in Sliceharbor's Pinetown District, about a block-and-a-half from the New Market. The New Market sold hot food—baked bread, roasted peanuts, grilled chicken. The food was cooked outside, of course. The buildings facing the market had outdoor ovens and barbecue grills sheltered under palm-thatch awnings. Hot food tastes best when you eat it in the rain.

When the wind was right, it would blow the smell of the food all the way to the kids in the apartment. They got the smell, but not the food.

Puji, the oldest, Bendoko's sister, said that they once had two mothers. Bendoko could only remember one. Puji said that was because the other one had run out on them when he was still a baby.

Bendoko could remember their two fathers—tall, laughing men with rapiers on their hips. They were sailors and only came home during hurricane season. Sometimes they got caught at another port and wintered there instead. But the children and their mother loved them because they were so jolly and they always brought home fruit and money.

Their fathers died at sea. Bendoko had assumed they were killed by pirates, because blue people can't drown. But when he was older, Puji had explained that their fathers had been killed when their ship smashed into some rocks in a storm.

We have to be conscious to breathe under water, she explained. *That's why we never sleep there. We'd suffocate.*

Their mother wasn't around to explain it to him because by then she'd jumped out the window.

But they still had Puji, and Puji took care of them. She was like their mother after that, except they still just called her "Puji".

Hertha called her "Mommy Puji" once, but Puji had slapped her for it. Then Puji had cried and promised never to slap any of them again. She'd kept her promise, but to be safe, they'd never again called her "Mommy".

No one ever thought of calling Bendoko "Daddy", but he was the one left in charge when Puji went off to work—in charge of three hungry little brats with no food in the house. He made up games for them. Like, he'd take a rag and tie it up into a ball and they'd toss it around the apartment. Or they'd take the stools and put them on top of the tiny dining table and pretend they were on a ship—brave sailors like their fathers had been. That game had stopped when the table leg broke. Bendoko got in trouble, but Hertha had the worst of it. She'd fallen from the highest stool and slammed her face so hard that she'd split her lower lip and broken a tooth. She still had the scar.

Puji had cried over that, too. Not about the table leg—Bendoko had borrowed some twine from a neighbor and sort of fixed it—no, she cried over Hertha's scar, because she didn't have enough money to pay for a healer. But anyway, even if she had, the healer might have started asking questions and sent them to a judge.

They lived in fear of judges. Puji said that a judge had the power to split them up, give them all to different homes. She said that anyone who found out they were living without parents could take them to a judge. That's why they always had to play indoors. They only went outside once a day, to swim in the canal.

Their mother had been afraid of judges, too. That was because they were all illegitimate. Their parents had never married because they couldn't afford to buy a house together. That was what you had to do to get married in Sliceharbor—

own a house. If a wealthy family ever found out, they could adopt the children and take them away from their mother.

Bendoko and his siblings had been seen bathing, but no one ever took pity on them. At least, not *that* much pity.

Bendoko thought maybe he'd been born bad. His mother hid out with all those illegitimate kids. His fathers went to sea to do Justice alone knew what. (Once he understood they hadn't been killed by pirates, he harbored a secret hope that they had been pirates themselves.) It was no surprise he was bad, too. Really, it was a miracle that he was the only one.

He hadn't known he was bad until he was fourteen. It happened in Orangemonth—the winter Orangemonth.

Winter days usually weren't too cold in the apartment, because they were on the top floor. Any warmth in the building tended to come up to them. But this day had settled in with a damp chill. Hertha and Tamba were fighting over whose turn it was to sweep the floor, and little Jambi, only seven, was crying and crying because he was so hungry.

The wind was just right, blowing the smell of roasted chicken from the New Market. Bendoko couldn't stand it anymore.

He told Hertha she was in charge, and then he just walked out. He'd never done that before. He was supposed to stay and watch the children—keep them quiet if a judge visited the building, or something. But he just left them. Maybe because he felt sorry for Jambi, but mostly because he had to get *away*.

He'd followed the smell to the New Market. That chicken was incredible. His mouth watered. His stomach groaned. He *ached* for that roasted chicken and its sizzling fat. Bendoko would be forever grateful that he had been too poor to own a knife, because in that moment he would have killed for that roasted chicken, if he'd only had the means.

He didn't have a knife. But he did have sharp eyes. He could tell which people were watching their wares and which were distracted by customers. The market was quite busy. It was excellent weather for selling hot food.

Bendoko took one walk across the market, like he was going downtown on an errand. Then he doubled back through an alley. As he had hoped, the barbecue he had his eye on was momentarily unattended. He snatched a roasting chicken and sprinted around the corner. It burned blisters on his hands, and he dropped it—almost dropped it in the street, except that he had the reflexes to spread his knees and catch the falling roast in the skirt of his sari.

Wrapped in cloth like that, the chicken didn't burn his skin. He carried it back to the apartment, licking his fingers to salve the burns and to taste that delicious fat.

Only when he stepped inside the building did he worry about what Puji would say. She was still at work, but she would find out somehow. Three little kids couldn't keep a secret forever. And then he realized he was a thief, a criminal. The judges would come for him. And even if they didn't—even if he was never caught—the God of Justice would remember this day and punish him for all eternity.

His feet slowed as he climbed the steps. The chicken wrapped in his clothing was only a light burden, but the weight of his crime made it feel stone-heavy. He stopped halfway between the second and third floors. He almost turned back. He almost went back to the market to confess.

And then he heard seven-year-old Jambi whimpering. Not crying anymore, just whimpering. And Hertha was making the sort of motherly sounds that Puji sometimes made when she wasn't too tired and wanted them to know she loved them.

Bendoko continued up the stairs and pushed open the apartment door. He took the big plate from the cupboard and set it on the twine-repaired table. Then he unbundled the chicken from his skirts and dumped it on the plate.

The three kids stared in amazement. How had he gotten a chicken?

He'd found a chicken vendor who needed him to run an errand. (After theft, lies turned out to be easy.)

They were all too hungry to ask any more questions. They ate the whole chicken, all the gristly bits, and most of the smaller bones.

And they smiled. Those little kids laughed. And Bendoko was happy. Because *he* had done it. He was the one responsible for that happiness. He had done something horribly, horribly bad—

probably the worst thing anyone in his family had ever done—and it had turned out to be wonderful!

Fourteen-year-old Bendoko was a criminal, and he was happier than he had ever been.

* * *

In the present, Bendoko reached the New Market. He'd timed it right. Puji was at the baker's stand, buying bread on her way home from work.

* * *

The happiness couldn't last, of course. Happiness is for good people.

Puji found out. She made him promise to never steal again. He broke his promise. She yelled. He ran away.

And he came back, sorry. He apologized and promised again.

After a week, he convinced himself that the problem was getting caught. If Puji didn't know he was stealing, she could be happy too.

He couldn't bring home roasted chickens anymore. The little kids would tell on him. They were hungry, but they were honest. Puji was raising them to be good kids, and he admired her for that.

He figured he could steal money, though. Puji wouldn't notice if an extra coin or two was added to her money string while she slept.

So he taught himself bumping. He would blunder into someone untying a money string. Coins would scatter on the paving stones. Bendoko would apologize and help pick them up. (Bendoko thought he invented bumping, but he was not Slice-harbor's only practitioner.)

Bumping was exciting because there were so many ways to win. The most obvious trick was to palm one of the coins as he helped pick them up, but suspicious people looked for that. The neatest trick was to catch a coin in the air during the moment of impact. He also liked the trick of grasping a coin with his toes and tucking it in between his foot and his sandal.

Bumping was something he could do when he took the little

kids swimming. He'd leave them in the water and slip off around the corner. He'd come back a tiny bit richer. He knew it wouldn't pay to get greedy—one coin, two at the most. Sometimes he took flatrings, but mostly he took sixths.

After two weeks of this labor, Bendoko had accumulated a small string of money. He couldn't spend it on anything, of course—that would give the game away. So he started slipping coins onto Puji's string while she slept.

But Puji counted. She was always calculating the balance between food and rent. She knew every coin personally.

The first coin confused her. She thought she'd miscounted.

The second coin made her suspicious.

When Bendoko slipped the third coin on her string, she caught him in the act.

Puji shouted. Bendoko ran away. He felt sorry. He came back and promised never to steal again.

Things went around like this three or four times before Bendoko finally left for good. By then, he had mastered bumping and was getting good at string cutting. (He'd been caught once, but he'd been able to afford triple restitution, which was his only punishment. After that, he was less afraid of judges.) He could take care of himself on the street.

He left because he'd realized that any happiness he stole for his younger siblings would always come at the expense of Puji's pain. He was tired of hurting her.

* * *

"Good evening, young lady, may I buy you a roasted chicken?"

His sister nearly dropped her string. She whirled to look at him.

"Ben!"

Her face rippled with conflicting emotions. He waited for her to say something more, but she couldn't.

"It's good to see you again," he said, because he wanted to hear somebody say it.

"What do you want?"

He shrugged. "I want to buy you a chicken."

She shook her head.

"I'll pay for it with real money," he said.

"And where did you get the money? No. Don't answer. Please." She turned to the baker and handed him two sixths. "Another loaf, please."

Puji purchased the bread, again refused to let Bendoko purchase a chicken, and led him back to the apartment.

The building hadn't changed much in the seven years since Bendoko had moved out—or left, or run away, or whatever. It was a "mushroom"—a cylindrical, three-story, white-brick building with a fat, conical roof (thatched in the orange school). Some of the pineboard storm shutters had rotted away from the windows, but their absence was only noticeable because they had been replaced by fresh boards. This wasn't the Shacks. This was civilization, where landlords took care of their buildings. Of course, they charged for it.

Bendoko followed Puji up the stairs, skipping the eighth step above the second-floor landing because it squeaked. Puji pushed open the door to the apartment and called, "Get a third plate. We've got company."

Bendoko peeked over her shoulder into the room.

Jambi's face lit up with a smile. "Ben!"

Jambi was fourteen now, with long hands and feet. His arms were skinny, and they always would be if he grew up like Bendoko.

"I bought you a chicken," Bendoko said, "but Puji ate it."

Puji rolled her eyes and set the loaves on the table next to a bowl of—

"Are those peaches?" Bendoko asked.

"Bought 'em yesterday," Jambi said, still grinning. "Help yourself."

Puji reached into her shopping bag and pulled out something wrapped in a lily pad leaf. She set it on the table and unwrapped it.

"Cheese?" It was Jambi's turn to be surprised. "You bought cheese?"

Puji looked at Bendoko with an apologetic smile. "We're celebrating," she said. "Jambi got a raise this week."

"A raise?" said Bendoko. "I didn't even know you had a job."

"I'm working for Vomozhibo on the Pinetown Canal," Jambi said.

"You're a canal mucker?"

Jambi shrugged. "Gotta start somewhere."

"And now he's going somewhere," Puji said. "He's up to seven flatrings a week."

Bendoko took the measure of his little brother. He remembered what it was like to be young and eager and finally able to help the family. "Good for you," he said.

Jambi beamed with pride.

Puji was smiling, too. She reached out and squeezed Bendoko's hand.

"Let's eat," she said.

They sat on the same old wooden stools around the same old table—the same except that the twine-bound table leg had been replaced. As Bendoko helped himself to their hard-earned food, Puji told him about the other siblings. Hertha was still living in Lowtown, working in that net-making shop with the bundle-thatched roof. She was thinking of moving into a different apartment, one where she would have fewer roommates. Tamba was still in the Republican Navy and hadn't ported at Sliceharbor since Bendoko's last visit. Puji had gotten a letter from him in Redmonth, though. He'd said his ship had been assigned pirate patrol, but they hadn't seen any pirates.

"Tell him *your* news," Jambi said.

Puji waved her hand dismissively. "There isn't any 'news'."

"Yes there is." Jambi looked at Bendoko. "Puji is going to quit her job."

"Good!" said Bendoko.

"I haven't quit yet."

"But you will soon?" Bendoko asked encouragingly. He hated Puji's job. She wove gauze.

"At the end of the month," Puji said. Her gaze drifted to the cheese. "I think we'll have enough money saved up by then."

"I can almost cover rent now," Jambi said.

Bendoko smiled at him. "Good for you."

Jambi looked to Puji. "Well, it's just because the landlord keeps our rent so low. He's been giving us a discount these last couple years, because he found out that we're orphans. Things aren't as bad now as they used to be."

"I'm glad," Bendoko said. He *was* glad. Of course, the truth was that Bendoko had been paying most of the rent—one way or another—for the past two years, and he'd just spent his up-front money on twelve more months. But Jambi didn't know that. Bendoko certainly wasn't going to tell him.

Bendoko looked at Puji. She wasn't meeting his eyes. Bendoko realized that she knew.

Well of course she knew. She'd never been stupid. Bendoko hadn't been able to get away with slipping a flatring onto her money string, so of course she knew that the landlord hadn't cut their rent by five-sixths out of kindness. But she hadn't said anything about it. At least, not yet.

"Puji, tell him what you're going to do," Jambi urged. "After you quit your job."

"I'm going to apprentice to a healer," Puji admitted.

"A healer?" Bendoko said. "You can be a healer? Doesn't that require some sort of—" he wiggled his fingers, "—talent?"

"Hujiki says the healing touch comes from the soul, not the fingers," Puji said. "And she says I have the talent—enough to learn on, anyway."

"Oh." Bendoko was surprised. He'd never thought of anyone in his family as being particularly magical.

"It won't pay as much as her weaving job," Jambi said. "Not to start. But she'll be making good money in a few years."

"Well," said Bendoko. "That's wonderful news, Puji."

She lowered her eyes. "Thank you."

And you couldn't be doing this unless I'd started helping with the rent. That really bothers you, doesn't it? I'm sorry, big sister. But taking help from a bad person doesn't make you bad, too. You deserve this chance, no matter how you got it. Don't worry. I'll never tell.

"So how about you, Ben?" Jambi asked. "What's new with you? I see you've got a new sari."

It wasn't *that* new. He'd bought it a couple months ago. But it was still nice-looking. Bendoko lived in the Shacks, but he didn't have to *look* like he lived in the Shacks.

"I bought it from a weaver on the Dock Road. He doesn't

charge too much."

Puji fingered the cloth automatically. "He does good work," she said.

"Yeah," said Bendoko.

And now they were out of things to talk about—except for the thing that Bendoko had come to talk about.

"Are you eating all right?" Puji asked.

"What? Yeah. Yeah, I'm doing great."

Jambi asked, "Are you still living in … ?"

"The Shacks, yeah," Bendoko admitted. "You know how it is, you can …" *You can either eat or pay rent* was how the saying went. But Bendoko didn't want Jambi to start examining how he and Puji were now able to do both. "Well, you know how it is."

"Yeah." Jambi nodded reassuringly. "Yeah, we know how it is."

Bendoko poked at his peach pit, trying to figure out how to begin.

Puji pushed the remains of the cheese to Jambi. "Better finish it up," she said. "You know it won't taste this good in the morning."

Jambi shrugged and began spreading it onto a chunk of bread.

"So the reason …" Bendoko began.

They looked at him expectantly.

"That is. Um. Puji, I need your advice. On … something."

Puji and Jambi exchanged glances.

"Maybe you should go for a swim," Puji suggested.

Jambi frowned. "I want to hear this," he said. But he got up from the table, still chewing his bread.

Jambi went to the door and slipped into his sandals. Puji frowned at the back of his head.

"All right," she said.

Jambi turned. "What?"

"You can stay. Sit back down."

Jambi left his sandals by the door and returned to his stool.

"He's doing an adult's job," Puji said. "He can hear what adults have to say."

Bendoko shrugged. "Fair enough."

"Well?" said Puji. "Go on then."

"All right. I've got a problem."

Puji waited.

"Well, let me back up," Bendoko said.

"You haven't gone anywhere yet," Puji said.

"Well, it's not exactly *my* problem," Bendoko said. "I did—" he looked at Jambi, "—some work. And I was pleased with how it turned out. But it seems to have made some other people unhappy."

Puji said, "Your 'work' always makes people unhappy."

"Yeah," said Bendoko. "I guess you could look at it like that. Except that this time, there's a lot of people unhappy."

"Oh no," said Puji. "You need us to hide you here, don't you?"

"What? No. Nothing like that." Bendoko thought a moment. He was pretty sure he was in the clean current. "I don't think so anyway. No, the problem is that … well, what if I don't want all these people to be unhappy?"

"Then you shouldn't have stolen whatever it was!"

"Yeah, yeah," Bendoko admitted. "But—" He looked at Jambi. Oh, well. The kid knew. "Look, I had to steal it because I was paid," Bendoko said. "I'm a professional. It was nothing personal. But I didn't realize that I'd be causing problems for so many people."

Puji looked at him suspiciously. "How many people?"

"Um … a lot of people?"

Puji looked at Jambi. "Go swimming."

"But you said—"

"I know what I said. Go swimming. Now."

"All right."

Jambi got up.

"Good seeing you again, Ben."

"Good seeing you, too, Jambi. Congratulations on your raise."

Jambi smiled. "Thanks, Ben." He went out the door.

Puji got up and looked out the window. Bendoko sat and waited for her to see Jambi leaving the building. He didn't have to wait long. The kid did what he was told.

"You stole the Sun Scroll, didn't you?"

Bendoko shrugged. "Yeah."

"And now you're sorry."

"Well, I wouldn't say I'm 'sorry'. I just ... wish people hadn't gotten so excited."

"You know there was a fight at the lumber yard today?"

"There have been fights all over."

"One of my coworkers had to leave early so she could care for her husband. He needed stitches in his leg."

"Yeah," said Bendoko. "A lot of stuff like that today."

"Why did you do it?"

"Puji, I didn't know, all right? It was just another job. A little trickier than a normal job, but just a job, right? I didn't know that everyone would get so excited about it."

"So what do you want from me?" she asked. "Do you want me to forgive you? Do you want me to say, 'That's all right, Ben. I know people are usually *happy* when you steal their things'?"

"No," Bendoko said. "I want you to tell me what I should do."

"What you should do? You shouldn't have stolen it!"

"Maybe not," said Bendoko. "But I did. So now ... suppose I wanted to do the right thing. What do you think that is?"

"The right thing? Now you want to do the right thing?"

"Yeah."

"No you don't, Ben. You don't want to do the right thing. Because if you wanted to do the right thing, you would have given it back."

"That's it? That's the right thing?"

"Yeah, Ben. That's the right thing."

"Oh."

"What? This surprises you?"

"Well, yeah," Bendoko admitted. "I thought you would tell me I had to turn myself in."

"Well, obviously you should turn yourself in," Puji said. "But you aren't going to do that either."

"I'd rather not," Bendoko admitted. "Every orange in the city is looking for someone to beat up. I don't really feel like telling them that I'm the guy."

"You wouldn't get beaten up," Puji said. "You might get imprisoned. You'd probably get sentenced to public labor until you'd paid your debt. But they wouldn't let anyone beat you up."

Bendoko didn't like the idea of public labor. Depending on the value the judge assigned the scroll, he could be working for the rest of his life. But he wasn't going to say that to Puji. She'd been weaving gauze since she was twelve.

"Let's go back to this return-the-scroll idea," he said. "Would that really make things right?"

"I don't know," Puji said. "Oranges are so touchy about everything lately. There's a lot of problems you didn't create and you can't fix. But yes, if you return the scroll, that will help a *lot*." She looked at him quizzically. "Do you still have it?"

"No," said Bendoko. "I gave it to the guy who hired me. But I'm thinking now that I might try to get it back."

* * *

At the Senatorial Palace, the three judges concluded that the Sun Scroll was not hidden in any of the senators' suites. The library inventory confirmed that it wasn't in the library, either. The senators concluded that the Sun Scroll had been stolen by someone outside the palace, and they made plans to announce their findings.

By the time Gusty and Tisha were free to go, it was time for them to start their second watch. They went looking for the Crane.

* * *

Bendoko knew Puji had given him the right answer. He walked toward the docks, sandals shuffling a quick step against the paving stones. He was going to see Mendu.

And Mendu would give him his fifty imperials—or make some excuse—and then Bendoko would ask if his client liked the scroll. And Mendu would say something, and then Bendoko would ask how come his client knew so much about holy scrolls. And then Mendu would … tell him to mind his own business or he'd be squished like a bug.

No, that wouldn't work. Getting information out of people wasn't Bendoko's area of expertise. That's why he worked for guys like Mendu. Mendu had the contacts. He knew the guy who wanted to buy the holy scroll.

But Mendu had let *that* slip, hadn't he? Bendoko knew the client was an expert on holy scrolls. And he knew the client was a guy. He *was* a guy, wasn't he? Hadn't Mendu said he was a guy? The inside man was a guy.

Bendoko thought about the inside man. He'd talked fancy, and he'd known all about the library. And he'd known about the plan.

And when Bendoko had mentioned the inside man was there, Mendu had gotten mad at Bendoko. He hadn't said anything bad about the inside man.

Mendu almost seemed afraid of the inside man.

So ... the inside man was the client. Bendoko was sure of it. Well, pretty sure. It seemed like a good bet, anyway.

If Bendoko kept his ears open tonight, maybe Mendu would let slip who the inside man was. Maybe he'd give Bendoko a clue about where the scroll had been taken.

And then ... then Bendoko could put it right. Once he knew where that scroll was, he could steal it back. He could break into the library again and put it back where he'd found it. Then they'd have their scroll again, and everyone would calm down.

The only hitch that Bendoko could see was that it was the right thing to do. This bothered him because he wasn't so good at doing the right thing. And also he was a little worried about Big Zeemo.

Bendoko had asked Big Zeemo to look after his immortal soul. In return, Big Zeemo expected certain standards of behavior. Big Zeemo didn't care much about doing the right thing. Big Zeemo wanted you to keep your word.

If you said you would steal a thing, you were supposed to steal it. And if a guy said he'd pay you half up front and half when he got the thing, he was supposed to pay you.

So far, so good. But what would Big Zeemo think if—after you got paid—you went and stole the thing back? Was that all right? Or was that like switching goods after sale? (Big Zeemo frowned on swindles if you swindled someone under the protection of Big Zeemo.)

Bendoko realized his plan was a little iffy.

Doing the right thing wasn't a good enough reason for Big Zeemo. Big Zeemo probably wouldn't like it if Bendoko stole the scroll back just to do the right thing. Now, if he did it for money ...

Bendoko wondered if anyone would pay him to do the right thing.

* * *

The docks were home to criminals of all kinds—smugglers, swindlers, shakers, as well as the usual mix of string cutters and bumpers that you could find elsewhere in the city. It was a dangerous place to patrol, and Captain Kosho tried to distribute this danger fairly.

Gusty and Tisha had rotated into and out of dock patrol several times over the years, and so Gusty knew a few things about Bendoko the Crane. He was a loner, didn't have any friends. He lived in the Shacks. He made his living by burglary, and his skills were for hire.

Going to the Shacks was out of the question. The Shacks were technically not part of the city, so anything that happened in the Shacks was technically out of the Urban Cohort's jurisdiction. But the real reason they wouldn't go into the Shacks was that urbies who went to ask questions in the Shacks didn't come out again.

The difference between the Shacks and Lowtown was that in Lowtown, the honest people were on your side. They knew there were a lot of criminals in the district, especially by the docks, and they wanted the urbies around to keep the criminals from getting out of hand. In the Shacks, the honest people might kill you out of fear that someone would think they had cooperated with an urbie.

So Gusty and Tisha hoped to find someone who had seen the Crane in Lowtown. The first people they found were their fellow urbies, Stormy Colorpot and Woto, his blue partner. Stormy and Woto said they had seen the Crane pay a visit to Mendu's warehouse last night. Maybe Mendu knew where to find the Crane.

Gusty and Tisha went to look for Mendu.

The door of Mendu's warehouse was closed for the night, but a high, tiny window lit by lamp glow suggested that someone was inside and awake. Tisha knocked. Gusty prepared for trouble.

They heard hushed voices coming from behind the door, but no one opened.

Tisha knocked again. "Urban Cohort," she said. "We're here to see Mendu."

Sandals shuffled toward the door—the strides of an orange person. Mendu employed Tiny and Sunny Too-Tall as warehouse security. It was a good job for them. Before, they had been shakers, oranges who pick up smaller people and shake their money strings loose. Gusty was glad they had finally taken a legitimate job—even though he wasn't sure all of Mendu's dealings were legitimate.

"Mendu's not here," said a voice on the other side of the door.

"Where is he?" Tisha asked.

A pause. Too long. "Away on business."

Tisha looked up at Gusty.

"We need to talk to *you*, then," Gusty said. "Sunny Too-Tall? If that's you, open up."

The sandals shuffled away. There was another muffled conference.

Gusty looked at Tisha and waggled his club.

She shrugged.

Gusty rapped his club on the door. "Open up or we come in anyway."

"I'm coming, I'm coming," called an irritated voice. Gusty guessed it was Sunny's brother, Tiny Too-Tall.

Gusty heard the wooden scrape of a bar being removed. The door opened and a short man stepped out and shut it behind himself too quickly for Gusty to catch a glimpse of the interior.

"What do you need to talk about?" Tiny asked.

"We're looking for a man named Bendoko the Crane," Tisha said.

Tiny backed against the door protectively. "He's not here."

"We know he's not here," Tisha said. "We want to know where he is."

Tiny looked down on her with a belligerent air and said, "I don't know."

"Can you tell us how to find him?"

Tiny looked from Tisha to Gusty, but he said nothing.

"How does Mendu contact him?" Tisha asked.

"All right," said Tiny. "I can see you two mean business, so I'll tell you everything I know. If you want to talk to the Crane, you have to go to the Dock Market and stand under the palm trees. If the Crane wants to talk to you, he'll meet you there. If he doesn't come, try again tomorrow night. If you stand under the palm trees three nights in a row and the Crane doesn't come, then you'll never find him. He's a very secretive man, and no one can find him when he doesn't want to be found."

* * *

It was quiet enough inside the warehouse that Bendoko could hear Tiny's story. He was certainly sending those urbies chasing after feathered snakes!

Bendoko appreciated an artful lie. He would have appreciated this one more if his head hadn't been in the grasp of Sunny Too-Tall, who was ready to snap his neck if he made a sound.

The urbies left. Tiny came back inside. Sunny released Bendoko's head, and Bendoko sagged to the floor.

He wanted to rub his neck with relief, but he couldn't. His hands and feet were tied.

He should have been suspicious when Tiny let him come inside without asking Mendu first. Well, he *had* been suspicious. Bendoko was always suspicious when dealing with bad people. But he should have been *more* suspicious.

Tiny strode toward them, his sandaled feet scuffing on the dirty stone floor.

He said, "We're running out of time, Crane. The urbies are looking for you now. You must have gaffed the job."

Bendoko knew he hadn't gaffed the job. The urbies were just guessing. When you're the best burglar in Sliceharbor, you get suspected of everything—even the jobs you actually did.

Tiny placed his sandal on Bendoko's foot and gently rocked forward, crushing Bendoko's toes.

Bendoko grimaced.

"Now that you understand the hurry we're in," Tiny said, "maybe you'll tell us where to find the scroll?"

"I told you, I— Ahh!" It was hard to talk with a giant standing on his foot. "I don't know where it is. I came here to find out from Mendu."

"So Mendu was gonna tell you what he did with the scroll?" Tiny seemed offended. "He didn't tell *us*."

Sunny glanced at the corpse on the floor beside Bendoko. "Maybe that's because I broke his neck too hard."

"Mendu could have told us earlier," Tiny said. "Like last night, when the Crane brought it in. He could have told us, Sunny, but he didn't. That hurts my feelings."

He shifted his weight and two bones in Bendoko's foot ground together.

"He wasn't planning to tell me anything," Bendoko said. "I just thought—unh!—that he would let something slip."

"Now what makes you think that a careful man like Mendu would let something slip?" Tiny asked.

"He'd already ... told me a few things."

"A few things." Tiny looked to his brother. "Do you hear that, Sunny? Mendu told the Crane a few things."

"What things?" Sunny asked.

"That's a good question," Tiny said. "Yeah, Crane. What things did Mendu tell you? Is there anything *you* would like to let slip?"

He leaned forward. Bendoko's eyes watered from the pain.

"There was an inside man," Bendoko said, speaking fast. "A blue. He knew the layout and he knew the scroll had been moved."

"Go on," Tiny said. He shifted his weight.

"Aaaangggh!" said Bendoko.

"Maybe he doesn't understand 'go on'," Sunny suggested.

"That's all I know!" Bendoko said. "I think the inside man has the scroll now. I think he's the guy who contracted with Mendu."

"What do you think, Sunny?"

"I think we need to know the inside man's name," Sunny said.

Tiny looked down at Bendoko. "Yeah, Crane. Tell us the inside man's name."

Bendoko shook his head. "I don't know, Tiny. I don't know. Mendu just said you don't want to mess with him. He's too big."

Tiny looked at Sunny. "Is he saying I'm not big?"

Sunny shrugged.

Tiny looked down at Bendoko. "Is that what you think, Crane? You think I shouldn't mess with this guy because you don't think I'm big?"

Bendoko cried out in pain.

"What was that? I didn't understand what you said."

"You're big, Tiny! You're big!"

Tiny nodded slowly. "Damn right I'm big. I'm bigger than you, Crane, and I'm very, very disappointed. Are you disappointed, Sunny?"

"Yeah," Sunny said loyally.

"We're disappointed, Crane. We're disappointed because we thought you could tell us more than that. We were expecting *more*. Weren't you expecting more, Sunny? I was expecting more."

"Look, if you let me go, I can help you," Bendoko said. "I can steal the scroll back and— and give it to you."

"Really?" Tiny asked. "How can you steal it back if you don't know where it is?"

"I— I'll find out! Give me a chance to find out! How can I find out if I'm— if you don't let me go?"

Tiny Too-Tall stepped off Bendoko's foot. The pain eased, but didn't stop. Bendoko's toes were bleeding under his toe nails.

"He says he'll find out, Sunny. What do you think?"

"What do *you* think?" Sunny asked warily.

Tiny nodded with satisfaction. "I'm glad you asked that, Sunny. I think he's told us all he knows."

"I have!" Bendoko said.

"And so I think we should kill him now," Tiny said. "We don't need him anymore, do we, Sunny?"

"Nope."

"You need me to find it for you," Bendoko said. "And steal it back."

Tiny frowned. "He thinks we can't find it, Sunny. He thinks he's smarter than we are."

Sunny said, "No blue's smarter than you are, Tiny."

"No, I think you can find it," said Bendoko. "You can find it. But you need me to steal it back for you."

Tiny thought for a moment. "No we don't," he decided. "You already touched our sacred scroll once. We don't need your slimy hands on it again."

Tiny Too-Tall knelt down at Bendoko's head. Meaty fingers gripped Bendoko's face and gently directed his gaze to the dead body beside him.

"You see Mendu?" Tiny asked.

Bendoko didn't want to see Mendu, with his eyes bulging out like that and his neck contorted. When Bendoko saw Mendu, he saw his own brief, ugly future.

Tiny's grip tightened. "You see Mendu?"

"Yeah. Yeah, I see him."

"That's what happens to blues who touch our scroll."

He let go of Bendoko's face and stood up. "Make it quick, Sunny. I hate to see people suffer."

Bendoko realized he wasn't going to be able to talk his way out. They were oranges, and he was the blue who had stolen their sacred scroll. That was sacrilege, wasn't it?

Bendoko was theoretically protected from Judgment. He'd given his soul to a nature spirit, which meant that the deities couldn't mess with him after death. That was the theory. And now he was going to find out how it worked in practice.

Bendoko was afraid to die. He wanted to ask Big Zeemo to save him, but really, how much had Bendoko done for Big Zeemo?

Just then, they heard a noise coming from Mendu's office.

Bendoko was too distracted by his own thoughts to pay much attention to the noise, but later he would retroactively recognize it as the sound of a blue woman in a cane skirt forcing her hips through a high window with help from an orange man standing in the street. Next came the thump of the woman hitting the stone floor, accompanied by a feminine grunt. And then she was standing in the office door shouting at the surprised brothers:

"Urban Cohort! You're all under arrest!"

Bendoko couldn't believe it: She had come to save him!

... All by herself. One little urbie against two professional thugs.

Sunny looked at Tiny. Tiny looked at Sunny.

The urbie's eyes widened and she ran for the door.

Bendoko's feet were tied together, but he rolled himself upright and began hopping after her, shouting, "Take me with you!"

The woman ignored him. She reached the door and lifted the bar. The door opened, revealing two orange urbies and another blue one.

Behind Bendoko, Tiny said, "Grab Mendu."

Afraid that he would also be grabbed, Bendoko hopped desperately toward the entering urbies.

"Save me!" he cried.

He lost his balance and fell on his face.

Giant feet ran past Bendoko's head.

Bendoko rolled over. The blue woman helped him sit up. One of the copper fins on her helmet was crumpled. She had saved his life.

The other three urbies were running toward the shadowy crates in the back of the warehouse.

"Do you have urbies waiting at the secret exit?" Bendoko asked the woman. She had beautiful lips and she had saved his life.

"We didn't know about the secret exit," she said.

"Oh," said Bendoko. "Well, you'd better hope your friends don't find it, then."

"Why?"

"Because if they start running through the back alleys, they'll learn that three against two can get evened out in a hurry."

The woman glanced toward the back of the warehouse. Her worried frown was very pretty, and she had saved his life.

* * *

Tisha considered running after her colleagues. But Gus was smart. He wouldn't let himself get hurt by the Too-Tall brothers. Besides, she had the man Gusty wanted to see right here.

"Are you Bendoko the Crane?" she asked.

The man shrugged and said, "Yeah."

He didn't look much like a notorious thief. Bound hand and foot, with abrasions on his face, he looked like a helpless boy. His body was barely full-grown. But man or boy, he was untrustworthy. And if his bonds came off, he might prove to be dangerous as well.

Tisha did not offer to untie him.

A short while later, Gusty came back into the warehouse. He was followed by Stormy and Woto.

Tisha smiled with relief.

"Glad you came back," she said.

"We had to let them go," Gusty explained. "I didn't like the looks of that alley."

"Good thinking," said Tisha. She nodded at the tied-up man and said, "This is Bendoko the Crane."

Gusty grunted an acknowledgment.

He knelt down to look in the Crane's eyes.

"Sunny was carrying something," he said. "I didn't get a good look. Did you see what it was?"

The Crane shook his head. "No. I don't know what he was carrying."

Gusty nodded.

Tisha had seen a man with a horrifically twisted neck lying on the floor next to the Crane. The body wasn't there now, so that had to be what Gusty had seen. She didn't say anything, though, because she had a feeling that Gusty already knew what he had seen. He just wanted to learn if the Crane would cooperate.

"What were you doing in the warehouse this evening?" Gusty asked.

The Crane held up his bound hands. "Knitting."

Gusty frowned.

"I'm looking for something you took last night," Gusty said. "Is it here?"

"I didn't take anything," the Crane answered.

"I thought Bendoko the Crane was a thief," Gusty said. "If you don't take anything, how do you make your living?"

The Crane didn't answer.

Stormy spoke up. "It smells like somebody died in here. Can't you smell it, Gusty?"

"Yes," Gusty said.

He had a good sense of smell. Tisha's was better under water.

"So ask him who died," Stormy said.

"I was hoping he'd just tell us," Gusty said. "But he's not being very cooperative."

The Crane made no reply.

Tisha decided that perhaps a gesture of kindness was called for. She said, "Let me cut your feet loose."

From her belt she drew her combat knife. The short stout blade was designed for fighting under water. Ashore, it wasn't much good against a club or a rapier, but it could still come in handy when she needed a knife. She sliced the knot. As she unwrapped the rope from the Crane's feet, she noticed fresh blood on his toes.

"What happened to your foot?" she asked.

She reached out and he flinched.

"All right," she said. "I won't touch it."

She looked up at Gusty. "We should take him to a healer before we lock him up."

"Lock me up?" said the Crane. "Sunny and Tiny are the ones you should be locking up. They—"

He was about to tell them. He was just about to tell them.

Tisha put her hand on his shoulder. "They did what, Crane? What did they do?"

"They … tied me up," he mumbled.

"They killed Mendu, didn't they?" Tisha asked.

"Look, I'm really sorry," the Crane said. He looked into her eyes, and for a moment, the suspicion was gone from his face. "Don't think I'm not grateful. I am. I'm grateful. You saved my life. But if they find out I told you anything … I just don't think I should tell you anything."

Tisha patted him gently. "You're scared," she said. "We

understand. But if they've committed a murder, someone will have to investigate. Cooperating with the investigation is the best way to make sure they can't hurt you."

"What if they find me before you find them?" the Crane asked.

"If you aren't cooperating," Woto said, "then we might not be able to convince a judge to investigate. And if no one's investigating, then they're sure to find you before we find them, because we won't be looking."

"I need some time to think this over," the Crane said.

Gusty shrugged. "Fair enough. We can't see a judge until morning anyway. Can you walk?"

"What? I—" The Crane moved his foot and grimaced with pain. "I think ... maybe I can," he said.

"Don't worry about it," Gusty said, kneeling to scoop the Crane up. The young man looked even skinnier in Gusty's great arms.

"A healer?" Gusty asked.

Tisha nodded. "A healer."

* * *

They left Woto and Stormy to watch the warehouse in case someone tried to take advantage of Mendu's sudden disappearance. And they found another pair of urbies to help Woto and Stormy in case the Too-Tall brothers came back. Tisha didn't know much about the Too-Tall brothers, but she didn't think Woto and Stormy should stand guard alone.

The Too-Tall brothers had crushed the Crane's foot. Tisha didn't know why. The healer on Nailmaker Street said nothing was broken, though, so that was good news. He was able to reverse the swelling. The notorious thief would be fine in a day or two.

The Crane limped along between them as they walked through Lowtown. They had removed the rope from his wrists and bound his hands behind his back with regulation leather manacles. The Crane looked unhappy about this, which Tisha saw as a good sign. Hopeless people didn't try to run away.

Gusty took an unusual route across the Main Canal. He

chose to cross on the Mikogi Footbridge, which was so narrow that they had to walk single file. It wasn't the sort of place anyone went at night.

Tisha was in front. Gusty was behind the Crane. She heard the men's footsteps stop at the midpoint of the crossing. She turned to see Gusty kneeling behind the Crane, holding his manacled hands.

Gusty asked, "Do you want to jump, Crane?"

"What?" Tisha asked.

Gusty said, "We'll tell the captain that he jumped. You went after him, but you couldn't catch him. Somehow he got out of his manacles."

"Gusty, what are you talking about?"

"We're gonna let him go, Tisha. All he has to do is tell us who has the scroll, and we'll let him go."

"But what about the murder, Gus?"

Gusty asked, "You didn't kill anybody, did you, Crane?"

"No," said the Crane.

"And when you got there, Mendu was already dead."

"Well ... yeah."

"That's the truth," Gusty told Tisha. "Think about it: The Crane was seen going to Mendu's warehouse last night. After the theft, right, Crane?"

The Crane didn't answer. The half of his face illuminated by the silver moonlight appeared conflicted.

"So the Crane gives the scroll to Mendu," Gusty said. "Mendu puts it somewhere. Then the mongzhi-wearing Too-Tall brothers find out the Sun Scroll has been stolen. They get mad. They kill Mendu. Then they realize they killed the man who knows where the scroll is. When the Crane shows up— Why did you show up, Crane? To get your money?"

The Crane's eyes shifted nervously. He was afraid of the man holding his manacled hands. The Crane didn't know that Gusty would never harm a helpless man.

At least, Tisha didn't think Gusty would harm a helpless man. But she had thought he would never ask her to let a prisoner escape and then lie about it.

"So he goes back tonight to get his money," Gusty said.

"And the Too-Tall brothers let him in, tie him up, and try to torture the information out of him. Right, Crane?"

The Crane said nothing.

Gusty was right, though. It all made sense once he put it together.

The mongzhi-wearing Too-Tall brothers. She'd noticed Tiny's mongzhi. How could she miss it? His exposed navel was at her eye level. But she'd just assumed he was following orange fashion.

Apparently not. Apparently the Too-Tall brothers felt some sort of cultural connection to the Queenies, and they had disliked the idea of their boss stealing a scroll containing the revelations of their Mother Goddess.

Pious criminals? Was it even possible?

It was possible. In Tisha's experience, criminals came up with all sorts of ways to pretend that what they did was right.

"So we know the whole story already," Gusty finished. "The only thing you have to tell us is who Mendu gave the scroll to. Then we'll let you go."

The Crane looked to Tisha. "Is he telling the truth? Will he really let me go?"

Again, he seemed to trust her. This shifty-eyed, suspicious criminal trusted Tisha, the veteran urbie.

She said, "Well ..."

"I knew it."

"Wait," she said. "Gusty and I need to sort something out."

Gusty looked at her. Suspiciously? *Gus, what's happening to you?*

"I can't lie to the captain," she told him. "You know I can't."

The corners of Gusty's huge mouth drooped in dismay. "Then tell the truth. I don't care. Tell him it was my idea to let the Crane go."

"But Gusty, if he confesses to the theft ..."

"There's no law that says we have to keep him. He can go free until he's sought for judgment."

That was true. They didn't *have* to keep him. But they should. The Crane didn't seem like the kind of criminal who would stick around to face judgment.

"I'm not confessing to any theft," the Crane said.

"Tell us who has the scroll!" Gusty said, and he lifted the burglar's hands, which were still manacled behind his back.

The skinny blue man cried out in pain.

Tisha was so shocked, it took her a moment to find her voice: "Gus! Gus, he's helpless! Let him go!"

Gusty, too, was stunned by his own actions. He let go of the Crane and staggered back. "I'm sorry, I— Tisha, we're so close! He knows! He knows who has it. I'm sure he knows!"

"I don't know!" the Crane said. He looked to Gusty, then to Tisha. "Tell him I don't know!"

"You don't know," Tisha repeated. "I believe you. You don't know who has it. Just tell us what you do know. Did Mendu give you any hints? Did he let anything slip?"

"Undo the manacles, and I'll tell you," the Crane said, backing toward her.

Tisha hesitated.

"He's going to kill me. Please undo the manacles."

Tisha realized he meant Gusty. "He's not going to kill you. Just calm down. I'll undo the manacles, but … promise you won't bolt."

"All right. I promise."

You're a liar, Tisha thought, but she undid the manacles. She didn't trust the Crane, but if he trusted *her*, she might be able to salvage this wreck.

"See?" she said. "Gusty's staying right there. He's not going to hurt you. And now, you'll tell us what you know."

The Crane said, "There was an inside man … Mendu said. I didn't steal anything, right? This is just stuff Mendu let slip."

"Right," said Tisha. "We understand. Tell us what Mendu said about this inside man."

"He was in the library last night," the Crane said. "He wasn't one of us—not from Sliceharbor, I mean. He was blue, but not one of *our* blues. He knew where the scroll was kept. It wasn't where Mendu thought, but this guy knew where it had been moved to.

"He didn't want the scroll last night. Mendu got it. But I think Mendu got it for the inside man. He put it someplace safe for him. That's what I think, and it's more than what I told Tiny."

In a voice full of doubt and dread, the Crane finished with, "Can I go?"

Tisha looked to Gusty. "Is that good?"

"Yeah," Gusty said, in a quiet voice. "That's pretty good."

She reached out and put a hand on the Crane's shoulder. He had stayed close beside her. Tisha would bust the helmet of any rookie who let an unrestrained prisoner stand that close, but she was no rookie, and she thought she had a good read on this guy.

"There is one more thing," she said. "We told our colleagues that we were bringing you in because of the murder investigation. If you can cooperate with us on that, we can let you go."

"The Too-Tall brothers would kill me," the Crane said. "I'd rather be locked up."

"Listen," Tisha said. "Gusty already figured out everything. Mendu was dead when you got there. And the only other people there were the Too-Tall brothers. Is that true?"

The Crane said nothing.

"Just say, 'Yeah,'" Tisha said.

"All right," said the Crane. "Yeah, that's the way it was."

"And now you have cooperated with the murder investigation," Tisha said. "So we don't have to bring you in."

He looked at her.

"That's it," she said. "Come on, Gusty."

Timidly, Gusty squeezed past the Crane. "Sorry I hurt you," he mumbled. "I shouldn't have."

* * *

Gusty Longbread glanced back at the narrow bridge. The Crane still stood there in the middle, alone in the moonlight.

Gusty hated to let him go—he'd stolen the Mother Goddess's sacred revelations!—but the information was worth the price. Now he knew that Senator Aura Wisebrow's suspicions had been correct: One of her colleagues had stolen it.

Walking beside him, Gusty's partner asked, "What did you think you were doing?"

Gusty shrugged. "I needed him to talk."

"That doesn't justify anything."

She was right. The Crane had been helpless. Gusty could have dislocated the little man's shoulders.

"I said I was sorry."

"To him. What about to me?"

"What?"

"You wanted me to abet his escape! And then lie about it!"

That's what she was so upset about? "If you wanted him in custody, why did you let him go?"

"I let him go because you promised we would, but I'm not going to *lie* about it."

"So what will you say?"

Tisha looked away. "I'll tell Woto and Stormy that we let him go once he agreed to cooperate with the murder investigation."

"What about Captain Kosho?" Gusty asked. Captain Kosho had assigned Gusty to investigate the theft from the library. If he found out they had been talking to the Crane, it wouldn't take him long to figure out why.

"I don't know, Gus. If the captain asks, we have to tell him the truth, don't we? We'll have to tell him we had the thief in our hands and we let him go."

"He won't like that," Gusty said.

"*I* don't like that!" Tisha said. "Why did you make that promise? We had cause to hold him. You know we'll never be able to find him again."

"I know," Gusty said. "But when we were at the healer's, I got to thinking: If anyone figures out why we arrested him tonight, we'll have a mob at Cohort Headquarters by morning. People will want him dead, Tisha. And they won't care how many urbies they have to go through to get to him."

"I don't think it would be *that* bad."

"Listen to me, Tisha: It would be *that* bad."

She frowned up at him. "What about you, Gus? Do you want him dead?"

Gusty clenched his fists. "I want the guy who hired him."

4 Yellowmonth

SENATOR FANJEI, representative of the ancient port of Thom-Hizo, stood on the steps of the Senatorial Palace with the other eight senators. Early morning sunlight glinted off the blue scalps of the citizens who had assembled to hear the Senate's announcement. Off to one side, a crowd of hairy, unruly Children of the Sun grumbled as Senator Washirko gave the unanimously approved speech.

Fanjei wasn't really listening to the speech, but he was not so rude as to talk when others needed to hear. The Children of the Sun shouldn't be grumbling. People needed to know that the Senatorial Palace had been searched. People needed to know that the senators and their staff were proven innocent of all wrongdoing.

Fanjei considered himself to be innocent as well. More than innocent, he was a hero! For now, he must remain silent about his deed. But someday, when people had calmed down enough to realize the magnitude of the sacrilegious disaster the Senate had been considering, then they would understand how *necessary* his actions had been. Historians would admire his courage.

As Senator Washirko brought his speech to its conclusion, the grumblings among the Children of the Sun grew louder. One of them bellowed, "So where's the scroll?"

Another called, "Yeah! Find the scroll!"

Others took up the cry and it became a chant—"Find our scroll! Find our scroll!"—overwhelming Senator Washirko's closing words.

Frowns were directed toward the disturbance. A few people shook their fists and shouted, but whatever they said was buried under the ox-like bellowing of the Children of the Sun.

Senator Fanjei wasn't afraid of them: He had stationed two lines of Republican Navy sailors between the palace steps and the Sliceharbor crowd. He wasn't afraid, but his heart was pounding with exhilaration. Because now everyone would see how dangerous Children of the Sun could be.

Their cry changed: "Find our scroll!" became "Save the Motherland!" And then, to Senator Fanjei's delight, five of them began pushing forward.

People scrambled to get out of the way. The five giants—all women—lumbered toward the palace steps. Other Children of the Sun surged forward in their wake. Sailors put their hands on the hilts of their rapiers.

Yes. This was the reason the Reconciled Queendom must never see aid from Fanjei's republic.

* * *

"Gusty, I don't like the looks of this."

Gusty had said they should attend the official announcement so they could study the faces of the senators, but now Tisha had other concerns. A delegation of five orange women was striding purposefully toward the palace steps.

"That's Lily Trueknife," Gusty said, "from the Enclave."

Tisha nodded. She recognized the woman from their encounter on the Palace Road the day before.

"And that's Mama Grace," Gusty said.

"Who's she?"

"She's trying to get help for the refugees living in Lowtown. And that one is—"

The women should have told the rest of their people to stay back. A crowd of giants flowed in behind them, looking ready to storm the palace. The greenscarves on the steps looked scared. If they drew their rapiers, this public protest would become a battle.

"We need to get in there," Tisha decided. "Watch my back."

They didn't have to push their way through the crowd. The people had left a gap between themselves and the greenscarves, and Tisha and Gusty used this as their own exclusive pathway.

Tisha's strides were so long and quick that she was nearly

bounding. But she wouldn't run. No, when an urbie ran, it was an emergency. And Tisha was determined that this situation would not become an emergency.

Some bosun or ensign or something stepped forward and held up his hand to the oranges.

"Halt!" he cried.

Exactly like a greenscarf. Don't try to find out what is wrong. Don't invite dialogue. Just assert authority.

And what if the oranges decided the Navy's authority was no longer worthy of their respect? Tisha wasn't going to let a pompous greenscarf start a fight in *her* city.

"Lily!" Tisha called. "Lily Trueknife!"

The five women turned at the sound of Tisha's voice. Their steps slowed. The other oranges surged around them, but then they stopped, too, as all eyes were directed to Tisha and Gusty.

Tisha strode up to them and stopped in front of Lily. "Are you here to speak for the Enclave?" she asked.

Lily opened her mouth to reply, but a glowering woman with rusty hair and a hawk-like nose answered, "We're here to speak for *all* the orange citizens of Sliceharbor."

Lily frowned for a moment, but then she turned to Tisha and nodded.

"Of course," Tisha said. "Forgive me for implying otherwise."

A shorter woman, who seemed to be compensating by growing her hair to ridiculous proportions, said, "We demand to be heard by the Senate!"

Tisha glanced toward the palace steps. The greenscarves still looked ready to draw. On the veranda, Senator Aura was watching the scene with concern.

Senator Aura's eyes met Tisha's. Tisha gave her an imploring look and beckoned with her head.

Senator Aura descended. When she reached the line of greenscarves, she said, "Excuse me."

The sailors looked to one of the senators. He scowled. Then nodded.

The greenscarves moved quickly aside.

Tisha said, "Thank you, Senator Aura."

"My people are always welcome to speak with me," Senator

Aura replied. "It's a bit crowded here," she told the orange women. "Would you care to take a walk?"

The senator turned, as though inviting them to come along. Lily and the hawk-nosed woman took a few steps, but the short woman said, "We want to speak in the Chamber."

"The Senate will not be gathering in the Chamber until later," Senator Aura said. "In the meantime, I am going to the Broad Market, and then to a goldsmith on Tumble Street. You are welcome to come along with me. We can discuss anything you like."

She started walking. After a moment's hesitation, the five women followed her. The rest of the crowd broke into small conversations. Those people closest to the line of greenscarves began edging away.

Tisha let out a breath: one more fight averted. And technically, it wasn't even her watch!

* * *

Bendoko the Crane did not hear news of the senators' announcement. He slept through the morning and most of the afternoon. But Bendoko didn't need to hear the news to know that the Sun Scroll wasn't in the palace. The inside man didn't want to be caught with it. That was why he had told Bendoko to take the scroll to Mendu.

Bendoko awoke when the afternoon thunderstorm rolled in. He was in his sister's apartment.

It was the only place he could think of to hide. Yeah, maybe some people knew he had a sister who lived in one of the "mushrooms" in the Pinetown District, but the Too-Tall brothers didn't know. And anyway, everybody knew that oranges didn't like to squish people in front of their families. Oranges were big on family. Weren't they?

They'd probably go for him when he went to the canal for a swim. Everybody knew that blues have to submerge themselves at least once a day. But Bendoko had once gone three days without a swim. This time he'd go longer, if he had to.

His skin itched already.

Bendoko went to the window and bared his skin to the raindrops blowing in through the gauze. So maybe he wasn't getting wet, but he was at least damp. Yeah. He could keep this up forever—or at least for the rest of his life.

* * *

The storm had long passed when Bendoko's brother came home.

Jambi said, "Hi, Ben. Glad you're still here."

"Yeah, me too," Bendoko said. "Sorry I missed you leaving this morning."

Jambi grinned. "You were sleeping like a stone!" He took six oranges from his shopping bag and set them on the table. "Want one?"

"No, I'll wait till Puji gets home."

"That might not be for another lithic," Jambi said. "I get off work early because I'm a kid."

"All right," said Bendoko. He picked up an orange and used the knife on the table to quarter it. "We'll split it?" he asked, wiping the knife clean with the table rag.

"Sure," Jambi said. "Oh!" He rummaged in the bottom of his shopping bag. "Some guy wanted me to give this to you."

He held out a small cloth bundle a little bigger than Bendoko's fist.

"What guy?" Bendoko asked.

"An orange guy."

Bendoko dropped the knife and the cleaning rag onto the table.

"Did you tell him I was here?"

Jambi's face grew worried. "He just said, 'Give this to your brother.' I thought he already knew you were here."

He does now, Bendoko thought.

"Jambi, no one's supposed to know I'm here. All right?"

Jambi nodded, wide-eyed. "All right. I'm sorry. Puji didn't tell me."

She probably thought you didn't need to be told. "It's all right," Bendoko lied.

Jambi offered the bundle again. Bendoko took it. It was light.

It didn't have to be from the Too-Tall brothers. Maybe it was a warning from one of his friends. Well, Bendoko didn't have any friends, but maybe it was a message from someone friendly.

"This orange guy," Bendoko asked hopefully, "was he an urbie?"

"I don't know," Jambi said. "He wasn't in armor."

"Did he have a woman with him, though? A blue woman about Puji's height? Maybe taller?"

"I don't … think so," Jambi said. "But, you know, there were blue women around. So … maybe."

It had to be a message from the urbies. It just had to be. They'd let him go, and then they'd followed him. That's what it was. The urbies had followed him and tracked him to his sister's house, and now they were just sending him a note asking to arrange a meeting. Or something.

It couldn't be the Too-Tall brothers. No one at the docks knew he came from Pinetown.

Well, at least *most* people at the docks didn't know …

* * *

"The criminal is ordered to pay triple restitution."

Fifteen-year-old Bendoko watched as coins were removed from his money string and handed to the carter. The broad-shouldered orange man counted them carefully, then slipped them onto his own string.

"I thank you for your time," the orange man told the judge. "May the God of Justice smile upon us all." He looked at Bendoko and sadly shook his head.

He wasn't angry that Bendoko had tried to cut his string. He wasn't happy that Bendoko had paid triple restitution. He was sad. Bendoko couldn't tell if the orange man felt sorry for himself, for Bendoko, or for Sliceharbor in general.

The judge put a hand on Bendoko's shoulder and looked into his eyes. "May the God of Justice bless you and inspire you to reform before you face your ultimate Judgment. Case closed."

The onlookers began talking among themselves. (Impromptu justice always draws spectators on the streets of Sliceharbor.) The carter returned to his heavy cart and resumed pushing it up the road. The judge was approached by two men who wanted to know the fairest way to exchange poultry for timber-cutting labor.

Bendoko, glad that he was no longer the center of attention, turned to go. He was confronted by a blue man wearing an iron medallion on a gold chain.

"Have you been saved?" the man asked.

Bendoko looked at him suspiciously. "Saved for what?"

"For eternity," the man replied.

"I'm sorry," Bendoko said. "I don't know what you're talking about."

He made to push past, but the man placed a hand on his arm and said, "I'm talking about your immortal soul."

"Oh."

"I heard the judge's blessing. *Will* you be inspired to reform, do you think?"

"Oh yeah," said Bendoko. "Yeah, I'll never do that again."

He'd counted on the carter needing both hands to push the cart, and he'd expected the carter's reactions to be slow. Next time, whether his victim was orange or blue, he wouldn't cut the string until they were in a crowd that could give him some cover.

"Forgive me if I doubt your sincerity," the man with the gold chain said.

"All right. Can I go now?"

"Your body can go where it likes. But where do you think your soul is going?"

"Hey. I said I'll reform, all right?"

"Many young criminals think they will reform. But they always intend to reform *later*."

"Yeah? So?" Bendoko didn't want to admit it, but this was, in fact, his plan.

"They think that once they have achieved enough wealth, they can become honest people and earn their way back into favor with the deities."

"So what's wrong with that?"

The man with the iron medallion shook his head. "Your ultimate judge will be the God of Justice—there is no God of Mercy."

"Well, maybe I've given my soul to the Goddess of Luck," Bendoko said.

The man chuckled. "How good has your luck been lately?"

Bendoko rolled his eyes. "I don't have time for this."

"Ah, so you realize that you may be short on time," the man said. "Good for you. Most young criminals plan to live forever. Foolish, really. The lives of criminals are often quite short."

"Look," said Bendoko, "if you wanted to scare me, you've done a good job. Really. But this is between me and the deities. It's no business of yours."

"But it doesn't have to be between you and the deities," the man said. "Their standards are for Heaven. They don't understand what a poor boy has to do to survive on the streets of Sliceharbor."

"You're right there."

"Have you ever considered putting your soul in the hands of a more worldly entity?"

Bendoko finally got it. "You're a shaman, aren't you?"

"I am."

"And you want me to give my soul to the nature spirits."

"Not just any spirits," the man said. "I have a particular spirit in mind."

"Yeah, well, sorry," Bendoko said. "I'm not gonna run off into the jungle and marry a tree. I appreciate the offer, but that's just not my thing."

"I understand," the man said. "But that's not what I'm proposing."

"So ... what then?"

"Are you aware that we have nature spirits right here in Sliceharbor?"

"You mean ghosts."

"No. Ghosts are people who have died and don't know where they belong. Souls who have a place become spirits. Have you ever heard the legend of Big Zeemo?"

"Wait," said Bendoko. "You're asking me to give my soul to Big Zeemo?"

The shaman smiled. "Think of it as a business opportunity."

* * *

So, yeah, Big Zeemo's shamans knew where Bendoko had come from. And he'd probably told a few other people. He was just a kid then. He hadn't yet learned to clam up. But who would *remember* something like that? Who would care that the Crane had siblings in Pinetown?

Every contractor he'd ever worked for, that's who. People like Mendu made their living by knowing stuff like that.

So, all right, maybe it was possible that some contractor on the docks knew Bendoko had a brother named Jambi. And maybe the Too-Tall brothers had asked around and gotten lucky and found him.

But more likely it was the urbies. They'd had a chance to follow him. He'd been pretty careful, but somehow they'd followed him last night.

That had to be it. The cloth bundle had to be from the urbies.

Bendoko set it on the table and untied the string. He unwrapped the folds of cloth.

There, in the center, was Mendu's ink-stained finger.

* * *

Tisha and Gusty walked down the Palace Road. Since parting ways that morning, Tisha had been home, seen her family, gone swimming, and slept all afternoon. Now the sun was setting and her body was ready to begin patrol.

But she wasn't on patrol. For the second night in a row, she was investigating the theft of the Sun Scroll. Or rather, helping Gusty investigate. He seemed to have some idea of how to go about it. He was outlining their strategy for approaching Senator Aura.

"First we'll need to ask her where the other eight senators stand on helping the Queenies," he said. "See if she thinks she has any support, and find out where her opposition is."

"All right," said Tisha.

"And then we'll ask her about the older senator—the one who hesitated before telling the greenscarves to let her pass."

"Sst."

"All right," Tisha said.

"It's important to ask about everyone before we let her know which one we suspect. Otherwise—"

"Sssst!" A man was hissing at them from the alley they had just passed.

"Crane!" Gusty said.

"Not so loud," the Crane pleaded. "Come here."

Gusty looked at Tisha. She shrugged.

Gusty peered suspiciously into the alley. He gave a grunt that meant it looked safe enough.

They entered the alley. The Crane turned and began walking deeper into the shadows. Tisha and Gusty did not follow.

"I don't want us to be seen from the street," the Crane explained over his shoulder.

Tisha and Gusty stood their ground.

"We'll talk here," Gusty said.

The Crane's eyes, shining white in the gloom, looked from Gusty to Tisha. His shoulders slumped.

"All right," he said.

He slunk back to them.

Gusty said, "You start by explaining how you found us."

The Crane shrugged. "I asked around. The urbies down on the Canal Road said you'd start your watch about now. So I guessed you'd be on the Palace Road, coming down from your headquarters."

"You talked to urbies?" Tisha asked.

"Well if I talked to anyone else, it might get back to Sunny and Tiny."

That was true. But Tisha was still surprised he would talk to urbies. He must have really needed to find them.

"All right," she said. "You found us. Did you remember something you forgot to tell us?"

"What? I thought the stuff I gave you last night was good enough. 'Pretty good.'" He nodded at Gusty. "That's what *he* said."

"Yeah, it was pretty good," Tisha said. "All right, then. Why are we here in this alley?"

The Crane unslung his shopping bag from his shoulder and fished something out of it. It was a small bundle of cloth.

He offered it to Tisha. She took it.

The bundle was light. Tisha squeezed it. She felt something

like a small, desiccated carrot.

"It smells like rotting meat," Gusty said.

"Open it," the Crane said.

Tisha unwrapped the bundle and spread it open on her palm. "Is that a finger?" she asked. In the gloomy alley, it was hard to tell.

"Mendu's finger," said the Crane. "See the ink stains?"

"Not really," she said. She handed it up to Gusty.

Wrinkling his nose, Gusty studied the severed finger. "Are those ink stains, or just rot? In this weather, this thing isn't going last too long."

He gave a tiny sniff. "All right," he said. "I guess I do smell a little ink. You think this is Mendu's?"

"Yeah," the Crane said. "An orange man handed the package to my little brother this afternoon. He asked him to deliver it to me."

The Crane had a brother? Tisha had imagined him without family. He had a reputation for being a loner.

"And your little brother knew where to find you?" Tisha asked.

"I was staying with him and my sister," the Crane said.

"All right," Tisha said.

Gusty retied the bundle and offered it to the Crane.

"You can keep it," the Crane said. "For the investigation. But I need something in return."

As far as Tisha knew, the investigation into Mendu's murder had not yet begun. The finger would probably be maggot food before Mendu's family found a judge—if Mendu had any family. So the finger was useless.

But the judge might need the Crane's testimony, so it didn't hurt to string him along.

"All right," Tisha said. "What do you need?"

"I need a place to hide! I can't stay with my sister—not when the Too-Tall brothers are coming to kill me."

Gusty asked, "Why us, Crane? Why don't you get help from one of your dockside friends?"

"I can't trust *them*," the Crane said. "They're all criminals!"

"That's the big disadvantage of being a burglar," Gusty said. "All your friends are as dishonest as you are."

"Yeah," the Crane agreed. Gusty's words had been so close to the truth that the Crane hadn't noticed he was being mocked.

Tisha asked, "What were you thinking we could do, Crane? Do you want us to arrest you for stealing the Sun Scroll? Headquarters is right next to the Enclave. I'm not sure our prison doors would be stout enough to protect you."

"What if I snuck in?"

"Breaking into jail?" Tisha asked. "You're really desperate, aren't you?"

"I saw what happened to Mendu. I don't want to end up like that."

"I understand," Tisha said. "Gusty, do you have any ideas?"

Her partner was sniffing the breeze.

"Gusty?"

"I smell smoke," he said. "And it's not a barbecue."

The Crane looked from Gusty to Tisha. He frowned. "I'll be right back."

The Crane reached inside his shopping bag and withdrew some spiky iron things that he strapped to his hands and feet. Then, like a gecko, he clambered up the wall of the alley and disappeared over the edge of the roof.

Tisha and Gusty looked up and waited.

The Crane's head appeared silhouetted against the alley's narrow crack of sky. "Nothing to worry about," he called down to them. "The fire is down at the docks. It's a long way from here."

A fire! Tisha looked at Gusty. His nostrils flared and his eyes grew big and round.

"We gotta go," she said.

As they ran out of the alley, the Crane called, "Hey, wait! I need your help!"

* * *

Although the Urban Cohort spends most of its resources on policing the streets, it is, by necessity, a multi-purpose force. If a Child of the Sun or a foreigner is drowning in one of Sliceharbor's many canals, an urbie dives to the rescue. If a cart loses a wheel and spills lemons all over the street, an urbie directs people around the mess until the carter has recovered his or her fruit. If a cat gets stuck in a tree, an urbie helps the owner coax it down. And when a fire starts in Sliceharbor, urbies run to organize the bucket chains.

Bendoko knew this, but he didn't realize urbies would run so *far*. He tried to catch up to Gusty and Tisha, but after a couple blocks, he realized they planned to run all the way to Lowtown. Bendoko decided he preferred to walk.

Oh, he'd been so close! She had pretty much agreed to help him, hadn't she? Of course. She *had* to help him. After all, he'd given her all that good information, right?

On the other hand, she'd already saved his life once. Really, she didn't owe him anything.

Bendoko's footsteps slowed. It was crazy, really, going to the urbies. Maybe he should just hide out on the rooftops.

But he'd have to come down and eat sometime. And anyway, the Too-Tall brothers knew him: They'd be checking roofs.

No, getting help from Tisha and Gusty was still the best plan. He felt safe around Tisha, and maybe he could help Gusty track down the inside man. Maybe he could even steal the scroll back for them. Yeah. That would work. A business arrangement. Maybe they wouldn't even turn him over to the judge afterwards ... or at least, maybe Tisha would say something nice on his behalf.

So he'd go down to the docks, find Tisha and Gusty, maybe help them with their fire, and then make his business proposition. Yeah. That was a good plan.

So everything would be all right, if he could just find them again. But that wouldn't be too hard. He knew where they were, right? Just look for the fire, follow the bucket chains, and he'd find them. Yeah.

Unless Tiny and Sunny found him first.

Bendoko realized he was walking all alone in the middle of the Canal Road. He decided he preferred to swim.

* * *

Bendoko emerged from the canal, sari dripping wet. He hurried along the Dock Road. Flames glowed brightly in the distance. He heard excited voices ahead.

Bendoko had not seen many fires in Sliceharbor, but he had taken advantage of the few he had attended. People were so distracted by the smoke and the flames that they paid little attention to their money strings.

As Bendoko neared the site of the blaze, he scanned the people in the bucket chains. Here and there, flickering firelight glinted off a copper-finned helmet, but Bendoko didn't see either of *his* urbies.

An orange woman wearing nothing but a loincloth and a breastband stepped into his field of vision. "Come with us!" she told him. "We're starting a chain to wet down the warehouse across the way."

Bendoko followed, hoping to catch sight of Tisha, but she was not among the people gathering on the Long Dock.

The tide was out, and the dock was high above the water level. Two blue men in the water were filling empty buckets and hooking them to ropes held by strong orange men. The oranges hoisted the buckets, then lowered their hooks for the next load. Runners were carrying full buckets to the chain and returning with empty buckets to toss down to the swimmers. The scantily clad orange woman was adding people to the end of the chain so that the runners would not have to travel so far.

Bendoko was assigned a spot between an orange man and a blue man. The orange could handle a bucket with one hand, swing it across his body to the other hand, and pass it on to Bendoko. Making full use of his armspan, he was doing the work of three Bendoko-sized people.

Bendoko caught the heavy buckets as they descended on him and tried to keep their momentum going as he passed them on to the blue man. Catching buckets required his full attention and occupied both hands. Anyone could steal his money chain easily. For that matter, Sunny Too-Tall could slip up behind him and snap his neck before he even noticed. His last words would be, "Sorry for not catching the bucket."

But leaving the bucket chain was out of the question. The orange giant was working so hard that even a miscreant like Bendoko would be ashamed if he didn't do his own tiny part.

… Catch. Pass. … Catch. Pass. … Catch. Pass. …

Bendoko had no idea where the buckets were going. He had only a vague awareness of the people behind him passing the empty buckets back. Someone brought more buckets for the chain and the pauses between pass and catch became shorter.

Orange flames continued to lick the night sky. The wind blew the smoke inland, which was a pity because the mosquitoes were getting thick on the docks. Bendoko rubbed his ankles together to shake the insects off.

The flames had spread to several buildings, but Bendoko thought he could tell where the fire had started. It was the warehouse of Gisherwoku, the cotton importer who traded exclusively with the Mogadrel. At the Dock Market, Bendoko had heard oranges complaining that Gisherwoku was single-handedly funding the Mogadrel's invasion of "the Motherland". But that was just something people said, right? Nobody would set his warehouse on fire over it.

Well, a crazy person might.

Two crazy brothers might.

Bendoko kept catching the orange man's buckets. Most of the oranges weren't crazy.

* * *

Bendoko the Crane wasn't the only one who realized the fire might have been intended as a message. Chonder—a Broad Market merchant who imported Mogadrel iron work, Mogadrel leather work, and Mogadrel cloth—had long feared that angry oranges would do something violent to disrupt his business. When he heard the news that Gisherwoku's warehouse was on fire, he left the pool where he and his spouses had been enjoying the evening and hurried to check on his shop.

Chonder found no sign of fire, but his front door had been pried open. He rushed inside and lit an oil lamp.

At first, nothing seemed amiss. All his wares were still in the shop. He saw no sign of vandalism beyond the front door.

Then he found the body of Gisherwoku, whose neck had been broken.

* * *

The warehouse fire spread to adjacent buildings, but it did not spread fast. The thatch was wet from the afternoon's rain. The walls of the adjacent buildings were mildewy and moss-covered. It took a while for them to dry out in the heat of the warehouse fire.

Bendoko's bucket chain saved an adjacent warehouse by keeping its walls damp. Eventually, the urbies brought round the water engine—a huge barrel reservoir with a pump worked by two orange giants—and Bendoko was relieved of duty.

Urbies directed people toward the fires down the dock. Bendoko went with them, but he allowed himself to fall behind. His arms were tired, and his foot was still sore from being crushed last night.

He walked past the ruins of Gisherwoku's warehouse. Steam hissed from charred beams as the water engine sprayed the smoldering wreckage. A salty sea breeze met the deep, black heat and blew flaming palm fronds into the sky.

Nothing to worry about, really. It had rained that afternoon, and all the roofs would be too damp to catch fire.

Except for the net maker's shop where his little sister, Hertha, worked.

Bendoko forgot about his sore foot and broke into a run. The net maker's workshop was on the other side of the block. He passed through a bucket chain by ducking under the legs of an orange woman and ran around the corner … right into an urbie wearing a helmet with one crumpled fin.

"Crane, what are you doing?"

Tisha! He'd found her!

"Tisha, there's a net maker's workshop on Sailor Street. I need you to get buckets there."

"Crane, I think we've got this fire under control now. It isn't going to cross the warehouse alley."

Bendoko pointed at the flaming palm leaves dancing skyward. "What about that?"

"One or two stray embers aren't going to start anything," Tisha said. "Not tonight. The thatch is damp."

"But the net maker's workshop is bundle-thatched!"

Tisha looked at him blankly.

"It has lots of loose ends that catch fire easily. And the under layers stay dry."

"What are you talking about?"

"Just trust me, all right?"

Tisha studied his face. "All right," she said. "I'll try to get some buckets to Sailor Street."

"Thanks," Bendoko said. "I'll meet you there!"

The alley behind the net maker's had a stack of rotting crates (which was illegal because it was a fire hazard). Bendoko used the crates as steps and reached the eaves with a jump. He could smell the fires already.

As he had feared, the ends of the thatch had dried quickly after the rain, and the dry crackle of the layers under his feet told him the rain had not soaked in. Two spot fires were blazing, and another flaming palm frond had landed on the other side of the roof.

Bendoko curled his toes and kicked the frond off with the sole of his sandal. All right, that fire wouldn't start. But what about the other two?

Bendoko took off his sari and wrapped it around his hands. The big spot-fire looked like more than he could handle, so he started beating at the smaller one. It was mostly in the top layers. The flames couldn't penetrate very deeply into the tight thatch.

Bendoko focused on his work and tried not to worry about the bigger circle of flames. It was expanding, but there was nothing he could do without water. He glanced over the edge of the roof and saw Tisha's helmet with the tell-tale crumpled fin.

"Tisha! I need the water up here!"

She looked up.

"How?" she asked.

"There are crates in the back alley! You can climb up."

A moment later, Gusty's copper-finned helmet and coppery eyebrows rose above the edge of the roof. He heaved a bucket up.

Bendoko grabbed it by the handle. Careful to keep his weight on the frame poles, he dragged the bucket into position above the flames.

He dumped it. Water rushed down and met the flaming

thatch. A cloud of scalding steam blew up in Bendoko's face. He staggered backward.

Dammit, dammit, dammit!

"Crane?" Gusty called. "Are you all right?"

"I'm fine!" he called. His face felt blistery.

Smoke was still rising from both spot fires, but the flames were weaker now.

"I need another bucket."

* * *

The net maker's workshop had the only flammable roof on Sailor Street. *Only the Crane would know something like that,* Tisha thought with a smile.

With Gusty's help, the skinny young man had put out the spot fires—although not before they had burned big holes in the thatch. Until the net maker got a thatcher, his workshop would have an indoor shower.

Gusty was guarding the roof, armed with a pole to push off any stray embers. The Crane was sitting on the street, and Tisha was tending his blistered head.

She soaked the edge of his singed sari in a bucket of water and draped the wet cloth over his scalp.

He winced.

"That was real brave, you know," she told him.

"This is going to sting for a week," he said.

"Probably," she agreed. "I said it was brave, not smart. You could have let it burn, you know. No one was inside."

"I know," he said. "But my little sister works there. I didn't want her to be out of a job."

So he *did* have people he cared about: family. Maybe his family were the only people who cared about him.

"I've been thinking about your problem, Crane."

"Which one?"

"The men who want to kill you."

"Oh, yeah. Will you help me?"

"Yeah," Tisha said. "You can hide out at my house."

"Really?"

"Yeah."

"That's— that's very kind of you. Thanks."

"Well, it won't be that great," Tisha said. "You'll have to stay locked in the cellar."

"Locked in the cellar?"

"I've got two spouses and two kids at home."

"Oh." He thought about it. "Yeah, I see your point. All right, that's fair."

Tisha took the cloth off and soaked it again. She draped it gently over his face.

"Tisha?" he asked, voice muffled.

"Yeah?"

"You'll catch those guys, won't you? Tiny and Sunny?"

"Yeah, probably. Unless they ship out."

"I doubt they'll ship out," the Crane said.

"We'll catch them, then," she said. *She* probably wouldn't, but other urbies would. Word of Gisherwoku's broken neck had already reached the docks, and his family would be pressing judges for an investigation at first light. The Too-Tall brothers would be apprehended for questioning as soon as they showed their faces.

"Good," said the Crane. "I don't want to stay locked in your cellar forever."

Tisha laughed. "Trust me, Crane. I want you out of my house as soon as possible."

"Yeah," he said.

She dipped the cloth in water again.

"Tisha?"

"Yeah, Crane?"

"Could you do me one more favor?"

She chuckled. "What now, Crane?"

"Do you think—? Never mind."

"What, Crane?"

"Do you think you could call me 'Bendoko'?"

* * *

Senator Fanjei, representative of the ancient port of Thom-Hizo and admiral of the Republican Navy, spent the evening at the Senatorial Palace, where he received several messages.

The first message came from Fanjei's own ship, the *Thom-Hizo Warrior*. Captain Tu reported flames on the waterfront.

Admiral Fanjei sent his thanks and invited Captain Tu to supply more details.

Captain Tu was a thorough man. His second message was quite informative:

The fire had started in a cotton warehouse. The owner—who had not yet been located—was well known for his commerce with Mogadwen. Supporters of the Reconciled Queendom believed his cotton purchases were helping fund the Mogadrel invasion.

Captain Tu drew no conclusions in his message, but he did not need to. The implication was clear.

Senator Fanjei began to work up a speech, pacing through the rooms of his suite as he mumbled to himself, seeking the proper balance between nuance and accusation.

A little later in the evening, a messenger came to see Senator Washirko, Sliceharbor's true senator.

Washirko had people all over the city. Fanjei's only people were in the Republican Navy, but because the Navy guarded the palace, Fanjei was notified whenever one of his colleagues received an interesting visitor.

Seeking truth, Fanjei knocked on the door to Washirko's suite.

Washirko opened. His face was grave, and Fanjei surmised that he had already heard the messenger's news.

The messenger herself—a well-dressed woman of middle years—was still in the room. She retreated to a corner, as though she wished to stay out of the senators' way. Her face was troubled.

"Have you heard the news from the docks?" Fanjei asked.

"Yes, I was swimming at the Shady Glen," Washirko said. "I came back here so that people could find me if there was any new information."

Fanjei looked at the messenger, who had backed so far into the corner that she was nearly standing behind the potted palm. Fanjei asked, "And is there new information?"

"Well ..."

Washirko didn't want to tell him, but being a true Child of Justice, he was an honest man.

"I've just had word from the Broad Market," Washirko said, glancing at the messenger. "Had you heard that the fire started in the warehouse of a cotton importer?"

"Yes," Fanjei said.

"Well ... the cotton importer's body was found in a Broad Market shop."

"His *dead* body?"

Washirko nodded. He looked miserable.

"How did he die?"

"His ... neck was broken."

Difficult to snap a man's neck, Fanjei thought. *Unless one is nine feet tall with hands like dinner plates.*

"Who found the body?" Fanjei asked.

"The shopkeeper," Washirko said. "Like the cotton importer, he's done a lot of business with Mogadwen."

"So the body was a warning," Fanjei said.

Washirko nodded.

"Or perhaps even a message," Fanjei said. " 'This is what happens to Children of Justice who do business with the Mogadrel.' "

"Something like that, yes."

Fanjei considered. Yes, this was definitely material he could work with.

Fanjei looked into the other man's eyes. "Senator Washirko, this is indeed a tragedy."

"It is."

"And it is not yours to bear alone," Fanjei said. "This is not just a crime against the honest merchants of Sliceharbor. It is a message aimed at our entire republic, at everyone who would trade freely around the Sunward Sea."

"I ... ah ..."

"Senator Washirko, I have taken the liberty of preparing a speech to bolster the spirits of those who have been fighting the fires on the docks. With your permission, I would like to deliver it tonight."

"Well ... ah ... I'm sure the citizens of Sliceharbor will be glad to listen to anything you have to say … ah …"

"Thank you, Senator Washirko. I'm glad we are in agreement on this."

* * *

Senator Fanjei arrived at the docks shortly after the last of the flames had been vanquished. The Republican Navy built him a platform out of crates temporarily commandeered from one of the warehouses the Urban Cohort had saved.

Gusty Longbread watched these preparations closely. He recognized Fanjei as the senator who had reacted strangely when the crowd of oranges began surging toward the Senatorial Palace that morning. Eight senators had tensed; this one had taken a half-step forward, as though eager to order the greenscarves into battle. And then, when Aura had wanted to pass through the greenscarves, this senator had hesitated before giving his consent. Gusty wanted to know more about him.

The senator opened with congratulations for the people who had worked so hard to stop the blaze. He offered condolences to those who had lost property. And then …

"We weep most for the family of Gisherwoku, the owner of the first warehouse that was set ablaze. If you have not already heard, Gisherwoku was the victim of a brutal murder this evening. His body was found with injuries that could only have been inflicted by a mad person of gigantic strength. In the days to come, we will hear those who say that Gisherwoku brought it upon himself—that he deserved his fate because of his business choices. But I ask you: Does anyone deserve this?"

Senator Fanjei gestured at the black gap where the cotton warehouse had stood. Several blues in the crowd shook their little bald heads.

"Do honest merchants deserve to die because they choose to engage in lawful commerce?" Fanjei asked. "Is that what we mean when we speak of our reverence for justice?

"Foreign influences seek to intimidate the honest citizens of our republic! They say that their enemies must be our enemies, that their war must be our war. But we are no longer their subjects! We are free people. And we will not let their violence obstruct our justice!

"These foreigners have tried to bring their war to our port. They have tried to bring their war to our warehouses. They have even tried to bring their war to the Senate! But we will not let them sway us. We will not allow justice to be swept aside by brutality. We will stand against them.

"And when we senators stand against the foreigners, we stand for the Republic. We stand for you! We stand—" and here his voice grew quiet and somber, "—for one Sliceharbor merchant who was just trying to make an honest living. Tonight the Ultimate Judge has granted his soul passage into Heaven.

"But what of us? How will *our* souls be judged? How can we face Judgment unless we stand up now and tell these foreigners, 'No more!'? No more demonstrations. No more arson. No more murders. From this night forward, let justice rule!"

Gusty felt the crowd's applause like eels swimming in his guts. This was *his* town! These were *his* people. How could they let this senator from Thom-Hizo call Gusty a foreigner?

But they cheered like they had heard a different speech.

Maybe they had. Gusty wanted to believe that of them. He wanted to believe that the blues didn't realize Senator Fanjei had labeled their fellow citizens as foreigners. He wanted to believe that they hadn't heard the implication that everyone who supported the Reconciled Queendom was an accomplice to murder. He wanted to believe that "justice" was more than a word in Sliceharbor—that it was a principle which applied fairly and equally to blues and oranges alike.

But as he looked down on their ugly bald heads, he knew they all hated him. And he discovered, deep inside, a part of himself that hated them, too.

A tiny blue hand touched his arm.

"Gus!" Tisha said. "Bendoko says it's him!"

"Huh?"

The Crane was beside her, looking nervous and shifty-eyed— a shining example of blues' dedication to justice!

"That guy on the boxes," the Crane said, in a voice so low Gusty almost couldn't hear it. "He's the inside man."

The inside man! The man who stole the scroll! Gusty had suspected, and oh how he had hoped! But now, with the Crane right here to bear witness—

"Don't look at him like that!" the Crane said.

Gusty looked down into their worried blue faces.

"We're gonna do more than look at him," Gusty said. "We're gonna arrest him!"

There was fear in Tisha's voice: "On what grounds, Gus?"

"On the grounds that he stole the Sun Scroll!"

"Could you pleeeease speak quietly," the Crane begged.

Gusty put his face down to theirs, touching helmets with Tisha. "We aren't going to let him get away, are we? Shouldn't we take a stand? Shouldn't we let justice rule?"

"Gus, I don't blame you for being upset."

"Upset? You think I want to arrest him because he made me upset? Tisha he—"

"He's surrounded by twenty greenscarves," Tisha said quietly. "If you march up to him with the look you have on your face right now—"

"What? What look do I have on my face right now?"

"Like," the Crane squeaked, "like you want to kill someone?"

Tisha nodded.

Gusty straightened up. He looked at Senator Fanjei, surrounded by his sailors.

Yeah, all right. Gusty *did* want to kill him. Or at least give him a good shaking. But he wouldn't, of course. He was still an urbie. He would uphold the honor of Sliceharbor. He would walk calmly up to the senator and—

One of the sailors was looking at him suspiciously. Gusty realized what Tisha meant. If he tried anything against Fanjei after a speech like that, the sailors could stick him with two dozen rapiers and claim they'd averted a "foreign" assassination attempt.

Gusty held the sailor's gaze long enough to prove he wasn't afraid. Then he turned back to Tisha.

"All right," he said. "Maybe we shouldn't get him now. But when?"

"We've got to catch him with the scroll, Gus. It's the only way."

"What if we can't find it?" Gusty asked. "What if he's already destroyed it?"

"I don't know," Tisha said. "Maybe Senator Aura will have some ideas. All I know is that if we arrest a senator on the word of a criminal—sorry Bendoko—"

"It's all right."

"—if we arrest him without overwhelming evidence, then he'll go free and we'll be handing in our helmets."

Gusty snorted. "And that's 'justice' is it?"

"No," the Crane said. "That's just the way it is." He shrugged and added, "Sorry I'm not more respectable."

* * *

Bendoko had never been in love—at least as far as he knew.

He'd been pretty close. There'd been that girl with the interesting scar on her shoulder, whom he'd often met in the canal when he took the little kids swimming. She'd even let him touch the scar once. Then Hertha had told Puji that Bendoko was talking to other kids, and Puji had forbidden him to ever go swimming at that time of day ever again.

Because, you know, the girl might have had a parent who was a judge or something. It seemed stupid now, but at the time, Puji had been only thirteen, just doing the best she could to keep her family together. Bendoko didn't hold it against her. But he did sometimes wonder what had happened to the girl with the scar.

After Bendoko had moved out, he could swim with any of the pretty women. He certainly had looked at them. But things never went much beyond looking because Bendoko assumed they wouldn't be interested in him. The pretty ones were probably good people. Most people were.

Bendoko had once had a girlfriend for an entire week. She'd been a swindler. From her he had learned that when a woman of twenty-four is interested in a boy of sixteen, it's probably because she's heard that he recently fenced a set of solid gold drinking cups. Once she had Bendoko's money, she disappeared.

So, yeah, Bendoko had never really been in love before. So he couldn't say for sure that this wasn't it.

Tisha was so … kind! She'd soaked his head! And now she was taking him into her home.

It was a beautiful home. You didn't have to walk up any stairs to get there. You just brushed your mosquitoes off at the front door and stepped inside.

Tisha lit a lamp and reminded him to be quiet. The house was nice on the inside, too. The gauze on the windows was tight. The table was laden with leftover food. The hardwood floor was clean, and Bendoko's charred sandals left marks.

Tisha took off her cane skirt and wrapped it around a wooden stand in the corner. She hung her belt—with rapier, sword-breaker club, and combat knife—on the stand. Next she took off and hung up her cane-armor bodice. Finally, she removed her helmet and set it on top of the stand.

Standing there in the lamplight, wearing only a loincloth and a breastband, she didn't look like an urbie anymore. She just looked like an ordinary woman getting ready to take a swim— except for the funny wrinkles the helmet had left in her scalp.

She took her sari down from a peg by the door and began pleating the skirt about her hips.

"Help yourself," she said, nodding at the table. "The bread won't last, and I can't guarantee you'll have regular meals while you're here."

Bendoko thought about refusing to take an honest family's food, but he'd missed eating supper with his own honest family that evening. Bendoko sat down on a bench and broke off a chunk of bread.

A man stepped out of a darkened doorway into the lamplit living room. He rubbed sleep from his eyes. "Tisha?"

Bendoko stopped eating in mid-chew.

The man frowned at Bendoko.

"Hi," he said.

Bendoko swallowed. "Hi."

"Sander, this is Bendoko."

"Hi," Bendoko said again. That wasn't right. He shouldn't have said it again. Something was called for, but "hi" wasn't it.

"Bendoko, this is my husband, Sander."

Sander waved.

"And this is our wife, Vernda," Tisha finished as another sleepy person entered the room.

Like Tisha, they wore loincloths, and the wife had put on a breastband. They had probably gotten dressed on his account. Bendoko felt bad for waking them. It was hard enough to sleep on a night as hot as this.

"Bendoko's going to be staying with us for a few days," Tisha said.

"Yeah?" Sander said.

Vernda's eyes flicked from Bendoko to Tisha.

"He'll be staying in the cellar," Tisha said.

"In the cellar?" they said. Together. Bendoko could tell they were married.

"The cellar locks," Tisha said. "Oh, before I forget, Cra— Ben. I need your belt."

"What? Oh. Yeah."

Bendoko reached inside his sari and untied his tool belt. It didn't feel right. He was naked without it.

"Here you go."

Tisha hung it up on a peg behind her armor. "We'll keep it here," she said. "We'll give it back when you leave." She ran her fingers over his lockpicks. "Even though we probably shouldn't."

She looked at him with her head tilted to one side. "You don't carry any knives."

Bendoko shrugged. "I've got a putty knife."

Tisha shook her head. "I almost think you aren't dangerous."

"Ah, Tisha?" Sander asked. "Why would he be dangerous?"

"I'm a burglar," Bendoko told him. "But I don't stab people," he told Tisha.

"Even burglars have their standards?" she asked.

Bendoko shrugged. "I just don't think I'd like stabbing people."

Tisha chuckled and shook her head. "You're a funny man, Bendoko the Crane."

Vernda looked from Tisha to Bendoko. "So you've brought a *burglar* home? And you want us to keep him in the cellar?"

"Yeah," Tisha said. "It's complicated."

"You know, I'm suddenly feeling awake," Vernda said. "Maybe you could explain?"

"Yeah, I'm awake, too," Sander said. "Why don't you sit down and tell us about it. I'll go get us a crock of beer."

* * *

They had a *lot* to talk about. Tisha explained in general terms that Bendoko was sought by dangerous men and needed a place to hide until she could catch them. This made Vernda and Sander worried about Tisha, which led to a listing of other worries, most of which had nothing to do with Bendoko. He ate their bread, drank their beer, and didn't really listen.

"I need to go for a swim," Tisha decided, once she had explained everything. "May I show you to your room?"

"What?" said Bendoko. "Oh, yeah." He'd noted the cellar when Sander had fetched the beer.

"Do we have to lock him in the cellar?" Vernda asked. "He could sleep out here."

Tisha and Sander exchanged worried looks.

"I think the cellar will be fine," Bendoko said. "That will keep me out of your way. Really, you've done so much for me already."

"I suppose we could clear off a shelf for you to sleep on," Vernda said. "But it doesn't sound very comfortable."

Bendoko shrugged. "It will probably be better than some of the places I've slept." He thought about his molding wicker bed in the Shacks and added, "Better than home, really."

"Really?"

Bendoko nodded. "You have no idea."

5 Yellowmonth

BEHIND THE IRONMONGER'S SHOP on the Dock Market was a street so short that it didn't have a name. It provided access to three buildings, the middle one being a shabby boarding house that smelled of day-old fish.

The boarding house was three stories tall by blue standards, but it had only two actual stories because it was sized for oranges. It was home to unmarried orange men who no longer lived with their mothers.

Each man had his own reason for living alone, and Mama Grace, the proprietor of the boarding house, knew each man's reason. Blustery Chandler had moved out of his mother's candle shop after his oldest sister had married and taken over the business. Airy Freshmilk's betrothed had decided to marry a bigger man instead, and Airy had left his old neighborhood to hide from the shame. Willful Hammer had left home to row galleys around the Sunward Sea, but the orange captains had learned that he started fights with his crew members, so now Will was exploring a new career as a carter for a blue housebuilder.

In addition to her male boarders, Mama Grace had recently taken in two families of refugees, the Honeythroats and the Warmbloods.

Opal Warmblood was still adjusting to the shock of having her town destroyed by small, ferocious red soldiers. She'd been in charge of the town's food stores, and she couldn't understand why she had to give up her high status after fleeing to Slice-harbor. Every day she complained about "mainlanders" who lacked respect for her golden armband, which proclaimed her to be a member of the city-official caste.

She pretended she had money, but Mama Grace knew why

she had forgotten to pay rent for the past two months. Mama Grace had stopped feeling sorry for Opal Warmblood, but she still felt sorry for Opal's two frightened daughters, so she forgot to ask for the rent.

Patience Honeythroat had lost her mother in the war. She had escaped with her two rowdy brothers and her sober little sister. After purchasing passage to Sliceharbor, she was nearly out of coin. Mama Grace had offered to let her stay in exchange for housecleaning. Like Opal Warmblood, Patience Honeythroat was an armband-wearing member of the city-official caste, but she had been grateful for the opportunity pay her own way.

Mama Grace thought Patience could prosper in Sliceharbor, if she decided to stay.

Mama Grace was basically a kind-hearted soul. So when two desperate men came knocking on her door the morning after the big warehouse fire, she didn't turn them away. Instead, she hurried them inside.

Shutting the door, she asked, "What are you doing here?"

Sunny Too-Tall looked at the floor, kicked at a spider, and said, "Good morning, Mama."

Tiny met her eyes defiantly. "We need a place to stay."

Aware that the breakfast table conversation in the adjacent room had grown quiet, Mama Grace ushered the Too-Tall brothers into her bedroom, lit the lamp, and shut the door.

She said, "It was you, wasn't it?"

Tiny put his head on one side and said, "Now, Mama, you don't want to know that."

"You're right," she said. "I don't. What about the murder? Did you do that, too?"

Sunny inspected his hands. "Which one?"

" 'Murder' is a harsh word," said Tiny Too-Tall. "Think of it as a political statement."

Political statement. He was referring to Mama Grace's role as the leader of the Lowtown oranges who sought aid for the Reconciled Queendom and the refugees. Her dining room hosted meetings of like-minded people. She shouldn't risk their credibility by allowing Sunny and Tiny to stay here.

"That's not the way we make political statements," she said.

"Maybe you'd have better luck if you tried it our way," said Tiny.

Maybe she would. Yesterday, Aura Wisebrow had told her and Lily Trueknife, the leader of a similar group in the Enclave, that progress was only possible as long as oranges remained peaceful. So far, peaceful had gotten them nowhere.

But Sunny and Tiny had made things worse. All those puny bald heads nodding along at that ugly senator's despicable speech last night! Mama Grace's people had put out the fires, but some blues refused to see any good in an orange person.

Well, those blues would never offer help for the refugees. Mama Grace couldn't worry about them.

And as for Sunny and Tiny ... well, they were wrong. Heavens help them, they were wrong. But their mother had drowned in that fishing boat accident when they were still boys. They'd been raised by wayward men. When Mama Grace had found them, she'd done her best to set them straight, but by then, they had been too far gone.

Or maybe she just hadn't been good enough.

Sometimes she thought the Mother Goddess had made her infertile so she could take care of a bigger family. Sometimes she thought it was because the Goddess knew she would be a bad mother.

Had she failed these boys, or had they been born bad? It didn't matter. They needed her help, and she could help them.

"The only place I have for you is the attic room."

Sunny's face grew morose. The attic room was only pleasant in winter. In summer, it was steaming hot.

"We'll take it," Tiny said.

"And you can't stay long."

"It's all right, Mama," Tiny said. "This will all blow over in a week or so."

Mama Grace doubted that, but what else could she do? They were her boys.

* * *

Gusty went to the Senatorial Palace without Tisha. She liked to sleep mornings. And anyway, they weren't on duty until evening.

So there was nothing wrong with what he was doing. He could go anywhere he wanted when he was off duty. He just happened to want to go to the Senatorial Palace. That was all.

He wore his sari instead of his armor, and he carried no weapons. He wanted to look humble and harmless.

The greenscarves guarding the entrance eyed him suspiciously, but he must have looked innocuous enough, for they agreed to relay his message to Aura Wisebrow. She sent her secretary to escort Gusty inside.

"Do all the senators have suites in this wing?" Gusty asked as the secretary led him down a smoky, dimly lit hallway.

"Yes," said the secretary. "Even the two who represent Sliceharbor. Here we are."

They stepped inside quickly and shut the door. The secretary cleansed the infiltrating smoke and infused the room with a light citrus scent. Gusty was impressed. His own skill at magically manipulating scents did not extend far beyond his own body.

The room was designed to receive mixed company. Orange-sized wicker stools from the Sun Island sat beside locally carved, solid-wood stools sized for blues.

The only daylight came from a doorway into what was, presumably, Aura Wisebrow's study. A rainbow-glass ceiling lamp, suspended from a brass chain anchored high among the rafters, augmented the natural light with a warm glow that suffused the cheery yellow walls and their woven pine-needle paneling.

Senator Aura Wisebrow stepped out of her study and crossed the receiving room to greet Gusty.

"Thank you for finding time to see me," Gusty said.

"Is this about the investigation?" she asked.

"Yes."

"Good," she said. She turned to her secretary and said, "Thank you for showing Gusty Longbread to my suite. I won't be needing you right now."

The secretary nodded and left, letting in some of the smoke from the smoke pots in the hallway.

Aura Wisebrow invited Gusty to sit down and asked, "What news do you have for me?"

"May I ask a few questions first?"

She seemed surprised, but she said, "Of course."

"How many guards are in the palace hallways late at night?"

"It varies," she said. "When I come back from the pool house, sometimes I see a guard, but usually I don't."

"How easy would it be for a senator to leave his or her suite and walk to the library without being seen?"

"At night, you mean?"

"Yes."

"I suppose it would be quite easy," she said. "People bustle about the hallways in the daytime, but at night, we tend to stay in our rooms."

"So on the night the scroll was stolen, anyone could have gone to the library without being noticed."

"I suppose so. But you found evidence that the thief broke in through the roof."

"The burglar said he was working with somebody on the inside."

Senator Aura sat upright. "You caught the burglar?"

"Tisha and I caught him, with help from another pair of urbies."

"You should have informed the Senate at once."

"Maybe," said Gusty. "But I didn't want to alert the inside man."

"Oh." She considered this. "Who's the 'inside man'? Do you know?"

"I was hoping you could tell me," Gusty said.

"I'm afraid I don't know," Aura Wisebrow said. "I didn't see anyone in the halls the night the scroll was stolen."

"You were in the halls?"

"I came back rather late from swimming at the Shady Glen. The guards let me in. I came here and went to bed."

"I see," Gusty said. "I didn't expect that you would have witnessed anything. But if I told you one of your colleagues had arranged to have the scroll stolen, which one would you suspect?"

"I'm not sure it's proper for me to speculate—"

"Please, Aura Wisebrow. You know these people better than anyone else. Are any of them likely to hire a thief?"

"No," she said.

"All right," Gusty said. It had been worth a try.

"Hiring a thief is the same as stealing," Aura Wisebrow said. "They would never steal. Although ..."

"Yes?"

"Well ... some senators see this as a religious issue. They believe giving the Sun Scroll to the ambassador would be a sin."

Gusty gave a noncommittal grunt. The Queenies wanted to use the sacred secrets against the Mogadrel. Maybe that *was* a sin.

Gusty wasn't sure. Mostly, he was glad that he did not have to decide. But he did see how a pious blue senator might be able to justify the theft.

"So you're suggesting I look for the senator who's the most pious?" he asked.

"I'd say the most self-righteous."

"And who would that be?"

Aura Wisebrow threw up her hands. "Oh, all right. I think it was Fanjei. He hates all oranges. He's glad the Reconciled Queendom is losing the war. And if theft was the only way to keep the Sun Scroll out of their hands, then he would justify it by claiming he was only adhering to the will of the deities."

"And why didn't you want to tell me?"

"Because everyone knows that Fanjei and I are enemies. If I say anything against him, the others will just suspect me of trying to undermine him."

"I see."

"Have you found evidence against him?" she asked.

Gusty had seen Senator Fanjei react strangely when it looked like the oranges might clash with the sailors in front of the Senatorial Palace. And he had heard him imply that all oranges were responsible for the fire at the docks. But those were just reasons to hate the man. They weren't evidence.

"That's the problem," Gusty said. "Right now, the only evidence I have is the word of the burglar."

"Does he know where the scroll is?"

"No. He gave it to a middle man."

"And have you questioned the middle man?"

"The middle man is dead."

"Oh," said Aura Wisebrow.

"The middle man was killed by his orange employees after they discovered what he had done."

"Oh."

"We're still looking for them," Gusty said. "But they don't have the scroll, either. They were trying to get the burglar to tell them where it is."

"I doubt it is in Fanjei's suite," said Aura Wisebrow. "The search of his suite was as thorough as the search of my own."

"Right," said Gusty. "So he must have hidden it somewhere else."

"Well, Senator Fanjei is the admiral of the Navy. He has a personal ship in the harbor."

"Right," said Gusty. He'd been thinking the same thing. "But the Urban Cohort doesn't have the jurisdiction to search Navy ships. Can you get me aboard?"

"I don't know," Aura Wisebrow said. "If I bring the matter before the Senate, the others will assume I'm just harassing Fanjei. Do you have any evidence stronger than the word of a burglar who confessed only under coercion?"

"I didn't coerce him." *Not much. At least, not last night, when he identified Fanjei.*

"You said he confessed, but you haven't brought him before a judge. I was in city government long enough to know what that means."

"All right," said Gusty. "Maybe I lost my temper. But he didn't change his story after I let him go."

"Let him go?"

"Yes."

"But he stole the Sun Scroll!"

Gusty flinched.

"He didn't even know what it was," Gusty said, trying to explain. "I know where to find him. We can take him to trial at any time. But if we want to avoid mobs and riots, we need to get the Sun Scroll first."

For a moment Aura Wisebrow wore the stern face of a mother about to pass judgment. Then her shoulders sagged and she glanced at the door to the hallway.

Leaning forward, she said very quietly, "That's also the reason I don't want to go after Fanjei right now."

"But if I can search Fanjei's ship—"

"And if it's not there?"

She was right. If a search of the ship found nothing, every blue in the city would turn against her. And then the oranges would turn against the blues.

"So what can we do?"

Aura Wisebrow's voice became even quieter. She said, "What if I told you there is a second Sun Scroll?"

"What?"

She held up a hand. "I'm just guessing now, but let me tell you what I know. See what you think."

"All right."

"Matyu Gloria Sunrise, the ambassador from the Reconciled Queendom, has not been nearly as anxious about the scroll's disappearance as I would expect."

Gusty grunted to show she had his attention.

"Today she has been making plans to visit the Order of the Holy Shield."

The Order of the Holy Shield was sort of like urbies for the jungle. Their headquarters was a day's walk inland. Mostly they protected villages from dangerous animals, but they would help the Urban Cohort apprehend fugitives, and they were sometimes called upon to investigate rural crimes.

So the Order of the Holy Shield was kind of a police force, but it was also a religious secret society. Only Children of the Sun could join.

"The Order of the Holy Shield hasn't been very supportive of the Queenies," Gusty said.

"That's right," said Aura Wisebrow. "The order's First has publicly supported the Senate's stance of neutrality. Ostensibly, Gloria Sunrise is traveling to talk to her."

"But you think the visit involves the Sun Scroll?"

"The revelation was originally given to a matyu from the Blessed Order of the Noonday Sun. Ambassador Gloria is also a matyu of that order."

Gusty grunted. That was an interesting piece of information.

The Blessed Order of the Noonday Sun had been at the fore-front of the movement to conquer the mainland. They believed that all the peoples of the world should be led by the Children of the Sun. Their philosophies had shaped the Empire.

After the Revolution, the Lunaslip Republic (with the en-thusiastic support of the Order of the Holy Shield) had expelled the Blessed Order of the Noonday Sun from the mainland. The Noonday Sun had been eradicated so completely that most blues didn't even recognize the name anymore.

"She might have knowledge about the Sun Scroll that we do not," Aura Wisebrow said. "Perhaps from her order, perhaps from family lore."

Right. The ambassador was a Sunrise, and the name of the matyu who had received the revelation had been Ruby Sunrise.

Gusty asked, "So what does this have to do with visiting the Holy Shield?"

"I believe that's just an excuse," said Aura Wisebrow. "I believe she is actually visiting the Temple of the Noonday Sun."

"We don't have one," Gusty said. "Not anymore."

"No," said Aura Wisebrow. "But in Imperial times, the Noonday Sun had a temple inland, not far from the great-house of the Holy Shield."

"And you think a second Sun Scroll might be found there?"

"I think Matyu Gloria is unconcerned with our investigation and is suddenly very keen on going into the jungle."

"Well, that's interesting."

"Is it interesting enough that you and Tisha would be willing to escort the ambassador on her expedition?"

"What?"

"I convinced her that she would need two guides—one orange, one blue."

"Oh," said Gusty. "Well, I can't speak for Tisha—"

"No," said Aura Wisebrow. "But Captain Kosho can. I'll send a message asking him to assign both of you to escort duty."

"Oh," said Gusty. He didn't want to give up on Fanjei so easily.

"If Matyu Gloria finds another Sun Scroll, I need you and Tisha to make sure that Sliceharbor has jurisdiction over it."

"What?"

"Our people need to see us helping the Queenies, Gusty. If the Republic can't do it, maybe Sliceharbor can."

"So you think the Queenies should use the scroll against the Mogadrel?"

"No," said Aura Wisebrow, in a voice sharp enough to make Gusty blink. "Gusty, this scroll belongs to *us*. To Sliceharbor, do you understand?"

Gusty nodded, though he wasn't sure he understood.

"But once we have the Sun Scroll, then we get leverage. The city can offer aid—provided the ambassador relinquishes her claim. Sliceharbor can send food, clothing, even weapons! We can close the port to the Mogadrel. The scroll gives us something to bargain over. And it leaves Sliceharbor in a position to put pressure on the Senate. Do you see?"

"Maybe."

"Get me that scroll, Gusty Longbread, and I'll be able to give our people what they really want."

* * *

Tisha held baby Chobo down with one hand as she wrapped a clean cloth around his chubby loins. Her son loved being changed. For him, it wasn't hygiene; it was sport.

Six months ago, she would lay him on a bench to change him, but now she changed him on the floor. It was the only flat surface he couldn't wiggle off of.

Sander admired the squirming baby. "He's gonna be a gator wrestler."

"A gator wrestler?" Vernda asked. "Nobody eats alligator meat anymore."

"They do in the jungle," Sander said.

"My brother lives in the jungle," said Vernda. "They're just as civilized as we are."

Jodi, their three-year-old daughter, growled like a panther and jumped on Bendoko's back.

"And how civilized is that?" Sander asked.

"Jodi," Vernda called.

"It's all right," Bendoko said as the wild child hooked a leg around his ribs and grabbed his neck.

"You got good toes," Bendoko said to Jodi. "That's the secret to climbing—good toes."

Tisha certainly wasn't raising her daughter to be a burglar, but she smiled in spite of herself. She was glad she had let Bendoko out of the cellar for a while.

Vernda said, "It's all right for you, Ben. But I was hoping to put her down for a nap."

She was smiling, too, though.

"Yeah, you don't want to see what she's like when she misses her nap," Sander said. "Almost as bad as Tisha."

Tisha said, "Thanks, Sander."

She let Chobo go, and he toddled off to Vernda. His loincloth was crooked. Oh well. It would be changed again soon enough.

"Oh, that's right," Vernda said. "Tisha was sleeping when the committee came to visit."

"Committee?" Tisha asked. "What committee?"

"Just some people from around the neighborhood," Sander said.

"A *mixed* group of people from around the neighborhood," said Vernda. "They're organizing a march."

The cool hardwood floor suddenly felt cold. "What kind of a march?"

"A unity march," Vernda said. "Do you know what happened at the docks last night?"

Sander said, "Vernda, she was there. Remember?"

Vernda waved this fact away. "But maybe she didn't hear the speech. Apparently, there was this senator—"

"Yeah," said Tisha. "I heard him."

Sander rescued Bendoko by pulling Jodi off his head. "Is it true?" Sander asked. "Did he really say all oranges should be exiled?"

"What? No."

"Well, that's what we heard," Vernda said. "And they say he accused oranges of starting the fire."

"Oh," said Tisha. "Well, oranges were probably involved. While we were working on the fire, a shopkeeper found …" She looked at Jodi bouncing on Sander's knee. "He had reasons to think that."

Bendoko looked a little sick. He'd been there when an urbie had told Gusty and Tisha about Gisherwoku's murder. He was thinking it could have been his own broken-necked corpse.

Vernda looked at Sander. "Maybe we shouldn't go."

"You were planning to join the protest?" Tisha asked.

"It's not a protest," Sander said. "It's a unity march."

Whatever it was, it sounded like trouble for the Urban Cohort. She asked, "What's the difference?"

Vernda said, "Well, the idea— At least the way the neighbors explained it— We all show up at the New Market at noon, oranges and blues, and then we march to the Broad Market. To show this senator that we won't tolerate hateful rhetoric."

Sander said, "But if the things he said were true ..."

What *had* he said? He'd talked a lot about justice. And about keeping out foreign influences.

Tisha said, "It wasn't so much what he said. It was more about what he implied."

"Like what?" Sander asked.

"Well, he kind of called all oranges foreigners, without coming right out and saying it."

"So what should we do, Tisha?" Sander asked. "We thought, you know, being such good friends with Gusty, that you'd want us to join this march ..."

"Oranges and blues?" Tisha asked. "All marching together?"

"Well, yeah," Sander said.

"Not calling for any action in the Queenies' war?" Tisha asked. "Just marching together because we can?"

"Just because we can," Sander said.

"All right," Tisha said. "Yeah, I guess we should go."

* * *

Senator Fanjei would occasionally meet with members of the general public, but only in odd-numbered years, when the Senate convened in the ancient port of Thom-Hizo. This was the first time he had ever met with anyone from off the streets of Sliceharbor.

He had never heard of the League of Revolutionary Completionists, but their delegation—two men and one woman—had asked to see him while expressing scorn for their own representative, Senator Washirko. So Fanjei had decided to allow their visit. He was curious.

"Senator Fanjei," their leader began, "we've come on behalf of the League of Revolutionary Completionists to congratulate you on your speech last night."

"I was there," added the female member of the delegation. "Well done."

"Thank you," Fanjei said. "After your fellow citizens worked so hard to put out that terrible fire, it was the least I could do."

"We've come to offer our services. If there is anything you need the Completionists to do, we'll be happy to comply."

"I see. Well, thank you for your support."

"We can't stand by and let these oranges murder our merchants. We're ready to do something about it."

"I see," Fanjei said. "What support do you have from the town council?"

"Not enough," the second man grumbled.

"Most people are blind to the problems caused by the oranges," the leader said.

"Well," said Fanjei. "After last night, perhaps they will begin to see."

"*You* made them see," the woman said.

"So we've come to offer our services," the leader said again. He looked at the other two.

"And to warn you," the second man said.

"Warn me?" Fanjei asked. "About what?"

The second man looked to the first. The first looked at the woman. "You tell him," he said.

The woman stepped forward and inclined her head, as though she were about to present a public speech. "Senator Fanjei, our organization has discovered certain elements of this city organizing a march."

"Children of the Sun?" Fanjei asked.

"No, Senator. A mixed group of oranges and blues marching together."

"I see. And what is the purpose of this march?"

"To show 'unity'," the woman said. "Some blues think we can just get along with oranges. Those of us who have been victims of their violence know better."

Yes we do, Fanjei thought. "Thank you for bringing me this information," he said. "Do you have anything more to add?"

"Just that we offer our services," said their leader.

"Thank you," said Fanjei. He nodded toward Hesho. "If you would care to tell my secretary where you can be found, I will be sure to keep your offer in mind."

They stood around for another awkward moment.

"You may go," he told them.

"Thank you," they said.

And they left.

People marching together to show unity? It was a foolish gesture, but there was nothing Fanjei could do about it. People had a right to protest. People had a right to say what they believed, as long as they were not advocating demon worship.

And yet ... these things could swiftly get out of hand. The Children of Justice might be able to hold a peaceful protest, but when Children of the Sun demonstrated their beliefs, they broke merchants' necks and burned down warehouses.

The woman was right: Everyone in Sliceharbor would be assaulted by a Child of the Sun sooner or later. Fanjei had been assaulted on his first day in port.

He had been an ensign on his first naval voyage. In the foolishness of his youth, he had been excited to set foot on the docks of the wildest port in the Lunaslip Republic.

Bakers and citrus vendors hawked their wares, trying to separate Fanjei from his coins, but he was wary. He knew that better prices could be found farther from the docks.

The scent of baked lemon-rolls lured him down a side street. He was following his nose, unaware of the man following him. Then two huge hands grabbed him by the hips and spun him upside down.

Fanjei didn't know what was happening. The skirt of his sari came loose and fell down over his face. His rapier slid free and clattered in the street, but Fanjei gave no thought to the weapon.

The hands were wrapped around his ankles now, and they were shaking him so roughly that he couldn't catch his breath. His head bounced against the paving stones. He lost his new green bandana. The shaking didn't stop until his money string crashed to the ground.

Then Fanjei was tossed against a building, left lying in a heap, while a hairy, grotesque Child of the Sun ran off with his coins.

No one had protected the young sailor from this brutal assault. But now Fanjei was the admiral. He had the power to protect others—the power and the responsibility.

Violence *would* break out again—perhaps even during this unity march. As a pious man, it was his duty to stop any violence that the belligerents started.

So he would send his sailors. And if their presence incited violence? Well, that would be unfortunate, but it could not be helped. The Children of the Sun would use any excuse to start a fight.

* * *

Bendoko returned meekly to the cellar. It made Tisha feel terrible—locking up a man who had been playing happily with her children—but he was a burglar. They had valuable things in the house. She couldn't take chances, not when her family was involved.

Jodi was fascinated to have a stranger in the cellar. And she was so pleased when Tisha bolted him in: "He'll be here when we come back!"

Yes, Jodi, Tisha thought. *He'll still be there.*

* * *

Gusty Longbread didn't hear about the march until later. While Tisha and her family were getting ready to leave for the New Market, Gusty was at home, catching up on his sleep. He didn't wake up until well after the lunchtime rush.

Gusty rolled out of his hammock and reached for his sandals. His hand stopped when he saw the rolled-up paper he had left lying beside them—Aura Wisebrow's message to Captain Kosho.

Well, he *had* to deliver it, didn't he? He couldn't refuse the senator's request.

Captain Kosho could say no, of course. But that was his prerogative, not Gusty's.

Gusty put on his sandals and went into the other room. It was tidy. On the main counter, the mixing bowls were sitting in a row, top down so they wouldn't catch any bugs that happened to fall from the ceiling. The flour bin was sealed and stowed away. The baking pans had been scraped, and his mother was putting the last of them into the cupboard.

"I hope I didn't wake you," she said.

"You didn't," Gusty said.

He went to the little table in the corner that held their personal food, set the senator's message on it, and helped himself to bread and cheese.

His mother brought him a jug of milk from the coolbox under the floor. "What's that you have there?" she asked.

"A message for my captain."

"You have to go on watch early again today?"

Gusty shook his head. "No. I'll deliver it this evening."

"You don't sound very happy about that."

Gusty grunted.

She was right. He wasn't happy. He wanted to catch Fanjei with the Sun Scroll. Instead, he was being sent off into the jungle.

"The paper looks nice," his mother said, studying it without touching it. "And that's a fine ribbon."

"It's from Aura Wisebrow."

Gusty's mother smiled. "Ah. Are things going well with her?"

Gusty grunted.

"Does that mean 'yes' or 'maybe'?"

"I don't know," Gusty said.

His mother put a hand on his shoulder. "Maybe you should tell me about it."

Gusty grunted. Yeah, maybe he should. He felt like he was confronting what blues called "an ethical dilemma". Blues loved ethical dilemmas—to the point that philosophers could actually earn a living writing treatises about them. But Gusty was an orange boy. And oranges with problems didn't consult philosophers, they talked to their mothers.

"Aura Wisebrow wants to send me into the jungle," Gusty said.

"Will you come back?"

"What? Yeah. It's only for a few days."

"So what's the problem?"

"The problem is that I think I know who has the Sun Scroll."

"You do?" Her eyes widened. "Gusty, that's wonderful!"

"No it's not," Gusty said. "He's so powerful that I can't accuse him."

"What? This is Sliceharbor. No one is above the law."

"Yeah, well, he's not from Sliceharbor. So I've got some jurisdictional problems."

"Oh."

Gusty hadn't wanted to tell her that a senator had stolen the Sun Scroll, but from the sound of her voice, he suspected she had figured it out.

His mother asked, "Have you told Aura Wisebrow? Did you ask her for help?"

"Yeah," said Gusty. "That's why I went downtown this morning."

"And?"

"She said I could do more good by escorting the ambassador through the jungle."

"Wait. The ambassador? You didn't say anything about an ambassador."

"The ambassador from the Reconciled Queendom needs an escort to the Order of the Holy Shield's greathouse. Aura Wisebrow thinks Tisha and I should do it."

"That's good, isn't it? You've been chosen for an important mission."

"But it's not really my job, Mother. I'm an urbie. I'm supposed to keep the peace and catch criminals."

"And you're frustrated because you've found a criminal you aren't allowed to catch."

"Yeah, I guess so."

"Will he still be here when you get back?"

"I think so." The senators would be leaving for their home ports at the end of the month, but Gusty expected to get back within a week.

"Then have faith, Gusty. Maybe he's too powerful for you to go after right now, but give Aura Wisebrow some time to work on him. Maybe she can cut him down to size. And in the meantime, if she thinks that escorting ambassadors in the jungle is the best place for you, then go escort the ambassador. Have faith in Aura Wisebrow. She knows more about this than we do."

"I hadn't thought of it like that," Gusty said. "I guess you're right."

"Of course I'm right. I'm your mother."

* * *

Tisha and her family joined the other marchers mustering in the New Market. The day was hot and lazy, so the march got going about a quarter-lithic later than planned. They followed secondary streets—a wise choice, since the primary streets were busy with carters heading home for an afternoon nap. Some people complained about the sun and said that next time they'd march at midnight, but the mood was convivial. It didn't really feel like a protest. It just felt like an afternoon stroll with a few hundred other people.

Baby Chobo fell asleep in his sling with his head pillowed on Vernda's breast. Jodi rode on Tisha's shoulders so she could see better.

Really, there wasn't much to see. Lily Trueknife was somewhere in front; Tisha and her family were somewhere behind. In between were a lot of blue heads and orange backs.

As they entered a narrow, twisting street between wicker weaver shops, the crowd pressed together more tightly.

"Stay together," Tisha murmured, letting people push past her. Sander and Vernda stayed with her as the pace slowed. The rear of the unity march was barely moving.

When the pace picked up again, Tisha knew the main body of the march had turned onto the wide street leading to Breadbaker Bridge—the only way to cross the Pinetown Canal in this part of town.

As the press of bodies eased, Tisha relaxed. When she turned the corner, the sun hit her full in the face, but at least she had some space around her again.

Sander wasn't carrying anybody, so he decided to push ahead. Tisha glanced at Vernda. She wasn't puffing, but a person with a baby in a sling can only walk so fast.

"Sander."

Sander glanced over his shoulder. Vernda caught up and put her hand on his back. Tisha stayed close behind with Jodi's fingers tapping on her scalp.

The pace slowed again as the front of the march reached the bridge. People crowded together again. On the other side of the bridge, someone shouted.

Tisha heard raised voices—oranges and blues—but she couldn't make out any words. The oranges between her and the front of the march were craning their necks like they thought they could see something. The blues couldn't see anything, so they began murmuring to each other.

"There's more of them in the canal!" shouted an orange near the railing.

More of what? What was happening up there?

"Mommy?"

"Sander, take Jodi."

Tisha passed her daughter off. Jodi wrapped her arms around Sander's neck.

Vernda put a hand protectively over Chobo's head. Her eyes were wide.

Tisha didn't know what was going on, but she knew she wanted her family out of it.

She turned to face the people behind her and said, "I'm with the Urban Cohort. Everyone back off!"

They blinked at her in confusion. She wished she were wearing her armor and helmet instead of her pretty green summer sari with the yellow embroidery.

The marchers on the bridge were shouting. Someone screamed.

Tisha turned to her spouses. "Get the kids out of here."

She didn't need armor to have authority with them. Sander

and Vernda began pushing their way toward the rear.

"Back off!" Tisha shouted. "We need to clear the bridge."

Beside her, an orange man with age-wrinkled hands turned to follow Sander and Vernda.

"Back off! Back off!" he said. He gestured as though shooing a flock of chickens, and the people came to their senses. As voices on the bridge rose, the crowd at the rear began to flow away, with Sander and Vernda and the babies somewhere in that flow.

Hoping they would be safe, Tisha started jostling toward the railing of the bridge. Someone had seen something in the canal, and she wanted to know what it was.

The noise of the crowd changed abruptly. Tisha looked up and saw that everyone on the bridge was now surging toward the rear.

She got out of the way, stepping behind a stone column at the edge of the bridge to screen herself from the onrushing mass of blue and orange people.

Some of the blues escaped the press of the crowd by jumping off the railing into the canal. One blue woman fell down, but an orange woman picked her up and carried her. Tisha was only a half step away from the stampede of bodies.

Nearby, someone shouted, "Halt! Halt!"

Men and women with rapiers were climbing out of the canal to form a line along the bank. Tisha recognized them as greenscarves, even though their wet heads were bare.

There's more of them in the canal. These were the *them* the orange man had seen more of. That implied he had also seen greenscarves on the bridge.

What could turn a peaceful protest into a fleeing mob? Only the diplomatic skills of the Republican Navy.

The greenscarves on her bank were forming a line to … to do what? Attack the marchers' flank? Their cries of "Halt!" were not being heeded.

Tisha moved with the flow of fleeing marchers and put herself between them and the line of sailors. The sailors had steel rapiers. Tisha had her pretty summer sari.

"Urban Cohort!" she said. "What's going on here?"

"You're under arrest!" shouted the sailor closest to the bridge. "You're all under arrest!"

"Keep moving!" Tisha told the people behind her.

"I'm with the Urban Cohort," she told the leader of the sailors. "You're out of your jurisdiction."

"You are out of uniform," said the leader.

"You don't have the right— Don't move!" she said, pointing to the sailor at the opposite end of the line. They were all out of the water now, about twenty of them, dripping wet, rapiers drawn. They could hurt a lot of people with their steel blades, but then, this march had a lot of people who could hurt them, too.

"Hold your line," she told the leader. "Everyone's leaving. We don't want anyone else to get hurt."

He glanced at the bridge. Tisha kept her eyes on him. He met her gaze and nodded.

"Hold the line," he ordered.

The rapier points lowered a little. His sailors didn't want to kill anyone.

The leader said, "You leave with them, or I'll have you arrested."

Tisha had a reply for that, but she kept it to herself. Much as she hated to let him save face, this was not the time to provoke a response.

Tisha fell in behind an orange couple, running to match their pace. The woman was wailing, "She's dead. She's dead."

"Who's dead?" Tisha asked. "Who's dead?"

The orange man looked down on her and his pace slowed. Tisha suddenly felt very blue.

He said, "They killed Lily Trueknife."

* * *

A sailor who had joined the Navy to fight piracy said it happened like this:

The sailors had orders to look for arsonists leading a march on the Senatorial Palace. They confronted the marchers on the bridge and began asking questions. At the same time, another detachment of sailors emerged from hiding in the canal and cut off the arsonists' escape.

On the bridge, Captain Tu tried to ascertain which Children of the Sun were the leaders, but it quickly became clear that Children of Justice were also leading the march. Because they were not arson suspects, the captain discounted them, but one Child of Justice insisted that the sailors arrest all of them or none.

He struck Captain Tu. The mob surged forward. The sailors, trapped between the rails of the bridge, drew their rapiers. Some thrust in self-defense.

The mob backed off, leaving four behind.

The Child of Justice who had struck the captain was dead from a rapier thrust to his eye.

The other wounded civilians were Children of the Sun. Two men were crippled by puncture wounds in their legs. One woman was dying from a rapier stuck hilt-deep in her abdomen. She said she was a healer and would tell the sailors how to save her, but then she passed out from the pain. She died of her wound before a healer could be found.

One sailor had been knocked unconscious. She didn't remember what happened, but her rapier was the one inside the body of the dead woman.

The sailor who told this story shared it with only a few comrades in arms. His story did not spread well, and it was not widely heard in Sliceharbor.

It was not what people wanted to believe.

* * *

In the Enclave, the story took on many variations, but the most popular was the story from a friend's cousin "who was really there":

Oranges and blues were marching together to show that the people of Sliceharbor were tired of being ignored by the Senate. As their protest reached Breadbaker Bridge, they were ambushed by a group of blue sailors who charged them with arson, kidnapping, and disturbing the peace.

The sailors drew rapiers. Some of the blues in the crowd ran away, but Lily Trueknife held her ground to ensure that the men with rapiers did not stab the fleeing blues in the back.

So the sailors stabbed Lily Trueknife and left her to die on the bridge.

Some said it wasn't sailors, it was urbies. Some said it was blues who looked like sailors, but were really blue urbies in disguise.

People believed whichever version they liked best.

* * *

After careful consultation with Admiral Fanjei, Captain Tu gave this story to the Senate:

The Republican Navy had received word that some of Sliceharbor's residents (he avoided the word "citizens") were organizing a march on the Senatorial Palace. Because the march threatened the safety of the senators, he ordered two squads of sailors to observe the protesters and stop them if they were hostile.

The squads met with the protesters on Breadbaker Bridge and attempted to ascertain their motives. When Captain Tu began asking people what they knew about the warehouse fire, the leaders turned defensive and belligerent. Among the protesters were several Children of Justice, who tried to calm the leaders down. This only made them angrier.

When the mob surged forward, the sailors had to draw their rapiers in self-defense. Regrettably, one of the blue bystanders was pushed onto the point of a sailor's blade. The woman who pushed him was particularly belligerent and had to be killed. Two others were injured, but the rest turned to flee. The injured belligerents were questioned and then released.

Many additional details were supplied as blue lips passed this story around the city. In one version, an orange woman knocked a sailor unconscious, seized the sailor's rapier, and began swinging wildly, slicing the throat of an innocent blue bystander and killing him instantly.

This wild, orange woman swiftly received her Judgment: Her fellow oranges were in such a frenzy to attack that they stampeded over her. As she fell, she was impaled on the stolen rapier.

This last version achieved wide popularity among the blues of Sliceharbor. Blues like stories with morals.

* * *

The Lowtowners met at Mama Grace's boarding house after supper. Mama Grace didn't need to call a meeting. They just showed up. They brought friends. The dining room was crowded.

Crowded, but not loud. People murmured to each other, quietly comparing stories, trying to figure out what had happened.

Eventually, someone asked if the Trueknifes were seeking justice, and Splashy Brownbread said, "There isn't going to be any justice for Lily Trueknife."

Everyone grew quiet to hear what Splashy had to say. He worked as a gardener at the Senatorial Palace.

Splashy said, "According to the Senate, the sailors were just defending themselves. They say Lily Trueknife was belligerent. Case closed."

The voices in the dining room grew louder. That wasn't the way it had been. They were all in agreement, but there were no blues to argue with, so they argued with each other, competing to be a better defender of Lily Trueknife's name.

When they finally began to quiet down, Mama Grace asked, "Was anybody there?"

No one spoke up.

That was the problem with Lily Trueknife's people. They thought they were the only oranges in town. It hadn't even occurred to them to get oranges from Lowtown to join their march.

On the bright side, none of Mama Grace's people had been stabbed.

"So we don't know what happened," she said. "And we probably never will."

One of her boarders, Airy Freshmilk, said, "All we know is that Lily Trueknife thought she could march in peace with the blues, and now she's dead."

That drew murmurs of agreement.

"What did Aura Wisebrow say?" a woman wanted to know. "Did she buy the story that the sailors were just defending themselves?"

"Oh you know Aura Wisebrow," Splashy Brownbread said, obviously pleased that this woman was giving him the chance to speak as an authority. "She goes along with whatever the blues say."

This assessment produced some head nodding and some grumbling about Aura Wisebrow. Mama Grace didn't like it. The gardener was just making things up to feel important.

Now maybe Mama Grace had also disparaged Aura Wisebrow once or twice, but yesterday morning, when the orange senator had said she was looking into ways the Republic could help refugees, Mama Grace had believed her. Aura Wisebrow cared. She just couldn't be very effective in a blue senate.

"Does the Senate even have jurisdiction?" a woman wanted to know. "Lily Trueknife was murdered on the streets of Sliceharbor. The urbies should be looking into this."

A man said, "My cousin in the Enclave says the sailors were really urbies in disguise."

"They'll believe anything in the Enclave," the woman said. Mama Grace recognized her as a citrus vendor on Sailor Street. She thought maybe the woman's brother was an urbie.

"The urbies won't arrest any of those sailors," said Willful Hammer, the former galley rower. "I heard they were all blue."

Heads nodded in agreement. People started grumbling about "blue justice".

Will's opinions had carried little weight at recent meetings. Mama Grace's people were angry with him for starting the fight that got all oranges banned from the pool house on Nailmaker Street. Mama Grace was not sure she was glad that people were agreeing with him now.

As their voices faded, Tiny Too-Tall asked, "So what are you gonna do, then?"

All heads turned to look at him and Sunny standing in a corner in the back of the room. Mama Grace's boarders were allowed to attend the meetings, but she had hoped that Sunny and Tiny would stay discreetly in the attic. A foolish hope—the attic was too hot, and Tiny liked the smell of trouble. She hoped no one recognized them.

Tiny looked up at his brother and said, "I think they're gonna have to decide, Sunny."

"Yeah," Sunny agreed. "Decide what?"

"I think they're gonna have to decide whether they want to stay good little oranges and follow the blues' laws or if they want to actually change things in this mucksucking town." He shrugged and pushed his way to the stairwell. "I know what I'd choose."

Mama Grace's people were quiet and thoughtful as they watched the Too-Tall brothers leave the dining room. Tiny was right. The laws weren't working for them.

But Tiny's alternative was hopeless violence. She wondered if she was the only one in the room who could see that.

Mama Grace wished she'd been hard-hearted enough to turn him away this morning.

* * *

Fanjei thought Captain Tu's report to the Senate had gone well. It was important to present an official version of the story that had spawned so many conflicting variants that afternoon.

Fanjei was sorry the confrontation had turned violent, but not surprised. Children of the Sun were violent people. He did not regret his decision.

Suppose these agitators had been allowed to march all the way to the Palace District? Then they would have brought their violence to the steps of the Senatorial Palace itself.

Fanjei reminded himself that his actions were for the good of the Republic. The Senate must not allow itself to be intimidated by bullies. The Republic's ports must not be ruled by violence.

His actions had shown what beasts the Children of the Sun truly were. The truth was unpleasant, but it had to be revealed. He had done the right thing.

* * *

When Tisha arrived at Cohort Headquarters that evening, she went straight to Captain Kosho's office and told him and Gusty everything.

She concluded with, "I want to arrest Senator Fanjei."

Captain Kosho stared at her. "Senator Fanjei didn't stab anyone on Breadbaker Bridge."

"As admiral of the Navy, he's responsible," Tisha said. "And he's behind the theft of the Sun Scroll."

"Your evidence for that is the testimony of a burglar who will not testify," Captain Kosho said.

"What if I convince him to testify?" Tisha asked.

"You won't even find him again," Captain Kosho said.

Tisha glanced at Gusty. His face remained carefully blank.

"Finding him is not a problem," Tisha said. "The problem is convincing him to talk about his crime. But he might. For me."

"Tisha, how would that look? The Urban Cohort arrests a senator on the word of a criminal? The other cities in the Republic would accuse Sliceharbor of interfering with the Senate."

"The Republic is committed to justice," Tisha said. "If some people are immune to justice, then there is no justice for anyone."

"The final Judgment is in the hands of our Creator," Captain Kosho said. "Ultimately, there will be justice for all."

Tisha said, " 'Ultimately' wasn't soon enough for Lily True-knife. Now she's dead, and her murderer makes our laws."

Captain Kosho studied her for a long moment. Finally, he said, "Tisha, I don't think this is about Lily Trueknife. Nor is it about Senator Fanjei. You're upset because your family was there."

"Damn right I am!" Tisha said. "The greenscarves could have killed them!"

Kosho looked at Gusty. Gusty frowned.

Captain Kosho sighed. "I'm giving you both the night off," he decided.

"What?" Tisha asked.

"You need to spend the evening with your family," Kosho said. "You need some rest, some time to cool down. And ..."

He looked at Gusty again.

"... you need your sleep," he finished. "You and Gusty are getting a special assignment—a *diplomatic* assignment. You leave Sliceharbor tomorrow at sunrise."

* * *

Tisha wasn't used to walking through her own neighborhood in the evening. Lithfield was laced with the scents of barbecued pork and chicken. Conversations bubbled through the privacy fence of the local pool house. She heard a little brown bat flitting overhead, and from the corner of her eye, she caught a glimpse of his blurred wings against the twilit sky.

So she had the night off.

A punishment for proposing something politically dangerous? A reward for her hard work on the Sun Scroll theft? A brief respite to calm her anxieties? Or a necessary rest in preparation for an important mission?

Maybe it was all of these.

Gusty had known—not about Tisha's part in the Breadbaker Bridge incident, but about the mission. That was why he'd been in the captain's office when Tisha got there.

But after Kosho had explained the details and dismissed them, Gusty hadn't said any more about it. She didn't blame him. Gusty was usually pretty quiet anyway, and Tisha had been too upset to be worth talking to.

So. She'd go home and spend the evening with her family, just as though it were her night off. And then in the morning she and Gusty would go off to the jungle, as an escort for the Queenies' ambassador.

Maybe by morning she wouldn't feel like her blood was fizzing.

Tisha's house looked comforting and inviting. Lamplight shone in the gauze of the windows. She could hear Sander's warm, quiet voice. No one was giggling, crying, or screaming, which meant that the kids were already asleep.

Tisha took down the palm branch hanging over the door and brushed her mosquitoes off. Sander went abruptly silent.

She hung the palm above the door again.

"It's only me," she said, opening the door.

Then she stopped, standing there in the open doorway.

The lamp was in the center of the table, and the three of them were sitting around it: Sander and Vernda together on one bench, and Bendoko the Crane on the opposite side.

They all looked scared. And guilty.

"Why isn't he in the cellar?" she asked.

Vernda nodded at the door. "Tisha. Bugs."

Tisha stepped inside and closed the door. "It was *your* idea, wasn't it?" she said to Vernda. "You let him out."

"I let him out," said Sander. "And it was Jodi's idea. After you left for work, she wanted to play with 'the cellar man'."

"Why aren't you at work?" Vernda asked.

"That's not what we're discussing here," Tisha said. "We're discussing why *you* decided to open the cellar when I wasn't here to protect you." She knew it had been Vernda's idea, no matter what Sander said to defend her.

"Sander can protect us, too," Vernda said. "Maybe he doesn't have a rapier and armor, but—"

"It's not my rapier and armor that protect you," Tisha said. "It's my experience. I've dealt with hundreds of criminals. I know—"

"You know, Ben is sitting right here," Sander pointed out.

"He knows he's a criminal," Tisha said. "Tell them, Ben."

"I— I'm a criminal," Bendoko said. Fear shook his voice— fear, guilt, and shame.

"He's a person," Vernda said. "He doesn't deserve to be locked in our cellar. He's not going to murder us in our sleep."

Tisha sighed and took off her weapons belt. They were right, of course. Bendoko wasn't a murderer. But he had fooled them into thinking he was a good guy. They had to learn the truth.

"Ben, where does Sander keep the shopping money?" she asked as she hung up her cane-armor skirt.

"In the earthenware pitcher in the top corner of the cupboard," Bendoko admitted in a miserable voice.

"What is Vernda's most valuable piece of jewelry?" she asked.

"Her toe ring," Bendoko said.

Vernda looked at him.

His shoulders sagged. "It's gold," he said.

"Do we have anything else worth stealing?" Tisha asked as she slipped out of her cane-armor bodice.

"I could eat for a month if I fenced your helmet," he said sadly. "Copper fins."

Tisha took the helmet off and put it on her armor stand.

"And that's why we keep him locked in the cellar," she explained.

"But he's not going to steal from us," Sander said. "You weren't planning to steal from us, were you, Ben?"

"I—" The skinny young man shook his head. "I don't think so. Maybe. I don't even know."

"But ... you played with our kids," Sander said. "We're friends."

Bendoko cried, "I don't have friends!"

"Baby," Vernda warned.

"I don't have friends," said Bendoko, quieter, but still angry. "People like you get to have friends. People like me just get ... locked in the cellar."

He stood up. "I'm sorry, Tisha. I didn't mean to trick them, but I guess I did. I'll go back."

Sander wore an expression of incredulous horror. Horror at the idea that Bendoko might steal from them? Or horror at how Tisha had demolished the man?

Vernda's face held remorse and pity.

Well, Tisha felt sorry for him, too. She wasn't heartless. But really how could they—

How could they treat him like a person?

That was all they had done. They had let a nervous young man spend the evening with them and treated him like a person. And maybe he would have stolen their money. Maybe he would have stolen their things. But Tisha could have found him and gotten most of it back.

Vernda was right. He wasn't dangerous. He was just a sad, worthless little man.

"Wait, Ben. I'm the one who needs to apologize here. Sit back down."

"No, I think it would be better if—"

"Sit," Tisha said.

Bendoko sat.

She sat down beside him.

"All right," she admitted, "I was a little hard on you guys. I guess I'm still upset about what happened on the bridge today."

Vernda reached across the table and put her hand on Tisha's. "I think we all are."

Tisha looked to Bendoko. "I'm sorry I humiliated you. That wasn't necessary. I just wanted— Oh, never mind what I wanted. I'm sorry."

Bendoko hunched his shoulders. "It made sense to me."

"I knew Jodi wanted to keep playing with him when I locked him in tonight," Tisha said. "And I should have guessed she'd find a way to talk you into letting him out. It's just too much temptation for a three-year-old."

"So we don't have to keep him in the cellar anymore?" Sander asked. "I mean, if he promises not to steal anything?"

"Crane, would you lie to us?" Tisha asked.

"I don't know," Bendoko said miserably. "I don't want to lie to you. But I don't know."

She smiled. "At least you're honest."

She patted his arm. Her hand was sticky from the evening's heat, but he didn't seem to mind.

She sighed. "Although frankly, I don't know what to do with you. Captain Kosho just gave me and Gusty a mission that's going to take us out of the city for a few days."

"Is it dangerous?" Vernda asked.

"Will you miss your night off?" Sander asked.

Tisha looked at him. "Yeah, Sander. If I'm not in the city, then I won't be home for my night off this week."

"Oh."

"I'm sorry," Tisha said. "I like spending the evening with you guys. I guess *this* is my night off."

"It's been fun so far," said Vernda.

"Yeah, well, anyway ..." Tisha said.

"... what do we do with the criminal?" Bendoko finished.

"Yeah," Tisha agreed. "I could be gone for a week. We can't keep you locked in the cellar the whole time."

"Right," said Sander. "That's where we keep the beer."

Tisha chuckled. "Yeah, right. So if I'm going to trust you not to steal from my family, I'm going to need a better promise than 'I don't know'."

"I'm good at making promises," Bendoko said. "Just not

good at keeping them."

"Yeah," said Tisha.

"I don't suppose you've caught ... those guys yet?"

"No," Tisha said.

"Didn't think so."

She didn't really want to throw him out, but she kind of had to. He had to see that, but he was going to make her say it.

"Look, I can't let you stay here," she said. "Otherwise, Vernda and Sander will start thinking we need another husband."

No one laughed at her joke. Vernda and Sander didn't meet her eyes. Oh no. They'd actually been *thinking* it. Bring a guy home for one day and— No. That was ridiculous. They didn't really want him for a husband. Like Jodi, they were thinking of him as a house pet.

"I see," Bendoko said. "Do I have to go now? Or can I stay one more night in the cellar?"

"You can stay one more night," Tisha said. "But in the morning ..."

"It's back to the streets," Bendoko said.

"Yeah. Unless you want to come to the jungle with me."

"Really?" he asked. "You'd take me with you?"

"What? No, I was joking. It's an Urban Cohort mission. Gusty and I are guarding this ambassador on her trip through the jungle."

"Why does an ambassador want to go into the jungle?" Sander asked.

"I don't know," Tisha said. "Maybe she thinks she'll find people who will go help in the Queenies' war."

"Does she need a jungle guide?" Bendoko asked.

"I don't know," Tisha said. "Why?"

"Because you could take me along as a jungle guide."

"Do you know anything about the jungle?" Tisha asked.

"Sure," the Crane said. "I've heard lots about it."

"Yeah. 'Heard lots.' Well—"

"He could be your scout," Sander said.

"My 'scout'?" Tisha asked.

"He's a burglar, right? Sneaky? Stealthy? Climby? He could go ahead and tell you where the danger is."

Tisha laughed. "He doesn't want to go ahead and look for danger. If he weren't afraid of danger, he wouldn't be staying *here*."

"But you'll take him if he wants to come?" Sander persisted.

Tisha shrugged. "Yeah, I guess so."

He wouldn't want to come.

Sander asked, "What do you say, Ben? Do you want to be Tisha's scout?"

"Panthers, vipers, and alligators," Tisha said.

"I don't know," Bendoko said. "It still sounds safer than going back to the streets."

6 Yellowmonth

MATYU GLORIA SUNRISE, ambassador for the Reconciled Queendom of the Goddess of the Sun, stood in the middle of the dirt road and considered the skyline of Sliceharbor. On the left edge of the sunward horizon, an arc of bright sun was beginning to rise above the thatched roofs of the city.

Her assistant, Matyu Iris Daylight, paced the road like a chicken scratching for bugs. "Where is the native guide?" Iris asked. "She was supposed to be here by now."

The other guide grunted. Matyu Gloria could not tell whether he was supporting, disputing, or just acknowledging Iris's statement. Gusty Longbread was not very communicative.

Of course, men didn't need to be communicative—not in general. Her bodyguards, Pious Rock and Clever Rock, rarely spoke at all. They were standing in silence now—arms folded, feet shoulder-width apart, faces hard-edged. She had ordered them to leave their weapons behind and pretend to be merely porters, but they did not look like bored laborers waiting for the day's labor to begin. They looked like they were guarding the supplies.

Most of the supplies were food: loaves of bread, net-bags of citrus, small crates of dried apples and apricots, and two caged laying-ducks. The food was heaped on a litter which also held Gloria and Iris's sea chests.

Iris had invited the guide to put any of his equipment on the litter, too, but it seemed he planned to wear it all. He wore a copper-finned helmet, an iron breastplate, a cane skirt, and cane shin-guards with iron knee-covers. He carried a stout wooden paddle that he gripped like a club. Apparently, he thought *he* was her bodyguard. Perhaps she could use that to her advantage.

Gusty Longbread was Aura Wisebrow's man. Gloria had no

doubt of that. Aura had not recommended her best guide; she had recommended her most loyal spy. The true guide was this native that they were still waiting for.

Gusty Longbread, with his club and his armor, was not even pretending to be a guide. This meant that Aura knew that Gloria knew Gusty was a spy.

Aura must have confidence in him. Gloria wanted to know this man who inspired such confidence. And then she would take his loyalty to Aura and make it her own.

* * *

Gusty Longbread saw Tisha before the sun cleared the horizon. She wasn't really that late. The Queenies were just impatient because they had all arrived early.

Like Gusty, Tisha was in uniform. Sunlight glinted off her copper-finned helmet. Sunlight also glinted off the bald head of the skinny blue man beside her.

The Crane? Why had she brought the Crane?

The Rock brothers focused on Tisha, sizing her up. Yeah, those guys weren't really porters. They acted too much like soldiers.

Gusty decided he was glad they were wary of Tisha. He wanted them to take her seriously. She looked too small to be a fighter, but she wore her weapons well.

Tisha approached smiling, with her hands nowhere near her weapons. She said, "Good morning, Ambassador Gloria. It's good to see you again. I am Tisha of the Urban Cohort. We met at the Senatorial Palace."

Ambassador Gloria Sunrise was a tall woman with elegant yellow skin and a proud, flat nose—traits common among the matyu caste in the Motherland. Her carrot-orange hair was oil-dressed and piled atop her head in a mound of elaborate curls decorated with nine jeweled combs surrounding her gold circlet. She looked down on Tisha with the full pride of the Sunrise dynasty and said, "I assure you, I have not forgotten."

"You are late," her assistant said.

Tisha kept her smile and looked to Gusty. He realized she expected him to complete the introductions.

"Ah, Tisha, this is Iris Daylight," Gusty said. "And these are the Rock brothers, Pious and Clever."

The ambassador's assistant looked offended by these last words. Maybe he wasn't supposed to introduce people from the laboring caste. Or maybe they didn't count because they were men.

"And who is this?" the ambassador asked, looking down on the Crane.

He was dressed in the yellow sari that Tisha sometimes wore when she met Gusty for an off-duty visit to a pool house. It looked nice on the Crane, because it was a nice sari. And he still managed to look bedraggled in it, because he was a bedraggled little man.

Gusty said, "Ah, this is Bendoko the ..."

"The guide," the Crane finished. "Bendoko the guide."

The ambassador looked at Gusty curiously. "I thought this Tisha was our native guide."

"Gusty and I are the escort," Tisha said. "And we can act as liaisons. But Bendoko will be our guide—or scout, if you prefer."

"What use have we for a scout?" the ambassador asked.

"To watch for unstable ground," Tisha said. "And to spot signs of predators. The jungle can be a dangerous place."

So to make it less dangerous, you decided to bring a burglar? Gusty thought. "Glad you could make it," Gusty said.

"Yeah," said the Crane. "Me too."

Gusty looked from one blue to the other. Oh well. He wasn't going to get the story out of them while the Queenies were listening.

"I think we're all here now," Gusty said.

The ambassador's assistant sniffed.

The ambassador just said, "Very well. Let us go."

The Rock brothers knelt down on either end of the litter and hoisted the load. In addition to food, the ambassador and her assistant had brought two sea chests—one mahogany chest decorated with carved manatees, and one cedar chest decorated with gilt-painted seascapes that flashed in the morning sunlight. The litter's wooden poles sagged with the weight, but the Rock brothers seemed to bear it effortlessly.

Iris Daylight looked to Gusty. He was expected to do something. Maybe take the lead?

"Ah," Gusty said. "You can lead ... Bendoko. Go on ahead and scout."

"Right," the Crane said. "Where are we going?"

* * *

"Where could they be going?" Senator Fanjei asked.

Hesho, his secretary, said, "I do not know. They apparently had food for several days."

Fanjei had asked Hesho to keep track of the Reconciled Queendom's ambassador. Ambassador Gloria had become quiet once the scroll was removed from her reach. Instead of storming into the Senatorial Palace demanding that it be found, she had stayed in the guest suite of the City Palace and consulted with Aura. The other senators attributed the ambassador's silence to Aura's diplomacy, but Fanjei suspected that Ambassador Gloria was working on a secondary plan.

"We need to find out what she's doing," Fanjei said.

Technically, the Republic's inland territory was under the jurisdiction of the individual ports. Sliceharbor's jungle belonged to Sliceharbor, and Fanjei's navy couldn't touch it. But technically, anything involving the Reconciled Queendom was "relations with a foreign power", which was definitely a matter for the Republican Navy. In fact, since the Urban Cohort was confined to Sliceharbor and the jungle villages had no soldiers of their own, Fanjei could claim that involving the Navy was necessary.

"Hesho, please send a message to Captain Tu. Tell him I want the services of his best jungle tracker. Tell him I need someone quiet."

* * *

The Moko River Road is broad and rutted in the vicinity of Sliceharbor. It curves between the orchards, fields, and timber stands that support the Lunaslip Republic's largest city. The landscape is crisscrossed by canals designed to aid drainage into the river. Many of the fruit trees have been magically shaped into varieties that are more flood tolerant. In other words, the rural landscape outside Sliceharbor is as artificial as the city itself. But to a city dweller, any place without paving stones is wild jungle.

Gusty Longbread watched the Crane's wary advance. The burglar expected a panther in every tree, and because they were passing through an orange grove, the panthers of his paranoia had many places to hide. But the Crane didn't let his paranoia slow him down. In fact, his nervousness propelled him up the road, far ahead of the rest of the party.

Gusty had to admit that the Crane made a pretty good scout. He wasn't a *convincing* scout. He wasn't *reassuring*. But Gusty was certain that if there were trouble ahead, the Crane would find it long before they got there.

Gusty and Tisha strolled at their typical patrolling pace. The ambassador and her people followed along behind. The Queenies weren't particularly friendly, but Gusty didn't mind. As long as they stayed aloof, he and Tisha could talk privately.

"So why did you bring him?" he asked.

"Because I couldn't leave him at my house," she said.

"You could have told him to go back to the Shacks," Gusty pointed out.

"I did," Tisha said. "But he didn't want to. You think the Too-Tall brothers have stopped looking for him?"

Gusty shrugged. He suspected the Too-Tall brothers had other things to do now. After the skirmish on Breadbaker Bridge, the sailors of the Republican Navy were probably in more danger than Bendoko was.

"Yeah, I don't know either," Tisha said. "So I told him that if he didn't want to go home, he could come with us."

Gusty grunted.

"So why are we visiting the Order of the Holy Shield?" Tisha asked.

Gusty said, "The ambassador wants to talk to the Holy Shield's First."

Tisha didn't need to know that there might be a second Sun Scroll. At least, not yet.

"Oh," Tisha said. "I thought there was some kind of trouble between the Holy Shield and the Queenies."

"Yeah," said Gusty. "That's right."

When Mogadwen invaded the Sun Island, the First of the Holy Shield had said that the Republic shouldn't get involved—with the implication that the Queenies had it coming.

Tisha asked, "So the ambassador is trying to mend nets?"

Gusty grunted. He hoped Tisha would take that as a yes.

Maybe Aura Wisebrow had made a mistake by asking that Tisha come along. It wasn't easy to keep things from her.

* * *

Later that morning, they reached the river for which the Moko River Road was named. Like the river, the road grew narrower as they progressed upstream. By midday, it was little more than a cart track. Farmers who lived this far from the city did not drive their carts to town very often. Barges were more efficient.

Villages were sparser here. Fields were hidden in forest clearings. A few fruit trees lined the road, but the travelers saw no more great orchards.

People were small here, and the jungle was thick. Now even Gusty was wondering where the panthers might be hiding. Branches hung high overhead, suspending clumps of jungle moss.

The forest kept the sun off their heads, but mosquitoes were thick in the shade. When the ambassador called a halt for the midday meal, Gusty suggested that Tisha and the Crane eat with the Rock brothers. The two men had a strong mosquito-repelling scent.

The ambassador's assistant, Iris Daylight, went off to eat by herself. She obviously considered herself to be too important to eat with the others. Gusty thought guides and soldiers must be like porters—part of the laboring caste. Iris seemed offended that she was not allowed to sit with the ambassador. Or maybe she was offended because Gusty *was* allowed to sit with the ambassador.

Allowed? No. Gusty's company was required. Technically, the ambassador had invited him, but Gusty did not think the invitation was refusable.

* * *

Gloria Sunrise sat on a picnic mat beside a wicker food basket finely woven by tiny native hands. Gusty Longbread, Aura's spy, sat on the other side of the basket emitting a sharp scent to keep away the mosquitoes. The scent seemed to be working for him, but he lacked the skill to fully encloud them both. Gloria discreetly resonated with the scent so that it enclouded her as well.

She gave him an encouraging nod and told him, "I will start with bread."

Gusty didn't move.

"Either loaf will do," Gloria prompted.

"Oh," said Gusty. "I'll take this one, then." He snatched a loaf from the basket and a lemon rolled out onto the picnic mat.

"Sorry," he said.

He picked up the stray lemon and then—yes, it was true; Gloria saw it with her own eyes—he returned the dropped lemon to her basket!

Customs were different on the mainland. Gloria understood this. Gusty had not meant to insult her. But he would have to be taught.

"Food that leaves a matyu's basket is never returned," she said.

"Oh," said Gusty. "Sorry."

He reached for the lemons, but hesitated because he couldn't tell which one it had been.

"Let us pretend the lemon never fell out," Gloria suggested. That was better than throwing out every lemon—and much better than throwing out the entire basket, which was the protocol her mother insisted on. Protocol had to be relaxed in certain situations. Gloria was a pragmatist.

"When you share a meal with a matyu, you may take one of anything she has already taken." It was like explaining manners to a child. "So when I ask for bread, you may take the other loaf as soon as you have handed me mine."

"Oh," said Gusty. He offered her the loaf he was clutching. So tight was his grip that his fingers had poked holes in the crust.

"Perhaps I shall eat that one," she said, indicating the bread still in the basket. She didn't want to embarrass him, but she couldn't bring herself to take torn bread.

Gusty withdrew the intact loaf from the basket, and Gloria took it before he could mangle it or drop it or do who-knew-what-else.

"Good," she said. At least, it was a start.

The bread had cured nicely during the morning's walk. The inside was firm and spongy. The crust was delightfully chewy, while still managing to retain a hint of crunch.

"You may eat your bread, too," she told him.

"Oh. Right. Thank you." He took a bite.

"Does your mother bake bread like this?"

"Yes," Gusty Longbread said.

Seeing that he wouldn't elaborate, Gloria prompted, "Is it as good as this?"

"Better," Gusty said. "But this is good, too."

Gloria smiled. "What Mother makes is always best. You are a good son."

"Thank you," Gusty said.

"I understand that customs are different here," she said. "I do not judge you for concealing your navel."

Gusty looked down at his iron breastplate. It extended nearly down to his hips.

"It's a regulation uniform," he mumbled.

"I understand," Gloria said. "Even on the Sun Island, we now have soldiers who cover their navels. The Mogadrel are barbarians who will stab their swords into any opening, no matter how sacred."

"You've seen the fighting?" Gusty asked.

"Not personally, no," she said, pushing the image of her brother's corpse from her mind.

Gusty was studying her curiously. He was a soldier. Would talk of the war open him up to her?

She said, "The fighting is on a sparsely populated coast of the island. Our frontier, really. If the Mogadrel had tried to attack the city where I live, they would have been slaughtered while still aboard their ships."

Gusty grunted.

"Have you heard much news of the war?" she asked.

"Some," Gusty said. "I haven't talked to anyone from the Motherland, but I've heard stories second- and third-hand."

"What are people saying?"

"They say we're losing."

So it was *we*, not *you*. Interesting.

"It's true," she said. "We are. That's why I was sent here."

Gusty frowned.

"To get the Sun Scroll," he said.

"That is correct," she said. "Why does this make you frown?"

Gusty shook his head. "I'm sorry. I didn't mean to frown."

"You don't approve of my mission?"

"It's not for me to say."

"But Aura Wisebrow has given you *her* opinions," Gloria said.

"What?"

"It is not for you to say, because it is Aura Wisebrow's decision. Is that what you meant?"

"I guess it's nobody's decision now," Gusty said. "The Sun Scroll is gone."

"You were looking for it, weren't you?"

"Yes. With Tisha."

"Did you find it?"

"Not yet. You'd know if we had."

"So why did you quit looking?"

"You needed an escort."

"Yes," said Gloria. "So Aura Wisebrow told me."

She knows! … But how much do you know, Gusty?

Gloria said, "You know why this expedition is so important, don't you?"

"Not really."

"But you can guess."

"Would you like to tell me? Tisha and I are here to help you. We can do that better if we know what you're trying to do."

Again he mentioned the native girl. Gloria looked at her. She sat on the road, sharing a basket with the nervous jungle guide and the Rock brothers.

Gloria asked, "Tisha is important to you, isn't she?"

"Of course," Gusty said. "She's my partner."

"And you trust her?"

"Of course."

"With everything?"

"Yeah. Most things, anyway."

"Gusty Longbread, you know we are losing the war in the Motherland. This expedition could tip that balance. Our people's lives depend on our success. With so much at stake, I can't jeopardize my plan by revealing it to people who may be unsympathetic to the cause."

Gusty glanced at the native woman. Worry was in his eyes.

Gloria said, "I can tell you our purpose only if you promise not to tell anyone else."

Gusty sighed. "Then you'd better not tell me," he said. "I can't keep anything from Tisha."

* * *

Bendoko took a lemon. He bit off the end and spat it out onto the road. He tore apart the peel, sending pungent droplets bursting into the air. The aroma blended into the citrusy smell of the two porters.

Clever Rock and Pious Rock. Oranges had funny names, but those were two of the funniest.

Bendoko didn't laugh, though. Only their names were funny. The men were steel sharp.

They ate with none of the lazy insolence that Bendoko expected from muscular orange thugs. The Rock brothers sat like men ready to stand in an eyeblink. They looked like soldiers. Their eyes were wary. Bendoko was glad that most of their suspicion was focused on Gusty.

"It bothers you that he sits so close to the ambassador," Tisha said.

The brothers turned their alert eyes to Tisha.

"Are you afraid he might harm her while you are sitting too far away to help?" she asked.

"We fear nothing," said Pious.

The brothers were easy to tell apart. Pious was the one with the scar on his chin.

"All right," Tisha said. "But you're watching for something."

"We're just eating our lunch," Pious said.

"All right," Tisha said.

The brothers *had* been eating their lunch, but now neither was eating anything. Their hands were empty, ready for action.

Bendoko chewed on his lemon, waiting for the next move.

"Is it the club?" Tisha asked. "I can tell him to leave it with me the next time he's alone with the ambassador."

Pious glared at her.

"That would be better," Clever said.

Pious looked at him in surprise.

Clever shrugged. "It would be."

Pious shrugged and fished a piece of dried apple out of the basket.

"We're all here to help the ambassador," Tisha said. The earnestness of her face was pretty. Bendoko had figured out that he wasn't in love with her after all, but he still thought she looked pretty.

"We can work together," Tisha said.

Clever looked her up and down. "I do not think so," he said. "You are too short to hold up your end of the litter."

She smiled—very pretty. "That's not what I meant."

"Then I am afraid I do not know what you mean," Clever said.

He wasn't cold. He wasn't coy. He was still pretending to be a porter, even though he had just admitted he was a bodyguard.

An honest liar. Bendoko found himself liking the man.

Gusty and the ambassador stood up.

"Finally," Pious said.

Tisha glanced at Bendoko and gave him a little grin.

Bendoko didn't grin back. He didn't want the Rock brothers to think he might be laughing at them.

The brothers hastened to the ambassador's side, ostensibly to pick up her basket and picnic mat.

Tisha smiled and shook her head. "I hope they relax a little once they get to know Gus."

"I don't think those guys relax," Bendoko said.

"I suppose not," Tisha admitted. "But they might calm down a little."

"Yeah," said Bendoko. "I suppose."

Tisha picked up their picnic basket and stood up.

Bendoko said, "That was smooth, by the way."

"What was?"

"The way you called their bluff without making them angry."

Tisha grinned. "I don't think Pious appreciated it."

"No, but he didn't slap anyone's head off either."

"Oranges are just as reasonable as we are," Tisha said.

"Hey, I wasn't saying anything about oranges. I've known plenty of blues who wanted to slap my head off, too."

"All right, Ben."

She eyed him.

"So how does it feel to be out of reach of the Too-Tall brothers?" she asked.

Bendoko checked to be certain that none of the Queenies were within hearing distance.

"To tell the truth, this place makes me nervous," he said.

"It shows," Tisha said.

"How bad?" If the Queenies knew he wasn't really a jungle guide …

Tisha brushed some mosquitoes off his neck. "Let's just say I hope no one calls *your* bluff."

* * *

The Rock brothers packed up the supplies, and the expedition left. By that time, the ants had already found the bread crumbs. They organized a supply chain to haul the bread back to their queen.

After the shadows had moved, a pack rat discovered a pretty piece of orange peel glowing in a patch of sunlight. He took it away. He already had two pebbles, three feathers, and a fern leaf in his junglemoss nest, but he needed a nice piece of orange peel.

At about mid-afternoon, a man paused at the picnic site. He knelt to examine the bit of lemon rind Bendoko had spat out. Then he continued following the tracks.

* * *

Gusty Longbread walked along the cart track, flattening the soft ruts with his sandals. Ferns rustled against his cane shin-guards. Junglemoss drooping from overhanging branches brushed against the fins of his helmet.

"So what did you learn?" Tisha asked.

She was walking beside him, staying close because the road had narrowed and because Gusty could repel mosquitoes. He extended his elemental senses out through his breath and altered the scent of the air ahead of them. The mosquitoes fled the scent-cloud.

"I didn't learn much," Gusty said.

That was the truth. He wasn't lying. Gloria Sunrise just hadn't told him very much.

But he *had* learned something. He'd learned that Gloria Sunrise, despite her majestic bearing and diplomatic masks, could be shaken by the idea of a man getting stabbed in the navel. Gusty suspected she had seen the wounded … or perhaps the dead.

The navel was sacred to the Queenies. Well, it was sacred to all oranges, because it represented the connection to one's mother, but only a Queenie soldier would want his navel exposed while charging into battle. This would put a great round hole in his armor right at a Mogadrel's eye level. No wonder the red men took advantage of it.

But to a Queenie, it would look like the Mogadrel had abandoned all decency, like they had no good left in their hearts. Any person who stabbed another in the navel was probably in league with the demons. (Being civilized, the Queenies preferred to club their enemies in the head.)

So unsealing the Sun Scroll was justified. At least in Gloria Sunrise's eyes. She didn't have to wait for the demons to enter the world; her people were already fighting creatures from Hell.

"Oh, he looks so ridiculous," Tisha said in a voice that held more fondness than ridicule.

The Crane was bounding along the road, slapping mosquitoes off his bald head. Periodically, he would crouch low and peer into the undergrowth. Then he would scan the branches above.

Tisha shook her head. "I'm surprised the Queenies haven't said something about him yet."

What could they say? Something like, *I don't think your guide is really a guide*? Then Gusty could say, *I don't think your porters are really porters*. And then the Queenies could say, *I think you're really a spy for Aura Wisebrow*.

No one could say anything because they were all pretending to be something else.

Except Tisha, of course. She was an urbie with every breath she took.

So was Gusty, really. He wasn't really a spy for Aura Wisebrow. Not really. Or at least, not yet.

They passed a field—peas or lentils or something—on the edge of another village. There were many villages along the Moko River Road. This one looked small and smelled musty, which didn't really distinguish it from the others.

Chickens strutted out of their way. A group of muddy blue children stopped doing the thing that was making them muddy. They stared like they'd never seen oranges before, but Gusty could tell from ruts and sandal marks in the road that an orange carter had passed through earlier in the day.

Tisha waved. The children waved back, flashing white smiles in their muddy blue faces.

Another road met theirs in the center of town. Instead of staying on the Moko River Road, the Crane took this side branch.

"What's he doing?" Tisha mumbled.

Gusty grunted to indicate that he didn't know.

"Ben!" Tisha called. "Wait up."

She hurried to catch up to the Crane. Gusty strode along beside her.

The Crane waited for them.

"You're going the wrong way," Tisha said, when she was close enough to not be overheard. "The Moko River Road is the other one."

"We leave the road here," the Crane said.

"Maybe we should ask for directions," Tisha said.

"I got directions," the Crane said.

"From whom?" Tisha asked.

"From other people in my line of work," he said.

"How many burglars need to visit the Order of the Holy Shield?" Gusty asked.

"Their greathouse is on the way to the other … place."

"The other … *place?*" Tisha asked.

"Yeah, just some place, right?"

Gusty asked, "The burglars have a hideout in the jungle, Crane?"

"Hey, I didn't say that."

"But you do know how to get there," Gusty said.

"I know how to get to some places in the jungle," the Crane said. "Not hideouts. Just places, right?"

"All right," Tisha said. "You know places."

"Yeah," said the Crane. "Because I'm your guide, right?"

"You're the guide," Tisha said.

The Queenies were close enough to hear them now.

"So follow me," the Crane said. "And have a little trust."

Gusty grunted.

Tisha smiled and shook her head.

They took the Crane's road out of the village. It passed through some lime orchards—or maybe they were green lemons. Gusty hoped the Crane knew what he was doing.

Urbies often heard "he's gone jungle" when asking for the whereabouts of a Sliceharbor miscreant. It was used almost as often as "he shipped out". Usually, the fugitive was just lying low in the Shacks, but criminals *did* go jungle sometimes. Otherwise, it wouldn't have been a good lie.

In popular legend, criminals who went jungle lived in the swamp, wrestled alligators, and wore panther-skin loincloths. In practice, they either stayed with relatives in a nearby village, or they camped out in the ruins of some old building.

There were quite a few ruins around Sliceharbor. In Imperial times, settlement had extended farther inland. After the Revolution, a lot of places had been abandoned.

Like the Temple of the Noonday Sun.

* * *

About half a lithic after the expedition left the village, a man crept through the lime orchard. His plan was to circumvent the thatch-roofed huts and rejoin the Moko River Road on the opposite side.

At the edge of the orchard, he found a trail leading away from the Moko River. On the trail, he found seven sets of footprints. So he abandoned the Moko River Road and instead followed the footprints into the jungle.

* * *

The trail had grown so narrow that they were forced to walk single file. Gloria's bodyguards walked in the rear, because they were pretending to be porters. To keep them from getting nervous, Gloria had to walk in the rear, too, letting Iris walk ahead of her. Gloria's view was mostly obscured by Iris's hair. The only break to this monotony was the yellow spider that had somehow fallen in among Iris's long, orange locks.

The spider crawled along the edge of Iris's golden circlet. As it reached the back of Iris's head, it became immersed in her hair and disappeared from view.

Gloria watched and waited. Her patience was rewarded when the spider crawled out along one of Iris's bouncing locks. The spider reached the end and jumped off. Such courage! Or perhaps it felt its predicament was so severe that it had nothing left to lose.

The spider descended, swinging on its silken thread, dropping a thumbwidth with every bouncing step. It was halfway down when Iris turned to speak over her shoulder, whipping the spider through the air.

"I believe he is lost," Iris said.

"Our native guide?" Gloria asked.

"He is no guide," Iris said. "He acts like an urban child on his first trip into the jungle."

"True," Gloria agreed. "But he convinced Gusty Longbread and the native girl that he knows where to go."

"We have not seen a village since he led us off the road," Iris said. "He could be leading us to a gang of kidnappers."

"First you say he is lost, and now you say he is deliberately leading us astray."

"I do not trust him."

"Very well," Gloria said.

"He is misaligned. Did you notice?"

"I noticed he is aligned with Nature, yes."

"How can we trust a man who has rejected the deities?"

"We do not have to trust him," Gloria said. "But we do have to follow him. He is the one who claims to know the way. Perhaps the nature spirits are guiding him."

"I do not trust the nature spirits, either."

Gloria let Iris have the last word in hopes that it would placate her.

She had lost track of the spider.

No. There it was.

The yellow spider had abandoned its thread and was now crawling down Iris's back, heading for the waistband of her loincloth.

Would it climb over or try to duck inside?

Gloria found herself hoping for the latter.

* * *

Tisha tromped up the jungle trail, taking long strides so she wouldn't slow the oranges down. Even with long strides, she wasn't gaining ground on Bendoko. He was moving fast, and he was no longer looking back.

Close behind her, Gusty asked, "Do you think he's lost?"

"You think he's moving fast because he's hoping the next bend will prove he's been going the right way?"

"Yeah," Gusty said.

"All right," Tisha said. "So what do we do, Gus?"

Gusty made a grunt that meant he didn't know.

"I don't think it's a good idea to tell the ambassador that we're lost," Tisha said. "I don't think she trusts us 'natives' much."

"Yeah, well, she doesn't have much reason to," Gusty said.

"What's that mean?"

"Nothing," Gusty said.

"No, Gus. Tell me what's wrong. Why can't she trust me?"

"It's not you, Tisha. It's the Senate. She came here looking for a way to help her people, and the Senate has given her nothing."

"The Senate is supposed to look out for the Republic, Gus. It's not there to bail out the Queenies if they get themselves on rough seas."

"So you think it's all the Queenies' fault?" Gusty asked.

The Queenies had invaded the mainland. And now the Mogadrel were punishing them for it. And maybe the punishment was harsh, but it wasn't any worse than what the Queenies had tried to do in Mogadwen.

Had Gusty forgotten that?

She asked, "What do you think, Gus?"

"I think people are dying over there," he said. "I don't blame the ambassador for wanting to end the war."

"Are the Queenies trying to end the war or win the war?"

"Both, Tisha. They don't want to give up land to the Mogadrel."

"And you think that justifies opening the Sun Scroll?"

"I don't know," Gusty said. "No one knows what's written there."

"Because the Goddess of the Sun told us not to read it."

"She told *us* not to read it. But she gave the words to the Sunrise line. They are matyus."

"That doesn't make them exceptions to divine law."

"That's not for us to decide!" Gusty said. "Matyus have direct contact with the deities. Deciding questions of divine law is *their* job! But now a blue senator has taken divine law into his own hands and stolen the scroll away! And that's why we can't trust … the Crane."

Oh.

Tisha wanted to believe that her partner had not been about to say that he couldn't trust her. Maybe they disagreed about this one thing, but that didn't mean—

Actually, yeah, it did. This wasn't a little thing. For Gusty, this was a big thing. And because she was blue, he couldn't trust her.

But he hadn't said it. So they could pretend he hadn't meant it.

"I'll go check on him, then," Tisha said.

She jogged ahead, trying to put some distance between herself and the oranges.

* * *

Bendoko hurried along the trail, hoping to find a sign around the next bend.

All right, maybe the next one, then.

He scanned the tree trunks on either side, even checking the undergrowth in case the mark had been placed too low for him to see it easily. But he found no marks.

This had to be the right trail, though. He'd seen the "ruined temple" mark on the doorpost of that house on the village square. That meant he was supposed to leave the main road and follow the road that went past that house, right? That was the code, right?

The code was invented by Big Zeemo. Knowing its secrets was one of the benefits of giving your soul to him. In the city, criminals left signs on houses to pass on important messages: *Don't mess with this house—a judge lives here. This house is under protection of Big Zeemo. You can lie low here, if you can afford the rent. This house has nothing of value.*

Bendoko had left this last message more than once.

In the jungle, the code was supposed to tell you where to go. Bendoko had been following signs marking the route to the ruined temple, but he hadn't seen one since turning down this path.

Maybe he'd read the mark wrong. Maybe it had meant, "You're on the right track," instead of, "Now turn here." Or maybe it hadn't been left by Big Zeemo's people at all. Maybe some kids had seen the mark on a tree somewhere and copied it on the doorpost of their house one day when they were bored.

Maybe Bendoko was lost.

Maybe he could fake his way out of it.

Panting and the clacking of a cane skirt caused him to turn around. Tisha was jogging toward him.

"How's it going?" she asked.

"Smooth," Bendoko said. "It's going smooth."

"So you know where we are?"

"Yeah," Bendoko said. *We're in the middle of the jungle,* he thought.

She gestured to indicate they should keep moving. Bendoko did so. She walked behind him, armor clacking, weapon scabbards creaking as they swung on her belt.

"How long till we get there, do you think?"

"Oh … I'd say about …" Bendoko pretended to check the sky. Any heavenly body that could have told him the time was completely obscured by junglemoss-covered pine boughs. "About another lithic," he decided.

That was safe. If he said two lithics, then the Queenies might want to make camp here. Bendoko did not want to spend the night in the jungle. The cellar hadn't been that great, but at least he hadn't worried about panthers.

"All right," Tisha said. She sounded sad.

"But it might be sooner," Bendoko said.

She didn't reply. Nor did she fall back to walk with Gusty.

Bendoko glanced over his shoulder.

She met his gaze with somber eyes. Yeah, she was sad about something.

"Look, I'm pretty sure we'll get there," he said.

"All right, Ben. I trust you."

"Really?"

A pause. "Well, no. Not really. But until you admit you made a wrong turn back at that village, I'll keep following you."

"I don't know," Bendoko said. "It seemed like the right way at the time."

"I bet you say that a lot."

Bendoko thought about it. "Yeah. Maybe I do."

* * *

Gusty Longbread walked along the jungle trail, wading through ferns and ducking low-hanging branches. He was supposed to be staying alert for any dangers that might be concealed in the vegetation, but he was distracted by what Tisha had asked him: Would it be right to end the war by opening the Sun Scroll?

Aura Wisebrow wanted him to claim the second Sun Scroll for Sliceharbor. *She* didn't think it was right for the Queenies to open it. But Aura Wisebrow thought like a blue. You had to, to be successful in politics.

The navel oranges said that urbies thought like blues, too. Maybe they were right. Gusty didn't know anymore which thoughts were his and which thoughts were blue thoughts that had been put in his mind by the Urban Cohort. It was simplest to follow orders and not think at all.

Someone shrieked on the path ahead.

Gusty froze.

It wasn't Tisha shrieking, though. It was the Crane.

"Kill it!" the Crane shouted. "Kill it!"

Gusty broke into a run. He held his club in one hand. With his free hand, he pushed aside branches that got in his way. He caught up to the blues at the marshy shore of a shady lake.

"It went in there," the Crane said, pointing to a hollow log lying among the rushes.

Tisha was standing with her hands on her knees, peering at the log dubiously.

"I think it was just a garden snake," she said.

"It could be a viper!" the Crane said.

"Well, maybe," Tisha said. "But it's gone now."

She looked up. "Hi, Gus."

Gusty grunted a greeting.

Tisha said, "I think you were a little too loud, Ben. You made Gusty run."

"It jumped at me!" the Crane said.

"It jumped at you?" Tisha asked.

"Yeah. Or, at least, it jumped."

"I jumped, too," Tisha said, "when you started screaming."

"Yeah. Well."

"I'd better go tell the ambassador's bodyguards they can stand down," Tisha said.

Gusty thought that was a good idea. The Rock brothers wouldn't be keen on all the screaming. Pretending that the Crane was a competent jungle guide was going to be real hard now.

Except …

"Hey," said Gusty. "You found it."

"Found what?" the Crane asked.

He looked where Gusty was looking.

"Oh," he said. "Yeah, I guess I *did* find it."

Beyond the trees on the opposite shore of the lake was the greathouse of the Order of the Holy Shield.

* * *

The Order of the Holy Shield had boats. They were large, flat-bottomed dories designed specifically for carrying Children of the Sun across the swampy lake.

The Republican Navy's jungle tracker arrived at the edge of the lake just in time to see the ambassador and her companions disembarking on the opposite shore. Monks of the Holy Shield were greeting them.

So now he knew where she would be staying the night. Was this visit the reason for her journey, or would she be traveling again the next morning?

He waited until everyone had left the docks. Then he slipped quietly into the water.

* * *

Gloria Sunrise thought the Holy Shield's greathouse was rustic. The vegetable gardens grew close to the walls, as though huddling around the building for protection against the jungle. The fruit trees were pruned, but that did not make them ornamental.

However, the building itself was heavily decorated with wood carvings representing various aspects of the deities. Here was a string of coins representing Wealth. There was a sword representing Lith. The carvings were well done, although they seemed somewhat primitive because they were unpainted.

Sun motifs appeared often on the greathouse's facade, and always in places of high distinction, but the most common carvings were two-panel scenes depicting acts of justice: a thief stealing money and a judge requiring restitution; a healer stooping to help an injured man and then receiving new sandals as a reward; a dragon threatening a village and then being speared by a monk of the Holy Shield.

Matyu Gloria's order, the Noonday Sun, also served all the deities, but they understood that the highest honor must always go to Mother Sun. The Holy Shield, in their centuries of service on the mainland, had been forced to make concessions to the customs of the natives.

The interior of the greathouse was as dark as the jungle. Fish-oil lamps burned in lamp nooks, illuminating the carvings that decorated the support posts. The interior theme was dangers of the jungle: panthers, alligators, vipers, and the dragons that the Order of the Holy Shield had finally eradicated after centuries of hunting. The order claimed to serve Heaven, but their concerns were so worldly.

Of course, Gloria's own concerns were worldly, too, now. She realized this as she spoke with Stormrain, the Holy Shield's First. They did not discuss spiritual matters. They talked only about the war.

"I'm sorry we can't be more help to you," Stormrain said, after Gloria had told her everything she knew about the battles that had been lost and the territory that had been seized. "The Holy Shield must be aloof from politics."

Gloria nearly choked on the irony. The Holy Shield had remained on the mainland only because of their deep involvement in the Sliceharbor Insurrection. If they had not chosen the rebels' side so forcefully, they would have been expelled from the mainland just like the Blessed Order of the Noonday Sun. In fact, if they had not betrayed the Queen's forces, the Insurrection would most likely have failed and no one would have been expelled at all.

As a matyu of the Noonday Sun, Gloria knew well these events, though they had happened ten dozen years before. But this was not a time to renew historical quarrels. Only the oldest people remembered the Insurrection first hand, and they had been children at the time.

"I did not come here to beg for political help," Gloria said. "I just wanted to ask directions."

The corner of Stormrain's mouth twisted in a grin. "Directions?" she asked.

"I wish to visit the Temple of the Noonday Sun," Gloria said. "My grandmother told me that it was near your greathouse." *At least, geographically.*

Stormrain's eyes widened, and she nodded. "Ah. So that is why you came in on the back trail."

"Was that the back trail?"

"It's mostly used by blues. They don't mind swimming across the swamp." Again her mouth twisted. "But in Imperial times, it was a cart road to your order's temple."

That was interesting. The skinny native guide had seemed surprised to find a lake between them and the greathouse. Gloria suspected he'd been leading them on second-hand directions. Did he know that following the trail onward would take them to the Temple of the Noonday Sun?

Perhaps she could have asked to be taken there directly. Then she would not have had to reveal anything to this order of traitors.

But no. This way was better. This way she could leave the two natives behind in the village that supported the greathouse.

And Longbread's son? Should she leave him here, too?

No, she decided. If she left Gusty behind, his obligation to Aura Wisebrow would require him to interfere. But if she took him along, then she could make him part of her expedition.

By showing him trust, she would make him her ally. She was a diplomat; recruiting allies was her job.

As Gloria laid these plans, Stormrain continued speaking of local geography and geology—facts that Gloria felt free to ignore now that she knew the way to the Temple of the Noonday Sun. Until:

"Excuse me, Stormrain. Could you repeat that?"

"I said that if your order's architect had hired spelunkers, she would have realized that your temple was built on unstable ground."

"How unstable?" Gloria asked.

"Thirty years ago, most of the building collapsed into a sinkhole."

7 Yellowmonth

THE NEXT MORNING, Gusty Longbread got his first glimpse of the ruined Temple of the Noonday Sun.

Tisha and the Crane had been left behind, so Gusty was in the lead as the ambassador's expedition reached the edge of the clearing. Except it wasn't truly a clearing. The thick jungle was open to the blue sky not because someone had harvested the timber but because the ground had given way beneath it.

The earth had collapsed, creating a lake in a market-sized hole surrounded by jagged, white limestone cliffs. Trees clung to the edge with roots reaching down to the water fifteen feet below. The lake's surface was placid, reflecting the cliffs and the blue sky above, but Gusty could not see into the depths. One part of the jagged cliff-face was interrupted by a hole at the waterline that gave the impression that a great maw had opened to drink the lake.

On the opposite side stood a wall of the temple. The view through the windows was not a glimpse into the interior; it was a glimpse *out*, to the jungle beyond. Gusty was looking at the inside of the back wall.

The rest of the temple had crumbled away. Chunks of tiled floor tilted on the edge of the sinkhole. Below was a trail of rubble leading down into the dark water.

Iris Daylight came to stand beside Gusty. She stared at the ruins in horror.

"This is worse than what the First described," she said. "Much worse."

"She said she hasn't visited this site for many years," the ambassador replied. "I had hoped more of the temple would be intact."

The two porters also arrived at the edge of the gaping hole, but said nothing. They carried the digging tools that the ambassador had purchased from the village by the greathouse, but they were not prepared to excavate an underwater heap of rubble.

"It is gone," Iris Daylight said. "It is just … gone."

Gloria Sunrise looked at Gusty. "Not necessarily," she said.

"Was Ruby Sunrise's cell in the part that is left standing?" asked Iris Daylight.

"No," said Gloria Sunrise. "Her cell had a sunward window."

"So it is gone," Iris Daylight said.

"I believe it is still down there," Gloria Sunrise said. "And Gusty can swim."

Gusty looked at her in surprise. It was true. He could swim a little. Everybody in Sliceharbor could.

Iris Daylight looked down into the water. "He will never find it," she said. "And I am certain the water has already destroyed it."

Gloria Sunrise smiled and asked, "Is that why you are so willing to talk about it in front of Gusty?"

Iris Daylight looked up, alarmed at the idea that Gusty might be intelligent enough to figure out she was talking about a copy of the Sun Scroll. She gave Gloria Sunrise a guilty look.

"Forgive me," she said.

Gloria Sunrise smiled and shook her head. "You have done nothing wrong. The time has come for Gusty to know."

She put her hand on Gusty's armored shoulder and drew him back a few steps from the edge.

"Gusty Longbread," she said, "when I first met you, you had been given a task—to find the Sun Scroll. I was given the same task by the Queen Matyu. One copy was held in the library of the Senatorial Palace, and I was well on my way to securing it when it was stolen.

"But there was a second copy. When the Mother Goddess revealed her secrets to Ruby Sunrise, Ruby wrote them down twice, precisely because she feared one copy could be lost. The second copy, the one we came here to find, was hidden beneath the floor tiles of her cell, on the sunward side of the temple.

"Matyu Iris now fears that copy has also been lost. But I believe it is right here. The Mother Goddess has led us here, you and me, and brought us together on the same mission. I am here because our people must have that scroll. And you are here to help me get it."

Divine warmth filled Gusty's lungs, and in that instant, he knew Gloria's words were true. The Mother Goddess wanted this second scroll to be found. And she had guided him there for that reason.

"What is it?" Gloria Sunrise asked.

"I felt ..."

"Did the Mother Goddess touch your soul?" Matyu Gloria asked.

"Yes."

She smiled. "Then you have been blessed," she said with satisfaction.

Gusty looked at her in wonder. "Is that what it feels like to be a matyu?"

"Yes," she said. "On the best days."

"So will he help us?" Iris Daylight asked.

"Of course," Gusty said. "But ..."

They waited for him to continue.

"Ambassador—Matyu Gloria—I can swim, but only a little. We don't know how deeply the rubble is submerged."

"The Mother Goddess would not give you this task were it beyond your abilities," Matyu Gloria assured him.

Gusty would have liked for that to be true, but the brief touch of the Mother Goddess had left him. He was on his own again. He knew what the Mother Goddess wanted him to do, but he didn't see how. The tea-dark water could be impossibly deep. Gusty, like all oranges, tended to float.

"Matyu Gloria, Tisha swims so much better than I do."

"Your abilities will be enough," Matyu Gloria said. "We need not share this with her."

"We have already had one scroll stolen," said Iris Daylight. "We must not let them know about the second."

"Tisha would never steal a sacred scroll," Gusty said.

"And what of her skinny friend?" asked Iris Daylight.

Well, Gusty couldn't vouch for the Crane's character, of course. And if they left him alone in the village, he'd probably sneak up the trail and spy on them. Maybe they could leave one of the Rock brothers with him.

But then Gusty realized something. The Crane wasn't brave enough or stupid enough to steal the second scroll while two urbies were watching—at least, not if he wasn't being paid. And besides, the Crane didn't seem particularly happy about what had happened after he stole the first scroll.

"I won't say we can trust him," Gusty said. "But I don't think he'd try to steal it for himself. In fact, I think he would be happier if he helped us find it."

"That is out of consideration," Iris Daylight said. "If the scroll can be found, we must find it ourselves. What if these natives find it and decide to destroy it?"

"Why would they do that?" Gusty asked.

"Did you know that the guide is misaligned? He serves nature spirits!"

Clever and Pious Rock exchanged concerned glances.

Gusty said, "It's just a local religion common among … people like Bendoko. They don't serve the deities, but they don't commit sacrilege, either."

This was true. Sliceharbor's criminal class committed everything else, but usually not sacrilege.

"Will you not even try?" asked Matyu Gloria.

Gusty said, "Yes, I'll try, Matyu. If that's what you want. But I doubt I can dive much deeper than Pious and Clever. Has the Mother Goddess told you that I'm the only one who can find it? What if my job is helping you work with the people who can dive?"

Matyu Gloria considered this. Even Iris Daylight was considering.

"The deities made the nine peoples different so they could help each other," Matyu Gloria said.

"But when you consider how little help we have received so far …" said Iris Daylight.

"Nevertheless, we will give them another chance to help us now," Matyu Gloria said. "Gusty Longbread is right. I would never consider diving into that pit myself. Would you?"

"No," said Iris Daylight.

"So we need to call upon the people who were created to be divers."

"At least let Gusty Longbread try it first. He said he would. Give him one day. Or even two. Let us not call on the natives until we are certain Gusty cannot find it."

"No," said Matyu Gloria. "That would be a waste of time. And we must not waste more time. We have an enemy in the Senate. Perhaps more than one. The more time we spend here, the more we risk being discovered. We need to return to Sliceharbor before the natives notice we are missing."

* * *

Coated in mud to conceal his skin and ward off mosquitoes, Ensign Shuver of the Republican Navy crept through the jungle parallel to the path. The ground was soft, and he couldn't risk leaving a footprint. Only Children of the Sun had gone up the trail this morning, and his normal-sized track would stand out among the prints of their giant sandals.

Because the ambassador had left the two Children of Justice at the village inn, Ensign Shuver didn't expect her to travel very far. And he was right. The thumping of the ground told him the Children of the Sun were coming back down the trail.

Ensign Shuver flattened himself against the ground, wriggling his mud-covered legs into the bracken. Though he knew the whites of his eyes might give him away, he kept his head up, watching the trail. This was his first chance to get a close look.

The one in front brushed through the ferns with a clattering hiss. Cane shin-guards. Of course. He was with the Urban Cohort. Shuver had noticed a strange indentation by his tracks sometimes. He now realized the impression had been left by the giant leaning on his paddle-club.

The next one moved like a cat. He didn't have any armor— nor any weapons that Shuver could see—but he moved like a killer. He was male. Shuver could tell by the knees.

The next giant was a female. Fine leather-crafted sandals. She was probably the ambassador. Only rich people could afford leather. Poor people had to buy something that could be worn in the rain every day.

Next came the small-footed giant. She stopped, right where Shuver could get a good view of her orange ankles.

"I smell swamp mud," she said.

Damn! Shuver thought. *Damn the giants for their sense of smell, and damn me for forgetting about it.*

His camouflage and insect protection had come from the marsh by the greathouse. Of course he smelled out of place. If the sniffing giant bent down and poked her head into the bracken, he was sunk.

The woman ahead of her said, "We are getting close to the lake, Matyu Iris."

"Not that close," said the woman with the small feet. She had leather sandals, too, but they weren't as nice as the other's.

"I have made up my mind," the woman ahead called. "Accept that. And stop dragging your feet."

"I am not dragging my feet," she grumbled. She resumed walking down the trail.

The last giant said nothing. He, too, paused to sniff the air, but he did not linger.

They left behind a sharp odor that was said to repel insects. Amazing they could smell anything at all when they stank like that.

Ensign Shuver waited for his heart to stop pounding before backtracking them to find out where they had been.

* * *

Tisha awoke earlier than she would have liked, but well after everyone else had arisen and left the women's quarters. She carefully rolled herself out of the hammock and managed to land on her feet.

Staying at an orange inn was like visiting a foreign country. Women and men had to sleep in separate rooms. No beds were available, only hammocks. And these were built for women much larger than Tisha.

But at least the hammock had been stable. Tisha hadn't fallen out once.

Tisha studied the sleep marks the hammock had left on her grubby skin. She wanted a swim before she got dressed.

She looked at her weapons and armor sitting in a pile by the wall. No one would steal them. Well, Bendoko might, under other circumstances, but he probably wouldn't steal them today.

Tisha checked her breastband and her loincloth to be sure everything was decently covered. Then she left the inn.

The village was awake with people working in gardens or hanging out laundry. A group of children—some of them as tall as Tisha—were chasing an escaped pig, trying to trap it against one of the wooden fences. Three old women watched the sport from benches by the well.

Their eyes turned to Tisha as she walked by. Maybe she should have gotten dressed. She had heard that jungle people were more casual about dressing to go swimming, but maybe that was only true of blue jungle people. Everyone here was dressed. She wished she'd brought a sari.

Tisha realized she saw no mongzhis. Maybe the Order of the Holy Shield really was on her side.

Sides. Is that what it was all about? Were there two sides in Sliceharbor now?

The path to the water was easy to find, and at the end of it she also found one of her saris—the yellow one she had loaned to Bendoko. He must be in the water somewhere.

A waterfall dropped five feet off a ledge and splashed into a round pool deep enough for bathing. From there, the stream meandered off into the darkness of the jungle.

Tisha slipped quietly into the water, submerged, and listened for sounds of Bendoko swimming. The splash of the waterfall was too noisy for her to hear anything.

Well, he wasn't in the pool. It was so clear that she would have seen him. She gave a dolphin kick and undulated downstream.

The slow, cool water was deep enough for underwater swimming. Tisha settled in at crayfish depth and listened for Bendoko the Crane.

A wave pushed against her head. It wasn't the reflection of her dolphin kick; it was a sudden, quick motion about thirty feet downstream. She was under the jungle canopy now, and her eyes had not adjusted to the shadows, but she could hear this wave perfectly well.

Tisha blew out her air and started breathing the water. Overhead, her air bubbles popped on the surface.

The body downstream jerked at the sound. Something burst out of the water and splashed its way onto the bank.

Tisha pushed her feet off the slimy stream bed and poked her head up to see what had made such commotion. It was Bendoko, sitting on the bank, backing away from her, wild-eyed.

"Tisha!" he gasped.

She expelled the water from her lungs and took in a breath of air so she could speak.

She asked, "Who did you think it was?"

"An alligator."

"We're only five hundred yards from the greathouse. The Order of the Holy Shield wouldn't let alligators move into the village stream."

"You never know," Bendoko said. "Sometimes one even slips into Sliceharbor."

"Well, I'm not an alligator," she said.

She let the current carry her downstream toward him. "Come back in," she said. "I'll protect you."

She had meant it as a joke, but he asked, "Are you wearing your alligator knife?"

"It's called a 'combat knife'," Tisha said, "and I left it at the inn. I guess I'm a risk-taker."

"Yeah," said Bendoko, taking her seriously again.

"You coming back in, or you gonna lie there like mosquito bait?"

Bendoko slipped back into the water.

"Want to see what's downstream?" Tisha asked.

"No, let's go back to the pool," Bendoko said. "I don't want to swim where I can't see."

"You'd hear an alligator," Tisha said, as she turned to go back with him. "They're pretty big."

"You ever seen one?" Bendoko asked. "A live one?"

"No. Have you?"

"No," said Bendoko. "And I don't want to."

They walked on the bottom and pushed their way upstream.

Bendoko didn't drop his head into the water, so Tisha didn't either. If he wanted to talk, she was happy to talk back.

"I guess we have the day to ourselves," Bendoko said.

All right. She hadn't really wanted to talk about *that*.

"Yeah," she said.

"Sorry," he said.

"For what, Ben?"

"For ... whatever is making you sad."

"I'm not sad, Ben."

"Oh. All right."

They reached the pool. Tisha ducked under and dove down to the rocky bottom. She rolled over onto her back and looked up at the ripples of light and the Crane's water-treading legs.

She floated back up to him.

"Why do you think I'm sad?"

"I don't know," he said. "Yesterday on the road ... And then now when I mentioned ... Is there trouble between you and Gusty?"

"No," she said. "Gus and I get along fine."

"All right," he said.

A kingfisher landed on a nearby branch, scolded them for being in his pool, and flew away.

"You have any orange friends, Ben?"

"I don't have *any* friends," Bendoko said.

"Sander and Vernda like you all right."

"Yeah, I like them, too." He tipped his head back, so that only his mouth and nose were out of the water. "But they're good people. Criminals can't be friends with good people."

"I guess you're right," Tisha said. But maybe he didn't hear her. His ears were under water.

"I'm worried oranges and blues can't be friends anymore, either," Tisha said.

Bendoko popped his head up again. "Why do you say that?" He sounded almost defensive.

"This whole war thing. Not just the Sun Scroll, Ben. All of it."

"But you and Gusty are friends. Right?"

"Yeah," Tisha said. "We're friends."

"But what?"

"I didn't say 'but'."

"All right," he said.

They were friends. They were.

"I don't know," Tisha said. "Maybe he just needs space right now."

"Space?"

"He seems to want distance from me."

"Oh," said Bendoko. "I thought the Bossy One ordered him to leave us behind."

"Yeah," Tisha said. "I guess."

"Look," said Bendoko, "has he started talking about 'the Motherland'? Has he decided to wear a mangy?"

"Mongzhi."

"Yeah. One of those."

"No," Tisha said. At least, she *thought* Gus still wore a sari. It had been a while since they had seen each other in street clothes. They hadn't gone to a pool together since Redmonth.

"Well, as long as he's not flashing his navel around, you know he's still a Sliceharbor boy."

"Yeah, I guess."

"But what?" Bendoko asked.

"But there's something going on here, Ben. Something he's not telling me."

"Like what?"

"I don't know," Tisha said. It had something to do with that ruined temple they were visiting, but she didn't know what.

"Have you asked him?"

"No," Tisha admitted.

"Why not?"

"Because then it's all over, Crane! Then he either tells me what's going on, or he admits that he's keeping secrets. And then ..."

"And then what, Tisha?"

"And then I've lost my best friend."

"Why?" Bendoko asked. "Can't friends have secrets?"

"I don't know," Tisha said. "I suppose."

"Maybe you're right about him wanting some distance right now," Bendoko said. "But does that mean he doesn't love you?"

Love? That was a funny word coming from the Crane. It wasn't the wrong word, though. She and Gusty did love each other, in a sister-brother kind of way.

"I don't tell everything I know to people *I* care about," Bendoko said. "Mostly because I care about them."

"You're an odd man, Bendoko."

"Yeah," he admitted. "But maybe Gusty is feeling the same way right now. Maybe he trusts you but doesn't trust himself. Or maybe he's got some other reason for not telling you everything. Instead of worrying about whether he trusts you, maybe you need to ask yourself if you trust him."

Tisha brushed a mosquito off his head. "Thanks, Ben."

"Uh ... what for?"

"For being my friend."

"Uh ... all right."

He shot a glance at the path to the pool. Tisha followed his gaze. Gusty stood there. He'd come back early.

"The ambassador needs two divers to help her find something," Gusty said. "Would you come?"

* * *

Ensign Shuver crouched in the ferns, watching the ambassador's expedition tramp back up the trail. This time they had the two Children of Justice with them. He wondered what it was all about.

The first pair of blue feet were male, the second pair female. The four blue feet halted in Ensign Shuver's window of vision.

"What is it, Ben?" the female asked.

"I feel like we're being watched," the male said.

Some of the giants sniffed, but this time Ensign Shuver had been careful to stay downwind of the trail.

"Doesn't he always think he's being watched?" a giant's voice murmured.

"Yeah," the female said.

"What if it's a panther?" asked the blue male.

"Ben," said the female, "if there were panthers out here, the monks at the greathouse would have told us."

The expedition resumed walking. Ensign Shuver had explored the trail, so he knew they were going to the lake with the ruined temple. But he still needed to figure out why.

* * *

Gloria Sunrise and Matyu Iris stood a safe distance from the edge of the sinkhole, watching the natives descend on a climbing line. The guide had brought it with him—preparedness that Gloria had not expected. Perhaps he was not a fraud after all.

The men—her men—stood together near the edge, as though they could help if something went wrong. But really, it was all up to the natives now.

"You shouldn't have told them they were looking for the Sun Scroll," Iris said.

Gloria stared at her assistant.

"You should have told them to bring up anything of interest."

"That would take all day," Gloria said. "I believe the water holds plenty of antiques."

"You could have just said, 'Look for a scroll.'"

Gloria shook her head. "They are not stupid, Matyu Iris. There is only one scroll anyone cares about right now."

"I wish they *were* stupid," Iris said. "We should never have brought the natives along. Nor that Longbread's son."

"Thank you for your counsel," Gloria said, barely hiding her smirk.

Iris scowled.

Gloria saw no need to explain herself. The foolish woman should have realized that Gusty Longbread was the key to the whole thing. The natives would fetch the scroll and entrust it to him. Then the Mother Goddess would ensure that he handed it over to Gloria Sunrise.

* * *

Bendoko the Crane enjoyed swimming in the lake. The water was cool and clean—at least compared with the canals of Sliceharbor. The water was clear, too, but dark as tea. Tisha said it was colored by the rotting bark of the trees that had fallen into the sinkhole over the decades. It tasted bitter, but it smelled clean.

Bendoko floated lazily above the bottom like a catfish. He took breaths infrequently, because expelling lungfuls of water disturbed the fine algae coating the rubble. He was over ten feet down, and everything was calm and peaceful. The only currents came from the swishing of Tisha's arms and legs as she searched beside him.

He saw her in occasional glimpses—a foot, an arm, a dull flash of light from the hilt of the alligator knife he had asked her to bring. He felt safer knowing that she was armed. Funny. Armed urbies had never made him feel safe before.

But Tisha wasn't really an urbie anymore. Well, yeah, she was still an urbie, but not to him. She had been his rescuer, and then his jailor. But this morning, in the pool below the village, she had confided in him. Did that really mean they were friends?

Sander and Vernda like you all right, she had said. She hadn't included herself. But she did like him. And he liked her. Funny, really. If things had been different …

But they weren't. They weren't different. He had made his decision to be a criminal long ago.

* * *

Ensign Shuver had belly-crawled to the very edge of the pit. Shrubs grew vigorously here, as though they were glad to have found a place where the trees didn't steal all the sunlight. From this cover, Shuver could see the pile of debris sloping steeply down into the water. Periodically the woman would emerge and tell the Children of the Sun that she and her partner hadn't found "it" yet. Ensign Shuver wondered what "it" was.

The water was so dark that he couldn't see what they were doing. He wanted to get closer, see where they were looking. But there was no way to drop fifteen feet into still water without being heard and no way to climb down a bare limestone cliff without being seen.

He waited … and was rewarded at midday when the divers came out for the noon meal.

No one was watching the hole now. He slipped over the edge and climbed carefully down the cliff.

He slipped slowly into the water. Then he dove for the

bottom.

Ensign Shuver rolled, looking up at the shafts of sunlight shimmering in the tea-dark water. The shimmering would grow calm again. The surface ripples would be gone by the time the divers returned.

* * *

About a quarter-lithic later, papa alligator swam through his underwater tunnel to see if anything good to eat had fallen into his pit.

* * *

"Hidden under the floor tiles of a sunward-facing room" wasn't really much to go on once the room had collapsed and the floor had tumbled to the bottom of a lake. Tisha swam above the ruined temple's rubble pile, looking for the ceramic-tiled chunks of its limestone floor. Whenever she found one, she tapped it with a tiny hammer, listening for a hollow sound.

She'd borrowed the hammer from Bendoko. The man had a lot of tools on his belt! She wondered what this one was for. It was too light for driving nails. Maybe it was for tapping floor tiles to see if any of them made a hollow sound.

She could hear Bendoko making his own taps with his putty knife. Why did he need a putty knife? As he had said, it wasn't the sort of thing a criminal would draw in a knife fight.

Tisha couldn't imagine Bendoko in a knife fight. But she supposed he had run away from a few.

Tap, tap, tap. Tap, tap, tap. Tap, tap, tap.

No hollow spots on this chunk either.

Tisha wondered how big the temple had been, how small the room had been, how small the scroll's hiding place had been. Her parents had stopped teaching her arithmetic once she'd learned to make change, but she had a feeling that it would take a long time to tap on every floor tile in the temple. And most of them were buried under rubble.

The idea had seemed exciting. Every Sliceharbor kid grew up hearing about treasure hunts. And now Tisha had been asked to find a sacred piece of history!

Gusty and the ambassador had acted like they expected it to be sitting right on top, plain for anyone to see and miraculously undamaged by the water. Tisha—well, she hadn't really thought about it. She'd just been so grateful that Gusty trusted her enough to let her in on the secret. But now she was beginning to realize that finding the scroll would require incredible luck. Ambassador Gloria had promised to pray for success.

Tap, tap, tap. Tap, tap, tap. Nothing.

Yeah, well, prayers were good, if you were the praying type. Tisha wasn't really. It seemed a bit like cheating. She figured she should just do her best, accomplish what she could in life with her own skills, and then accept the Judgment of how well she had done.

Was there a way to find this scroll without luck and without divine assistance? If there was, Gusty could figure it out. She hoped he was putting his mind to it right now.

Tap, tap, tap. Tap, tap, tap. Tap, tap, tap …

* * *

Bendoko was glad Tisha was using his sounding hammer. He felt safer knowing exactly where she was and how far away.

He stuck his arm inside a hole and sounded around with his putty knife: *pingk … pingk … pingk.*

No wooden scroll case in there. No hollow slab of flooring. At least, nothing he could reach.

These ruins had been a hiding place for Sliceharbor criminals ever since the temple had been abandoned. Doubtless some of the blue ones had poked around in this lake, if only because hiding out was so boring. Most stuff within easy reach would probably have been found by now, but Bendoko still liked the idea that he might find something of value. It was fun to look. Way more fun than lying in Tisha's cellar. And if he happened to find that damned scroll—no, that *blessed* scroll—then at least he could brag to Puji that he had done a good deed.

Pingk … pingk …

And from Tisha he heard his sounding hammer:

Tap, tap, tap. Tap, tap, tap. Tap, twap, twaap.

Had those last two taps been distorted?

A wavefront hit him. Something was moving through the water. Something big. And it could have been Tisha swimming, except that she was still tapping, just floating in place.

* * *

Ensign Shuver had tucked himself inside a limestone crack that seemed small and narrow, but was actually deep and narrow. He didn't have much light down here, but he was near enough to the rubble pile that he could hear the divers clearly.

They were sounding the rubble, and the echoes of their instruments told him precisely how they were moving about. They were definitely searching for something. A certain construction material perhaps?

Their full purpose was still a mystery, but Ensign Shuver now had plenty of information. He knew they were staying in the village by the greathouse of the Holy Shield. He knew they had made contact with the Holy Shield, but that contact was not central to their mission. He knew they were sounding the ruins of some abandoned building. And he knew they were searching for something.

He didn't know what it was, but he was just an ensign. Maybe Captain Tu and Admiral Fanjei could figure it out. Ensign Shuver's job now was to deliver the information as soon as possible.

But first he had to get out of here without being seen. That wouldn't be a problem, as long as they didn't come tapping around his crevice. He could wait until they took another break. For food, for rest, for darkness—it didn't matter. They would leave the water sometime. And once they were gone, he would climb back out.

Something rippled between him and the divers' tapping. Ensign Shuver caught the scent of alligator.

* * *

The wavefront hit Tisha on the soles of her feet and rippled up her back. Something big was coming up behind her, moving very fast.

Tisha twisted and rolled to face it, tucking her knees to protect her abdomen.

A scaly snout was rushing at her. Tisha raised her arm. Toothy jaws opened.

Tisha's hand caught the creature on the side of the face. Scales slid against her forearm as she pushed herself out of its path. The alligator passed, and she spun in its wake.

That's what it was: an alligator. Its sticky scent filled the water. She guessed it must outweigh her by at least three to one.

She righted herself, caught a flash of the alligator's underbelly as it turned back toward her. This time she remembered her knife. She pulled it from her belt. Designed for underwater combat, the short, stout blade shone silver in the tea-dark water.

The alligator came from above this time, a brown shadow against the rippling surface of the sunken lake. Tisha raised her left hand to protect her head. She poised her knife hand to strike.

Jaws opened. The tail curled. Tisha thrust, but came up short.

The tail ripped through the water, and the alligator lunged forward. Teeth sawed through Tisha's skin, and the jaws clamped shut.

Her left arm was crushed, as though caught between two boulders. The alligator rolled, wrenching her elbow. Tisha rolled with it, trying to outmaneuver the pain.

Light and darkness spun around her. Her feet slapped a chunk of rubble. The alligator was spiraling down, trying to drown her. But she was a Child of Justice. She could breathe under water, as long as she stayed conscious.

Her flailing knife hand slammed into stone. Tisha let the knife go. Keep breathing. That was all she had to do—keep breathing the water, and spin with the alligator so it wouldn't rip her arm off.

It couldn't drown her. Her arm was full of pain, but as long as she stayed conscious—

Tisha's head struck a limestone outcropping. Light flashed through her brain, and her thoughts went silent.

* * *

Ensign Shuver knew the smell of alligators. They were common in the river on which he had grown up, on the other end of the Republic.

An alligator had once attacked his best friend, and Shuver, then only fifteen years old, had jumped into the river and saved his life. (The friend had needed healers to save his foot.)

Shuver the boy had not hesitated then, and Shuver the man did not hesitate now. He drew his jungle knife, pushed himself out of his hidden crevice, and swam toward the churning waters of combat.

A cloud of disturbed silt and algae obscured his vision. Waves told him where the combatants were, but in the chaotic thrashing, he could not distinguish smooth, blue limbs from scaly, brown tail.

The alligator and whomever it was fighting seemed to be heading down. The speed of their descent indicated that the gator was in control.

Ensign Shuver slipped into their wake, but even with the favorable current, he still could not dive as fast as the alligator.

He had known alligators to stash carcasses under logs, storing food for later. If this victim was already a carcass, then he shouldn't be going after the gator. His orders were to stay hidden and report back.

But if the person was still alive, he had a duty more important than his mission. Ensign Shuver kept swimming, following the trail of the gator's spirals.

* * *

Bendoko burst from the water and clambered up the pile of rubble.

From atop the limestone cliff, Gusty called, "Did you find something?"

Bendoko expelled the water from his lungs and took a deep breath of air. But he didn't waste any breath on answering Gusty's question. Instead, he seized his climbing line and began scaling the cliff.

"What is it?" Gusty asked.

"Alligator!" Bendoko yelled. "Pull me up!"

He didn't wait for the oranges to obey. He kept climbing. And it was a good thing, too, because the ingrates weren't lifting a finger to help him get out of the damned hole.

"Where's Tisha?" Gusty wanted to know.

Bendoko hoped Tisha was right behind him, but he wasn't going to wait for her. Climbing with two people on the line was trickier, and Bendoko wanted to be out of the hole before Tisha started climbing.

Really, he was helping her. If he got off the line quick, then she'd have it all to herself when she came out of the water. Yeah, he was doing her a favor.

Bendoko seized a shrub at the top of the cliff. He hooked a knee over the rim. His other hand grabbed some orange person's ankle. And he just kept crawling through the vegetation until he was certain he was farther away from the pit than an alligator could jump.

Could alligators jump? Probably not. At least, they probably couldn't jump up a fifteen-foot-high cliff.

Bendoko grabbed a pine tree, pulled himself to his feet, and stood there, panting.

"What makes you think you saw an alligator?" Gusty asked.

"I didn't have to see it," Bendoko said. "I could feel it. Something big is down there, and it's not me or Tisha."

Gusty frowned. "If she's in trouble, you have to go in after her."

"It's an alligator!"

Gusty glared down at him. For a moment, Bendoko thought the urbie was going to pick him up and throw him back in. But he didn't.

Instead, Gusty said, "All right. I'll go."

Bendoko looked him up and down. In the water, a man shaped like Gusty would have all the grace and agility of a coconut. Either he'd float on the surface leaving his giant toes hanging above the alligator's jaws like tasty persimmons, or his iron breastplate would drag him to the bottom where he would never be seen again. There was no way an orange built like Gusty could ever match a blue like Bendoko in a contest of deepwater combat.

But Bendoko was no match for an alligator. "Better you than me," he said.

* * *

Ensign Shuver followed the spiraling wake along the craggy limestone lake bottom. The water smelled of rock algae, alligator, and blood. Ensign Shuver hoped he was not too late to perform a rescue.

The alligator heard his approach. Ensign Shuver felt the creature's body whip through the water as it turned to face him. He curled into a defensive position and waited for the gator to attack.

Faint waves rippled against his skin. The alligator's feet were making tiny paddling motions. The person—whoever it was—was no longer struggling. Ensign Shuver prepared to exact revenge.

The tail lashed. The gator lunged. Ensign Shuver threw up his forearm and caught the alligator under the jaw. A claw too dull to draw blood scratched against his scalp. Ensign Shuver kicked himself away from the alligator's powerful tail.

The gator spun back on him. Shuver's feet found a slimy rock, and he pushed himself up. The alligator pursued. Shuver tucked his legs and twisted, bouncing off the side of the alligator's snout. He shot out his hand and grabbed the alligator on the knee.

The alligator rolled, but Shuver hooked his legs around its back and rolled with it. He let go of the leg and ran his hand up the gator's smooth belly.

There. There was its jaw. He pushed it closed, wrapped his hand around, and held it shut.

Now you are mine.

The alligator jerked its head to the side, but Ensign Shuver held on. A foot caught on his loincloth, but he dug his heels into the alligator's lumpy back and didn't let go.

He stabbed into the gator's underbelly. He ripped the knife up. The alligator's tail thrashed.

Now it was time to let go.

Ensign Shuver swam away, and the dying alligator sank to the bottom.

* * *

"Will that line hold him?" the orange woman asked. Tisha referred to her as "the ambassador", but Bendoko thought of her as "the Bossy One".

"Yeah," Bendoko said. "It'll hold him."

It probably would, too, but it didn't really matter. So what if it snapped and Gusty fell fifteen feet onto jagged blocks of stone? Was that worse than being eaten by an alligator?

But maybe the alligator was gone now. In the time it had taken for Gusty to unbuckle himself from his weapons, helmet, and armor, the water had grown calmer. Neither Tisha nor the alligator had been seen.

Gusty gave a tug on Bendoko's climbing line. "Tell me where you saw her last," he said.

"She was working that side of the rubble pile," Bendoko said, pointing. "But it's dark down there. You won't find her by looking. You'll have to use your ears."

"Look," said Clever, the bodyguard who pretended to be a porter. "Toward the middle of the lake."

Concentric circles were spreading, like those made when a fish slurps a dragonfly from the surface of the water.

"Those are air bubbles," said the Bossy One.

"Her last breath?" asked the other orange woman, the Scowling One.

"Tisha would be breathing water," Gusty said. "Not air."

"So it must be bubbles from the alligator," said the Bossy One.

At least she believed there *was* an alligator. That was some comfort.

Gusty seized Bendoko's slender climbing line in his thick, orange fingers. He looked behind himself uncertainly and lifted one foot.

"You shouldn't go," Bendoko said. "If she were alive, she would have come out of the water with me."

"Tisha's not a coward," Gusty said.

"She's not stupid, either," Bendoko said. "She wouldn't stay in the water if she could get out."

"But 'can't get out' is not the same as 'dead', Crane. What if she's hurt? What if she's unconscious but still alive?"

"Then she won't be alive much longer," Bendoko said. "We suffocate under water if we get knocked out. I should know. I lost both my fathers in a shipwreck."

"Then I have to get her out quick," Gusty said, taking a step down.

"You'll never find her."

Gusty's foot slipped and he flailed about for purchase.

"Dammit, you can't even climb," Bendoko said.

But you can, Bendoko. And you can find her before she suffocates. Maybe. If she's still alive.

A vision of Jodi flashed into his mind—Vernda and Sander trying to explain why Mommy Tisha wasn't coming home.

"Hell," he said.

Bendoko turned to Clever and Pious. "Help him up. I'll go look for her myself."

The orange men looked to the Bossy One.

She nodded.

They heaved Gusty back onto flat ground. Bendoko took the line, slipped over the edge, and descended.

"Strong toes," he called up at Gusty. "The trick is strong toes."

Bendoko landed on the rubble pile. He clambered down to the water's edge. He couldn't see any alligators in the brown water. He dipped his head under to listen.

All was calm now. If Tisha was still struggling, she was struggling quietly. On the other hand, he didn't hear any reptiles snapping her bones.

Bendoko eased himself into the water, careful to not disturb the silence.

* * *

Ensign Shuver padded his hands carefully along the lake bottom. The alligator's victim should be somewhere close.

He was fairly certain there had been a victim. The alligator had been dragging something to the bottom. It was most likely the body of one of the two divers.

He should give up. He had already risked too much by killing the alligator. If he found a dead body what would he do? He would have to leave it and complete his mission.

And how likely was he to find anything but a dead body down here?

Shuver felt a wavefront push against the soles of his feet. Another alligator? Or one of the divers? Shuver pushed his way back to one of the deeper cracks and tucked himself in.

* * *

Bendoko dolphin-kicked toward the place where they had seen rising bubbles. He didn't want to find the alligator, but that was the best place to look for Tisha.

In his right hand he held his putty knife. He knew it would be no good against an alligator. He was just carrying it for reassurance. It wasn't very good at that, either.

He tasted blood in the water—faint at first, but growing stronger as he drew closer to his target. Suddenly it was too strong. He hit a cloud that tasted like blood and entrails.

Tisha's intestines. In his mouth.

Bendoko vomited and swam away. He took great liquid lungfuls of water, trying to clear the taste from his body.

Oh she was dead! So very, very dead. And she was going to stay there. Devout Children of Justice were supposed to be interred in running water, but still water would have to be good enough for Tisha. There was no way he was going anywhere near that corpse. Not again. He hoped her spirit would forgive him.

Bendoko curled into a ball and sank to the lake bottom, trying to recover even a little of his composure. He didn't want to tell the others what had happened—what he had tasted. He had washed the worst of it from his mouth, but the flavor of Tisha's entrails was stamped into his memory. And he could still smell her blood.

Actually, this blood smelled clean.

He wasn't in the huge cloud of blood and entrails. He was just catching a whiff of a small, concentrated bloom. Somewhere nearby.

He reached out a hand and felt a face.

Bendoko screamed—something he had learned at a young age not to do. The water rushing from his lungs scoured his tight vocal cords, causing great pain while producing only a puny sound.

Calm down! he told himself. *This is good! This face is Tisha!*

And that meant that the bloody entrails had belonged to the alligator.

* * *

"That is blood," Iris Daylight said.

"I hope not," the ambassador said. "I hope it is simply sediments stirred up from the bottom."

"It is blood," Iris Daylight repeated.

Gusty hated the morbid, morbid woman.

Out toward the middle of the lake, the clear, brown water was suffused by a darker cloud. Gusty had seen enough pool-house brawls to recognize blood spreading through water. Iris Daylight was right, and that made him hate her more.

Gusty squeezed his fists. He should have gone with the Crane. But he couldn't swim. Not really. Not the way blues could.

A bald head broke the surface.

"Is that the male coming up for air?" Iris Daylight asked. "Or is it the corpse of the female? They're so hard to tell apart."

Gusty recognized Bendoko. The blue man opened his mouth and spewed out the water that had been in his lungs. He was swimming strangely.

Bendoko leaned back, and another bald head broke the surface. Tisha!

Alive or dead?

Bendoko looked over his shoulder, the wild whites of his eyes visible even at this distance. He didn't call out. He just started backpedaling toward them, holding Tisha's head out of the water. Alive or dead, she wasn't doing any swimming of her own.

Tisha floated limply. Bendoko glided toward the rubble pile, towing her along.

Gusty watched. That was all he could do.

Finally, Bendoko dragged her ashore. Standing on the exposed rubble of the ruined temple, Bendoko grabbed Tisha's legs and lifted them into the air. Water flowed from her lips and ran in rivulets among the broken ceramic tiles.

Tisha's chest heaved. Her body convulsed, and water gushed from her mouth.

"How disgusting," said Iris Daylight.

But it wasn't. It was the most beautiful thing Gusty had seen since his little sister's birth. Tisha was alive!

* * *

It was like a maze, but a simple one: up, out, in, out, up, out, in, out, up ...

Tisha realized she wasn't looking at a maze. It was a pattern on the ceiling, carved into the wood. A high ceiling. No gauze. Where was she?

It was nighttime. Cicadas buzzed outside the window. Her room was lamplit. Flying bugs cast flickering shadows on the walls.

"Tisha, are you awake?" A kindly voice. A huge, gentle hand against her shoulder.

"Gusty?"

A smiling orange face with a huge tuft of curly blond hair came into view. She was a woman. Not Gusty.

"He's waiting outside," the woman said. "Would you like me to invite him in?"

"Yes, please."

The face left. Tisha walked the maze with her eyes. Oh, she was tired! How long had she slept? She felt like it hadn't really been "sleep".

She was on a huge cot. She could feel the wicker ridges under the heavy cotton sheet. Another sheet lay atop her. She was wearing a loincloth and breastband, but they weren't hers. Too clean.

The breastband was loose. She tried to retie it. Then she discovered her left arm was splinted and her fingers felt numb.

"You shouldn't be sitting up yet," the blond woman called from the doorway. "Lie back down or no visitors."

You're not one of my mothers, Tisha thought. But she lay back down.

The woman led Gusty in. The room was big enough to hold lots of people, and Gusty didn't have to duck to go through the doorway.

I'm in the women's half of the hospital wing in the greathouse, Tisha thought.

"She remembers you," the blond woman told Gusty.

"Hi, Tisha," he said. He waved his fingers like he was greeting a three-year-old.

"Hi, Gus."

"Do you remember what you were doing before you came here?" the blond woman asked.

"Looking for buried treasure," Tisha said.

The woman gave Gusty a concerned look.

"Tisha," Gusty said. "Do you remember the ruined temple?"

"Yeah."

"Do you remember the ambassador asking for some help with her archaeology project?"

Archaeology project? What in the world? ... Oh! She wasn't supposed to talk about what she'd been doing.

"Oh, yeah," she said. "I remember now."

"Flora Warmhands says you hit your head, and it might have knocked some of your memories out of you."

"Most of the memories will find their way back," the blond woman added. "Your head has already been healed."

"Oh," said Tisha. "Thank you."

"I can only heal the body," the blond woman said. "Your mind will have to heal itself."

"All right," Tisha said. "I'll get right on it."

Tisha looked at her arm.

"My fingers feel numb," she said.

"Can you move them?" the blond woman asked.

Tisha tried. They moved. "They feel tingly."

"Be sure to wiggle them periodically," the blond woman said. "So they don't forget they are fingers."

"But don't move your arm too much," Gusty said.

"She should be fine as long as she doesn't put any weight on it," the blond woman said. "Your bones have just begun to knit," she told Tisha. "So keep the splint tight or my mends will separate."

"That doesn't sound good," Tisha said. What had she done to her arm?

"I'll work on your bones again tomorrow," the blond woman said. What had Gusty called her? Warmhands? Flora Warmhands. That was it.

"In the meantime," Flora continued, "exercising the muscles—within reason—is the best way to help your arm remember which way it is supposed to grow."

"All right," Tisha said. "I'll wiggle the fingers and bend the elbow, then."

Flora smiled.

"Can I talk to Gus alone for a little bit?"

"Certainly. But don't talk too long. You need your rest. I'll see you first thing in the morning."

Flora Warmhands glided out of the room. She walked gently, considering she was nine feet tall.

"Lucky you, getting visited first thing in the morning," Gusty said.

"Yeah." Tisha grinned. "Just before bedtime."

Gusty's smile gave way to worry: " 'Digging for treasure'?"

"Sorry," Tisha said.

"Do you remember what we were looking for?" Gusty asked.

The Sun Scroll. Right. Ambassador Gloria thought the ruined temple might have a second copy. "Yeah, I remember now," Tisha said. "Sorry. My head feels a little murky."

We were diving and then ...

"Gus, was there an alligator?"

"I think so. I didn't see what happened. It was all under water. But, yeah, I think you were attacked by a gator."

"And it bit a chunk out of my arm?"

"Flora Warmhands said it just crushed your arm. Most of the pieces missing are the ones she had to cut off so everything would grow back the right way."

"Oh. That doesn't make me feel better, Gus."

"Sorry."

She'd been diving. The alligator had attacked her ...

"Gus! What happened to Ben?"

"Nothing," Gusty said. "Although I thought about smashing

his face in."

"What for?"

"He wouldn't go in after you," Gusty said. "He left you to fight the alligator all alone and wouldn't go back to help you. At least not at first."

"And then?"

"Then he changed his mind."

"Or you changed it for him?"

Gusty shook his head. "No. No, he just changed his mind. Decided to go back and help you. He was so scared. It was actually really brave, Tisha. But don't tell him I said that."

"So Bendoko the Crane saved my life?" Tisha asked wonderingly.

"Yeah," Gusty said. He looked deflated. Like he'd lost a Tisha-saving contest.

Tisha reached for his hand. "I'm glad you're here, Gus."

He gave her hand a gentle squeeze. "I'm glad you're here, too."

"Was the ambassador mad that I quit work early?"

Gusty shook his huge, copper-haired head.

"Gus … what would have happened if we had found it?"

"What do you mean?"

"The ambassador seems to think this one is hers. But doesn't it really belong to the Republic?"

Gusty sighed. "Senator Aura thinks it belongs to Slice-harbor."

"Oh." Well, that case could certainly be made. The ruins were in Sliceharbor's section of the coastline. "Is that why Senator Aura wanted urbies here?"

"Yeah."

"So we're really supposed to get the scroll for Sliceharbor."

"Yeah. That's right."

"Why didn't—?" No. She shouldn't ask.

"What?"

"Why didn't you tell me?"

Gusty's coppery eyebrows lowered. His mouth contorted as though the words on the tip of his tongue were fighting over which had to be the first ones out.

"I don't know," he said. "I guess I thought that if Aura Wisebrow had wanted you to know, she would have mentioned it in her message to Captain Kosho."

"I see," Tisha said. "That makes sense."

"You understand?"

She didn't really. But it didn't matter. "Yeah, Gus. It's all right."

His broad shoulders relaxed a little.

Tisha said, "Really, this is our first chance to talk since we got our assignment."

"Yeah," said Gusty. "I guess you're right."

"Have you told Bendoko?" Tisha asked.

"Told him what?"

"That we aren't really going to let the Queenies have the scroll."

Gusty frowned and rubbed his neck. "Uh, no. I don't— I guess— Look, Tisha, I know you like him."

This didn't really have anything to do with whether Tisha liked Bendoko. But whatever.

"I guess I just don't trust him," Gusty said.

"Well, he is a criminal," Tisha said.

"Right," said Gusty. "I don't think he really needs to know about Aura Wisebrow's plans."

He had a point. She liked Bendoko, but if he knew that Gusty was planning to claim the scroll for Sliceharbor, he might try to get the ambassador to pay him for the information. Or he might want to be paid to keep quiet.

"Maybe you're right," she said. "Maybe it's best if he thinks we're just trying to help out the ambassador."

* * *

Bendoko the Crane sat on a giant-sized bench in the hallway of the Holy Shield's hospital wing. The wooden walls had been painted yellow here, and no one had added carvings of huge, toothy beasts that shredded people's arms. It was his favorite part of the greathouse.

He didn't have to be nervous about being in a religious order's greathouse. He was protected by Big Zeemo, right? The deities couldn't touch him, not even here.

What made him think that?

It's all right, Crane. Just go sit down on that sacred bench. Big Zeemo will keep you perfectly safe. Had anyone ever said that? Big Zeemo was a long way away. And the deities seemed close.

Yeah, well, Bendoko was a good guy tonight. He'd pulled Tisha out of the water. That counted for something, right? Of course, when you counted up all the things that counted against him ...

"She wants to see you, Crane."

Gusty came strolling down the hall, his huge body throwing Bendoko's bench into shadow.

Bendoko stood up. "How is she?" he asked, in a voice still scratchy from his underwater scream.

"She's tired," Gusty said. He glowered down, coppery eyebrows scrunching together like two caterpillars wrestling. "Don't keep her awake. She needs her rest."

"All right."

Gusty grunted. His glower softened to a frown. The wrestling eyebrows decided to break up the fight and go their separate ways.

Gusty's fleshy hand settled on Bendoko's shoulder. His touch was warm and light.

Then the giant turned and strolled away toward the exit.

Bendoko could still feel Gusty's warmth on his shoulder. What had that been about?

Bendoko shrugged. Who knew why anybody did anything?

He entered the room with the rapid, smooth footsteps he used for crossing floors quickly and quietly. The sound of his sandals brushing against the floorboards would not carry beyond the open doorway.

Tisha was the only person in the room. She was lying down—asleep already? He wouldn't wake her. He just wanted to check on her.

She looked so tiny lying on the giant wicker cot, with her head bare and the cotton sheet covering her muscular body. Her maimed arm was in a splint. Her fingers were wiggling.

"Tisha?"

"Ben!" she said. "I didn't hear you come in."

"Yeah, well ..."

She grinned. "You were sneaking up on me!"

"No. I just walk softly."

"Is something wrong with your voice?"

"No," said Bendoko. "My throat's just a little sore."

"All right," she said.

From screaming when I touched your face, he didn't add.

She was smiling at him. Her eyes had kind of a moist glow. Probably something to do with her head injury.

"I'm healing up," she said.

She lifted her splinted arm and waved it at him. He flinched—mostly from the memory of what it had looked like when he had pulled her out of the water. It actually looked fine now, wrapped in a clean bandage, splinted with strong cane.

"Good," he said. "How's your head?"

"Murky," she said. "But maybe I just need sleep."

"Get your sleep," he said.

"Ben?"

"Yeah?"

"Thank you for saving my life."

Bendoko shrugged. "You were the one who killed the alligator."

"I did?"

"Someone did," Bendoko said. "And it wasn't me."

"I don't remember," she said.

The healer had said she might have trouble remembering some things—especially details about the alligator attack.

"Some things are better forgotten," Bendoko said. "Don't worry about it."

"I'm not," she said.

"Good," he said.

"Well," he said. She was awfully pretty with the lamplight reflecting off her forehead.

"Good night," he said.

"Ben," she said.

"Yeah?"

"It doesn't matter who killed the gator. You still saved my

life. Gusty told me what you did. It was very brave."

Damn right it was brave!

"Yeah, I guess," he said.

"So ... thank you."

"You're welcome," he said.

"Well," he said.

"Good night," he said.

"Good night, Ben."

Bendoko walked toward the doorway.

He stopped.

He turned and came back.

"Tisha?"

"Yeah?"

"Does this mean we're even?"

She smiled. "Yeah, Crane. If that's the way you want to look at it, you can say we're even."

8 Yellowmonth

SENATOR FANJEI HATED the bristly growth that appeared on his throat every morning. His beard had started growing when he was only thirty-five. He had refused to tolerate it. Beards were for old men.

So he had shaved off the black bristles every morning. And now that he was an old man, the bristles were white. And still he shaved them. He could not stop them from coming back, but he would never let them live long enough to become hair. Fanjei was no furry animal. He was a man.

As he shaved in his study this morning, he listened to his secretary, Hesho, reporting on the previous evening's events. For the third day in a row, Hesho had been sent to the Urban Cohort's headquarters at first light, and for the third day in a row, he had come back with nothing.

"… both combatants were taken into custody, after receiving treatment for minor contusions," Hesho said. His voice held a note of finality.

"Is that all?" Fanjei asked. "Three brawls, an attempted break-in, and a stabbing?"

"That is all from the Urban Cohort," Hesho said.

It was nothing—petty skirmishes. The Navy's defense at Breadbaker Bridge should have started riots. Instead, the Children of the Sun had mourned the dead woman for three nights.

"What of Captain Tu's report from the docks?"

"The same as last night, Senator."

"Foreigners meeting, but no action?"

"Precisely, Senator."

Captain Tu had a woman watching a boarding house near the Dock Market. Fanjei had been able to learn that the boarding house had taken in a number of Children of the Sun and the landlord was a secret foreign sympathizer.

She collected donations for a "war orphans" fund. She approached ship captains bound for the Sun Island and badgered them into delivering crates of bandages "for the wounded". And she openly admitted to—even bragged about!—harboring women who were highly placed in the administration of a city in the Reconciled Queendom.

Most damningly, she had been among the women who led the charge at the steps of the Senatorial Palace four days ago. There would have been bloodshed that morning had Senator Aura not diverted them. Perhaps the scene had been scripted to make Aura appear reasonable.

Aura had spoken with the women for some time, but no one knew what had been discussed or agreed upon. The Children of the Sun were planning something, and the meetings at the boarding house were part of it.

"There will be sabotage," Fanjei said. "You can count on it, Hesho."

"I hope not, Senator. Captain Tu is watching them most closely."

"We cannot sit by and watch, waiting for them to attack," Fanjei said. "Tell Captain Tu I want them arrested."

"All of them? The sailor on watch last night counted seventeen people, and those are just the visitors. Many of the boarders are doubtless part of this conspiracy as well."

"Doubtless," Fanjei said. "But no, it is not necessary to arrest all of them at the same time. Have the captain take just a few as they gather for the meeting."

"On what grounds?"

"The investigation of the warehouse fire. The city has not yet challenged our jurisdiction on that."

"But we have no evidence that any of these people were involved in the fire," Hesho said.

"No," Fanjei agreed. "But they were probably at the scene."

Hesho said, "Your pardon, Senator. Are you suggesting we arrest them for having been at the scene?"

Fanjei considered this. "Of course not, Hesho, that would be going too far."

Perhaps his zeal for justice was overcoming his piety and his good judgment. This worried him. As a pious servant of Justice, Fanjei had to restrict himself to actions that were just.

Only a few of the conspirators were guilty of the warehouse arsons. The majority were guilty of conspiracy, and that was what they should be arrested for.

But conspiracy was difficult to prove.

Assault, however, was simple to prove, and the Breadbaker Bridge incident had shown that the Children of the Sun would let themselves be goaded.

"Hesho," he said, "we won't *arrest* them for being at the scene of the fire. We will simply *detain* them, as part of our investigation."

Hesho looked doubtful, but Fanjei was beginning to see how to make this work.

"Tell Captain Tu to send a lone sailor. The sailor will approach a few of the conspirators and ask them to come to the brig for questioning."

"Very well. You did say a single sailor?"

"Yes, Hesho. You see, the Children of the Sun, believing themselves to have a physical and numerical advantage, will resist. Then a hidden crew of sailors can be called in to arrest them for assaulting a deputized investigator."

"Ah. I see. So the sailor will have support in case the conspirators resist."

"Yes."

"What if they do not resist?" Hesho asked.

"They are violent creatures," Fanjei said. "They will allow themselves to be provoked."

"Very well," Hesho said. He seemed troubled.

Fanjei put a hand on Hesho's shoulder. "If they offer no resistance, then Captain Tu's sailors can simply release them after questioning. No harm done. Understood?"

"I ... think I understand, Senator."

"Either way, they will know we are watching them," Fanjei said. *And then they will be forced into action. They will be forced to reveal what beasts they truly are.*

Someone knocked on the door of his suite.

"I shall see who it is," Hesho said.

Fanjei nodded.

Hesho left the study, crossed the receiving room, and opened the door.

"Good morning, sailor. Your business?"

"I have orders to report to Admiral Fanjei."

"Report? For what?"

"Ah ... to give him my report."

"Concerning?"

"Navy business. My apologies. I am not authorized to discuss it."

Fanjei went to the doorway of his study and looked across the receiving room. Hesho had kept the man standing in the hall, but Fanjei had a good view of him: a Navy man, his white bandana marking him as an ensign.

"You may let him enter, Hesho."

Fanjei's secretary stepped aside.

The ensign entered and saluted—three fingers to his earlobe. "Ensign Shuver reporting, Admiral."

Fanjei gave the answering salute—three fingers to his cheekbone. "Good morning, Ensign."

Ensign Shuver stood straight, but fatigue hung on his shoulders. His eyes looked sunken from lack of sleep. His white sari and white bandana, however, were spotless. He had obviously made an effort to look his best before coming to see his admiral.

Fanjei asked, "Are you Captain Tu's jungle tracker?"

"I am."

"Let us proceed to my study," Fanjei suggested. "I am eager to hear your report."

Hesho arranged comfortable stools for the three of them in Fanjei's study. Ensign Shuver looked uncertain when Hesho sat down, too. He was worried about discussing Navy business in the presence of a civilian secretary. Fanjei ignored the ensign's discomfort. Justifying Hesho's presence would imply that Hesho's presence required justification.

"Your report, Ensign."

"In detail?"

"In summary first, please."

"Yes, Admiral. On the sixth, I followed the ambassador's party inland to a greathouse of the Holy Shield. The next day, she went to a ruined building a short distance away. Most of this building had been consumed by a limestone sinkhole, and the pit was filled with water. But she had with her two Children of Justice."

Fanjei nodded. Hesho had already determined the party's composition from interviews with people who had seen them leave. One of these Children of Justice was from Sliceharbor's Urban Cohort. The other was dressed as a civilian, but Fanjei suspected he was the Urban Cohort's jungle tracker. Including the Child of the Sun in uniform, that made three soldiers. Obviously, Sliceharbor was losing control of the foreign sympathizers in its police force.

The ensign said, "These Children of Justice spent the morning swimming among the ruins searching for something."

"Searching for what?" Fanjei asked.

"I do not know, Admiral."

Fanjei looked to Hesho. The man would have some ideas. They would discuss it later.

"Very well," Fanjei said. "Continue."

"They resumed their search in the afternoon. This time they were tapping on chunks of rubble. Their search was interrupted when their tapping attracted an alligator."

"An alligator?" Hesho asked.

"Yes," the ensign said. He looked uncomfortable, but not with Hesho.

"The alligator attacked them," the ensign said. "I smelled its scent on waves emanating from the struggle. Forgive me, Admiral, but it was my duty to come to their aid."

Fanjei was too shocked to be angry. "Did Captain Tu not tell you to avoid all contact?"

"He did, Admiral."

"And you disobeyed?"

"No, Admiral. I chose to obey my conscience."

And now the ambassador knows I sent someone to follow her, Fanjei thought. *How will Aura use this against me in the Chamber?*

"They were two against only one alligator," Ensign Shuver said, "but it was a large alligator, and they seemed ... unused to the jungle. I doubt they had faced an alligator before. They needed my help."

"I fear you have put me in a very bad position," Fanjei said.

The ensign lowered his eyes. Hesho looked worried.

"But my alligator is only political," Fanjei said. "And I have wrestled with it before.

"You did the right thing. A sailor has a duty to protect the citizens of the Lunaslip Republic, and you should be proud that you accepted that duty, even though you risked ending your career by revealing yourself."

The ensign tensed.

"Do not fear, Ensign. You have not ended your career. In fact ... Hesho, let us send Captain Tu a letter commending the ensign's bravery."

"Yes, Senator Fanjei."

The ensign still did not look pleased.

"I trust you rescued them?" Fanjei asked.

"I killed the alligator, Admiral. But one of the divers was badly injured. I could not find the body. Then the other diver swam down and I hid."

"Did the other diver find the body?"

"I believe so," the ensign said. "After they left, I inspected the area where they climbed in and out. The pattern of blood on the rubble indicated that someone had been lifted in a sling."

"Wait," said Hesho. "You were still tracking them? I thought you made contact."

"I breeched concealment by killing the alligator," the ensign said. "But no one had seen me. I doubt they even felt my waves."

"That is not nearly as bad as I had feared," Fanjei said. "Well done, Ensign."

Ensign Shuver shrugged, "I wish I could be certain the victim survived."

"I am certain you did your best," Fanjei said. "You earned your commendation."

"Thank you, Admiral." He did not sound convinced, but he did seem less burdened.

Fanjei said, "And now the detailed report, if you please. Speak slowly so Hesho can write it down."

"Yes, Admiral. On the sixth of Yellowmonth, at two-and-one-quarter lithics, I was ordered to report to Captain Tu. The captain informed me ..."

Fanjei let his mind wander while the ensign gave the details to Hesho. Once they were two dozen lines into the report, he excused himself and left his suite. On his way to breakfast, he remembered that Hesho had mentioned a ruined temple as one possible destination for the ambassador's party.

Hesho had explained that the ambassador had some sort of familial or religious connection to the ruin, but Fanjei had dismissed the idea. He did not think Ambassador Gloria would waste her time on a journey with only sentimental significance.

But if she were looking for something ... something that was likely to be found in the ruins of a temple ...

Fanjei realized she was looking for a copy of the Sun Scroll.

Could there be a second copy?

What could he do if she found it?

Ah. Yes.

Fanjei hoped she *did* find it. Then he could arrest the ambassador for theft. He could arrest Aura for conspiracy. And he would be rid of both of them forever.

* * *

As Senator Fanjei was finishing his breakfast in Sliceharbor, Bendoko was lying in the men's quarters of the village inn, dreaming of a hurricane.

"Crane. Wake up, Crane."

It was a funny sort of hurricane. For one thing, it was dry. And it didn't sound very windy, either, even though it was blowing hard enough to shake the roof he was sleeping on.

"Crane." The insistent voice was Gusty's.

Bendoko opened one eye. He wasn't lying on a thatched roof; he was lying in a hammock. And the wind wasn't shaking the hammock; Gusty was.

Ha! Gusty, not the wind. Oranges had such silly names.

Bendoko opened his other eye and looked up at Gusty. The urbie was scowling at him. Bendoko decided to keep his joke to himself.

"You can't sleep the morning away," Gusty said.

Bendoko thought about this. "Why not?"

"Matyu Gloria wants to get an early start."

"On what?"

Gusty rolled his eyes. "You know on what. Get to your feet."

Bendoko rolled himself out of the hammock. "We're not going back to the ruin, are we?"

Gusty knelt down to bring his broad face close to Bendoko's ear. They were the only ones in the men's quarters, but Gusty spoke softly: "We're going back every day until we find it."

"But there's alligators in there!"

"You said Tisha killed the gator."

"Yeah, but what if it had spouses?"

"Alligators are monogamous."

"All right, what if it had one spouse and seven grown children?"

Gusty shook his huge helmeted head. "Let's go, Crane."

It wasn't fair. He'd saved Tisha's life, hadn't he? That should be good enough. He shouldn't have to go back.

"It ripped Tisha's arm off," Bendoko said.

Gusty stared at him. His caterpillar eyebrows writhed in thought. "All right, Crane, how about this: If we see any alligators, you don't have to go in."

"We didn't see the one that got Tisha."

"All right. If you *sense* any alligators, you can come out. And you don't have to go back in until someone kills them."

"How are you going to kill them?"

"That will be our problem, not yours. All right?"

"I want you watching," Bendoko said. "All the time I'm under water. And if you see anything moving, you have to toss in a stick to warn me."

Gusty's frown had softened. It was almost a smile. "All right, Crane. You don't have to go in if we see a gator. You can come out if you sense one. And I'll warn you if I see one."

"And you'll keep watch," Bendoko said. "A *close* watch."

"A close watch," Gusty agreed. "Do we have a deal?"

Deal?

"What's in it for me?" Bendoko asked.

"What do you mean?"

"Well, I agreed to be your jungle guide as a favor to Tisha." He almost wanted to say "my friend Tisha" but maybe that would be stretching it. "I didn't sign up to be an underwater explorer."

Gusty sighed and shook his head. "All right, Crane. What do you want?"

What *did* Bendoko want? He'd been promised fifty more imperials for stealing the Sun Scroll, but he didn't want to bring *that* up. He wished he'd never even heard of the Sun Scroll.

Actually, he hadn't heard of it until he'd stolen it. Maybe if he'd heard of it before, he wouldn't have taken the job.

"I want some information," he said.

"About what?"

"About this scroll. How do I know that stealing it won't anger the Sun Goddess?"

"You've been a thief all your life, and now you start worrying about the deities?"

"Look, I stole the one from the library, and bad things happened. I didn't know those things would happen, but they did. So now I want to know: Will finding this scroll put everything right again?"

"That's a funny question."

"I'm not laughing."

"You think it's that simple, Crane? You think that after stealing a sacred piece of my people's history you can somehow fix it?"

"So finding the scroll won't put everything right again?"

"I don't know," Gusty said. "It probably won't fix *everything*. But it will at least make Matyu Gloria happy."

"And that's good?"

"Of course it's good! She's a matyu."

"Yeah, well, I've never been too clear on what a 'matyu' is."

"She has direct contact with the deities."

Can't be too direct, or else they would have warned her about me, Bendoko thought. "All right, so she's pious," he said.

"Yeah, Crane. She's pious."

"And she thinks finding this scroll is a good thing."

"Yeah."

"But there are a lot of blues in Sliceharbor who don't want her to have it. Will they get mad if we find it for her?"

"Who needs to know, Crane?"

"No one, I guess."

"All right then."

"But—"

"Yeah?" The orange man's voice was nearly a growl.

"Well, if we find the scroll but no one knows it, then they'll still be just as angry as they are now."

Gusty said, "Look, Crane, we just have to find it, all right? We don't have to worry about what happens afterward. That's not our concern."

"Oh," said Bendoko. "But I heard that the Queenies want to open it."

"… Yeah."

"And I heard that the Sun Goddess said not to."

"… Maybe."

"So you think that's all right?"

"I think I'm not a matyu," Gusty said. "What do I know? And what do *you* know, Crane? You gave your soul to a dead crime lord!"

"All right, all right."

Big Zeemo preferred to be called a merchant or a nature spirit, but this wasn't the time to argue nomenclature.

"So will you do it?" Gusty asked.

"Yeah," said Bendoko. "I'll do it for six flatrings."

Gusty's mouth hung open. He looked somewhat like a carp. Bendoko wasn't sure why he was so surprised. He thought the price was fair.

Finally Gusty said, "All right, Crane. I'll pay you six flatrings. But only if you find it."

"All right. You got the money on you?"

"Yeah, I got it," Gusty said. "And I've counted it, so don't be trying to sneak off any extra while I'm sleeping."

Bendoko could tell Gusty hadn't counted the coins, but he probably would before he went to bed that night.

"I'm just an honest jungle guide," Bendoko said. "I don't steal."

"Right, Crane. Whatever. We have a deal?"

Bendoko thought about it. He should have asked for twelve flatrings. Gusty had caved too easy at six.

"One more thing," Bendoko said.

Gusty sighed. "What, Crane?"

"I want you to call me 'Bendoko'."

* * *

Bendoko figured there were two kinds of people in the world: good people, and bad people. And now he was working for the good people.

It felt good.

Yeah, he was a little worried about alligators as he swam above the chunks of rubble and tapped them with his putty knife, but Gusty was watching out for him, and Bendoko could trust Gusty. Because Gusty was a good person.

Of course, working for Mendu had paid better. But Mendu was dead.

At about mid-morning, something shiny caught Bendoko's eye. There hadn't been much that was shiny here—other criminals had picked it clean. So this thing, even though it was small, really stood out.

Bendoko dove toward it. Could it be so easy? Was this the second Sun Scroll?

No. It was the wrong shape.

What was—? Oh!

He smiled. It was his sounding hammer. Tisha must have been about here when she dropped it.

On second thought, maybe that wasn't anything to smile about. Still, he was glad to have his hammer. He plucked it out of the crack it had lodged in and headed up to lighter waters where he was sure his lookout could see him.

Tap, tap, tap. Tap, tap, tap. Tap, tap, tap.

He didn't find anything else that morning, but it was nice to have his hammer.

* * *

At midday Bendoko came up and shared a basket with the bodyguards. Gusty sat and ate with the Bossy One and the Scowling One for a while, but then he came to talk to Bendoko.

"Matyu Gloria wants to know how much has been searched so far," Gusty said.

"I don't know," Bendoko said. It seemed like he'd been all over the rubble pile.

"Well, do you think you've searched half of it?" Gusty asked. "A sixth? A twelfth?"

"Why does she want to know?"

Pious looked down at him and frowned.

"She wants to know how long it will take," Gusty said.

"Oh."

Bendoko thought about that. He'd been all over the rubble pile, and so had maybe three dozen fugitives before him. There was little chance he'd find the Sun Scroll.

But that didn't matter. The point was that these ruins were a lot safer than being in Sliceharbor, especially with all these oranges around to protect him. He wondered how long it would take before the urbies arrested Sunny and Tiny Too-Tall.

"Tell her two weeks," Bendoko said. "At least. Maybe three."

Did he want to be swimming in this hole every day for three weeks? He took a peach from the basket, bit into it. It was so sweet that the juice ran down his chin.

Yeah, this wasn't so bad. He could do this for two weeks. Maybe he could even ask for every sixth day off. And a later start time.

Gusty was studying him. He said, "Let's go for a walk, Bendoko."

Bendoko exchanged glances with the Rock brothers. He shrugged. "All right."

He and Gusty didn't walk very far. Just far enough into the jungle to be out of earshot.

"You're not even trying, are you, Crane?"

"I'm trying. And you said you'd call me—"

"You want to be called 'Bendoko' then you have to hold up your side of the deal."

"I'm trying."

"You spent most of the morning on the shallow end."

This was true. Bendoko wanted to stay close to his climbing line, and he knew that Gusty wouldn't be able to see alligators in the deeper waters.

"Yeah, well, I got a good feeling about finding the scroll there."

"That doesn't make any sense, Crane. Bendoko. Whatever your name is. Because, look, we know the scroll was in a sunward room:"

Gusty picked up a stick and drew a square atop a moss-covered rock.

"The entrance was probably in the middle." Gusty drew two lines in the sunward side of the square to delineate an opening.

"So the scroll had to be here or here." He pointed to the two corners of the sunward side.

"The sunward side fell into the sinkhole first," Gusty said. "And you're searching the stuff that fell in last."

"Well, if the sunward side fell in first," Bendoko said, "then the other stuff fell on top of it. So I'm not going to find it at all. It's buried."

"You're right," Gusty said. He looked thoughtfully at the square he had drawn in the moss. "Good thinking, Crane. Bendoko. Thanks."

"For what?"

"For helping me figure out where you should be looking."

* * *

While Bendoko ate another peach, Gusty explained his plan. The Bossy One agreed. The Scowling One agreed, too, but her opinion didn't matter much more than Bendoko's. Maybe that was why she scowled so much.

The ambassador handed Gusty some coins, and he went off down the trail. Bendoko took a nap. He awoke when Gusty returned with the supplies: ropes, grappling hooks, and a stout ladder.

The ladder was for the orange men, so they could climb down to the rubble pile. The ropes were so the orange men could pull slabs of rubble out of the way. The grappling hooks were supposed to help Bendoko attach the ropes.

Bendoko refused the hooks.

"Hooks slip," he said. "Especially on stone."

Gusty shrugged. "You can just attach it again."

"Yeah, and while I'm doing that, the rock slips and crushes me. Forget it. We'll tie on."

"What if you can't wrap the rope all the way around?"

"Trust me."

After some hesitation, Gusty said, "All right."

Bendoko knew that Gusty didn't *really* trust him, but Gusty did give him a chance to show that he knew what he was doing.

They began excavating, one piece at a time.

Bendoko wrapped each chunk of rubble carefully. He had three ropes to tie, and he made sure that each one could safely hold if the other two failed. Yeah, there were some chunks he couldn't wrap a rope around. So he left them there! Bendoko selected the pieces that were easiest to move, always trying to avoid shifting anything that looked like it was supporting pieces above.

The rubble did slide, though. You couldn't open a hole in a rubble pile without some of the stuff shifting. Because Bendoko was careful, it didn't shift much. To be on the safe side, he stayed near his climbing line while the oranges were pulling on their ropes. He didn't trust their ladder.

The rubble-moving project went well. Bendoko got to spend a lot of time carefully considering his next move, and then he got to spend a lot of time ashore, watching other people work. One of the first things they discovered was a stool that still had two of its three legs. Bendoko propped this against an outcropping of the cliff face, and then he had a place to sit while he watched the orange men work. Yeah, he hadn't been too sure at first, but now he was thinking that Gusty's idea was keen.

As Bendoko explored the expanding hole, tapping with his sounding hammer, he discovered other treasures: shards of a brewing crock, an intact deer antler, and a wooden beam carved with names of those who had hidden out in the abandoned temple before the sinkhole caved in.

But the best treasure came late in the afternoon. Gusty had ordered him to search around the edges of the rubble pile, because some stray chunks had tumbled down during the excavation. At the bottom of the lake, Bendoko found a light patch that he mistook for a piece of freshly-exposed limestone. Tapping on it produced a metallic *ting!*

He grabbed it. The object fit easily into his hand. It was a weapon. A stout dagger. Swimming up to better light, he saw that he had found Tisha's alligator knife.

It was an expensive chunk of metal. He knew Tisha would be glad to have it back.

* * *

The sun was so low that the entire lake was now in shadow. It wasn't dark—sunlight was still dancing in the treetops, and the yellow moon was high and bright—but it was time to quit for the day.

Gusty Longbread sent Pious and Clever up the ladder ahead of him.

Iris Daylight came to the edge and frowned down. "Why are you coming out?" she wanted to know.

"We're done for the day," Gusty said.

"You haven't found it yet," she said.

"No," Gusty said. "But we've moved a lot of rock, and we're done for the day."

Pious looked down from the ladder and gave Gusty a worried look. Clever just looked relieved that Gusty was sticking up for them.

Matyu Gloria came to stand beside Iris Daylight.

"The problem with mainlander men," Iris Daylight said, "is that they do not know their place."

My place is back at the inn with a chilled mug of beer, Gusty thought.

"They have worked hard," Matyu Gloria said. "Let them rest."

"They shall never find it, you know," said Iris.

"Do you think they are looking in the wrong place?" Matyu Gloria asked.

"They are looking under the water," Iris said. "If it was ever there, it has surely rotted away by now."

"I do not think so," Matyu Gloria said. "A scroll that important would be well purified and sealed in a tight case."

"Wood is porous."

"The case was probably lacquered."

"Lacquer cracks."

"The Mother Goddess always provides."

Gusty was pleased that Iris had no answer for that.

Bendoko the Crane emerged from the water, holding an object triumphantly in the air. He expelled the water from his lungs. Gusty hoped Iris Daylight had a good view.

Bendoko coughed out the last of the water and called, "I found Tisha's alligator knife!"

Above Gusty's head, Iris Daylight heaved a heavy sigh. "Why is that blue rooster always crowing about finding junk?"

Gusty went to meet the thief. He held out his hand. Bendoko gave the knife to him.

"That looks like Tisha's," Gusty agreed. "Where did you find it?"

"On the edge of the rubble pile," Bendoko said. "Where you told me to look." He was a little bit defensive.

Gusty knew Bendoko hadn't found it on the edge of the rubble pile. The alligator's bubbles—and its cloud of blood!—had come up in the middle of the lake. Tisha couldn't kill the alligator, swim back to the rubble pile, drop the knife, then swim back out to where Bendoko had found her. The Crane was lying about something.

But then, that was no real surprise, was it?

"Good work, Bendoko," Gusty said. He handed the knife back. "Let's go give it to Tisha."

* * *

The Bossy One insisted that Gusty discuss excavation plans with her, so Bendoko got to see Tisha alone. She was still in the hospital wing, but at least she was sitting up now. She even stood when she saw him.

"Ben!" She had a pretty smile.

"Hi, Tisha."

"How'd it go today?"

"I didn't find the … thing," he said. "But I did find this."

He reached inside his sari—her sari—and pulled out her alligator knife.

"My combat knife?"

"Yeah." Alligator knife, combat knife. Whatever.

He handed it to her. She took it, turned it over in her hands.

"That's my knife, all right."

She looked down at her waist. She had no belt. She was dressed in a giant-sized white sari folded double so it would fit her. Her blue skin made the plain white look pretty.

She handed the alligator knife back to him. "Can you put it with my armor?"

"Yeah."

Bendoko slipped it back inside his tool belt.

"How did you find it?" Tisha asked.

"Oh, I just kept my eyes open."

She grinned. "Yeah, but this isn't what you were supposed to keep your eyes open for."

Yeah. That. He wanted to talk to Tisha about that.

He moved closer to her and lowered his voice. "Is anyone else around?"

"This house can be a busy place," Tisha said. "But I don't think they'll overhear us if we keep our voices low."

"All right," he said. "Have you and Gusty talked about the thing we're looking for?"

Her face grew solemn. "Yes."

"Did he tell you to keep quiet about it?"

"Yeah," she said. "More or less."

"Do you think that's right?"

"What do you mean, Ben?"

"Well, if we find this scroll, and nobody knows about it, then everyone in Sliceharbor will still be angry, right?"

"I suppose so."

"And if the Queenies sail home with it, and someone finds out we gave it to them, then some people will be even angrier, right?"

"Yeah."

"So how is giving the scroll to the Queenies the right thing to do?"

"Did Gusty tell you we're letting the ambassador have the scroll?"

"He told me it's none of my business. But the way I see it, this is my chance to give the scroll back to the library."

"You want to get the scroll for the library?"

"Yeah." He mumbled, "My sister said that would make things right again."

"I see."

"It would, wouldn't it?"

"I don't know, Ben. I would be glad if it did."

"But if we're just going to secretly give it to the Queenies—"

"Listen, Ben. You don't have to worry."

"Well, I'm worried."

"No, Ben. Listen. Gusty doesn't want you to know this, but ..."

"Yeah?"

"He's not going to give it to the Queenies. He knows how angry everyone would be if they found out that the Urban Cohort had given the scroll away. And he knows that letting the Queenies use the sacred knowledge against the Mogadrel is wrong."

"You sure?"

"You have to trust him, Ben. Gusty's smart. He has a plan."

* * *

Tisha thought about Bendoko's questions long after he had gone to supper. She didn't have much to do except wiggle her fingers and think. Gusty came in as she was holding her arms above her head making fists.

"Are you supposed to be doing that?" he asked.

"Yes." She smiled. "Good to see you, Gus."

"You too," he said. He nodded at her splinted arm. "How long before ...?"

"Two weeks. That wretched Flora said she'd ask Captain Kosho to keep me off duty for two weeks."

Gusty grunted sympathetically.

"I'm not even allowed to swim with it," Tisha said. "But Flora might let me take a bath tomorrow if she's convinced that the wound has closed."

Thinking of the bath she had missed today made her skin itch. She tried to put it out of her mind.

Gusty said, "The Crane put your combat knife back with your other things."

"That's good."

"Do you remember dropping it?" Gusty asked.

"No," Tisha said. "Or ..."

To tell the truth, she had been keeping the gator attack out of her mind. It wasn't pleasant to remember.

"I think my hand hit a rock," she said.

She flexed her sword hand. It had been sore this morning, but a lot of hurts had faded under Flora's care.

She tried to recall.

"When the gator took my arm, it started rolling. I had to roll with it. Yeah. My hand hit a rock, and I dropped the knife."

"What did you stab it with, then?"

"I ... don't know. I don't remember stabbing it."

Gusty nodded.

"What is it?" she asked.

"Crane's story doesn't make sense," Gusty said. "He claims he found the knife by the rubble pile. But we saw the alligator blood in the middle of the lake."

"So what happened?"

"We may never know," Gusty said. "But here's my guess: I think the Crane found your knife as he was going after you. He picked it up and killed your gator with it. Then he decided to keep it."

"But you'd have seen my knife in his tool belt when he pulled me out."

"Could he have hidden it in his loincloth?" Gusty asked.

"That sounds ouchy."

Gusty nodded. "Right. So he probably didn't have it with him when he pulled you out. He stashed it, planning to get it later, keep it for himself."

"All right," Tisha said. "But then why did he give it back to me?"

"I guess he decided to come clean," Gusty said. "Or, you know, clean enough."

Tisha said, "Or maybe he dropped it accidentally and was too embarrassed to admit it. So when he says he found it, he's actually telling the truth."

"Maybe," Gusty said.

"You don't think so?"

"I don't think he'd lie about who killed the gator unless it was to cover up a theft."

Tisha shook her head. Bendoko was certainly a complicated man.

"All right, Gus. I guess that makes sense."

"Thanks for helping me sort that out," Gusty said.

"Are you going to confront him?"

"I don't think so," Gusty said. "He did the right thing in the end. That's what counts, isn't it?"

"Only Justice knows what counts," Tisha said. "But yeah, I don't think we should embarrass him. We don't want to discourage him from being honest."

"Mostly honest," Gusty said.

"Yeah," Tisha said. "Honest more or less."

Bendoko *was* honest, in a funny kind of way. And even somewhat trustworthy.

"Gus, I told him what you told me."

"About what?"

"About what Senator Aura sent you to do."

Gusty's face clouded over.

"Not the details, Gus. But he was worried that we were planning to give *it* to the Queenies. So I had to tell him we weren't."

Gusty grunted.

"I just told him you have a plan. I didn't tell him what it was."

Gusty grunted again. It meant, *I heard what you said, but I'm not going to show you how I feel about it.*

"He just seemed worried about what might happen if the Queenies got it, so I—"

"It's none of his business!"

His voice was loud. Flora wouldn't like that.

"I'm sorry, Gus, I—"

Gusty gave a low, dismissive growl. "I guess it doesn't matter," he said.

"I don't think he'll tell the Queenies, Gus. He's a criminal, but he's also a loyal Sliceharbor boy. At least, loyal enough. I think."

"All right," Gusty said.

"Are you angry with me?"

"I said it's all right."

It wasn't all right. He was angry—or at least annoyed. And he looked anxious, too.

She said, "It's not easy, is it?"

"What?"

"Working for Senator Aura while pretending you're working for the ambassador. You respect Ambassador Gloria, and you don't like keeping secrets from her. It troubles you."

"I'll be fine," Gusty said.

"All right, Gus."

"Get some rest," he said. "Captain Kosho will want you healed up quickly."

Tisha smiled at him. "All right."

* * *

At the boarding house, Mama Grace was cleaning up after supper. Willful Hammer and Airy Freshmilk already had their seats for the evening meeting. She could hear them arguing in the dining room—Airy was claiming that spiders were better than frogs at catching mosquitoes. Blustery Chandler had retired to his room to take a nap.

Opal Warmblood had also retired to her room, but she was hiding, not napping. The meetings made her nervous. Ironic, really. The meetings were for *her* benefit.

At least, that had been the original idea, when Mama Grace had first invited people to spend an evening in her dining room. She had wanted them to find a way to help the refugees and help the Motherland. But there was only so much help that poor, orange people could offer to a queendom on the other side of the sea. They needed support from the city and from the Senate.

They had expected the city government and the Lunaslip Republic to listen to reasonable requests, to do something to help solve the problem. But the governments had ignored them. And gradually, the people meeting at Mama Grace's boarding house had come to think of government as something that only worked for blues. For oranges, government was the enemy.

When Lily Trueknife was killed, they were proven right.

To tell the truth, Mama Grace's people hadn't quite gotten along with Lily Trueknife's people. How could they? The oranges in the Enclave thought they were better than everyone else. But in death, Lily Trueknife had become their hero. Every orange in the city could point to Breadbaker Bridge and say, "See? This is the proof that the blue government has failed us."

The boarding house would be crowded tonight. They were planning a foot blockade—a group of people so big that it could shut off access to a building, a street, or maybe even an entire market. They just needed a target.

Some people wanted to go straight for Senator Fanjei's suite in the Senatorial Palace. Mama Grace needed to find a gentle tack to dissuade them. The palace had armed guards, and she didn't want any of her people to become the next martyr.

The pool house on Nailmaker Street would be a safe choice. The door guard wouldn't be able to throw them out, because they wouldn't go in. And Mama Grace was certain that she had enough regular attendees at her evening meetings to block the entrance.

But more ambitious would be to blockade the entire Broad Market. It was the heart of the Palace District, so the City Palace and the Senatorial Palace would get the message, but it wasn't close enough to the Senatorial Palace that the Navy could claim they had jurisdiction.

Did she have the numbers? The dining room would be crowded tonight, but to close off the entire market, everyone would need to bring dozens of friends.

Mama Grace thought they could do it.

The door to the boarding house opened. That must be Patience Honeythroat, coming back with a bucket of water. The girl had certainly been slow tonight. Patience would need to hurry now to get the mopping done. Mama Grace expected people to begin arriving at any time.

But Patience didn't hurry in. She stayed in the entryway. Was she sobbing?

Mamma Grace heard Airy Freshmilk ask, "Patience, what's wrong?"

Mamma Grace dropped her cleaning rag, pushed past Airy and Will, who were standing in the entryway, and knelt to look at Patience. The girl had collapsed with her back against the door. Her shoulders were shaking. Tears were running down her cheeks. The water bucket was nowhere in sight.

"I feared they would kill me, Mama," she said, in her Sun-Island accent.

"Who?" Mama Grace asked. "Who, Patience?"

"The greenscarves," she said. "One of them stopped me as I was coming home. Oh, Mama! I forgot your bucket."

"Don't worry about the bucket, child. Just tell me what happened."

"She drew her sword, Mama, and pointed it at—"

Her hands were covering her navel.

"The greenscarf pointed her rapier at your belly," Mama Grace said. "And then what?"

"She told me to get down on my knees. I did. Oh, Mama, I thought she would stab me."

Patience didn't look like she was bleeding anywhere. She wasn't wounded, just terrified. Understandable. Short people with swords had killed her parents.

"What happened next?" Mama Grace asked.

"She said nothing more to me. She just pointed her sword at me until some of our people arrived. I believe she was waiting for them."

"Waiting for *our* people?" Airy asked. "You mean—?" He waved vaguely at the empty dining room where the early-arriving meeting-goers should have been.

"Yes," said Patience. "And then when they asked her why I was on my knees, she said she was arresting me for arson. Mama, I had nothing to do with those fires."

"I know you didn't, Patience. I know you didn't."

And the greenscarf knew it, too. Patience was just bait.

"They started arguing," Patience said. "And the greenscarf yelled. And a dozen more greenscarves came running. Maybe two dozen.

"Some of our people ran. Some wanted to fight. I saw a man get stabbed. The blue woman who stopped me—she was thrown into a wall. I think maybe she—" Patience shuddered.

"They were ignoring me," Patience continued. "I did not wish to die. So I stood up and ran. Oh, Mama, I led them straight here. I am so sorry."

"It's all right," Mama Grace said.

She stepped over Patience's legs and barred the door. A little late now. If the greenscarves had wanted to come in, they would have done so already.

Airy looked at her in alarm. "I'll get the back door." He ran into the dining room.

Will snorted.

There was a creak on the stairs, and Tiny Too-Tall came down to sit on the steps above the entryway.

He said, "And to think that just last night, you were trying to find a way to get the blues' attention."

9 Yellowmonth

GUSTY LONGBREAD DIDN'T HAVE TIME to visit Tisha in the morning. Matyu Gloria wanted to get out to the ruined temple as early as possible.

It was just as well. Tisha needed to sleep through the morning anyway. And Gusty wasn't sure he was ready to talk to her again.

As Bendoko, Pious, and Clever got the ropes organized for another day of rock moving, Matyu Gloria took Gusty aside.

"Have you thought about where to excavate today?" she asked.

"I was planning to work on the same place," Gusty said. "Bendoko says we're not at the bottom yet."

Matyu Gloria nodded. "I approve of your thoroughness, but today I would like you to search on the left side."

Gusty opened his mouth to speak. He much preferred to finish the area he was working on. But Matyu Gloria's tone left no room for debate. "Yes, Matyu Gloria."

"Have faith," she said. "Last night, the Mother Goddess blessed me with a vision."

"All right," he said. He couldn't argue with that.

She studied him. "You do not doubt me."

"I don't," he agreed.

"Some of the mainlanders have lost faith in the matyus," she said, "but your mother has raised you well."

"Thank you," Gusty said.

In truth, his mother had taught him little of the matyu caste. They had special access to the deities—especially the Mother Goddess—and that was about all Gusty knew. But he had no reason to doubt it.

"Have you ever been blessed with a vision, Gusty Longbread?"

"No."

"But you are close to the Mother Goddess."

"I just try to do what's right," Gusty said. "That's all."

"That's admirable."

Gusty grunted. He wasn't sure it was "admirable". It was just right. People were supposed to do what was right. And Gusty's job was to catch those people who forgot.

Unless they were blue senators. Then Gusty had to let them go free.

"My admiration troubles you?" Matyu Gloria asked.

"What? No."

"Then why do you frown so fiercely? Is your soul conflicted?"

"No," said Gusty. "Not really. At least …"

But his soul *was* conflicted, wasn't it? Tisha had pointed it out last night. Gusty admired Matyu Gloria and didn't like deceiving her.

"Yes?" She was expecting him to say more.

But what could he say?

"Maybe I should tell you the truth," he said.

"About what?" she asked, voice calm.

"About why Aura Wisebrow sent me with you."

"Very well," said Matyu Gloria. "Tell me the truth."

"Aura Wisebrow wants me to claim the Sun Scroll for Sliceharbor," Gusty said.

"There," said Matyu Gloria. "Do you feel better?"

"You aren't angry?"

"No," said Matyu Gloria. She wasn't even surprised.

"You are her soldier," Matyu Gloria said. "I understand why you feel you must serve her."

"Oh." Gusty hadn't thought he was serving Aura Wisebrow. He just wanted to do something that would make his city better. Aura Wisebrow had said she had a plan. And his mother had told him to trust Aura Wisebrow.

"So if we find the scroll …" Gusty said.

"Yes?"

Gusty glanced at Pious and Clever, standing on the edge of the cliff, just out of earshot. They were looking at him expectantly, ready to get started.

"If we find the scroll," Gusty asked, "what will you do?"

Matyu Gloria smiled. Kindly.

She laid a gentle hand on his cheek. "You know I will do what the Mother Goddess says I must. You are not afraid of what I will do. You are worried about what you will do."

She was right.

She said, "When we first saw this place, the Mother Goddess touched your soul."

Gusty nodded, ever so slightly, not disturbing the warm, motherly hand on his cheek.

"I believe you are pious," Matyu Gloria said. "You have faith in the deities. So have faith in yourself. When the time comes, you will do the right thing."

* * *

Bendoko sat on his salvaged stool and watched the three giants heave the slab of limestone out of the tea-dark water. Following Gusty's lead, they dragged it close to the cliff wall. Gusty untied the ropes. Then the three of them pushed it off so that it went tumbling back down into the water again.

The process churned up the rock scum, making the water murkier, but it was fun to hear the splash.

The three men looked at him.

"Right," he said. "My turn again."

Bendoko collected the ends of the ropes and dove into the water.

Gusty had them working on the left side of the rubble pile today. Bendoko didn't mind. He'd already found a stick of wood with a little gilt paint left on it. And he was sure he'd seen something metal under the slab the giants had just moved.

Bendoko swam down into the hole they were making. Sure enough. There was a piece of something shiny. He tapped it with his sounding hammer. It sounded like brass.

His fingers scrabbled against it. The object was stuck to the stone underneath, but with his putty knife, he was able to peel it off. He brought it to the surface to examine it in the light.

"It's a lamp!" he said. A brass lamp, squished flat by the rocks.

No one else was impressed.

Bendoko had the feeling this would have been more fun with Tisha.

He swam back down, tapping as he went.

Tap, tap, tap.

He let his ears and fingers work while his eyes tried to figure out what to move next. That looked like a pillar. The oranges could pull it out from under that slab of flooring if he tied the rope in the right place.

Tap, tap, tap.

But the deep end of the pillar was wedged between two slabs of wall. If he shifted one, the pillar might roll down that way.

Toap, toap, toap.

What was that?

He tried his hammer again: *toap.*

This slab was resonant—like it was hollow!

Bendoko forgot all about the troublesome pillar. *This* was the piece he needed to concentrate on.

He tied the three ropes to it. It was hard to be careful. His eagerness made him so hasty.

There! He had it secured.

He checked again. Yeah, that was probably secure. They'd brought up dozens of slabs so far, counting yesterday's work. He wouldn't foul it up now, would he?

He checked a third time. *Oh forget it! Let's just try it and see.* He went to the surface.

Bendoko thought he was real nonchalant when he told them they could pull it up, but Gusty gave him a suspicious eye. It was hard to fool Gusty.

The oranges pulled. The slab rose. Everything was going smooth.

The slab came out of the water. Couldn't they hear the hollow sound? Oh, it was sweet! Bendoko had found it. In all this huge pile of rock, this was the piece they were looking for.

The brothers began pulling it off to the side.

"Wait!" Bendoko said. "Don't dump this one."

They looked at him.

"Flip it over," he said.

"Why?" Clever asked.

Bendoko got off his stool. He swaggered over to the slab—as much as he could swagger on the uneven footing of the rubble pile. He ostentatiously withdrew his sounding hammer from his belt.

Toap. Toap.

They looked at him.

"It's hollow," he said.

They looked at the slab.

"All right," Gusty said. He was trying to sound calm, but his breathing was a little raspy. "Pull it up this way. That's right."

The edge dropped into a gap in the rubble.

Gusty said, "Hold it steady, Pious. Clever, you pull your end up … and up … and overrrrrr …"

The slab teetered on edge then fell onto its other side. Blue, white, and gold ceramic tiles flashed in the morning sunlight. In the very center of the slab, where three square tiles should have been, there was a rectangular hole just the right size for a scroll case.

It was empty.

* * *

Gloria Sunrise, direct descendent of the sister of Ruby Sunrise, would not give up. The Sun Scroll was here. She would find it. It would be hers.

Because she had faith.

She climbed down the ladder to examine the slab for herself. It was definitely a chunk of flooring. The ceramic tiles were of high quality. The hollow in the center was exactly the hiding place she had been expecting to find.

She put her hand in the hole, feeling its emptiness, willing the scroll to appear there. But it was not there. So where was it?

"It must be somewhere close," she said. "Move more stones."

Her bodyguards nodded.

"Bendoko has something," Gusty Longbread said.

The native guide emerged from the water holding two pieces of stone. After vomiting out water—a disgusting habit which, according to Gusty, could not be cured—the native guide announced, "I found the lid."

He was as pleased with this find as he had been with his squished lump of brass or the deer antler he had found the day before. The skinny little man failed to understand the gravity of their undertaking. That was just as well. The less he understood, the less likely he would be to cause her trouble when she found the scroll.

And she *would* find it.

The native guide took the two pieces of stone and showed how they fit together to make a rectangle—three ceramic squares, with the center square broken in the middle. He set this lid atop the hole in the slab. It was a perfect fit. The tiles on the lid matched the pattern of the floor.

"It must have popped open when the temple collapsed," the native guide said cheerily.

"Then the scroll is lost," said Iris. She had come down the ladder, too, though Gloria had not invited her.

"It's probably real close," the native guide said. "We just have to move a few more rocks. I wouldn't be surprised to find it in, oh, a day or two. Maybe three."

"Stupid man!" Iris said. "The scroll *case* may still be down there, but there will be nothing inside except a pulpy sludge."

The native guide shrugged. "Not if it stayed sealed."

"Sealed?" Iris said. "An unprotected tube of wood under huge slabs of rock?"

The native guide said, "Oh."

"We must have faith," Gloria said. "The Mother Goddess would not have led us here unless—"

"The Mother Goddess did not lead us here," Iris said. "You did."

Yes, maybe I did, Gloria admitted to herself. *But it felt right, then. And I will not give up now. Either I press on, or I can no longer claim to be a matyu.*

She turned to the young man with hair like copper. "What do you think, Gusty Longbread?"

He looked thoughtful. She now knew him well enough to know he would give her an honest answer without worrying about what she wanted to hear.

"I think Matyu Iris is right," Gusty said.

Iris looked shocked.

"Partly," Gusty added.

Iris looked suspicious.

"Let's say the lid popped off as the slab was falling," Gusty said. "If the scroll was inside at the time, then it could have fallen out."

"It *did* fall out," Iris said. "See? It is gone."

Gusty nodded. "So it falls out and lands in the water. What happens next?"

"It gets crushed by rocks that fall on top of it," said Iris.

"Maybe," said Gusty. "In that case, the scroll is gone, right?"

Iris threw up her hands. "That is what I said."

Gloria saw the ray of hope: "But if it did not get crushed, then it floated on the surface."

Gusty nodded. "Because it's sealed and full of air."

Iris rolled her eyes. "It could have become water logged and sunk later."

Gusty nodded. "But if it did, then the scroll is destroyed, so there's no sense looking for—"

"That is what I said!"

"There's no sense looking for it at the bottom of the lake," Gusty finished, giving a smile to Gloria. He could tell that she understood.

"You are saying we need to look on the surface," she said.

Gusty nodded. "If the scroll is still worth finding, then it must be floating on top."

"We have been staring at the surface for the past two days," Iris said. "It is not there."

Gloria pointed across the lake to the gaping black hole in the limestone. "We need to look in that cave."

* * *

Bendoko made them relocate to the side of the lake above the cave. They grumbled. There was no easy trail, and the bracken, shrubs, and fallen trees kept tripping the oranges' big feet.

But they did what he said because they needed him to look in the cave. And as long as they needed him to look in the cave, Bendoko was in charge.

Bendoko secured his climbing line to a tree so that it dangled down beside the opening in the limestone. No way was he going in there without a climbing line handy. He needed a quick escape route. The cave looked too much like a mouth.

The alligator probably lived in there, Bendoko thought. *I hope he was a loner like me.*

He climbed down the cliff slowly, carefully. If toothy jaws burst from the water to snap at him, he didn't want any downward momentum.

He put a toe in the water. Pulled it out. Waited.

Nothing.

He put in a foot. Wiggled the toes.

"Water too cold for you?" Gusty called from above.

Bendoko ignored the taunt. He was a professional. If he wanted to take his time, he would take his time.

Nothing came to his bait.

Bendoko lowered himself the rest of the way into the water—quietly. Pulling gently against the limestone walls, he entered the cave.

He couldn't feel waves reflected from the bottom. He guessed the bottom was at least fifteen feet under water. But Bendoko was supposed to find a floating scroll case, so he kept his head above the surface.

It was dark. He felt his way in.

The lake's debris had accumulated against the walls of the cave. His long fingers sifted through leaves, pine needles, and pine cones. This skinny round thing was a stick, not a scroll case.

He found another patch of debris at the back of the cave. By this time, his eyes had adjusted and he could make out shapes of things. But again, it was just tree bits that had fallen in from above.

He turned around to face the bright window of daylight. From this angle, it was easy to see that no scroll cases bobbed on the surface of the water. He wasn't going to find it here.

But he hadn't explored *all* of the cave. His head was at the back, but his legs were telling him the tunnel continued on, under the water.

Well, he was a blue wasn't he? If he wasn't meant to go under water, Justice wouldn't have given him lungs that could breathe down there. He expelled his air and submerged.

A tap from his sounding hammer told him that the cavern went back a long way. He'd heard of a guy who had broken into somebody's cellar by finding one of these limestone tunnels. Bendoko decided he should try it sometime.

He kept one hand on the cave's ceiling so he wouldn't get lost. He was swimming blind, but the wave fronts felt like they were reflecting from the sides of a tunnel. He could keep going deeper inside.

Bendoko knew what he was looking for: another chamber with a ceiling above the surface. Water levels in this lake probably went up and down depending on the rainfall. When the lake was low, stuff from outside could move deeper inside … then get trapped when the water came back up.

The cavern opened upward. His hand broke into air.

Bendoko didn't go up to breathe it. His sister Puji had told him not to breathe stale air pockets. Where had she gotten that from? No one went spelunking in Sliceharbor. Maybe one of their parents had been jungle born. Bendoko knew so little about them.

Regardless of how this bit of wisdom had come to him, Bendoko kept his head below water as his hands felt around for the Sun Scroll. His hands found nothing.

Well, he hadn't reached the end yet. Maybe he'd find another chamber farther back.

Reflections of his underwater strokes told him that the cavern twisted ahead. It was narrower here. He wasn't squeezed, but there was not much room to move his hands and feet. He grasped the craggy limestone and pulled himself around the twist.

Light was ahead—at first just a hint of a glow, but as he drew nearer he began to see the walls of the cavern as a jagged, black outline around the murky, brown water. The patch of brown grew larger, and larger. Then suddenly Bendoko was in a pool, looking up at a surface shimmering in the sunlight.

He went up and expelled the water from his lungs.

Head bobbing above the surface, he could see that this place was not like the ruined temple's lake. It was a small pool with gradual slopes, not sheer drops. Trees draped in jungle moss grew all the way down to the water. Some even grew *in* the water. Ferns and shrubs crowded the bank. A floating scroll case could be hidden anywhere in such a tangle of vegetation.

If the Sun Scroll was here, Bendoko wanted the credit for finding it. But a search behind every fallen log and through every clump of rotting bracken would take the rest of the day. Maybe several days. He'd need help.

Still, it couldn't hurt to give the water's edge a quick check. Maybe he'd get lucky.

The pool had an outlet. A shallow channel had carved itself into the limestone, but water was barely trickling through right now.

Near this outlet, a clear path led up the muddy bank and into the jungle. This must be where animals came to drink from the pool.

Bendoko wasn't really a jungle guide. So he didn't exactly recognize the tracks. He had a vague idea that deer should have hooves like goats or something, but these tracks looked like they'd been made by clawed toes. Didn't really remind him of a bird's foot, though.

Maybe kind of lizardy? No. It was an animal much bigger than a lizard.

In fact, now that he thought about it, the tracks looked exactly like what he would expect from an alligator.

The swim back through the tunnel was the fastest swim of Bendoko's life.

* * *

After so long a wait, Gusty Longbread was surprised by the suddenness of the Crane's return. For quite a while, the tea-dark water had shown not even a ripple. Then, with a splash, the burglar was scrambling up his climbing line, wide-eyed and empty-handed.

He opened his mouth, spewed water over the side of the cliff, and gurgled, "Gator!"

Matyu Iris wrinkled her nose in disgust. Matyu Gloria heaved a patient sigh.

The Crane coughed out the last of the water and told Gusty, "I saw its tracks. I'm not going back in."

Gusty didn't think Bendoko was faking his fear, but that didn't make his excuse credible.

"It left tracks under water?"

The Crane shook his head. "No. On land. I followed the tunnel. To a pool. In the jungle."

He waved vaguely toward the trees as he tried to catch his breath.

Gusty said, "And near this pool, you saw tracks."

"Yeah."

It was reasonable. Gusty didn't know much about gators himself, but when he'd been little, his father had told him some gator-wrestling stories. He knew that gators stayed near water, but they built their nests on land.

"Think you can take me there?" he asked.

"No," said the Crane. "The tunnel is narrow and mostly under water. Besides, you promised if I saw a gator, I wouldn't have to go back in."

"Through the jungle, Bendoko. Can you take me there through the jungle?"

The Crane opened his mouth.

Before he could speak, Gusty reminded him, "Because you *are* an experienced jungle guide."

"Oh. Right. Yeah."

Gusty asked, "Matyu Gloria, with your permission?"

The matyu sighed and nodded.

Gusty gestured toward the trees to indicate that the Crane should lead the way.

The Crane frowned. "All right," he said. "But bring your club."

It actually made sense, Gusty thought, as they tramped away from Matyu Gloria and her entourage. Alligators weren't like blue people. They couldn't breathe under water.

So the gator that had attacked Tisha must have come from somewhere else. The cave was the only obvious way to enter or leave, so it must have an outlet.

"I have no idea where I'm going," the Crane admitted. "I'm only walking this way so the Queenies will think I'm a jungle guide."

"Did the tunnel twist around any sharp corners?" Gusty asked.

"There was a twist or two," the Crane said, "but they were little twists."

"Then we're probably walking in the right direction. Tell me about these tracks."

The Crane described something that was more like a gator track than anything else, although his estimate of the size was obviously exaggerated. He also described a muddy path that sounded like the run a gator would make when building her nest.

"Did you see a nest?" Gusty asked.

"I got out of there as fast as I could," the Crane replied.

Gusty grunted. He was beginning to suspect the nest would be there. Maybe it was an urbie's hunch. Maybe it was divine inspiration. Either way, he was getting the feeling that if the Mother Goddess wanted him to find the Sun Scroll, a good place to keep it would be in a mother's nest.

"That's it," said the Crane. "I think that's the pool."

"See?" said Gusty. "Who says you're not a jungle guide?"

From the Crane's description, Gusty made a guess of where the nest might be. He took the lead now, circling the pool, picking his way across the marshy ground.

The Crane saw the gator at the same time that Gusty saw the nest. It was just a nondescript heap of mud and sticks, well camouflaged by the jungle's vegetation. Gusty saw it only because it was exactly what he was looking for.

Sitting atop the heap was a long, bumpy creature, like a log with wary eyes and lots of teeth.

"You were right," Gusty said. "There is a second gator."

"Yeah. So can I go now?"

"No," said Gusty. "We need to search its nest."

"Are you crazy?"

"No. I think the Mother Goddess has led us here because she wants us to find her scroll."

"In the gator nest?"

"Yes," said Gusty.

"You know," said the Crane, "crazy and religious are sometimes the same thing."

Gusty looked down on the little bald criminal. "How would *you* know?"

The Crane didn't reply.

"All right, Bendoko. I need you to distract the gator."

"What? No. I'm not the one who's religious."

"Do you want me to distract the gator while *you* poke around the nest?"

"No," said the Crane, peering through the trees at the wary alligator. "It might be unhappy if I did that."

"We have two jobs here. Pick one."

"Can't you just ... club it in the head?"

"No," said Gusty. "I don't think killing a mother on her nest is a good way to gain the favor of the Mother Goddess."

"Oh. Yeah. So ... want me to go back and get the Rock brothers?"

Maybe that would be better. If the Sun Scroll was here, it was none of the Crane's business.

Gusty wondered what made him think the scroll was here. It had probably rotted away long ago, as Matyu Iris insisted.

Something told him he had to look in the nest. And whatever that something was, the Crane was part of it. Maybe because he was the one who had started all the trouble in the first place.

"No, Crane. We're not going to get the Rock brothers. We're going to do this, just you and me, right now. Go into the pool and see if you can draw her off the nest."

"But you promised—"

"You promised to help us."

"Yeah, for six flatrings."

"I'll give you twelve, right now, just for doing this."

"And that will buy me a new arm after the gator chomps this one off?"

"You'll help me because you owe Tisha."

"Tisha said we're even."

"Then you'll help me because if you don't, *I'll* rip your arm off."

The Crane made a disgusted face. "All right. Twelve flatrings."

He held out his hand.

Gusty paid up, feeling guilty about his threat. Bendoko was a cowardly ball of slime, but he *had* saved Tisha's life.

"Just stay in the pool long enough to draw her off," Gusty said. "As soon as she moves, get out."

"I'm safe on land?"

"Yeah," said Gusty. Well, at least he would be *safer*.

"All right," said the Crane. "You better move fast, because you know I will."

* * *

Bendoko the Crane slipped into the water of the mama gator's swimming hole. He couldn't believe he was doing this for twelve flatrings. It felt more like fifty imperials' worth of danger.

That was the difference between skilled and unskilled labor. Anybody could be gator bait. He wondered when he could go back to his real job. He wondered if the urbies had caught the Too-Tall brothers yet.

He wondered if Puji would think that helping an urbie search a gator nest would count as doing the right thing.

How could he draw the alligator off her nest? Somewhat weakly, he called, "Here gator, gator, gator."

Well, that was how people in Sliceharbor called their chickens.

The gator didn't come. Or maybe she was coming and Gusty hadn't thought to mention it. Gusty should still have his eye on the gator, but from the pool, Bendoko could not see Gusty. Maybe he should—

Sliding smoothly down the muddy path, the scaly creature glided into the water.

Bendoko seized a clump of bracken and scrambled out of the pool.

With a twist of its body and a flip of its tail, the alligator propelled itself toward Bendoko.

Bendoko grabbed a tree with both feet and started climbing.

The gator's nose brushed the bank, but then it backed away. Once it reached the middle of the pool, Bendoko could see only its short snout and watchful eyes.

All right, so it wasn't going to climb the tree. Good. It was just going to wait until Bendoko came down.

Bendoko didn't feel like doing that.

* * *

Gusty Longbread approached the pile of mud and sticks. Was there a way he could search it without disturbing the eggs? If there was, he needed to do it quickly.

"Let me know if she decides to come back," he called.

"Yeah," said the Crane. "No problem." His voice came from somewhere up high. He seemed upset about something.

Gusty walked around the nest. He couldn't tear it apart. That would be wrong, somehow. He needed—

Oh.

There it was.

He heard no heavenly chimes when he saw the edge of the case poking out of the mud. There was no propitious shaft of sunlight spontaneously illuminating the golden seal. No burst of divine fire shot up his arm as he grabbed the case and extracted it from the muck.

But this was it. Inside was the sacred document that Matyu Gloria wanted to take back to the Motherland. And Gusty Long-bread was holding it. Right now, of all the people in the world, he was the one with the power to decide what would happen to it.

He started walking out of the marsh.

Through the trees, the Crane called, "So do you have a plan for getting me down?"

"Why don't you just climb down?"

"Because I don't want to be eaten by a gator?"

"Is she still in the pool?" Gusty asked.

"Yeah. Doesn't look like she's going anywhere."

Gusty considered the wooden cylinder in his hands. "Good."

He kept walking, back toward Matyu Gloria.

"Ah, Gusty? Funny trick of the jungle. It sounds like you're leaving me here."

Gusty stopped.

"She'll get bored and go back to her eggs soon."

"Gusty?" The tenor of the Crane's voice was pathetic.

"Oh, all right."

Waiting for the gator to go back to her nest really was the smart thing to do, but the Crane was jumpy enough to do something stupid. Gusty waded through the bracken toward the Crane's tree.

Gusty had to admit that the gator made *him* nervous, too. Even though he was big enough to defend himself.

"I'm hoping she'll stay where she is," he said. "I don't want to hurt her."

"The other one nearly ripped Tisha's arm off," Bendoko said.

"They aren't as dangerous on land," Gusty said.

"How come you know so much about alligators?"

"My father's family hunted them. He told me stories."

"Your father was a gator wrestler?"

"Yeah," said Gusty. "But that was before he married my mother and moved to the city."

"Oh," said Bendoko. "So it wasn't a gator that killed him."

No. He'd been crushed by a wall that fell on him when he was helping a neighbor rebuild a house. Gusty didn't like to talk about it.

"How'd you know he was dead?" he asked.

"Orphans can kind of spot each other, you know?"

Gusty didn't know. "I'm only half an orphan."

"You're lucky."

"Yeah, well. Are you coming down?"

"I guess. You ready?"

Gusty tightened his grip on his paddle-club. "I'm ready."

The Crane dropped, but caught himself halfway down the trunk. Then he leapt from the tree.

He landed on a rotten stump that crumpled with the impact. If the landing hurt the Crane, he didn't take time to say. He sprinted across the marsh, leaping over logs and splashing mud in his wake.

Seeing that no toothy-jawed monster was emerging from the pool, Gusty lowered his club.

Then the bracken began to rustle.

Gusty decided to follow Bendoko—quickly, but with more decorum.

* * *

"Bendoko," Gusty Longbread called. "You can come back now."

"Did you kill it?" Distance made the burglar's voice sound tiny.

"It's not coming after us," Gusty called.

Gusty heard nothing except the insistent buzzing of the cicadas.

"Bendoko?"

Gusty caught sight of the burglar among the trees as his bald, blue head passed through a patch of sunlight. The Crane was approaching warily.

Gusty waited for him.

"The others are back this way," he said, waving in the direction from which they had come.

"Hey," said Bendoko, "you found it?"

Gusty was still holding the scroll case in his left hand. It fit neatly into his palm.

"Yeah. The Mother Goddess led me right to it." Gusty wasn't sure why he said that. Maybe just to see the Crane's reaction.

The burglar's face showed surprise, then wary acceptance. "All right."

Gusty started off toward Matyu Gloria. The Crane followed in his wake.

"So," said the Crane. "Do you want me to hide it somewhere for you?"

"Hide it? You mean the scroll?"

"Yeah."

Gusty glanced over his shoulder. "I don't want you even *touching* the scroll."

"All right, all right. Tisha said you had a plan. I just want to know if you need any help."

Gusty grunted. He didn't need help.

After about fifteen paces, the Crane said, "Look, the reason I ask is that I'm worried about what might happen to you when you tell the Queenies we're keeping the scroll."

"*You* aren't keeping anything, Crane. Got that?"

"Yeah, I got it. But those Rock guys look pretty mean. What's your plan if they jump you?"

"They aren't gonna jump me."

"I don't know, Gusty. I think they'll do whatever the ambassador says. And once she finds out you want to keep the scroll—"

"Who says I want to keep the scroll?"

"Well, Tisha said—"

Gusty stopped, turned, dropped his club, and grabbed the little man by the arm.

The Crane winced.

"Go on," said Gusty. "What did Tisha say?"

"She said you wouldn't let the Queenies open it," the Crane said, wide-eyed. "Because— because you knew it was wrong."

"I see," said Gusty. "Tisha said it was wrong."

"Ah … yeah."

The Crane's voice was shaky. Gusty let go of his skinny blue arm in disgust.

"Did it ever occur to you that maybe *Tisha* could be wrong?"

"Ah …"

"You blues think that Justice made you infallible," Gusty said. "Everything you do is automatically good. Even a viper like Fanjei thinks his despicable bigotry is justified. Just because he's blue."

Gusty waved the scroll case in the blue man's face. "So now you're gonna tell me what to do with this? You *stole* the other one from the library. People have been *murdered* because of what you did. And now you're gonna tell me what to do with *my* people's scroll because you're blue."

"But Tisha—"

Gusty raised his hand. The Crane flinched.

"Tisha is just an urbie like me," Gusty said, lowering his

hand. "She doesn't know what's right. She'll want a judge to decide who owns it. And what color will the judge be?"

The Crane stared at Gusty, unblinking.

"What color?" Gusty insisted.

"Blue?"

"That's right, Crane. The judge will be blue. And we'll get blue justice. Just like Fanjei got once we'd found out he was the one who hired you. Now maybe blue justice works for crimes against blue people, but when the crime is committed against all the Children of the Sun, blue justice is no justice at all."

The Crane bit his lip.

"So I don't think I'm gonna let you tell me the right thing to do," Gusty said. "I don't think I'm gonna listen to you, or Tisha, or any other blue. Maybe I don't know the right thing to do, but I do know who owns this scroll. This scroll belongs to the Mother Goddess. And the only person around here who knows what's right is Matyu Gloria."

* * *

Matyu Gloria stood underneath a longneedle pine waiting for Gusty Longbread. She kept her face serene, but inside, she was so agitated that she could barely maintain her scent. Mosquitoes were getting close enough to buzz in her ears.

"They have been gone some time," said Clever Rock, waving mosquitoes from his face.

Gloria was glad she was not the only agitated person here.

Pious turned his head sharply. "They are coming back now."

Gloria caught the sounds of Gusty Longbread crashing deliberately through the jungle. His helmeted head came into view.

"What does he have?" asked Pious.

Sunlight flashed on gold, and Gloria knew that Gusty Longbread held the Sun Scroll.

Divine love warmed her lungs, and her soul filled with joy. Gusty had found the sacred scroll, and he was bringing it to her.

The native guide skulked along behind. He glanced at Gloria with doubtful eyes, then looked away.

Gusty met Gloria's gaze and did not look away. As he approached, Pious and Clever stepped aside.

Gusty stopped in front of her and passed the wooden case into her hand. Matyu Gloria's fingers closed around the Sun Scroll.

She had known this moment would come. The Mother Goddess had promised her that Gusty would do the right thing.

* * *

Flora brought Tisha a crock of drinking water, a dipper, and a cup. Tisha thanked her, although she had asked for a *pitcher*.

She didn't want water. She wanted a heavy stone pitcher to lift. The crock was too heavy and the dipper too light. But she didn't say anything to Flora. The woman thought Tisha's bones were made of egg shell.

After Flora left, Tisha walked to a lamp nook and picked up the oil lamp. It wasn't lit—the room was bright in the mornings. She wrapped her fingers around the bowl of the lamp and hefted it with her injured arm.

Yeah. She could hold it. Could she do any wrist curls, or would that spill the oil?

Flora was talking to someone in the hallway. Some sort of disagreement. "Didn't you hear me? Tisha is to be relieved of duty for two weeks."

Someone was coming. Tisha pushed the lamp back into the nook. The oil sloshed and a little bit dripped over the side.

Someone else would have to clean it up. Tisha returned to her cot and adopted an innocent pose—the sort of pose that wouldn't fool her for one eyeblink if a suspect were sitting that way.

Gusty entered the room carrying her armor.

He stopped when he saw her. "What are you pretending you didn't do?"

"Nothing," Tisha said. "Hey, is that my armor?"

Flora entered the room, followed by Bendoko.

"I thought you guys had left already," Tisha said.

"We're back," Gusty said. "Put this on. I don't want to carry it all the way to Sliceharbor."

Flora shook her head. "She's not putting anything on unless I say she can."

"I won't strain myself," Tisha said, standing up to take her armor.

Flora rolled her huge yellow eyes. "That's what patients always say."

"The armor of the Urban Cohort is surprisingly light," Tisha said, holding up her cane skirt. "At least for blues. We have to chase criminals through water, so we can't wear armor that would drag us down."

"Like an iron helmet?" Flora asked.

"We toss our helmets before we dive in," Tisha said.

"I don't want you lifting it," Flora said.

"One hand only," Tisha said, waving her sword arm.

"You'll forget," Flora said.

"What if Gusty helps me?" Tisha asked.

"I won't let her use the injured arm," Gusty promised.

Try to stop me, Tisha thought.

The healer sighed. "I need to go write a message to your captain. Please don't leave without it."

"I won't," Tisha said. "Thank you for everything you've done."

The orange woman grunted a grunt worthy of Gusty and glided out of the room.

"So what's the scuttlebutt?" Tisha asked. "Why are we leaving?"

Gusty shrugged. "We found it."

Tisha was surprised. "You found *it?*"

Bendoko said, "Gusty found it."

"That's great!" Tisha said. She looked up at Gusty. "You found it in the water, or ...?"

Gusty scratched his chin and looked away. "It was in an alligator nest. Bendoko helped, too. We'll tell you the whole story on the road."

Gusty looked uncomfortable. Bendoko looked miserable.

"So, I guess everyone's pretty happy?" Tisha asked.

Gusty grunted.

Bendoko said, "Some people are happy." He looked up at

Gusty. "I'm gonna tell her if you don't."

"Tell me what?" Tisha asked. "Gus?"

"Nothing to tell," Gusty mumbled.

Bendoko said, "He gave the scroll to the Queenies."

What did that mean? Gusty wouldn't meet her eyes.

She said, "We don't have much leverage here, Ben. We can't really press a claim to it until we get back to Sliceharbor."

"The Queenies will ship out before you can make any claims," Bendoko said.

"Ben, it's all right," Tisha said. "Gusty has a plan."

Gusty rolled his eyes. "Matyu Gloria wants to leave right away," he said. "I'll meet you outside."

Gusty left.

Bendoko watched him go, then turned back to Tisha. "I'm telling you, he's not gonna take it back from them. He told me blue justice can't be trusted and only the ambassador knows what's right."

"He said that?"

"Yeah."

That didn't sound like Gusty. As an urbie, Gusty knew that everyone in Sliceharbor was treated equally. There was no "blue justice" different from "orange justice". It was one law for everyone.

Except Senator Fanjei.

"All right," Tisha said. "I'll talk to him. Maybe I can find out what's on his mind."

* * *

They returned on the Moko River Road. Gusty Longbread could tell that Tisha wanted to talk to him, but he didn't give her the chance to have a moment out of earshot of the others.

Bendoko helped—though he probably wasn't intending to—by tramping along right beside them the whole way. Apparently he was done pretending to be a scout.

Whenever the road went close to the Moko River, Bendoko watched the undergrowth, like he was afraid an alligator would jump out of the river and eat them. Whenever they stopped for a break, Bendoko watched Matyu Gloria's travel chest.

These breaks were brief—Matyu Gloria was in a hurry—and the chest was never unguarded. In fact, whenever the Rock brothers set the litter down, one of them sat right on the chest. Not even Bendoko the Crane was going to be able to steal the Sun Scroll this time.

* * *

In the mossy alley behind the warehouse, Sunny Too-Tall ripped off the boards that were nailed across the back door. Mama Grace wished he didn't have to be so loud.

Tiny Too-Tall opened the door and led the way in. Feeble light from the alley reached only a few paces into the dark, cavernous warehouse. The stacked crates were visible only as shadowy forms.

"I'll get a lamp," Tiny murmured.

Mama Grace waited by the door, listening to Sunny breathe.

An oil lamp sparked to life at the other end of the warehouse, and Tiny Too-Tall returned, bringing its glowing warmth with him.

"What do you think?" he asked, gesturing expansively.

Mama Grace shrugged. "It's big enough," she said. No more crowding around the dining table.

"They won't find us here," Tiny said. Mama Grace noticed that her people were *us* to him, now, not *you*. "And if anyone tries to follow one of our people into the alley ..."

He looked at Sunny.

Sunny smacked his hands together.

"Yeah," said Tiny. "That's what'll happen."

"All right," said Mama Grace. "You were right. This is a good place for our meetings."

"I've been meaning to talk to you about that," said Tiny, taking her by the arm. "I've got some ideas for turning our meetings into doings."

Two days ago, Mama Grace had been trying to keep people calm, like Aura Wisebrow had asked her to do. Last night, a helpless young girl had been threatened by an armed sailor in order to goad Mama Grace's people into breaking the law. Now a half dozen of them were in a ship's brig, and the greenscarves were stopping every orange person in Lowtown for "questioning".

She found herself listening to what Tiny had to say.

* * *

Gusty Longbread thought they were making good time on the Moko River Road, but it was clear that they wouldn't reach Sliceharbor before sunset. Gloria Sunrise didn't want to enter the city after dark, so they stopped in a village for the night.

The inn was run by blues. It had accommodations for people of both sizes, and the innkeepers didn't care who slept where. But Matyu Gloria cared, and she was paying, so Gusty and Tisha were in different rooms.

This suited Gusty fine. He had to share his room with Bendoko, but the Crane wasn't going to give him any lectures on his duties to Sliceharbor, Senator Aura, and the Urban Cohort. Bendoko just wanted to indulge his own anxieties.

He asked, "You think they caught the Too-Tall brothers yet?"

"I don't know," Gusty said. "Stormy Colorpot and Woto will be watching out for them if they try to show up at the docks."

"Right," said Bendoko. "Right. I hope they caught them."

Gusty grunted.

"What about that senator? Do you think they might catch him with the Sun Scroll?"

"Not a chance," Gusty said.

"You sure?"

"Pretty sure. Senator Aura said they searched his suite thoroughly."

"He has a suite?"

"Yeah. In the Senatorial Palace. They all do."

"Oh," said Bendoko. "That explains how he got to the library so easily. I bet his suite is right next door."

"No," said Gusty. "The suites are in the other wing."

"But his is closest to the library, right?"

"No. He's one door down."

"Window on the front side of the building or the garden side?"

"Garden side." Gusty remembered sketching it out with Aura Wisebrow. "But why does it matter, Crane?"

"Oh, just making sure it was him, you know. Wanted to be sure he could get to the library from there."

Gusty wasn't buying it. "You wanted to break into his suite and look for the Sun Scroll."

The Crane shrugged.

"It's a nice thought," Gusty said. "But the scroll's not there. It's on his ship in the harbor, probably guarded by dozens of greenscarves. We aren't going to get it back."

"All right," Bendoko said.

Gusty thought, *First he steals the Sun Scroll and now he wants to steal it back. Tisha's right: Sometimes the Crane is almost honest.*

* * *

That night, two messengers left the inn.

The first messenger was Pious Rock. He stayed on the roads, walked through the moonlit streets of Sliceharbor, and arrived at the docks with a message for the captain of the ambassador's ship: *Be prepared to leave at sunrise.*

The second messenger was a sailor in the Republican Navy disguised as a cotton merchant. She also went to the Sliceharbor docks, and her message was for Captain Tu: *The ambassador's party is returning on the Moko River Road.*

10 Yellowmonth

"TISHA? TISHA?"

The Crane's voice sliced through Tisha's sleep like an iron saw through a sheet of copper.

What was he doing here? This was supposed to be her own private room.

"Tisha, you better get up," he pleaded. "The Queenies are leaving with us or without us."

Tisha checked her breastband to be sure she was decently covered. Then she sat up.

Bendoko's skinny outline stood in the doorway to the lamplit hallway.

"Dammit, Crane, couldn't you knock?"

"I did knock. You didn't answer."

Tisha shook her head. It felt like it was full of sand.

"What if I'd been sleeping naked?" she asked.

"Who sleeps naked in an inn?"

"Hmf," she said, stumbling toward her armor. She found it by feel. The room was dark.

"You sure it's morning?" she asked.

"I'll tell Gusty you're coming," he said. "Maybe he can convince the Queenies to wait for you."

Tisha put on her uniform, the ache in her arm reminding her to be careful lifting the helmet. She'd be glad to return to Sliceharbor. With luck, she could be home in time for breakfast, and then she could go back to sleep.

But as she tightened her weapons belt, she remembered what she'd overheard the ambassador say to Pious Rock last night: *Tell the captain to be prepared to leave at sunrise.*

That didn't give Tisha time to tell anyone that the Queenies had the Sun Scroll. And that was probably why the ambassador was in such a hurry.

Tisha nearly ran out of the inn.

Good. They hadn't left yet.

Pious was sitting on the ambassador's travel chest. Clever was standing beside the ambassador. Bendoko was standing alone, slapping at mosquitoes and shuffling his feet in the dust of the road.

Gusty raised his eyebrows at her. "You're looking lively this morning."

Tisha looked sunward. Sliceharbor was just a brown smudge on a pink horizon.

"This isn't morning," Tisha said. "This is bedtime."

Gusty grunted in agreement.

The ambassador's assistant came out of the inn.

The ambassador breathed the word, "Finally." Then in a more audible voice, she said, "Let us go."

They set off toward Sliceharbor.

Tisha waited until they had spread themselves out before she murmured, "Gusty, we need to talk."

"You're not getting Flora's message," Gusty said. "I'm delivering it to Captain Kosho, as promised."

"Really?"

"Really."

That wasn't fair. Her arm was getting better. And she didn't *need* two arms to be an urbie. She just needed the authority that came with the uniform.

But that wasn't what they needed to talk about.

"Gus, we need to talk about the Sun Scroll," she said.

"We can talk about it all you want as soon as Matyu Gloria is on her ship," Gusty said.

"Gus, we can't let her take it."

Gusty grunted.

Bendoko had fallen back to walk beside them. He watched them nervously. Tisha would have preferred more privacy, but she was out of time.

"What are you gonna tell Senator Aura?" she asked.

That made his shoulders tighten. He didn't like the idea of confronting Aura.

"I'll tell her the truth," he said. "I gave the Sun Scroll to Matyu Gloria."

"But Aura asked you to get the scroll for Sliceharbor."

"Yeah," said Gusty. "She'll be mad."

She could tell that Senator Aura intimidated him. But he would go through with his plan anyway. Gusty couldn't be deterred by fear.

"Mother will understand," he murmured.

"Yeah?" Tisha said. "I don't know, Gus. I thought your mother was awfully keen on Senator Aura."

"Tisha," he said, "*every* mother in Sliceharbor will understand. They all want to do something to help the Queenies. Because mothers are losing their sons over there."

He looked down into her eyes. "Everyone *wants* to do something, but I was the one who had the chance to actually *do* it. So I *had* to give it to her. Do you see?"

He was begging her to understand.

"So you believe it's all right to let them open it?"

"Tisha, *I* don't know. That question is too big for me, all right? All I know is that I did what I had to do—for all those people who wish that *they* were the ones who could do something to help."

He did what he had to do. And if Tisha managed to convince him that it was the wrong thing, then he'd still have to let the ambassador keep it, or he'd be letting down all the oranges in Sliceharbor. Tisha realized that all she could do was make him regret his decision.

She didn't want to make her friend suffer. She wanted him to do what was right, of course, but *she* didn't really know what was right. She just wanted to hand the decision over to someone else, like the Senate, or judges. But Gusty had shown the courage to make the judgment himself.

Tisha had to admire that.

And maybe she thought he was wrong. But maybe she just weighed things differently because she was blue.

Tisha made a judgment of her own: "All right, Gus. We'll do this your way."

Bendoko looked at her sharply. "I thought you told me his way is wrong."

"I'm not saying *I* think it's right," Tisha said. "But maybe Children of the Sun are better qualified to make this judgment than we are."

Gusty laid a gentle hand on her shoulder and said, "Thank you, friend."

* * *

Gusty Longbread hadn't realized that he had been carrying a burden, but now that it was gone, his chest felt lighter. Maybe Tisha didn't understand him, but she accepted him. She would support him. And she respected him.

That meant they could trust each other again.

As the sun rose, the sky above Sliceharbor turned golden. Gulls soared above the fields on the outskirts, calling songs of the sea. The city lost its smudginess as they drew nearer, and the thatch-roofed buildings sharpened into focus.

Gusty's sandals crunched along the road. The dirt didn't feel right. It should be soft, not crunchy.

"It hasn't rained since we left," he observed.

"Yeah," Tisha said.

"There's always trouble when the nights stay hot," Bendoko said.

Gusty had thought only urbies noticed that hot weather made people violent. But of course, Bendoko walked the same streets they did.

"Lucky thing for you that you get two weeks off," Bendoko said to Tisha.

She looked up at Gusty. "Are you *really* gonna give that message to the captain?"

"I promised Flora I would." He had the message rolled up and tucked inside his breastplate.

"Aw, Gus, I don't want to take two weeks off."

Gusty grunted. He didn't want to spend two weeks patrolling with some rookie. Or worse: Captain Kosho could make him do clerk duty until his partner came back. After two weeks of reading and writing, Gusty would be the one who needed time off.

"There's something that's been bothering me," Bendoko said. "It's about where I found Tisha's alligator knife."

"Don't worry about it," Tisha said. "It's all right."

"No, listen," Bendoko said. "Something doesn't make sense. I found your knife by the rubble, but I found you by the alligator."

"I know," said Tisha. "But it's all right. Gusty explained it to me."

"Explained what?" Bendoko asked.

"Ben," Tisha said, "we know you were the one who killed the gator."

"No I didn't."

"It's all right," Tisha said.

"No it isn't," Bendoko said. "I didn't kill any alligator."

His voice was convincing. Was the Crane really that good a liar?

Gusty wondered if there was another explanation. But who else could have killed the alligator?

"Wish you'd mentioned this before," he said.

"Are you sure it wasn't you?" Tisha asked.

"You're the one who got knocked out," Bendoko said. "If I'd killed an alligator, I'm sure I'd remember."

"But it wasn't me," Tisha said. "Because I lost the knife before the alligator knocked me unconscious."

"Yeah, I know," Bendoko said. "So what if it was someone else?"

"Who?" Tisha asked.

"I don't know," Bendoko said. "But remember walking up the trail that first day? It felt like we were being watched."

And Gusty remembered that Matyu Iris had complained of smelling swamp mud in a place where it didn't belong.

"So what are you saying?" Tisha asked.

"What if there was a spy in the water with us?"

A spy? Gusty remembered one of the inn's guests leaving after dark.

He scanned the road ahead. They were passing through a palmetto farm—knee-high palm trees producing fronds for thatch. Hiding a spy in there would be easy.

But how much could the spy know? They'd been cautious, hadn't they? Still, anyone who had seen Clever sitting on Matyu

Gloria's travel chest would know where to look, even if they didn't know what they were looking for.

"Keep moving," Gusty said. "I have to talk to Matyu Gloria."

He turned ... and stopped. Behind Matyu Gloria and Iris Daylight, a dozen greenscarves were creeping onto the road. Then a dozen more came from the palmettos ahead of Bendoko and Tisha.

Pious and Clever reacted without hesitation. They dropped the litter and knelt down. Each grabbed one pole of the litter and, with a quick jerking motion, snapped the pole free. Now each was armed with a staff.

So *that's* where they had hidden their weapons: in plain sight.

Matyu Gloria and Iris Daylight moved toward the litter. Bendoko retreated to the litter as well, hiding between the Rock brothers who stood at either end. Each brother was a one-man wall between a line of greenscarves and the Sun Scroll.

Tisha and Gusty were caught between Clever Rock and the sailors ahead. They were on the wrong side of the wall.

Gusty hefted his club, though he didn't think it would do much good against a dozen rapiers. The only one who could get them out of this was Tisha.

"Are you sailors or bandits?" she asked.

That was no way to calm things down. Gusty had forgotten how much Tisha disliked greenscarves.

A sailor in a blue turban and a blue sari stepped forward. "I am Captain Tu of the Republican Navy," he said.

"Why are you attacking us?" Tisha demanded.

"We are not attacking. My sailors have orders to only defend themselves."

"From what?"

"I beg your pardon," said Captain Tu. "But the three men with you do seem somewhat hostile."

"Captain Tu," Tisha said, "would you be hostile if another ship came alongside yours and caught it with grappling hooks? The same principle applies on land."

"Forgive my excessive display of force," Captain Tu said. "But I wanted the ambassador's attention."

"You have it!" Matyu Gloria said. She strode past Clever Rock and came forward. Half a step behind, Iris Daylight followed, leaving Bendoko to cower alone behind Clever and his staff.

Gusty let the women by. They took a stand beside Tisha.

"I represent the Reconciled Queendom," Matyu Gloria said. "Is this a declaration of war?"

"Of course not," Captain Tu said. "I merely need to detain you for a moment."

"On what grounds?" Tisha asked.

Iris Daylight's shoulders stiffened. She thought Tisha was talking out of turn.

"We are looking for property stolen from the Republic," Captain Tu said.

"We have *stolen* nothing," Matyu Gloria said.

"I am relieved to hear it," Captain Tu said. "Taking an ambassador into custody would be most embarrassing for everyone. If you would be so kind as to let us verify your assertion, we will be pleased to send you on your way as quickly as we can."

"You have no jurisdiction here," Tisha said.

"I believe, if you will review the law, you will find that the Navy has broad jurisdiction in matters of state. You and he are with the Urban Cohort?" He looked at Gusty.

"Yes," Tisha said.

"I would be pleased to have the Urban Cohort aid us in our search. That would assure the people of Sliceharbor that there has been no foul play or tampering with evidence."

No one said anything.

What could they do? Gusty had his club ready, but he wasn't going to charge those greenscarves. For one thing, they would impale him. For another, he wasn't a killer.

Oh, he was a soldier. He'd follow orders from Captain Kosho. But he wasn't going to bludgeon men and women from his own navy. At least, not unless Tisha's life depended on it.

Pious and Clever Rock, now, would do whatever Matyu Gloria told them to do. That could get a lot of people killed, and they still wouldn't get to keep the Sun Scroll because they would be among the dead.

"Matyu Gloria," Gusty said, "I don't think you have the numbers to win this fight."

She didn't look at him. She just stared at Captain Tu.

Then her shoulders sagged and she shook her head. "Why are the numbers always against us?" she asked. "Very well, Captain Tu. You have permission for your search."

"Thank you, Ambassador." He looked up at Gusty. "Would you assist me?"

Gusty shrugged. Now he knew the sick feeling that criminals felt in their stomachs when he caught them.

He and Captain Tu walked back toward Clever Rock.

"I would like to start with your travel chests," Captain Tu said over his shoulder.

Matyu Gloria nodded to Clever Rock. He lowered his staff and stepped aside.

Captain Tu pointed to Matyu Gloria's travel chest. "Start with that one, please."

Gusty knelt beside it. Pious Rock glanced at him, then returned his attention to the line of sailors that blocked off their escape.

"Open it, please," Captain Tu said.

Gusty opened it. Right there, on the very top, was …

Well, it was Matyu Gloria's green mongzhi.

"Remove the clothing, please."

Gusty thought he had seen her put the Sun Scroll on top, but of course she would have hidden it under her clothes. And her jewelry. And her cosmetics.

Gusty was nearly to the bottom of the travel chest when he realized that Bendoko was nowhere to be seen.

* * *

Bendoko the Crane walked through the streets of Sliceharbor with the sacred Sun Scroll inside his shopping bag, bouncing against his back. It felt good to have paving stones under his feet again. The stones were hot, of course. But that kept the mosquitoes asleep. It felt good to be home, even if the streets were dusty and the roofs were smelling dry.

The houses of the Pinetown District were so hot he could smell the pitch cooking in their wooden beams. The moss on the houses' walls was turning brown—even on the shady side.

It would come back. Moss always comes back.

Like Bendoko. Here he was in his old neighborhood.

He walked along the Pinetown Canal until he found the canal muckers. They were chest-deep in water and even *they* looked too hot.

He called, "Hey Jambi!"

One of the muckers looked up and gave him that beautiful grin. Bendoko loved it when his brother smiled at him.

"Ben!" Jambi turned to his boss and asked something.

His boss muttered something.

Jambi swam to the edge, and Bendoko helped him out.

"Ben, good to see you! I thought—" His voice quieted. "I was worried."

"I was worried about you, too," Bendoko admitted. "Did you see that orange guy again?"

"No."

"Good. Did Puji?"

"I don't think so."

"All right. Good."

"Are they still after you?" Jambi asked.

"Probably," Bendoko said. "But you won't have to worry about me. I'll be safe for a while."

"Yeah?"

"Yeah," Bendoko said. "So if you hear something about me … Well, just tell Puji not to worry, all right?"

"All right."

"Thanks, Jambi."

"Sure, Ben."

"Well, have fun mucking."

"Yeah. Ben?"

"Yeah?"

"You going somewhere?"

"Yeah, Jambi. I'm going to do the right thing."

* * *

Tisha settled her helmet back on her head again—using both hands despite the warning look she got from Gusty, who was strapping on his breastplate.

The Queenies didn't have to take anything off because their clothing was too skimpy to hide a scroll in, although Captain Tu had scrutinized each of them suspiciously.

Tisha picked up her weapons belt. They couldn't confiscate it unless they wanted to take her into custody, and now that Bendoko had disappeared with the Sun Scroll, Captain Tu clearly had no grounds to arrest them.

That Bendoko! Such a clever man. They would have a good laugh when he brought the scroll back.

Tisha buckled on her weapons belt. There: she was dressed again. She strode forward and interrupted the argument between the greenscarves and the ambassador.

"Stop," Tisha said.

They looked at her.

"Captain Tu," Tisha said, "we are leaving now."

"I fear that I really must insist—"

"No, Captain Tu. The ambassador and her assistant have dumped out their belongings for you to see. My partner and I have stripped down to our swimming clothes. We don't know what you are looking for, but we have proven that we don't have it."

"There is still the matter of your absent companion," Captain Tu said.

"There is no absent companion," Tisha said.

"My people saw—"

"*Two* people," Tisha said. "Two of your people *think* they might have seen a blue man with us when you sprang your ambush, but neither can say what he looked like, and neither can explain how he could have gotten past two dozen of the Republic's finest sailors."

Actually, that was easy to explain. In moving to block off the road, the sailors had left a path for Bendoko to sneak through the palmetto field. The sailors had all been looking at the big orange guys—the men they might have to fight. Tisha wasn't surprised that only two of them had noticed Bendoko jumping to hide behind her and Gusty.

"He was wearing a yellow sari," said one of the sailors.

"Then he should have been easy to spot," Tisha said. "But we didn't see him. Now, Captain Tu, you are out of time. We have complied with all your ridiculous requests. You have absolutely no grounds on which to detain us. We are leaving now. Either murder us or tell your people to step aside."

She looked up at Ambassador Gloria and her assistant. "Ladies? If you would follow me?"

Gloria looked over her shoulder. "Let us go," she said.

Warily, the porters slipped their poles into place on either side of the litter. They lifted their burden—somewhat tentatively, because the poles were no longer tied on.

Tisha strode forward, murmuring, "Step aside, please. Ambassador coming through."

The sailors looked uncertain. Tisha chose a gap between the two least certain, took one of them by the shoulder, and gently moved him out of the ambassador's way.

* * *

Matyu Gloria glanced over her shoulder. The little blue sailors were far behind now. Their captain had them searching among the palmettos.

"That was well done," Gloria said.

"Thank you," the native girl said. She looked worried.

"Are you and the native guide working for Senator Aura, or Senator Fanjei?"

The native girl looked up at her. "What?"

She seemed surprised, perhaps puzzled.

"You have successfully taken the Sun Scroll from me," Gloria said. "I want to know what your plans are."

Gusty Longbread looked from Gloria to the native girl. He was incredulous. So: if there had been a plot to steal the scroll, Gusty had not been part of it. Good.

"I didn't take the scroll," the native girl said. "Bendoko did."

"So you deny that the two of you are working together?"

"I was as surprised as you were."

Matyu Iris said, "I believe all three of you were conspiring."

Gloria's bodyguards exchanged wary glances. She calmed them with a gesture.

"Gusty Longbread," she asked, "was this inspection part of Aura Wisebrow's plan?"

He shook his head. "Those were sailors in the Republican Navy," he said. "Fanjei's men."

"Is it possible that the natives were working with Fanjei?" she asked.

Gusty looked at the native girl.

She returned a look of horror and disbelief.

"Tisha wouldn't," Gusty said.

"What about the one who took the scroll?"

Reluctantly, Gusty said, "Well, he has worked with Fanjei before."

"Gus, no!" The little native was distraught. "Ben wouldn't. He just *wouldn't.*"

Gloria was beginning to believe that this little woman had not been party to the theft. She was dangerously manipulative, but she was not deceptive. Her indignation at being stopped on the road had not been feigned.

"He wanted to get his hands on that scroll," Gusty said. "But I think Tisha's right. He wasn't working for Fanjei. Otherwise, he wouldn't have stolen it just when Fanjei's men were about to find it."

"He might have done so if he and this Captain Tu were rivals," Gloria said. "Perhaps they are competing to impress Senator Fanjei."

Gusty grunted.

"You doubt me?" she asked.

"I don't think it's likely," Gusty said.

"Then what *is* likely, Gusty Longbread?"

"I'm not sure, yet."

"Then let me put it this way," Gloria said. "Have we lost this scroll, too, or can you get this one back before it's too late?"

Gusty considered this. "I think I can get it back," he decided. "With Tisha's help."

* * *

As Tisha and Gusty hurried through the city, Bendoko the Crane was hiding in the gardens behind the Senatorial Palace. A groundskeeper was hauling water for the magnolias—not surprising given that it hadn't rained in the last four days.

Bendoko waited him out. The peach trees were shady, and he was feeling patient. He would do the right thing, but he was in no hurry.

The water cart was a big barrel on wheels. Once the barrel was empty, the gardener started pushing the cart back toward the canal. It was downhill with the empty barrel and then uphill with the full barrel. Bendoko didn't think that was fair, but that was the sort of injustice you had to put up with if you worked an honest living.

Bendoko was glad he'd been given the opportunity to pursue a career in crime. The judges might force him to give it up now—once he did the right thing—but he'd always have the memories. Even if they exiled him to a prison island and he died from forced labor, he'd still be able to tell everyone in the afterlife that he was the one who had stolen the Sun Scroll twice.

The gardener was gone. Bendoko couldn't hear the cart wheels anymore. It was time to go.

He crossed the garden quickly, but not furtively. If anyone glanced out a window, he wanted to look like he belonged there.

He reached the palace wall without hearing anyone call a challenge. Now he could be seen only by people who stuck their heads out a window, and no one did that during mosquito season because the windows were covered by gauze.

The limestone was well ornamented: A relief of stylized vines ran up the side of the building, and these provided Bendoko with solid handholds—and toeholds. That was the secret to climbing: strong toes. He reached the roof as easily as he had eight days ago.

The roof was hot and barren. Not even the lizards wanted to be out in this heat. The dry thatch crackled as Bendoko climbed carefully up the whole-stalk batten-weave. He hoped the senators would be too busy talking to notice the noise. Senators did a lot of talking, right?

If Gusty's information was accurate, Bendoko was now directly above Senator Fanjei's suite. He glanced over his shoulder at the gardens. He was in a good spot, not visible from where the gardener had been working.

Bendoko unwove the palms from the cane battens, trying to

make no more noise than a mouse eating the thatch. He hoped no one was directly below.

He set the battens aside and peered into the hole. The room below was dark—which probably meant it was empty. There was no hurricane roof underneath this thatch. It was just roof poles and then a twelve-foot drop.

Bendoko climbed in. He covered the hole as best he could. No need for him to give himself away with a bright patch of sunlight in the windowless room.

Standing among the supports, Bendoko tied his climbing line to one of the frame poles. He lowered himself down to the ceiling gauze, parted a hole, and descended to the cool stone floor. As his eyes adjusted, he saw he was in a small bedroom. The door was open to let in fresh air. Light from the window of the adjacent room provided dim illumination.

Bendoko tied a fist-knot to weight the end of his climbing line. With a sigh, he tossed it back up through the hole in the gauze. It wrapped around two cross-beams and fell back down, coming to rest on the gauze. It would not be easily seen up there in the shadows. It would not be immediately obvious how he had gotten in.

Of course, he couldn't reach the rope anymore, but that was all right. This time, Bendoko didn't need to get back out.

* * *

Once Tisha was sure they had left the Queenies behind, she asked Gusty, "So where are we going?"

"The Senatorial Palace," he said, not slowing down. His strides were difficult to match. Tisha was feeling a little sore from yesterday's walk.

"You think Bendoko is taking the scroll there?"

"Yeah. Last night he was asking me how to find Fanjei's suite."

Acid sloshed in Tisha's gut. Bendoko couldn't be taking the scroll to Fanjei. Yeah, maybe he hadn't been at Breadbaker Bridge, but he'd heard about what had happened there. After that ... well, he just wouldn't. Would he?

"You think he was playing us, Gus? You think he was in league with Fanjei the whole time?"

She didn't want to believe it, but really, how well did she know him? She'd first spoken with him only a week ago.

Bendoko had weaseled an invitation to join the expedition. He'd helped Gusty find the Sun Scroll. He'd bided his time. And then when Fanjei's thugs gave him the distraction, he'd run off with the prize.

Bendoko the Crane was a thief. Tisha was an urbie. She'd been a fool for ever thinking he might be her friend. He'd been using her.

"No," Gusty said. "I don't think so."

"He tricked us, didn't he? Everything he said, everything he did—it was all just an act."

"I'm not sure."

"Give it to me straight, Gus. Just tell me I was a fool."

"Tisha, you aren't a fool," Gusty said.

"I thought he was my friend," Tisha said. "I thought that no-good, conniving canal-rat was my friend."

"Tisha," Gusty said, "if Fanjei wanted to plant a traitor in our expedition, how could he have contacted Bendoko?"

"A senator has lots of ways to contact people."

"But you didn't learn about the expedition until the night before," Gusty said. "And Bendoko was either with you or in your cellar the whole time."

"… Yeah, I guess you're right."

"So I don't think he's working with Fanjei."

"But you said he was asking about Fanjei's suite."

"Yeah. But I don't think he's giving the scroll to Fanjei. I think he's hiding it."

"I don't get it, Gus."

"He's hoping someone finds it when they search Fanjei's quarters."

"But Fanjei's quarters were searched the day the scroll was stolen," Tisha said. "No one is going to search them again."

"Yeah, well, maybe he hasn't thought that far ahead."

* * *

Fanjei left the Chamber with Senator Washirko. Two of his sailors fell into step behind them.

"Did you really mean what you said about the wine tariff?" Washirko asked as they headed back to their suites. "Or was that just Chamber talk?"

"I assure you," Fanjei said, "I meant every word. The voyage to the Moonaway Coast is a perilous undertaking. Our merchants must negotiate with duplicitous wine sellers in Dupho, then sail past the pirates of two seas. When they finally bring the wine to our glorious republic, they should be rewarded, not punished with a tariff that nearly doubles the price of their product."

"The tariff is less than half of what they charge," Washirko said.

"Yes," said Fanjei. "It is less than half, but it is less by only a small amount."

"You know we need the revenue," Washirko said.

"And if we drive all the wine merchants out of business, the tariff will bring in nothing," Fanjei said. "Don't think like a farmer. Think like a merchant."

"I thought you were a sailor," Washirko said.

Fanjei glanced at the sailors escorting him through the palace.

"I am," he said. "And a good sailor knows his duty is to protect others."

They turned down the hallway of the residence wing. The lamps were lit. The smoke pots were burning. Two sailors stood guard at the doorway of each suite.

Washirko asked, "Is it necessary to have so *much* protection?"

"I fear that it is," Fanjei said. "Their numbers are for their own safety as much as for ours. We both know what can happen to a lone sailor in this city."

The sailor who had made the initial arrest at the boarding house was technically still alive, but her soul had been knocked loose from her body. Healers had reduced the swelling inside her skull, but they feared her brain might be too damaged to allow her mind to return to her head.

"This isn't the docks," Washirko said. "This is the Senatorial Palace."

"Yes," said Fanjei. "And the guards are here to keep it from becoming like the docks."

In truth, Fanjei believed the guards on the outside steps were sufficient to defend the palace. The guards in the halls were to defend Fanjei. He feared what Aura would do when she found out he had arrested the ambassador from the Reconciled Queendom.

It was nearing noon. By now, his secretary doubtless had a report from Tu detailing the arrest. If Aura's secretary had also acquired the information, Fanjei could be expecting a visit immediately. He wanted to be safely behind his door.

"You may dismiss your own guards if you like," Fanjei said. His personnel were stretched thin. He turned to one of the guards that had been following him. "Pass these orders to all stations: If a senator indicates he or she does not wish to be guarded, that senator's guards are to resume regular duties."

"Yes, Admiral."

That left Fanjei with only one personal bodyguard, but he still had the two at his door. And the bodyguard with him was Termisho, a burly bosun. Fanjei believed he was safe. He didn't think Aura carried a weapon.

"If you'll excuse me, Senator Washirko, I have a few things to take care of before lunch."

"Of course," Washirko said, distracted by the sight of another colleague. "Ah, Senator Shigo! Do you have a moment to discuss my idea for funding harbor improvements?"

Fanjei left the senators to their discussion and opened the door of his suite.

"Termisho, could you wait outside a moment? I need to discuss something with my secretary in private."

Termisho touched three fingers to his ear and took a stance of attention beside the other two guards.

Fanjei went inside.

"Hesho?" he called, closing the door. "Any word from Captain Tu?"

"Who's Hesho?"

A skinny man in a yellow sari stepped out of Fanjei's study.

"Who are you?" Fanjei asked.

"Who am I?" the stranger asked raising his voice. "Don't play dumb with me, Fanjei! I'm the guy you sent to steal this!"

He reached inside the shopping bag he carried and withdrew a wooden cylinder. The end was marked with a golden sun.

Fanjei recognized him now.

"What are you doing here, and where did you get that?"

"I stole it from the library, just like you told me to."

The man tossed the scroll case. It flew end over end toward Fanjei. He was tossing the sacred Sun Scroll like a juggling stick!

Fanjei caught it. His heart filled with rage. In three strides he crossed the room.

"You will treat this scroll with respect!" he said. Though angry, he spoke very quietly.

"Where's my fifty imperials?" the impudent man demanded, not quietly.

"Keep your voice down!" Fanjei hissed.

But the man just shouted louder. "Where's my fifty imperials? You promised fifty up front and fifty on delivery. Well, here's the Sun Scroll. Where's my other fifty?"

The door opened.

Termisho asked, "Senator, is there a problem?"

"No!" Fanjei shouted. "Shut that door!"

"We're caught!" the skinny stranger yelled. "Fanjei, you stinking corpse of a bilge rat! You should have told me there were people in the hall!"

Senators Washirko and Shigo were looking in, trying to see past Termisho.

"Take it!" Fanjei said, thrusting the Sun Scroll at the thief.

But the man jumped back as though from a viper.

"I'm getting out of here," the thief said. He ran into Fanjei's study. But instead of going out through the window, he dashed into Fanjei's windowless bedroom.

The fool. He couldn't get out that way.

Washirko yelled, "Guards! Stop that man!"

Fanjei's three sailors rushed past him and followed the thief into Fanjei's bedroom.

"Don't stab me! Don't stab me!" the thief yelled. "I give up!"

Washirko and Shigo came into Fanjei's suite, followed by the sailors who had been at Washirko's door.

"Fanjei?" Washirko asked, looking at the scroll case in Fanjei's hands. "What is this all about?"

* * *

Senator Fanjei did not tell Senator Washirko what it was all about. Fanjei insisted that none of the burglar's story was true.

But Washirko knew what he had heard, and Fanjei *was* caught in possession of the Sun Scroll. The Senate convened a "hallway committee" and voted to start an investigation immediately.

Three judges were sent for—the same three who had overseen the search of the palace. While waiting for the judges, the Senate considered several problems:

Senator Fanjei was to be confined to his suite. But who would stand guard?

Termisho, the bosun assigned to be Fanjei's bodyguard, said his first loyalty was to justice. He offered to hand pick a squad of guards whom he could vouch for.

The senators had misgivings about this, but Senator Shigo pointed out that if Fanjei fled justice, he would lose his reputation, which was the source of all his wealth and power. This didn't mean that Fanjei would not try to flee; it just meant that such flight would be a self-punishing crime.

So Termisho's hand-picked squad was given guard duty, and the rest of the palace guards were sent back to their ships.

Senators Aura and Washirko suggested that the Urban Cohort be called in to provide moral reinforcement for those guards who felt conflicting loyalties. This was agreed upon, and Aura's secretary was sent to bring back the first urbies she could find.

Next, the Senate discussed what should be done with the other prisoner, Bendoko the Crane. No one trusted *him* to sit quietly in a suite and wait for justice. He had no reputation to lose.

The burglar was bound hand and foot and kept in the hallway until urbies could be found to take him to Cohort Headquarters. A sailor was dispatched to find more urbies.

Then Senator Shigo raised an important question: Was it possible for urbies to escort the burglar the length of the Palace Road without drawing a mob that would rip his limbs off?

The senators realized that the prisoner needed to be transported in utmost secrecy. Their solution was to spread word throughout the palace that no one was to discuss the afternoon's events until the judges gave permission.

The problem with spreading words is that they don't always get spread evenly. The palace servants understood that the Senate didn't want anyone to know Fanjei had been caught with the Sun Scroll, but some of the orange servants got the impression that they were being ordered to keep silent forever. They believed this was unjust. They decided to prevent this injustice.

A short time later, the situation was as follows:

Messengers from the Senatorial Palace were wandering through the city looking for judges and urbies. They had not been told to be discreet.

Servants from the Senatorial Palace were sneaking through the streets telling orange people that a blue senator had stolen the Sun Scroll and the Senate was conspiring to hush it up.

Most of the guards from the Senatorial Palace were reporting to their ships in harbor, leaving the entrances to the palace completely unguarded.

It was a hot afternoon in the hottest month of the year, and the people of Sliceharbor had gone nearly a week without rain.

* * *

As Gusty Longbread and Tisha neared the Palace District, they heard news that a sailor was looking for two urbies to escort a prisoner from the Senatorial Palace. Some people said the prisoner was a senator who had stolen the Sun Scroll. Others said he was a thief the senator had hired. Either way, it was clear that Bendoko had gotten himself caught.

Tisha asked, "Do you think he got caught on purpose?"

Gusty grunted. It was certainly possible.

"That's a crazy way to come clean," Tisha said.

"Yeah," Gusty said. "But it's just like Bendoko."

"Yeah, it is," Tisha said. "So what do we do?"

"About what?"

"Do we tell them it's not the same scroll? Or do we let them use it as evidence against Fanjei?"

You're the blue, he thought. *Why are you asking me?*

"Do you want to get Fanjei bad enough to lie about the evidence?" Gusty asked.

"Yeah, I do," she said.

"Me too."

"But we can't, Gus. We're urbies."

"Yeah," said Gusty. "I guess this is what the philosophers call a 'dilemma'."

It wouldn't work, he realized. Matyu Gloria knew where the scroll had come from, and she would have no reason to lie about it.

But maybe he could convince her to keep quiet until Fanjei's ship had been searched. Suddenly, there were many possible ways to make a case against Fanjei. And Gusty had the Crane to thank.

"There he is," Tisha said. Bendoko was being escorted along the Palace Road by Goochu and Choppy.

Choppy, the orange urbie, had been Captain Kosho's partner back in the old days, but he'd been teamed up with Goochu since Goochu's partner retired—which was before Gusty's time.

Goochu was behind Bendoko, holding on to Bendoko's manacled hands. Choppy walked beside them carrying his paddle-club. He had Bendoko's shopping bag slung over one shoulder.

Bendoko caught sight of Gusty and Tisha, then lowered his eyes without acknowledging them. Maybe he wanted to protect them, or maybe he thought admitting he knew them would discredit his story. Either way, Gusty decided to play along for now.

Tisha also picked up on the cue. Ignoring Bendoko, she said, "Hey guys. We heard something about arresting a senator."

"The senator is just confined to quarters," Choppy said. He managed to pack as much contempt into the word "senator" as Gusty felt.

"For now," Goochu said. "But they're bringing in judges to investigate."

Choppy and Goochu didn't break stride, and Gusty and Tisha fell into step with them.

"Mind if we tag along?" Tisha asked.

"Not at all," said Choppy in his rumbling voice. "We were told to keep quiet about the connection between this guy and Senator Fanjei, but the news is already in the rumor winds."

"Yeah," said Goochu. "I just hope we reach Headquarters before the winds blow through the Enclave."

They were walking briskly along the Palace Road, which is one of the longest, straightest roads in Sliceharbor. But in Sliceharbor, even the straightest roads curve a little. So they had to walk a good distance from the Main Canal before they could see the part of the road that went up the hill to Cohort Headquarters.

The road was not clear. It was occupied by a mob.

* * *

Mama Grace was shopping at the Dock Market when Splashy Brownbread brought the news to Lowtown.

Splashy was a gardener at the Senatorial Palace. He was supposed to be at work. But instead, he was here at the Dock Market talking to a pair of orange fishmongers.

As Mama Grace crossed the market to join them, she noticed that a blue vendor was packing up his citrus stand, even though the market still held plenty of customers. Across the way, a blue jeweler was doing the same.

"Mama Grace!" Splashy called as she approached. "Did you hear what happened at the palace?"

"What happened at the palace?" Mama Grace asked.

"They caught that Senator Fanjei with the Sun Scroll," said a fishmonger.

Splashy waved a hand at him like he was trying to shoo a fly. "But that's not the big news," he said. "The big news is that the senators asked the palace staff not to tell anyone."

"Why not?" asked Mama Grace.

"Because they want to keep lying about it," said a fishmonger.

"They can't hide him this time," said Splashy. "They found him holding the Sun Scroll. Senators saw him. Their secretaries saw him. Everyone in the palace knows it was him."

"The blues will find a way to get him out of it," said a fishmonger.

"Not if I can help it," Mama Grace said.

The three men shut their mouths and stared at her. Mama Grace knew she had their attention.

"Splashy, you go down and get our people off the docks. I'll go find Will and Airy."

"Where should we meet?" Splashy asked. "At the boarding house or at Tiny's warehouse?"

Not the warehouse. The Too-Tall brothers had brought too many of their criminal friends to the warehouse meeting last night. Mama Grace was afraid she couldn't control her people if they met in Tiny's territory again.

But not the boarding house, either. Tiny and Sunny were lying low there this afternoon. Let them lie.

"Tell them to come here, to the Dock Market," Mama Grace said. "But it's no meeting. We're marching on the palace."

* * *

As Mama Grace gathered her people in Lowtown, oranges from the Enclave were marching down the Palace Road.

Even at this distance, Gusty could tell they were a mob. The mongzhi-wearing orange men were carrying heavy chunks of wood, and it wasn't because they wanted to build something. They were ready to kill—or at least, *some* of them were ready to kill, and the others were caught in the current.

They were still far enough away that they looked like one thing—not a collection of angry individuals, but an orange mass of anger marching down the hill.

The old-timers, Choppy and Goochu, exchanged worried glances.

Tisha said, "I think maybe we're on the wrong road."

Bendoko looked up and winced.

"Let's go this way," Gusty said. He pointed down a side street.

Choppy and Goochu looked at each other and came to quick agreement.

Gusty was glad they let him take the lead. Blues would have

said the older men were wiser and should have been in charge. Oranges would have deferred to the woman. But these people were urbies first. They recognized that Gusty had a plan and they trusted him.

Gusty wished his plan were more detailed than "Let's run away from the mob."

He took them into the nearest alley. The moss was still green here. It probably never saw direct sunlight. Tisha came behind him, puffing the way she did whenever he made her move too fast.

Gusty poked his head out into the street on the other end of the alley. He recognized it as Persimmon Street. He hadn't realized the alley would lead him here.

They followed Persimmon Street until it met Plum. Gusty wasn't sure they should cross Plum. They might be seen from the Palace Road.

He almost asked Bendoko to climb up on a roof and tell him where the mob was, but then he remembered that he and Tisha were pretending that Bendoko was a criminal. Well, he *was* a criminal but—

It was complicated.

Gusty stepped onto Plum Street. He glanced toward the intersection where Plum met the Palace Road. No one was there except a blue man, staring toward the Hightown District.

The blue man turned hastily and took three steps down Plum. Then he saw Gusty and froze. He turned and ran off the other way.

"Cross the street quick!" Gusty said. "Don't let them see us."

Them. His own people were a *them.* But, no. Those weren't his people. His people were right here: Tisha and Choppy and Goochu. And Bendoko.

They took longer than Gusty would have liked. Goochu was trying to push Bendoko along instead of letting him run. Gusty was tempted to just let Bendoko go. Then they could all get out of this alive.

An orange man came out of a bakery on the corner. He scowled at Goochu and Bendoko. Then he heard the tramp of feet and stepped out onto the Palace Road to see what was making so much noise. He looked up the Palace Road, then he looked down Plum Street at Gusty.

Everyone was across Plum now. Gusty stayed back, waiting to see what the orange man from the bakery would do.

The orange man cupped his hands to his mouth and yelled up the street: "They're down here! They're taking the thief on Persimmon Street!"

Gusty's people hadn't gotten very far up Persimmon Street. He caught up to them.

"Into that alley!" he said.

Tisha led.

Bendoko looked up at him questioningly.

Goochu yanked Bendoko's manacles roughly and shoved him into the alley.

Choppy followed Goochu, and Gusty was in the rear.

Without Gusty to set the pace, Tisha was moving too slowly. Gusty tried to push the pace, but he just ended up pushing his way to the front.

The alley had a curve, so he couldn't see more than five paces ahead. No wonder Tisha had been moving slowly. What were they heading into?

Gusty lengthened his stride. Whatever he was leading them into, he wanted to be far enough ahead to give them warning.

As the alley bent around, a sunlit street came into view. It was still Persimmon Street. The alley had made a loop around a block of residences.

"Hurry!" Gusty growled.

About a dozen orange men came into view two blocks ahead. They saw Gusty—how could they miss his shiny copper finned helmet?—and came striding down.

The three blues popped out of the alley behind Gusty. The dozen men quickened their pace.

"Move!" Gusty said. "Back to Plum Street."

They ran. Choppy, despite his age, outdistanced the blues easily. The blues stayed together, and Bendoko couldn't run very fast with his hands manacled behind his back.

"I think you *want* them to get you," Goochu said. "Move! Move!"

He pushed, and Bendoko tumbled to the paving stones.

Bendoko rolled. Tisha helped him up, and they kept running.

At the intersection of Plum and Persimmon, Choppy pointed away from the Palace Road and shouted, "Hurry! This way!"

Choppy didn't wait for them.

Gusty and the three blues reached the intersection and followed Choppy. Behind them, the dozen that had pursued them down Persimmon rejoined the bulk of the mob that was coming from the Palace Road.

Tisha had taken over the prisoner now. Goochu was running to catch up to Choppy. Choppy turned up Cherry Pit Avenue.

They followed.

"Come on, come on!" Choppy called over his shoulder. He was still pulling away from them.

Tisha yanked Bendoko up short. "Stop, Crane."

Bendoko stopped, chest heaving with exertion and terror.

Tisha unbuckled the manacles. "Now run, Crane!"

They ran. Choppy ran around a corner. Goochu was still trying to catch him. Moving faster now, Bendoko and Tisha followed the other two urbies around the corner.

Gusty saw orange men ahead. He looked over his shoulder: The ones behind him were gaining ground.

Gusty turned the corner, leaving shouting men behind him on Cherry Pit Avenue.

Choppy was nearly a block away. He looked up the next street, shook his head, and kept running straight. Goochu was catching up to him.

Gusty reached the intersection with Bendoko and Tisha. He looked up the street and saw men running on a street that paralleled Choppy. A few men were coming down.

He looked down the street and saw men coming up. They shouted directions at each other.

Behind Gusty came the mob from Cherry Pit Avenue. They were shouting, "Kill the urbies! Kill the urbies!"

Gusty caught up to Tisha and asked, "Think you can talk your way out of this one?"

She shook her head and kept running.

Choppy and Goochu ducked into an alley. Bendoko and

Tisha followed them.

Gusty came around the corner and nearly ran into Bendoko.

"Lift me up," Bendoko said, pointing toward the sky.

"Hey, guys!" Tisha called. "Ben has an idea!"

But Choppy and Goochu didn't stay to listen. They kept running down the alley and disappeared around a corner.

Well, Gusty didn't have time to chase them down and discuss tactics. He grabbed Bendoko and hoisted him to the eaves.

Bendoko clambered onto the roof.

Gusty picked up Tisha.

Ben offered her a hand, and now they were both on the roof above the alley.

"Now you," Bendoko said, reaching down a hand.

"I can't climb!"

Tisha said, "Quit arguing and get up here, Gus."

The voices in the street were getting louder. Gusty tossed his paddle-club onto the roof. He jumped and grasped at the eaves. His fingers ripped the thatch.

Bendoko and Tisha each took one arm by the wrist and pulled. Gusty's feet kicked the wall of the alley. Ineffectually.

"You really *can't* climb," Bendoko said. "Hang on to him, Tisha."

Bendoko dropped into the alley.

"Stop kicking," he said.

Gusty stopped kicking.

Bendoko slipped his tiny shoulders under Gusty's sandals. Slender fingers took hold of Gusty's ankles.

Bendoko said, "One, two, nnnnnggh!"

Gusty swung an elbow onto the roof. He grabbed thatch and pulled. Tisha reached over the edge and hooked the back of his breastplate, pulling him up as Bendoko lifted from below.

Gusty got a knee on the roof. It broke through the thatch, but at least it gave him the purchase he needed to go up the rest of the way.

"There he is! Get him!"

Gusty looked over the edge. An orange man was coming up the alley waving a spade. Bendoko was running away.

* * *

Bendoko had done one or two jobs in this neighborhood, so he remembered this alley. That was an advantage. But what he remembered was that the walls were difficult to scale. They had no hand holds, the eaves had too much overhang, and the alley wasn't narrow enough for him to wedge himself upward between two walls.

He needed his climbing claws, which were in his shopping bag, which had been confiscated by that orange urbie with the blond beard.

So Bendoko didn't climb. He ran. And he considered praying to Big Zeemo, but to tell the truth, he was feeling a little rushed at the moment. Anyway, he didn't need Big Zeemo. He just needed his tools.

Heavy feet pounded behind him. Oranges were faster than blues. Known fact. They had longer strides.

Bendoko followed the alley's curve around a corner. Up ahead, someone was shouting, "They aren't down here! Check the next street!"

But Bendoko *was* "down here". He wasn't sure, but he thought the voice giving directions belonged to the orange urbie who was supposed to be taking him to jail.

Bendoko was in a blind curve. He could hear shouts. On the ground ahead was a long stick—an urbie's paddle-club, actually. And there was a helmet, breastplate, shin-guards—the complete equipment for an orange urbie.

A filthy cotton drawstring caught his eye. He shifted the breastplate. Underneath, he found his shopping bag. He reached inside, and the first thing he touched was one of his climbing claws.

Bendoko took out the claw and strapped it to his right sandal. He slung the shopping bag over one shoulder and took a step back. He put his left foot on the breastplate.

Bendoko leapt, catching the mossy wall with his claw and pushing himself up to the eaves.

An orange pursuer came snarling around the corner, waving a shovel.

Bendoko hooked an arm over the eaves and flashed a kick at the orange man's face. The sharp climbing claw made his enemy jump back.

But the orange man was not easily discouraged. He grinned and drew back the shovel, preparing a skull-crushing swing.

Someone grabbed Bendoko's arm and yanked him up onto the roof. It was that odious urbie who'd been jerking on his manacles.

Bendoko clambered up toward the ridge pole.

Behind him, the guy in the alley was cursing and whacking at the eaves, but he was no threat now. Not unless he grew wings … or another guy came along to give him a boost. Bendoko hastily retreated along the ridge pole toward the place where he had left Tisha and Gusty.

The odious urbie followed him. "You could at least say 'thank you'."

Bendoko looked over his shoulder—the shoulder on which he carried his shopping bag with his tools.

"Thank you," he said, adding silently, *Big Zeemo*.

* * *

The thatch was as hot as paving stones. Men were shouting in the streets below. Tisha feared that any moment someone would spot them on the roof. Well, not her, because she was lying flat, hidden from the streets. But Gusty's helmet was shining like a beacon.

Gusty was having problems. One of his legs had fallen through the thatch.

Behind her, a familiar voice said, "That's the problem with batten-free twin-panel."

It was Bendoko! He was crawling along the ridge pole.

"How did you get up here?" she asked.

Bendoko grinned. "It's what I do."

Goochu followed behind Bendoko, trying to act like he was in control. But unlike his prisoner, Goochu was not accustomed to crawling around on all fours.

"Where's Choppy?" Tisha asked.

"He couldn't climb up," Goochu said. "After he set me on the roof, he took off his armor and joined the mob."

Tisha wasn't sure what that meant.

"He's leading them away," Bendoko said. "We might be able to escape by heading back toward the Palace Road."

By this time, he had reached a point on the ridge pole above Gusty. He began descending.

"The trick is to keep your weight on the frame poles," Bendoko said.

"The trick is to stay off of rooftops," Gusty growled.

"This is batten-free twin-panel," Bendoko said. "It's an orange technique. This roof will support your weight if you move right."

Gusty grunted.

"Put your left hand there," Bendoko said, pointing. "Good. Now put your right hand on the other pole and lift your leg out."

Gusty pulled his leg out of the hole. If anyone was inside the house underneath, they were too scared to say anything.

"Now follow me," Bendoko said. "Gusty, keep your right knee on my pole and put your left knee on the other pole."

Bendoko started climbing back to the roof peak. Gusty followed.

Tisha climbed up, too. She couldn't see the frame pole she was climbing on, but she could feel its support under the thatch.

They all reached the ridge pole. It felt more solid under Tisha's hands. She could see that their roof was part of a complex block of buildings sharing common walls. There was no break in the thatch between the roof they were on and the roof that Bendoko took them to next. He was working his way back in the direction the mob had come from.

At the end of the block, Bendoko stood up.

"All right," he said. "We're in the clean current. But we gotta move now before those guys decide to check back where they last saw us."

Goochu spoke up: "Gusty, you're probably the only one who can get through the crowd. You'll go to Cohort Headquarters and tell them we aren't coming. Tisha and I will take the prisoner back to the Senatorial Palace and explain what happened."

"I'm not sure the Senatorial Palace will be safe, either," Gusty said.

"All right," Goochu said. "If things are too hot at the palace, Tisha and I will take the prisoner to ... where should we go, do you think?"

Gusty was frowning.

"I think you should be the one to take word to Headquarters," Tisha said.

Goochu protested, "But if it's surrounded by oranges—"

"Then Captain Kosho will already know there's trouble, and you won't have to carry the word."

"What about the prisoner?" Goochu asked.

"If things are too hot for us in the Palace District, Gusty and I will take him to my house."

"*Your* house?"

Tisha shrugged. "I can lock him in the cellar."

Goochu looked uncertain.

"Good plan," Gusty said. "Let's go, Crane."

Gusty dropped off the roof onto the street. He helped Bendoko down and strapped his manacles on him. Then he helped down Tisha and Goochu.

Goochu looked worried.

"After this is over, we'll all get together in a pool house and laugh about it," Tisha said.

Goochu nodded uncertainly.

Gusty said, "Just as long as it's not the pool house on Nailmaker Street."

* * *

Mama Grace found Willful Hammer among the orange men tearing up the pool house on Nailmaker Street. That didn't surprise her. What surprised her was that she found Airy Freshmilk there, too.

"Airy showed us how to bust the pump that primes the siphon," Will bragged. "No one will be swimming here for a while."

Because it was a working-class pool house, it didn't have much furniture to smash, so the men were already looking for something else to do. Mama Grace's idea of marching on the palace sounded good to them.

She led them toward the Dock Market, but when she reached the Market Road, she saw that others were already on their way to the palace. She hurried to catch up.

"Mama!" called a man at the back of the crowd. "Good to see you. We were afraid you weren't going to make it."

It was Tiny Too-Tall. His hulking brother walked beside him, pounding his fist into his palm.

"We heard you were organizing a little protest," Tiny said. "So we went and got some of our friends from the docks."

Mama Grace scanned the crowd. It was hard to recognize people by the backs of their heads. The street held far more people than had ever come to her meetings. And there weren't enough women in the group to keep the men under control.

"Who's leading these people?" she asked. "You?"

"Oh, no," said Tiny modestly. "I just helped them get organized."

"Nobody's leading," Sunny said with satisfaction. "It's a riot."

* * *

Tisha, Gusty, and Bendoko hurried away from the Palace Road, leaving Goochu to warn Cohort Headquarters if he could. As soon as they were out of sight of Goochu, Tisha unbuckled Bendoko's manacles.

"We'll tell Goochu that he jumped into the canal," she told Gusty. "You jumped in after him, but you couldn't catch him. Somehow he got out of his manacles."

Bendoko looked at her quizzically. "That made more sense when he said it."

"And we aren't at the canal yet," Gusty said.

"Close enough," Tisha said. "Crane, we owe you one. You're free to go."

"You owe me one?" Bendoko asked. "I started a riot."

"That's our problem," Tisha said. "You just go find a safe place to hide."

"I was hoping to get to jail," Bendoko said. "I couldn't find a safe place when it was just Sunny and Tiny looking for me. How can I hide from the entire Enclave?"

"They'll want Fanjei more," Gusty said. "At least the oranges in Lowtown will. You heard that speech he gave after the fire."

"You mean the one where he said oranges are prone to senseless violence?" Bendoko asked.

Gusty grunted.

Tisha remembered Breadbaker Bridge. "Our sensible violence isn't any better."

Bendoko said, "Come on, Tisha. You know all blues are honest, justice-loving, and virtuous."

"Yeah," said Gusty. "Anyway, some people want to rip Fanjei's virtuous arms off."

Tisha asked, "Is that why you're taking us toward the Palace District, Gus?"

"Go in from the Lowtown side," Bendoko suggested. "There's more places to hide there."

"You should go back to my place, Ben. Vernda and Sander will—"

"You know," Gusty said, "I think we should all stick together right now."

"Really?" Tisha asked.

"Yeah," Gusty said. "You and I do a good job of keeping order. But to get through the chaos, we might need Bendoko."

* * *

Aura Wisebrow's secretary reported that oranges from the Enclave were running through the streets of the Orchards and oranges from Lowtown were marching up the Market Road. She had found the three judges, but they had decided to stay indoors until the Urban Cohort could restore order.

"How bad is it?" Aura asked.

"It's quiet in some places," said her secretary. "In other places, I hear it's bad."

Aura passed the information on to her colleagues, many of whom had corroborating reports of marchers coming from the docks. It was decided to meet the marchers on the steps and address their concerns.

And so Senator Aura Wisebrow, representative of the orange citizens of Sliceharbor, found herself standing on the palace steps as a mob of her constituents flooded the area. And as she studied the faces in the mob, she saw very few angry women willing to state their demands and dozens of angry men carrying gaff hooks, paving mauls, and clubs made from busted furniture. They looked ready to kill someone.

A handful of urbies, orange and blue, stood at the bottom of the palace steps. Stormy Colorpot, the man she had appointed as their leader, turned and looked at her uncertainly.

Senator Aura raised her arms for silence.

The crowd ignored her. Twenty paces from the steps, they lifted their improvised weapons and broke into a run.

Aura didn't want to see people murdered.

"Save yourselves!" she yelled at the urbies. Then she turned to her colleagues and yelled, "Run!"

She led them through the palace doors and into the foyer. They were scared enough to keep up.

"Evacuate!" Aura shouted as she passed the clerks' offices.

She turned down a narrow corridor and ran out the door to the palace gardens. A glance over her shoulder told her that her colleagues were following. She dashed down the garden path.

Her aunt's house was nearby. She could hide her colleagues there.

She counted them as they came down the path. One. Two. Three.

Four was Washirko. He was still carrying the Sun Scroll. Good.

Five. Six. Seven.

Where was the eighth?

Oh. Fanjei and his guards were still inside.

* * *

Senator Fanjei, representative of the world's oldest port, admiral of the Republican Navy, wished he were not alone in his suite. He heard shouts in the garden outside his window. Scuffling sounds at the palace entrance were echoing through the halls.

Fanjei went to his door. The palace custodian had nailed a board across so he could not open it, but he could still make his voice heard.

"Termisho! What is going on out there?"

Termisho's muffled voice replied, "It is a riot, Senator. I suggest you barricade the door."

A riot? At the Senatorial Palace?

Fanjei crossed his receiving room to look out his window. The guards outside were gone. Three Children of the Sun with paving mauls were roaming through the garden.

Fanjei drew himself out of sight and pressed his back to the wall beside the window. Had they seen him? What could he use to block the window?

An unearthly roar resounded through the hallway outside his suite. Dozens—perhaps hundreds!—of running feet stomped the floor stones.

"Halt!" cried Termisho.

The feet grew louder.

Some thumps. Some groans. The sound of an Urban Cohort soldier's helmet hitting the wall.

Someone cried in pain.

The roaring continued down the hall. Running feet passed by Fanjei's door. These rioters weren't yelling. He could hear them breathing—heavy panting breaths from huge men capable of extreme violence.

Fanjei's own breaths were coming in short, quick gasps.

The stragglers jogged by Fanjei's door. No one called out a challenge.

A distant crash echoed down the hall.

Outside Fanjei's door a man moaned.

"Here's one," said a voice too deep to belong to a Child of Justice.

Feet shuffled toward Fanjei's door.

"Spare me," begged the moaning man.

"Ow!" he said.

"No, please!" he said.

"Ah!" he said.

His last cry was only a breathy rasp.

A regretful voice said, "I don't think that was right, Sunny. He asked you to spare him, not spear him."

"It's a rapier, Tiny. Not a spear."

"Whatever. Say, why do you think there's a board nailed across the door?"

Fanjei jumped back. *Please, dear God of Justice, do not let them look at my door.*

"Probably to keep us out, Tiny."

"Well now I'm curious, Sunny. What's so important that we can't see it?"

"I don't know, Tiny."

"Let's find out, Sunny."

Nails ripped out of the wood.

The door opened.

Fanjei wished he had built a barricade. He wished he had thought to hide in his dark bedroom. He wished there were no giants roaming through the garden outside his window.

Fanjei could not move his feet.

Two Children of the Sun stepped into the room, wearing nothing but that disgusting strip of cloth that drew attention to their fat, orange navels. The doorways in the Senatorial Palace had been designed with Children of the Sun in mind, but the second one ducked as he came through. The first one was about a head shorter, but still at least eight feet tall.

The shorter one said, "I think we found a senator, Sunny."

"Good," said the huge one. "I've got some political grievances."

He swished a bloody rapier through the air and a tiny droplet flew across the room and spattered against the wall.

"Now, Sunny," said the shorter one. "Don't kill him. We need his vote."

"I'm not killing him," the huge one said, drawing the blade through the air with a high-pitched swish. "I'm just practicing with my rapier."

It was a standard military rapier, but it looked like a baton in his hands. The giant could fit only his thumb and two fingers on the hilt.

Swish. Swish. He stepped closer to Fanjei with every swipe.

Fanjei took a step back.

The giant with the rapier took a step forward. "I like this," he said. "It's light. Moves fast."

He feinted at Fanjei's face, stopping his backhand strike in mid-swing. The rapier screamed like a whip. The end broke off with a metallic snap and flew past Fanjei's ear to lodge point-first in the door frame of his study.

"Don't you think it might be somewhat dangerous?" the shorter one asked.

The huge one looked sadly at the broken end of his rapier.

"You found him!" A woman was at the door—another Child of the Sun.

"Yeah, we found him, Mama."

"You don't recognize him," she said.

"Should we?"

"This is the senator."

The shorter one looked down on Fanjei and smiled like an alligator. "Oh!" he said. "You're the *hostage*."

* * *

When people are in danger, they hide in their homes. But Matyu Gloria and her entourage did not think of the City Palace as "home". When they heard news of the riots, they tried to get to their ship.

They walked through a grimy neighborhood with dusty streets and ramshackle houses. With three dozen guards, Gloria felt confident that her party would be left alone. But the Rock Brothers were taking no chances. They led Gloria on detours to avoid bands of club-wielding men. Progress was slow.

In fact, it was so slow that Aura Wisebrow was able to catch up to them.

Aura didn't bring any bodyguards or secretaries. She came puffing up all by herself. Clever recognized the senator and looked to Gloria for instructions.

"Let her pass," Gloria said.

Her soldiers stood aside, but Aura remained where she was, wheezing, bent at the back, with her hands on her knees.

"Forgive me … Matyu … I—"

"Catch your breath, woman," Gloria said.

"Thank you." After a few wheezing breaths, Aura continued, "The Senate needs your help."

"Oh?" The Senate had done nothing for Gloria. But now that they needed her, perhaps she had some bargaining power.

"I have come to ask you to address the rioters at the Senatorial Palace," Aura said. "We hope you can convince them to disperse."

"Why should they listen to me if they will not listen to their senator?"

"They are rioting because a senator was found in possession of the Sun Scroll. They think the Senate is colluding to keep it from you."

"Ah," said Gloria. "And is that not true?"

Aura looked at her dirty toes. "Perhaps."

"And if I addressed these rioters, would you give the scroll to me?"

"Please understand—" Aura began.

"Will you enact a trade embargo against Mogadwen?" Gloria asked. "Will you blockade the Mogadrel ports?"

"Something can be worked out," Aura said.

"What?" asked Gloria. "What something?"

"Please understand," Aura said, "if we negotiate with you too soon, then our citizens will say that we gave in to the rioters' demands, that we allowed violence to overrule good judgment and lawlessness to overrule justice. But if you help us calm the streets now, then next year—"

"Bah! Next year our fields will be burnt and the Mogadrel will walk among our cities, swords dripping with our blood. I need your support *now*, woman!"

"I cannot give you support now," Aura said. "But next year—"

"You are no use to me," Gloria said. "Come," she told her entourage. "Let us go to our ship."

"You will not help us?" Aura asked.

"Your senate will not help me," Gloria said. "Tell them that this is justice."

* * *

Gusty Longbread looked around the corner of the Lowtown tailor shop. Bendoko was right. They were Queenies—a whole squad of soldiers marching toward the docks, surrounding a diplomatic entourage.

"It's the ambassador," Gusty said. "I think she's trying to get to her ship."

"We should see if she needs help," Tisha said.

"Is that really the best idea?" Bendoko asked.

"Oh," Tisha said. "Maybe not."

"Let's try this way," Bendoko said.

The Crane had been right about Lowtown: There were plenty of places to hide. Gusty and Tisha followed Bendoko through a shadowy alley and across a deserted courtyard.

Bendoko peeked around a building.

"There's an orange woman there," he said. "Really nice jewelry. Just standing in the middle of the street. I don't think she's a threat."

"Let me look," Gusty said.

He looked.

"It's Senator Aura Wisebrow."

"We should definitely ask if *she* needs help," Tisha said.

Gusty looked at Bendoko.

The little man shrugged. "Why not? My *last* conversation with a senator went pretty well."

They stepped out into the street and approached Aura Wisebrow. Her downcast face was forlorn. Her shoulders sagged with defeat.

"Senator," Tisha said, "you shouldn't be out on the streets right now."

"Oh," said Aura Wisebrow. "Hello."

"Do you need us to escort you somewhere?" Tisha asked.

"We believe the Senatorial Palace may be unsafe," Gusty said.

"It's been overrun," Aura Wisebrow said.

"Did any other senators escape?" Tisha asked.

"Yes," said Aura Wisebrow. "I have them in a safe place."

"Can we escort *you* to a safe place?" Tisha asked.

"I fear you and your friend are the ones who are in danger right now," said Aura Wisebrow.

She looked at Bendoko more closely. "Say," she said, "aren't you the one who——?"

"Who stole the Sun Scroll," said Bendoko. "Yeah, that was me."

"We're escorting him to Cohort Headquarters," Gusty said.

The three of them gave him a funny look.

"We're taking the long way," Gusty said.

Aura Wisebrow looked him up and down. "Very well," she said. "I hope you know what you're doing."

Gusty didn't, but he didn't feel like admitting it.

"Did the rioters get the Sun Scroll?" Tisha asked.

Aura Wisebrow shook her head. "No. But they do have Fanjei."

"Not for long," Tisha said.

"I beg your pardon?"

"Forgive me, Senator." Tisha looked embarrassed to have spoken out loud. "I doubt we will find Fanjei alive."

"Do you know Mama Grace?" Aura Wisebrow asked.

"No," Tisha said.

"Yes you do," Gusty reminded her. "She's one of those women you spoke to in front of the palace last week."

"Ah," said Tisha.

Aura Wisebrow said, "Mama Grace is speaking for the people who have occupied the palace. She says they will return Fanjei unharmed if the Senate agrees to aid the Reconciled Queendom and their refugees."

Gusty frowned. He wasn't sure if this was good news or not.

"And how does the Senate feel about this?" Tisha asked.

"The Senate will not give in," said Aura Wisebrow. "Understandable, really. They can just ship out and leave this mess behind them."

"Well, too bad for Fanjei," Bendoko said.

"Yeah," Tisha agreed. But she didn't sound sad. She sounded like she thought Fanjei had it coming.

He did, really. Gusty wasn't going to cry over him.

"Fanjei isn't worth a string of rat droppings," Aura Wisebrow said, "but I can't let them kill him."

She looked to Gusty. "*We* can't let them kill him."

"What do you need me to do?" Gusty asked at the same time that Bendoko asked, "Why not?"

"Because these people didn't storm the palace for Mama Grace," said Aura Wisebrow. "They stormed the palace for every orange man and woman in the Lunaslip Republic. So if they kill a blue senator, then every orange has killed that blue senator. And then we have problems."

"Bigger problems than we have right now?" Bendoko asked.

"Much bigger," Aura Wisebrow said. "What would *you* say if you heard some Lowtown oranges had killed a blue senator?"

Bendoko shrugged. "I don't know. I don't really follow politics."

"You'll have to forgive him," Tisha said. "He doesn't think like normal people. Gusty and I understand."

Gusty grunted. He understood: Killing senators was not a good way to help oranges and blues get along. He didn't like the idea of saving Fanjei's skin, but it would be better for everyone if Fanjei lived to stand trial.

"So what do you need us to do?" Tisha asked.

Aura Wisebrow deflated. "I don't know," she said. "I was hoping you could think of something."

"Well, where are they holding Fanjei?" Bendoko asked. "Is he still in his rooms?"

"I don't know," said Aura Wisebrow.

"He could be dead already," Tisha said.

But Gusty was curious. "Suppose he's still in his suite, Crane. What would you do?"

"Well, if I can get onto the roof of the palace, I can get in," he said.

"They have people outside," Aura Wisebrow said. "It might be difficult to reach the palace without being seen."

Bendoko shrugged. "So Tisha and Gusty make me a diversion."

Tisha laughed. "You mean just me and Gus trying to draw the attention of dozens of rioters with clubs? No, I don't think that's a good idea."

"All right," said Bendoko. "Then *you* think of something."

Gusty already had. "It doesn't have to be *us* making the diversion, Tisha. Maybe you can talk some people into helping us."

She was suspicious. "Who?"

"The Republican Navy."

Tisha was incredulous. "No way," she said. "We're not going to them for help."

Gusty sighed. Tisha always had trouble talking to sailors.

"I know you can do it," he said.

"Have you forgotten what they did on Breadbaker Bridge?" Tisha asked.

Aura Wisebrow said, "Tisha, if the Navy can help us—"

"Let somebody else talk to them," Tisha said. "I'm not going to go begging."

Gusty sighed and reached inside his breastplate. He pulled out the mandatory-rest order that Flora Warmhands had written to Captain Kosho.

"If you go talk to them," he said, "I'll give you this."

Tisha stared hard at the rolled-up piece of paper. Then she plucked it from his hand and tucked it into her bodice.

"All right," she said. "I'll do it."

* * *

Sunlight glared off the waters of the harbor. Wavelets lapped at the piles of the dock. Tisha stood at the very end and called to the ship anchored fifty yards out:

"Ahoy, the *Thom-Hizo Warrior!*"

Greenscarves watched her from the deck, but no one replied.

"I guess they don't want to talk," she said. Normally, she liked Gusty's plans, but seeking help from the Republican Navy was a bad idea. The Navy was the problem, not the solution.

"They're lowering a boat," Gusty said, shading his eyes from the glare.

Bendoko said, "Well that's a good sign. Right?"

"Yeah," Tisha said. "Great."

The boat moved away from the ship. It had two occupants: one sailor in the usual loincloth and green scarf and one with a white sari and white scarf. The boat moved slowly, but no more slowly than it would have, had they been rowing. They were pushing it by creating an elemental current. Magic. Tisha wished she'd learned that trick. But it wasn't the sort of thing urbies needed to know.

They slowed the boat as they drew close and stopped it precisely three feet from the dock.

"I am Ensign Shuver," said the man in white. "What can I do for you?"

"We would like to speak with your captain," Tisha said.

"Captain Tu sends word that he is at sea and not available to receive communications from the Senate."

"Captain Tu?" Bendoko asked. "Isn't he the one who—?"

"Shh," said Gusty.

Tisha asked, "Would this unavailability have anything to do with the Senate relieving the admiral of command?"

"The *Thom-Hizo Warrior* has not received official notice of such an action," Ensign Shuver said.

All right, thought Tisha. *So Tu knows his career is sinking, and he's decided to go down with Fanjei.*

"I haven't heard anything official either," Tisha said. It was mostly true. Senator Aura hadn't been speaking to them officially. "Could I come aboard if I promised not to deliver any messages?"

"Then why would you need to come aboard?"

"Think of it as a business proposition," Bendoko suggested.

"No," Tisha said. That made it sound like they thought Tu could be bought. "I just want a chance to discuss mutual interests."

"That's what I said," Bendoko mumbled.

"You represent the Urban Cohort?" Ensign Shuver asked.

"We're just some people from Sliceharbor," Gusty said.

That was true, too. Tisha didn't have authorization for *anything* she'd done since returning to Sliceharbor.

"Technically, I'm not even on duty right now," she said.

"She's injured," Gusty said.

Tisha frowned at him. She'd been referring to the time of day, not to Flora's presumptuous edict.

Ensign Shuver looked at all three of them in turn, his eyes lingering on their feet, for some reason. When he looked up, his eyes held recognition. Maybe he'd been one of the sailors on the road this morning. Tisha didn't recognize *him.*

He said, "I think Captain Tu may be interested in what you

have to say." He reached out with a gaff hook and pulled the boat against the dock. "You have permission to come aboard."

"Can I come, too?" Bendoko asked.

Tisha froze. That wasn't part of the plan.

"I've never been on a ship before," Bendoko said.

She looked at him. She was trying to negotiate a rescue plan with a hostile faction. She didn't need him around to complicate things.

"Please," Bendoko said. "Both my fathers died at sea and—well—I've always wondered what a ship was like."

"I don't think I should take more than two of you," Ensign Shuver said.

"Don't worry," Gusty said. "I'm happy to stay here on the dock."

"Very well," Ensign Shuver said. "Then you two have permission to board."

* * *

Tisha thought the *Thom-Hizo Warrior* was not much larger than a small trading vessel, but Bendoko's eyes glowed with wonder. He wanted to see everything. Ensign Shuver showed him around, leaving Tisha on the aft deck to speak with Captain Tu in private.

"Ensign Shuver mentioned we might have mutual interests," Captain Tu said. "Our interests did not seem to have much in common this morning."

"I know," Tisha said. "But things have changed."

"Very well," said Captain Tu. "What is your request?"

"We need help rescuing Senator Fanjei."

"Rescuing him?"

Tisha explained the riots.

Tisha explained Gusty's plan.

Captain Tu was skeptical. "Delivering the admiral to Senator Aura will not make things better."

Tisha asked, "Don't you think it's better than letting him be killed by an angry mob?"

"He could still be killed while he awaits trail," Captain Tu said.

"The Urban Cohort can keep him safe."

"Are you certain? At present, Sliceharbor seems quite dangerous."

"Well," said Tisha, "that is why we need the help of the Republican Navy."

But Captain Tu was not easily moved by flattery.

"I will not risk my people's lives unless I am convinced that the admiral will live to receive a fair trial."

"He will," Tisha assured him.

"In Thom-Hizo."

"What?"

"That is my price. If I help you rescue Admiral Fanjei, you must deliver him to me so that I can take him home. Let the Senate try him there."

That was out of the question. She couldn't let Fanjei get away.

But would he really be getting away? The Senate would meet in Thom-Hizo next year. No matter what city the Senate was in, it still had jurisdiction over the theft.

Did Tisha need revenge, or could she place her faith in the Republic's system of justice?

"All right," she said. "It's a deal."

* * *

Once Tisha and Bendoko were back on the dock, she explained it to Gusty.

"All right," he said.

"All right?" she asked.

"Yeah," Gusty said. "You did the right thing."

"Maybe," Tisha said. "But I hate to let him get away with everything."

"He only gets away if the job goes smooth," Bendoko said. "If we gaff it, then he's gaffed, too."

"That's not encouraging," Tisha said.

Gusty put a hand on her shoulder. "Listen, Tisha. Tu was right. Fanjei can't get a fair trial in Sliceharbor. Half the town will want him dead, the other half will say he's a hero for saving the scroll from the Queenies. Whatever the judges decide, someone will be calling for blood. If we want people able to walk the streets again, sending Fanjei away is a good first step."

"We're helping a criminal evade justice," Tisha said.

Bendoko asked, "Why let that stop you?"

"We're not evading justice," Gusty said. "Just delaying it."

"All right," said Tisha. "Thanks, Gus. I think I gave away too much, but I feel better knowing you back me up."

"Always."

* * *

For the second time that day, Bendoko found himself hiding among the peach trees behind the Senatorial Palace. Gusty and Tisha crouched in a hedge behind him, softly arguing.

"Gus, I can climb," Tisha whispered. "I got on board Fanjei's ship just fine."

Gusty grunted. Did he have to grunt so loud?

Tisha said, "It's hardly sore at all now."

"If you reinjure yourself, I'll tell Captain Kosho about Flora's message."

"I'm burning the evidence the first chance I get."

Gusty grunted again. Maybe that was a laugh this time.

Gusty said, "We need a lookout, all right? Just stay on the ground and warn us if anyone comes."

"You're just saying that because you think I can't climb."

"Tisha, please."

"Oh, all right."

Bendoko crawled over and stuck his head into their hedge. "Will you be quiet? I'm trying to concentrate."

"How many are there?" Gusty asked.

"At least three," Bendoko said.

He'd seen two men with clubs lounging by the palace's back door, but they were talking to at least one guy Bendoko couldn't see, someone sitting down.

"Three's too many," Gusty said.

One was too many. For the job to go smooth they needed to reach the roof without being seen.

Bendoko said, "Yeah, well, when the Navy comes, we'll see if they pull these guys to the front of the palace. But until then, be quiet! I'm working here."

Tisha said, "All right, Ben." There was a smile in her voice.

Bendoko crawled back to the peach trees and made himself comfortable.

* * *

A lookout spotted Captain Tu's sailors sneaking up Barbecue Street. He ran to warn those who held the Senatorial Palace. They mustered at the front steps to meet this threat.

When the sailors got close, the rioters charged. The sailors turned and ran. The rioters pursued.

The diversion worked perfectly.

* * *

Bendoko ran through the deserted garden. The claws strapped to his sandals scraped against the paving stones.

Like a squirrel, he scampered up the side of the Senatorial Palace until he reached the whole-stalk batten-weave.

Crouching with his weight on the eaves pole, Bendoko reached into his shopping bag and pulled out a rope ladder. It wasn't something he normally carried, but Gusty had pointed out that they needed one, and he'd been willing to look the other way while Bendoko acquired it from a closed shop near the Dock Market.

(Gusty had also made Bendoko leave six flatrings on a workbench to pay for it. It was the first time Bendoko had ever broken into a building to leave money.)

Bendoko lashed the ladder to the eaves pole and let it unroll to the ground.

Gusty was at the base of the palace by the time Bendoko got the ladder unrolled. The orange man climbed up, puffing. Bendoko didn't extend a hand to help him onto the roof—he didn't want the huge man to accidentally pull him off.

"I think we made it," Gusty said.

"Yeah," Bendoko said, pulling up the ladder.

"Won't I need that to get back down?" asked Gusty.

"If someone sees it dangling over the side of the palace, you might not like what you climb down into," Bendoko said. "But we'll leave it lashed in place in case we need to leave in a hurry."

"How often do you have to leave in a hurry on jobs like this?" Gusty asked.

"Rarely," Bendoko said. "But I don't usually work in the daytime."

"It's sunset," Gusty said.

"That's daytime with long shadows," Bendoko said. "Stay in the shade of the roof beam so your shadow doesn't give you away."

"All right," Gusty said.

They were on the shady side, but the air was still plenty hot. The yellow moon was rising—so bright that it cast faint shadows of its own, even in daylight.

Bendoko led Gusty along the roof. The dry thatch crackled as they climbed. Bendoko hoped the noise sounded quieter inside the palace.

"Wouldn't this have been easier if we'd gone in through the window?" Gusty asked.

"Maybe," Bendoko said.

"So why didn't we go in through the window?"

"Because I'm a roof man; that's my thing."

"All right."

And I want my climbing line back, Bendoko thought as they arrived at the hole he had used that morning. From the outside, it was easy to spot. He hadn't been able to reweave the thatch properly. His line was still lashed to the frame pole.

Bendoko lifted the thatch and stuck his head in the hole. A gecko scuttled out of the way—those things could climb anywhere.

It didn't look like anyone was in Fanjei's bedroom. Bendoko hoped the orange rioters hadn't decided to move Fanjei out of his suite.

Bendoko took his sandals off. He brushed the mosquitoes off his arms and legs.

He wiggled inside and closed the hole behind himself—no need to leave a shaft of light shining from above. If he had to creep through the palace, looking for Fanjei, he didn't want his entry point to be discovered.

His line was wrapped around the rafters, but it wasn't

knotted. He untangled it and dropped it through the hole in the ceiling gauze.

His eyes were adjusting. The bedroom still looked empty. Well, maybe Fanjei was in one of his other rooms. After all, who could sleep at a time like this?

Bendoko lowered himself, hand over hand. He was halfway down to the floor when he heard the voice:

"Shouldn't we have people in the garden?"

That was Sunny Too-Tall!

"They all went to fight the greenscarves."

That was Tiny!

"They should have left someone to watch the back door," Sunny said.

"You're watching the back door," Tiny said.

So Fanjei was dead.

He had to be dead, right? Everyone knew that Fanjei had stolen the Sun Scroll. If Sunny and Tiny were here, they must have killed him.

It was too bad. Bendoko would have liked to rescue Fanjei, restore sanity to Sliceharbor, and all that, but it wasn't going to happen. He'd just go up and tell Gusty.

And Gusty would point out that he was a coward.

And Bendoko would point out that he already knew this about himself.

And Gusty would say, are you more afraid of the oranges down there or the orange up here?

And Bendoko would say, the oranges down there, because they grab people's heads and snap them right off!

Well, all right. Mendu's head hadn't been snapped completely off, but he hadn't looked very pretty, either. And really, there was no point in Bendoko going down the rest of the way just to look at Fanjei's broken neck.

So why had his treacherous arms started climbing down?

It was that damn alligator, wasn't it?

Bendoko the Crane, renowned coward of Sliceharbor, leaps into one lake to rescue one woman from one alligator and now he thinks he's a hero. Well ... well this was a pretty stupid thing he was doing.

Bendoko set his feet ever so lightly on the reed mat covering the floor. He could feel the cold, hard stone underneath.

He released the climbing line and it made a whisper of a swish against his sari. Bendoko hardly noticed. He was listening to the Too-Tall brothers breathing in the next room.

They were in Fanjei's study. He was in the darkness of the bedroom. The door was partially ajar, as he had left it at noon.

A thin line of light defined the gap at the hinges. Bendoko put his eye to the gap.

Dammit!

Fanjei was alive. He sat on the floor near Bendoko's doorway, staring dully across the room.

There was no mistaking it. His eyes were open. His chest rose and fell with his shallow breathing. He even stuck out his tongue and licked his lips!

Damn you, Fanjei! Damn you for still being alive!

Bendoko didn't have to rescue Fanjei. Gusty couldn't make him. Bendoko could just climb right up the rope and say Fanjei was dead. Because otherwise Bendoko would be dead. Rescue was impossible.

He shifted his position, trying to get an angle on the Too-Tall brothers. Sunny was at the window, blocking the light like a thundercloud. Tiny wasn't in a part of the room that Bendoko could see.

The wall creaked. "I want some wine," Tiny said.

Damn! Tiny was leaning against the wall! Just a half-foot of wood and plaster separated Bendoko from Tiny's orange backside!

Tiny asked, "You want some wine, Fanjei?"

The senator's eyes widened and he shook his head.

Tiny crossed through Bendoko's field of vision. "You want some wine, Sunny?"

"What's he got?" Sunny asked.

Tiny left the study. Sunny was distracted. This was Bendoko's chance.

His chance to get really, really killed.

From the adjacent room, Tiny's voice called, "Moonaway Vineyards, Hicho White, Peachgrove Extra Fine, Winelands Original . . ."

"Anything from around here?" Sunny asked.

"Just imported stuff," Tiny called.

"Good," Sunny said. "Bring whatever you like and we'll split the bottle."

To Hell with it.

Bendoko stepped out of the bedroom, seized Fanjei by the wrist, and pulled the startled man inside.

He pushed Fanjei toward the climbing line and slammed the door.

"Hey, Tiny: Fanjei just went to bed."

Bendoko slipped his putty knife from his tool belt and jammed it under the door, giving it a kick with his heel to wedge it tight.

"He went to bed in a hurry," Tiny observed, from the other side of the door.

"Climb up! Climb up!" Bendoko whispered.

Fanjei stood there helplessly.

"Oh, Senator?" Tiny knocked daintily on the door. "Senator Fanjei? Didn't your mother ever tell you it's rude to leave before your guests have finished their wine?"

Well, Bendoko hadn't expected Fanjei to be able to climb. That was why he had brought Gusty.

Bendoko grabbed the climbing line and tied the end into a hoisting bowline. He felt around, found the senator's legs, and slipped the bottom of the loop behind the senator's thighs. He took the senator's hand and folded the fingers around the line that led up to the roof.

He wiggled the line. Nothing happened.

He wiggled it again. Gusty didn't respond to his signal. Bendoko resolved that the next time he helped an urbie rescue a hostage from the Senatorial Palace, they would definitely spend a little time going over signals.

Tiny pushed on the door.

The putty knife held.

"He's jammed the door, Sunny."

"That was silly," Sunny said. "Now you can't open it without breaking it."

"Yeah," said Tiny. "I was thinking that, too."

"Hoist!" Bendoko yelled. "Hoist, hoist, hoist!"

The roof opened to reveal a patch of blue sky with Gusty's copper-finned helmet in the middle. The line pulled taut around Fanjei's body. Fanjei rose into the air.

* * *

Even an admiral sometimes has to be hoisted from a boat. Fanjei knew how to sit in a hoisting bowline, and his Navy training took over his body as his mind tried to figure out what was going on.

It was a rescue.

He had given up hope, but this was certainly a rescue. The Children of the Sun were not going to kill him after all.

Dear Captain Tu. Dear, brave sailors of the *Thom-Hizo Warrior!* They had risked their lives to save their admiral from these bestial Children of the Sun. Fanjei should have been expecting it.

They were honest men and women. Decent people. They did what was right. Because they believed in justice.

Fanjei's head rose to the light. It was like going to Heaven.

An arm reached under his legs to pull him out of the darkness and into the glorious light of the roof. Sunset painted the clouds golden, crimson, and orange. Huge, orange arms gently took the climbing line from his hand. A huge, orange face filled his field of vision.

An *orange* face.

"Wh— what?"

"Don't worry," said the Child of the Sun. "Justice won't rule tonight."

* * *

Would Gusty have been strong enough to pull up two men at the same time? Bendoko, still on the floor in Fanjei's bedroom, realized he should have asked that. The next time he helped an urbie rescue a hostage from the Senatorial Palace—

Smash!

The door broke from its hinges and fell into the room.

The climbing line snaked downward through the rafters.

Bendoko leapt and caught it.

"Hey," said Tiny. "It's the Crane."

Bendoko frantically pulled the slack through his hands. The line went taut. He tucked a knee up and grasped the line in his toes.

Tiny stepped into the bedroom.

Sunny came in behind him and looked around. "Where's Fanjei?"

"That's a good question, Sunny." Tiny grabbed Bendoko by the ankle and asked, "Crane, where's Fanjei?"

Underwater archaeologists have strong kicks. Bendoko jerked his ankle free and pushed off Tiny's chest. He swung toward the wall.

He braced a bare foot on the wall and pushed off toward the corner. Using the line as a tether, he swung around Tiny and flew feet-first at Sunny's face. Sunny grinned and reached out to catch him.

Bendoko let go. He dropped below Sunny's guard and landed with both feet in Sunny's soft stomach.

Sunny went down, Bendoko on top of him.

Bendoko rolled off Sunny and into Fanjei's study. He hopped to his feet and ran through the open door. He crossed the receiving room, opened the door, and ran into the hallway.

Five people sat on the floor, playing dice. They looked up.

Bendoko pointed back into Fanjei's suite. "They need help in there! Fanjei's loose!"

The five orange dice players frowned.

Bendoko remembered that he was blue.

He turned and ran down the hall.

"After him!" yelled Sunny Too-Tall.

Bendoko dashed through the foyer and crossed to the library wing. He opened the library door and ran inside.

The library hadn't been touched. Every scroll hutch was still standing upright, and every scroll was still in its cubby.

No lamps had been left burning. As Bendoko ran deeper into the shadows, he realized he was becoming harder to find.

He took a left, a right, and a left. Light leaked in through the door he had opened, but now he was in a corner so dark he couldn't even see the scroll cases in their cubbies. Bendoko stopped running and listened.

Sandaled feet were shuffling through the room. Shifting shadows told him that people were carrying lamps, looking for him. Bendoko took advantage of these beacons and used their light to guide himself deeper through the darkness.

He had a plan now. He was on familiar ground.

Quietly, he retreated to the back wall. He remembered the roof hatch being right about here. He climbed up the scroll hutch. Dangerous: the top of the hutch was at an orange person's eye level. Well, it wouldn't matter—not if he'd picked the right place. Bendoko reached up for the hole in the gauze.

It wasn't there.

He felt around frantically. Where had he come through?

Or had they replaced it already? That was it. They must have replaced the gauze, or—

There. Stitching. The hole he had ripped had been mended.

He reached up with bare hands and parted a new hole.

"Found him," said Sunny Too-Tall.

Bendoko looked out over the library. The labyrinth of scroll hutches was dotted with private pockets of light. Sunny's lamp was raised above the hutches, illuminating Sunny's triumphant face.

Tiny stood on tiptoe and peered over the top of a scroll hutch. "So what are you doing up there, Crane?"

"Leaving," Bendoko said.

He jumped and slammed the heels of both hands into the hatch. It didn't budge.

Glowing lamps slowly converged.

Putty knife, putty knife, putty knife. Bendoko felt around his tool belt frantically. Where was it?

Oh, yeah. He'd used it to jam Fanjei's door.

Tiny said, "It's a wooden roof here, Crane. Not thatch."

Tiny came around the corner. Sunny was advancing along the wall.

Bendoko leapt across the aisle, landed on a scroll hutch, slipped, and tumbled off at the feet of an orange woman with a lamp. The woman was so busy trying to keep her lamp from spilling that she had no hands free to grab Bendoko. Bendoko sprinted down an alley of scroll hutches.

A lamp appeared ahead. Bendoko ducked behind a hutch.

"He's over here," said Sunny, peering at him over the top.

Bendoko braced his shoulder against the scroll hutch and pushed. It didn't tip over and crush Sunny. It didn't even move.

Heavy damn things.

Bendoko saw the open library doors. It looked like he had a clean current. He sprinted for the rectangle of light.

Tiny stepped into view near the librarian's desk. He blew out his lamp.

Bendoko veered around Tiny, bounced off a reading table, righted himself, and sprinted for the door.

Tiny tossed his lamp in a gentle underhand. It bounced out the doorway with a *clunk, clunk, clunk,* spreading oil on the floor.

Bendoko's foot hit the patch of oil. He couldn't stop. He skidded out the door, stumbled when his feet left the oil puddle, and fell sprawling into the hall.

Tiny Too-Tall appeared in the doorway. He stepped carefully out of the library. "Mind the puddle," he said over his shoulder.

Bendoko scrambled to his feet and ran.

The garden entrance. He could find it. He had a map of this place in his head, and he knew exactly how to get there. Yeah, his feet were still a little slick from the oil, but he was making up for it by running twice as fast.

Tiny Too-Tall said, "This is getting wearisome, Crane."

Bendoko glanced over his shoulder. Tiny Too-Tall was wearing a determined expression that suggested he was done playing games. Behind him, Sunny Too-Tall was picking up speed.

They say you should never take time to look over your shoulder, but this sight gave Bendoko a burst of vitality. He dashed down the hallway, slipped only a little at the corner, righted himself, and ran down a corridor dark as a closet.

He skidded to a stop. His hands found a door, right where he had hoped it would be.

Thank you, Mendu, for your wonderful map.

The Too-Tall brothers' running footfalls echoed in the dark corridor. Bendoko opened the door to the light and ran outside into a crowd of heavily armed people.

The first ones he saw were the giants—orange people with shin-guards and breastplates and clubs. Then he saw the wide, surprised eyes of blue people in copper-finned helmets. And he realized he was running through a crowd of a dozen-or-so urbies who just happened to be sneaking up on the back door.

"It's the Crane!" someone yelled. "Grab him!"

A hand snatched at his wrist. Someone tripped him and he fell.

An urbie yelled, "No. Grab *them*!"

Someone else shouted, "Grab *all* of them."

A heavy knee pressed into Bendoko's back, and his arm was twisted around behind him.

Bendoko lay still. But the scuffling was not yet finished. He heard grunts and the clack of cane armor. Someone snarled. And then:

"Sunny and Tiny Too-Tall, you are under arrest."

* * *

Tisha ran through the palace garden. "Let the Crane go!" she called to the urbies. "He's with us."

Goochu looked at her skeptically. "He's with *you*?"

Tisha glanced at Stormy Colorpot, who was putting the manacles on Sunny Too-Tall.

"He's our witness against these guys," Tisha said. "Tell them, Woto."

Stormy's blue partner said, "Yeah, he's a witness in a murder investigation. Haven't seen him for a week, though."

"He's been with me," Tisha said. "And he's helping Gusty and me rescue Fanjei."

"*We're* rescuing Fanjei," Goochu said.

Now it was Tisha's turn to be skeptical. There were only about a dozen of them. The rioters had them outnumbered.

"Looks like Gusty has Fanjei already," Woto said, pointing at the rope ladder. Gusty was holding it, and Senator Fanjei was climbing down on shaky legs.

"Great," said Tisha. "Look, you guys did great. We've made some arrangements to keep Fanjei safe until he stands trial, so the Crane and I need to go with Gusty right now. Can you take the Too-Tall brothers back to Headquarters?"

They let Bendoko get up. He started sidling away toward Gusty.

Goochu said, "I wish we'd known you guys had Fanjei. Captain Kosho is leading a frontal assault."

Tisha was stunned. "A what?"

Goochu said, "Well, we needed a diversion so we could sneak in the back."

"Yeah," said Woto. "We didn't know the garden was gonna be empty."

Tisha grabbed Bendoko by the wrist. "Tell Gusty I'm not coming. I've got to stop a war."

* * *

Gusty listened to Bendoko's explanation. It was brief.

"Should we go after her?" Bendoko asked.

Gusty looked across the garden. Tisha had already disappeared around the corner of the palace.

"No," Gusty decided. "We need to stick with the plan."

Fanjei stood there trembling.

"Do I need to carry you?" Gusty asked.

Fanjei shook his head.

"Then let's move!"

Gusty set off for the shipyards at a pace that the blue men could match only by jogging.

"Is the urbies' diversion going to gaff our plan?" Bendoko asked.

"No," said Gusty. With any luck, it was drawing attention away from them.

"I can't—" Fanjei said. "I can't run."

Gusty looked around. They were in the open. He didn't see anyone in the streets.

"All right," Gusty said. "Then we'll walk. But stay close to me."

It would be faster to carry him, but Gusty didn't want to touch him. Besides, the Crane might need a head start.

"You can go ahead and get on with your part of the plan," Gusty said.

Bendoko looked at him suspiciously. "What part is that?"

"The part you think I don't know about."

"Oh," said Bendoko. "I thought you didn't know about that."

Ha! Gusty thought. *I was right.*

"Well, I do," Gusty said. "So go."

Bendoko shrugged. "All right."

Bendoko jogged away.

That left Gusty alone with Fanjei. He wished Tisha were with him. He hoped she knew what she was doing.

* * *

Tisha ran across a plaza behind the Senatorial Palace, weapons clacking against her cane skirt.

Why did she need them? They were just slowing her down.

Tisha popped open the buckle on her belt. *If you have to draw your rapier, you lose,* she thought as her weapons clattered to the paving stones. She pushed her helmet off her head and it clonked to the ground behind her.

As she sprinted into the Broad Market, she saw dozens of orange men with improvised weapons milling about the palace steps, trying to organize themselves.

On the opposite side of the market, coming up the Palace Road, was the Urban Cohort. Not just some urbies. It was nearly the entire cohort, marching toward the palace, blues in front, oranges behind them with paddle-clubs at the ready. Captain Kosho was in the front rank.

The hostage-takers moved off the steps and formed something like a battle line between the market and the Senatorial Palace. The Urban Cohort entered the Broad Market.

At a shouted signal, the hostage-takers began to advance, brandishing their weapons menacingly. Iron shovels glinted in the golden light of sunset. Rakes cast striped shadows on men's angry faces. Gaff hooks clawed at the sky. And clubs that had once been table legs or gate posts slapped against calloused hands.

The Urban Cohort did not slacken their pace. The orange urbies lifted their paddle-clubs, adding three feet to their already

intimidating height. The blues drew their rapiers, forming a front
of spiny steel.

They were going to kill each other, right here on the streets
of Sliceharbor.

Not on my watch.

Tisha dashed into the middle of the market, between the two
forces. She held up her hands to either side and said the word
she had thought she would never say: "Halt!"

It was not an invitation to dialogue. It was a winner-take-all
bet on their respect for her authority.

Both lines halted.

Tisha, the unarmed urbie standing on the line between rage
and bloodshed, had authority.

"Captain Kosho!" Tisha said. "You can withdraw your
soldiers. The hostage has been released."

All the urbies looked to Captain Kosho.

On the hostage-taker side of the battlefront, the men were
making incredulous noises of confusion.

"Aura Wisebrow and Mama Grace have negotiated an agreement," Tisha lied, withdrawing Flora's medical-leave mandate
from her bodice and waving it in the air.

"Senator Fanjei has been released and is even now on his way
to Thom-Hizo." Tisha hoped that was mostly true.

She turned to address the hostage-takers. "In return, Aura
Wisebrow has retroactively authorized your entry to the palace.
None of you are guilty of trespassing. You cannot be charged."

Yeah, Aura would probably agree to that, if Tisha explained it
to her right.

"You are free to return to the palace," Tisha said. "Or you
can go home. No arrests will be made at this time."

Captain Kosho looked at her, eyes hard.

He held out his hand.

Tisha walked to the line of urbies and handed him Flora's
medical notice.

"Please," she murmured. "Please trust me."

Kosho untied the string. He unrolled the message. He read it.

Kosho nodded and slipped the message inside his cane-
armor bodice.

He shouted, "Rapiers sheathed!"

Dozens of rapiers slid into their scabbards.

"Cohort, at my tempo, withdraw!"

He turned on his heel and led the Urban Cohort back along the Palace Road.

* * *

Gusty Longbread took Fanjei to the shipyards at the mouth of the Moko River. These backwater docks were far from Lowtown, and Gusty hoped that the trouble at the commercial docks wouldn't have touched this neighborhood.

He heaved a huge sigh of relief when he saw the dinghy waiting for them at the rendezvous spot.

Ensign Shuver helped Fanjei into the dinghy. Then he turned to Gusty and held up three fingers, palm outward. Gusty returned the gesture. It was the salute Navy officers gave to an equal.

Fanjei and Shuver headed away from Sliceharbor, moving toward the *Thom-Hizo Warrior*, at anchor eight hundred yards off shore.

Good riddance, Gusty thought.

Gusty wanted to go find Tisha, but if things went well, Tisha would be coming to him. And so would Bendoko.

Gusty hoped things went well.

* * *

Senator Fanjei—Admiral Fanjei, commander-in-chief of the Republican Navy—was received aboard his vessel with full honors. It was good to be among Children of Justice again.

He had fought a good battle. True, he had taken heavy losses, but in many respects, he had won.

He had shown Sliceharbor the true nature of the people they had chosen to accept as fellow citizens. The bloody conflict would doubtless rage for months. Fanjei was confident he had shattered the illusion that Children of the Sun could peacefully coexist with his people.

Maybe Sliceharbor would even give up their "orange seat" in the Chamber. What a boon it would be to not have to deal with Aura next year!

Fanjei had underestimated her. Her plan to incriminate him with the second Sun Scroll had worked perfectly, but she had fallen afoul of her own people's violent proclivities. And once the librarians examined the case and discovered that it was not the original Sun Scroll, Fanjei's name would be cleared. Then suspicion would shift to Aura, and he could wrench her from the Chamber with the force of her own deceptions.

Better yet: could he arrange to have the *true* Sun Scroll discovered in her home over the winter? It was dangerous to send agents out with such an important document, but the justice of the plan might be worth the risk.

As soon as the boarding formalities were out of the way, Fanjei retired to his private cabin to check on his prize.

But in his cabin, something was amiss: His inkwell had been freshened, and a piece of writing paper was missing from his desk.

Fanjei rushed to his lockbox. It was still locked. Everything was fine.

Perhaps Captain Tu had run out of paper and borrowed Fanjei's desk to write a message. It was a terrible breach of privacy. And a breach of discipline! Tu should have kept better track of his own supplies.

But it had been a difficult day, and if Captain Tu had been desperate enough to borrow Fanjei's paper, then Fanjei would have to make allowances.

He took the key off his money chain. He opened his lock box.

The scroll was gone.

In its place was a note that read: *You should have paid me my fifty imperials.*

* * *

Gusty Longbread looked out across the harbor. Horizontal light from the setting sun spread a confusing glare across the rippling water, but the tiny splashes and the gleam of a wet, bald head told him where Bendoko was. He was coming to shore, just as Gusty had anticipated.

Behind Gusty, sandals swished through the shore grass and a sheathed rapier clacked against a cane skirt. It was Tisha.

"Hi, Gus."

Gusty grunted a hello.

"How'd it go?" he asked.

"No one died," Tisha said.

"Good."

"I told them that Senator Aura had negotiated amnesty for the hostage-takers."

"Good for Aura."

"Yeah, well, I lied. Do you think Senator Aura can back me up?"

Gusty tried not to grin. "Maybe."

Tisha came to stand beside him. She gazed out across the water. "Is that someone swimming?"

"It's Bendoko."

"Why is he swimming on the surface like that?"

"He has the Sun Scroll."

"What?"

"Why do you think he wanted to come with you when you visited the ship?"

Tisha was incredulous. "He was scouting the layout?"

"Yeah."

" 'Both my fathers died at sea,' " Tisha said mockingly. "Oh, I should have known."

Actually, Gusty believed Bendoko's fathers *had* died at sea. But he had recognized it as a weak excuse to get on board a ship.

"Gus," Tisha said, "Ambassador Gloria's ship can't be very far out yet. We might be able to get the Sun Scroll to her. Do you want me to run to find a captain that can catch her? She might even still be in port."

Gusty looked out at Bendoko's tiny splashes. He would be exhausted by the time he reached shore. Gusty could take the scroll from him easily.

But giving the Sun Scroll to the Queenies wouldn't solve anything. Maybe Matyu Gloria could use the information to repel the invaders. But maybe that would be a sin. The matyus were qualified to make that decision, but Gusty wondered if the invasion wasn't coloring their judgment.

Yesterday morning, Gusty had been glad to put the Sun

Scroll in Matyu Gloria's hands. It had felt good to have the power to defy all the blues and their politics.

But today, he had needed his blue friends. Bendoko had kept both scrolls out of the Navy's hands. He had found a way to bring down Senator Fanjei. And Tisha had stopped the Urban Cohort from slaughtering rioters in the streets.

Giving the scroll to Matyu Gloria would not help Sliceharbor. It wouldn't show the oranges that their government cared about them. And it certainly wouldn't make the blues less angry about the riots. It would make things worse.

For now, they needed that scroll here in the city. Because the city needed the truth.

"No," Gusty said. "I think maybe we need that scroll more than the ambassador does."

* * *

Bendoko swam back toward Sliceharbor, pleased that he had just pulled off his greatest crime: stealing the Sun Scroll out from under the noses of four dozen sailors! Well, actually, he'd just climbed up the side of the ship and slipped into Fanjei's cabin through the window. (Gusty was right. Windows were easy.) But still, it *was* the Sun Scroll. And he'd stolen it three times!

The only problem with stealing the Sun Scroll in the middle of the harbor was that he had to swim back with one hand. Holding the case above the water made his arm tired.

Bendoko switched hands for the dozenth time and kept swimming.

As he neared the shore, he became aware of something huge swimming toward him. Its bare, round belly glistened in the yellow moonlight.

Bendoko realized he was looking at an orange man—an orange man in the harbor doing the backstroke.

"Hello, Ben."

"Gusty? What are you doing here?"

"It looked like a long way to swim. I thought I'd help you keep the scroll dry." He held out a hand. "Pass it over."

Bendoko did so.

Gusty lifted it carefully into the air and began scissor-kicking back toward land. He wasn't very fast, but still ...

"I didn't know you could swim."

"Of course I can swim," Gusty said. "I'm a Sliceharbor boy."

Judgments

FANJEI WAS EXPELLED FROM THE NAVY and barred from ever serving in the Senate again. After the summer of 1670, his bitter schemes were confined to the ancient port city of Thom-Hizo, where his hatred of foreigners could ferment undisturbed.

He wrote philosophical treatises on the necessity of keeping peoples separate. This philosophy gained many followers. Whenever any of his supporters expressed condolences for his loss of power and status, he reminded them that the true Judgment would come in the afterlife.

When his soul was claimed by Hell, he was quite surprised.

* * *

No one in the Navy ever faced trial for the Breadbaker Bridge incident, and Matyu Gloria lacked the legal standing to bring a case against those who had accosted her outside the city. Nonetheless, Captain Tu retired shortly after conveying Fanjei home.

* * *

The Reconciled Queendom negotiated peace with the Mogadrel later that year. Under the treaty, they retained most of their ports, but surrendered frontier lands to the invaders. This peace lasted some time.

* * *

People in Sliceharbor calmed down once peace was announced. True to Tisha's word, Aura Wisebrow negotiated amnesty for those who had occupied the Senatorial Palace. Some people were convicted of other crimes committed during the riot, but most culprits were unidentified and so escaped judgment …

at least during their lifetimes.

* * *

Evidence connecting the Too-Tall brothers to the murder of Gisherwoku was ruled to be insufficient, but they did not escape punishment.

Tisha and Gusty testified that they had seen Tiny and Sunny with a corpse, and Bendoko testified that the corpse had been Mendu's. So the Too-Tall brothers were convicted of murder after all.

Mama Grace's boarders testified that Tiny and Sunny had bragged about the warehouse fire, and they were convicted of arson, too.

The Too-Tall brothers were exiled to a prison island. Bendoko was glad to see them go. So was everyone else in Sliceharbor, except Mama Grace.

* * *

Mama Grace's refugees returned to the Sun Island after the war. Opal Warmblood hoped to regain her lost status by ingratiating herself with the administrators of an unconquered city.

Patience Honeythroat went to help her conquered city rebuild under Mogadrel rule. She said she would make good use of the lessons she had learned from Mama Grace.

Mama Grace denied that she had taught Patience anything except how to mop floors. But for the rest of her life, the letters she received from Patience filled her with pride.

* * *

Captain Kosho was proud of the Urban Cohort. Some wounds from the riots took decades to heal, but Kosho's cohort remained strong and unified. His orange and blue soldiers always worked side by side.

* * *

Captain Kosho had the responsibility of investigating Tisha and Gusty's conduct. After a full lithic of asking questions like

"You took him home and locked him in your *cellar*?" and "Why did you let him get away *that* time?" he finally gave up and declared the investigation closed.

They had both done a good job, he said, and he made them promise to never do anything like that again. Also, he made Tisha take two weeks off, as per Flora's orders.

* * *

Bendoko the Crane reformed, of course—at least for two weeks, while the judges were sorting out his case.

Senator Aura hired him a skilled advocate who successfully argued that Bendoko's only crime had been the original theft from the library. By helping Gusty find the second Sun Scroll and by recovering the first from Fanjei, he had provided the Republic with double restitution, which, in the judges' opinion, was sufficient. No additional punishment or restitution was required.

To celebrate, Bendoko went to the New Market and stole a roasted chicken.

Acknowledgments

I'D LIKE TO THANK MY WIFE, SIERRA, for helpful and encouraging comments on an earlier draft of this novel. Scott Thatcher and Greg Patterson also provided help with earlier drafts.

Bryon Quertermous helped me find places where I could make the manuscript even better. I did my own copy editing, so any mistakes that remain are mine and mine alone.

I had help on setting research from Mark Spritzer, Lorraine Heisler, and Greg Patterson. If the book feels hot and muggy, it's their fault.

David T. Stewart at Animal Alley was kind enough to share his reptile knowledge with me. In the end, I decided to ignore some of it. I wrote the gators this way because I thought it was cool. I don't expect herpetologists to forgive me.

For the record, male alligators do not usually stay with their mates, and if one ever got hold of your arm, it would most likely keep it. Ditto for senators.

About the Author

JASON A. HOLT has a Ph.D. in mathematics. He is fluent in Czech, and he lives on a remote Montana cattle ranch. In other words, he is well qualified to write fantasy novels.

To learn more about Jason, visit `JasonAHolt.com`.

To learn more about the world of Edgewhen®, visit `edgewhen.com`.

Chronology of Edgewhen® Adventures

1002: The Dragonslayer of Edgewhen
1311: The Artificer of Dupho
1500: The Klindrel Invasion
1670: The Burglar of Sliceharbor